17 December

CW00969701

To Gary,

TRIVENT

PUBLISHING

with all good
wishes,

Jonathan

THEOSIS

Jonathan Harris

Mythologos, vol. 1

© Trivent Publishing, 2023

Theosis
Jonathan Harris
eISBN 978-615-6405-78-4
Mythologos, vol. 1
eISSN 3003-9614
Responsible publisher: Teodora C. Artimon
https://trivent-publishing.eu/72-mythologos

First published in 2023 by Trivent Publishing

Trivent Publishing
1119 Budapest, Etele ut 59–61
Hungary

For more information, visit our website: http://trivent-publishing.eu

In Memory of Justin Champion (1960-2020)

'A change took place in his character after he acceded to the throne … he became a man of great energy.'

Account of the life of Basil II in Michael Psellos, *Chronographia*, I.4, translated by E.R.A. Sewter in *Fourteen Byzantine Rulers* (London: Penguin, 1966), p. 29.

TABLE OF CONTENTS

MAPS

MAIN CHARACTERS

Throughout the book:

Basil II, Byzantine emperor
Constantine, his younger brother

(1018-24):

Angelos, a spy
Aziz, al-Wuzara's Nubian servant
John the Paphlagonian, Chamberlain to Basil II
Sayyid al-Wuzara, Egyptian envoy to Constantinople
Stephen Lagoudes, cupbearer to Basil II
Yazid, attendant at the Constantinople mosque

(958-989):

Anna, Basil II's sister
Anthony, a monk and later Patriarch Anthony III, Basil II's
    first teacher
Bardas Phokas the elder, father of Nikephoros II
Bardas Phokas the younger, nephew of Nikephoros II, later
    claimant to the throne
Bardas Skleros, brother-in-law of John Tzimiskes, later
    claimant to the throne
Basil Lekapenos, known as Nothos, chamberlain to Basil II
Demetrius Spondyles, fellow student of Basil II, later holds the
    office of strator

George Alypios, fellow student of Basil II, later holds the office of archivist

John Tzimiskes, soldier, later Emperor John I

Kalokyris Delphinas, fellow student of Basil II, later governor of Bari, a spy in the pay of Nothos

Leo Phokas, brother of Nikephoros II, later holds the office of count palatine

Leontios Diaphantes, Basil II's teacher, later bishop of Amaseia

Nikephoros Ouranos, friend and faithful supporter of Basil II, later holds the office of keeper

Nikephoros Phokas, soldier, later Emperor Nikephoros II

Outis, chief official of the Office of the Wine Steward

Pita, Basil II's nurse

Roupenios, an Armenian officer

Stephen Kontostephanos, known as Impy, fellow student of Basil II, later holds the office of domestic

Theodora, Basil II's aunt

Theophano, Basil II's mother

Byzantine Empire in 1024

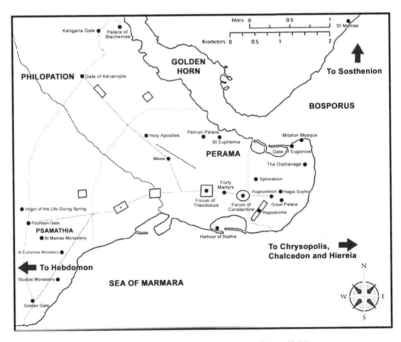

Constantinople in the time of Basil II

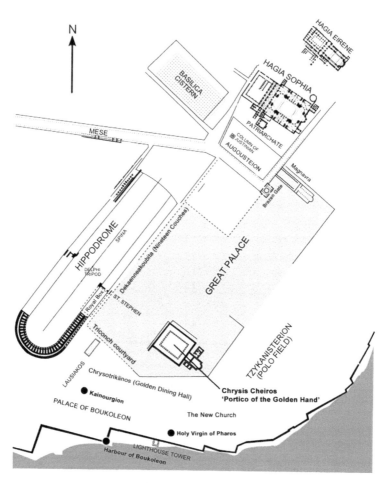

The Great Palace

1

The Caretaker
and the Ambassador (1024)

E very morning, summer and winter, as the sun was rising over Chrysopolis and casting a rosy light on the domes of the churches and monasteries of Constantinople, a man called Yazid would leave his narrow old house by the Sea Walls. He would walk to the Gate of Eugenios and wait there, ready to pass through once it was opened up for the day. When the custodian arrived, clinking his keys, he would greet Yazid cheerfully as he knew him well from when he had been a small boy and had used to pass through the gate with his father on the same errand. He and all the other Christians pronounced his name "Izid" and called him "the infidel" although not with any malice, for he spoke Greek just as they did and had lived in that quarter of the city all his life, just as they had. So, after some friendly words, Yazid would walk through the gate to the small mosque, the one known as the Mitaton. It stood close by, almost on the foreshore of

Constantinople's great harbour, the Golden Horn. It had a low dome and a narrow portico before the entrance but no minaret, for no call to prayer was ever made.

It was Yazid's job to take care of the mosque, first to sweep the porch and then to bring out the prayer rugs to beat them against the columns of the portico. He would brush the floor inside, carefully dust the great minbar that had been specially sent from Alexandria on a ship and make sure that everything was as it should be. At prayer times, some of the Arab merchants who lodged at the han on the other side of the Sea Wall would drift in. They too would greet Yazid cheerfully for many of them had been making the voyage to Constantinople regularly for years. And they too called him 'the infidel' because although he spoke Arabic, his accent was strange and he used childish words for grown-up things in a way that sounded very odd. Indeed when they returned to Alexandria or Tripoli they would regale their friends with stories of what Yazid had said, tears of laughter pouring down their cheeks. But when it came to prayer, Yazid knelt with them for he too was a Muslim, although his wife was Christian and his children looked as if they would prefer to be Christians too.

Not all the merchants were friendly. Some of those who came from Baghdad and Samarkand would take Yazid aside and demand to know why it was that in the Friday Khutbah the name of the caliph and Successor of the Believers was omitted and that of the Egyptian imposter mentioned instead. Yazid would shrug his shoulders and answer that he was a poor man and that God had not gifted him with wisdom, so they should ask the imam. But the imam is Egyptian, they objected, and doubtless appointed by the imposter. So Yazid would say that he was sure that God would hear the prayers in the mosque, whichever caliph was commemorated, if they were offered with a pure heart. At that the angry merchants thought he must be simple or cracked or both and they left him alone. He knew of course that the caliph in Cairo had a treaty with the emperor of the Romans who lived in the Great Palace up the hill from the Sea Walls. The caliph agreed not to attack his border in Syria and in return, the emperor promised not to attack him and let the caliph have control of the Mitaton. So it was only fair that it was this caliph who should be mentioned on Fridays, not the one in Baghdad. That was how Yazid came to be at this mosque. His father had travelled to Constantinople with the first imam when the treaty was made in the year 391, which is 1001 in the reckoning of the Christians. Yazid had been born in Constantinople and had inherited the position of caretaker from his father, so he was paid by the caliph of Egypt. But he did not say any of that to the angry merchants.

Now it happened that, every now and then, some great man used to come to stay at the han behind the Sea Walls. He would not be a merchant but the envoy of some potentate such as the caliph of Cordova or the emir of Aleppo. Yazid seldom saw much of these men as they spent their days in negotiations in the Great Palace and might join the congregation for prayer only once or not at all during their short stay. But one day an ambassador came who wished to speak to him. It was July and the days were long and as the mosque was always kept open in daylight hours, it was twilight when Yazid passed through the gate and the custodian closed it after him. As he walked down the dark lane to where his house leaned against the wall, Yazid noticed that a tall man was standing by the door. When he came closer the man greeted him in the Islamic fashion. He was a Nubian with a turban of brilliant white and a long blue robe that showed him to be, if not a man of importance himself, then at least in the service of a one.

'I am Aziz, servant of Sayyid al-Wuzara Abu Muhammad ibn Abd al-Rahman al Yazuri, the envoy of the caliph and commander of the faithful Abu'l Hasan Ali az-Zahir li Azaz li Din-illah.'

Yazid must have looked confused by this long speech for Aziz quickly rephrased what he had said, telling him that his

7

master Lord al-Wuzara was the envoy of the caliph of Egypt, the patron of the Mitaton mosque. His master, he went on, wished to speak with the caretaker and asked whether he would he accompany him to the han. Yazid knew that at this hour his mother, his wife and children would be outside, enjoying the cool of the evening with friends in the streets that led west to Perama so he was happy to postpone his homecoming. He was a little apprehensive though and he asked Aziz why it was that such a great man should wish to speak to him. The Nubian merely repeated his polite insistence and, without revealing to Yazid the reason for the summons, led him round the corner to the han. The courtyard was crowded with merchants relaxing at the end of the day, drinking sherbet and discussing the deals that they had struck in the markets of the Augousteion. Picking their way through the crowd, Aziz and Yazid walked up the stairs to the gallery that surrounded the courtyard and Aziz showed him through double doors into a spacious room whose windows looked out onto the waters of the Golden Horn. Yazid removed his skull cap and looked round to Aziz for reassurance but the Nubian had vanished. So he bowed awkwardly to the large man who was sitting among some plump cushions on the far side of the room, although he could not see him well as only one flickering oil lamp provided any light.

'Yazid ibn Mahmud, I am al-Wuzara, envoy of the Successor of the Believers. Is the mosque that has been entrusted to your care kept in the best condition?'

'Oh yes, Lord, I attend to it daily myself.'

As his eyes got used to the half-light, Yazid made out that his questioner's substantial form was clothed in a robe of multicoloured silk, such as was permitted only to the greatest of the servants of the caliph.

'And is the name of the Successor of the Believers commemorated there every Friday?'

'Oh yes, Lord,' said Yazid twisting his skull cap nervously in his hands.

That, Yazid supposed must be the end of the matter or if the Lord al-Wuzara had any doubts he could come to the mosque himself and see. But the envoy did not bring the interview to a close. It seemed to Yazid that he had something else to say and that he was not quite sure how to say it.

'Yazid ibn Mahmud, tell me about the emperor of the Romans, the one they call Basil.'

Yazid was surprised. Why was this great man asking him, a humble caretaker, about the emperor?

'But Lord, I have never seen him, nor the other emperor called Constantine, his brother. He rides out to make war for months on end and when he returns here he lives in the Great Palace and never goes out. On Sundays he goes to the cathedral of Hagia Sophia and then he can be seen but I am a Muslim and do not enter the church.'

'That is as it should be. What then do they say about him?'

Here Yazid was on firmer ground as the streets were rife with lurid tales of the man who had sat on the throne for nearly fifty years.

'Lord, he is very old and has ruled for as long as anyone can remember. He was already emperor when my father came to Constantinople. They say that he is not like other men. He scarcely touches the wine that the Christians drink so freely. He has no wife and not even a concubine. When he is not at war, he spends his days and night reading documents and decrees. He does all the ruling. The other emperor, his brother, lives a private life and takes no part in affairs of state. It was this Basil who conquered Bulgaria and Armenia. He wages war like a demon and is terrible in his anger. They say that after he had won a battle against the Bulgars a few years ago, he commanded that all men he had captured should have their eyes burned out. But at the same time he decreed that every hundredth prisoner should only lose one eye and those one-eyed men were then made to lead their comrades home. Another time, when he...'

'Yes, yes, yes,' interrupted al-Wuzara, 'I could learn all that in the souk and most of it is old wives' tales. What do they say about what the emperor knows?'

Now Yazid was all at sea. What was it that this man wanted from him? As he honestly had no idea, he simply answered 'Lord?.' The lamp flickered in a sudden puff of wind from the sea, making the shadows dance on the face of the visitor from Cairo.

'Yazid ibn Mahmud, can we trust you? Are you mindful that it was the father of the current Successor of the Believers who sent your father to Constantinople to care for our mosque as if it were a bright pearl on a dunghill of impiety? Does not the Successor of the Believers sustain you and your family to this day?'

Yazid acknowledged that that was indeed so and that he always remembered the Successor of the Believers in his prayers and asked God to send blessings upon him and upon his house. But for some reason he felt he should add as an afterthought that he lived among these Romans, that his wife was one of them and that would not wish them harm.

'No one is asking that of you. After all, the Successor of the Believers is not the enemy of the Christian emperor for he has had a treaty with him these twenty years. It is something else that we ask: they tell me that you speak Greek as the Romans do.'

'Yes Lord, I was born in this city and that is the language I find easiest to speak. But it is the Greek of the streets, not that of the palace which the great folk use when they write their documents and decrees.'

'It will suffice,' said al-Wuzara, 'Let me now tell you what I need you to do. I arrived in this city some ten days ago to carry out negotiations on behalf of the Successor of the Believers. We were received in the first instance, as is customary, by the vizier whom they call chamberlain I think.' His tongue stumbled over the long and unfamiliar Greek word: *parakoimomenos*. 'He is named John the Paphlagonian. We discussed our business through interpreters: he had his and I mine, a man called Jacob.

You do not need to know what the discussions were about as they would not interest you and you would not understand them anyway.'

At this point he broke off and glanced sharply at Yazid. The caretaker's mouth was slightly open and he was still twisting the skull cap. Reassured, al-Wuzara went on:

'As the discussions proceeded I became aware that the vizier was better informed than he should be. He had intelligence that he should not, indeed could not, have possessed, and yet possess it he did. It seemed to me that there was only one possible source of such details: my own interpreter, Jacob. He is, after all, a Christian, one of the Copts who reside in Cairo. He may have some residual sympathy for his co-religionists in this land and be passing information to them. How could I know what he was saying to the chamberlain? As I know no Greek, I would be none the wiser. Perhaps I am wrong and the man has been faithful to his task. Even so, I would be reassured and would count it as a personal favour if you were to come with us to the next meeting tomorrow. You will not need to speak, merely to listen and report to me if any untranslated discourse takes place between the Copt and the Romans.'

'But Lord, will they not think it strange that a humble mosque attendant is there at a meeting with the chamberlain, the greatest man in the land after the emperor?'

'I have thought of that, Yazid ibn Mahmud. You will go in disguise. I will be taking gifts for the emperor and six bearers will carry them. You will take the place of one of the bearers, wearing his turban and robe and no one will notice you. But be warned: it is not the vizier that we meet tomorrow, though doubtless he will be there. It is the emperor himself.'

As Yazid emerged from the room, Aziz was standing silently on the gallery overlooking the courtyard. He stared at Yazid without expression but slowly moved his head as if to impress on him that all would be well. And for some reason Yazid did feel reassured by that as he made the short walk home. Even so, when he got to the threshold of his house, he picked up a smooth pebble from a small pile that he kept underneath the wooden steps to the door. He walked back to the gate of St Eugenios and felt along the wall until he found a small recess. He placed the pebble in it and then went home to his wife.

So it was that Yazid rather unexpectedly found himself the next morning in a small procession that was winding its way along the narrow streets that lead uphill from the Sea Walls. In his unfamiliar turban and robe, he walked behind another man bearing on his shoulder a chest of cedar wood filled with gifts for the emperor of the Romans. Two other men were on the far side for it was a heavy burden. Behind him walked two other bearers holding smaller boxes in their arms and behind them the foreman. Ahead, he could see the litter in which al-Wuzara was being carried, closed off by curtains to shield him from the curiosity of passers-by, with Aziz and the Coptic interpreter Jacob walking alongside. An honour guard from the Great Palace escorted them, clearing a path for them as they went. It was certainly something of an adventure for Yazid but he fretted about the neglect of his duties at the mosque, even though the imam had been warned that he would not be there that morning.

The narrow streets gave way to broad boulevards and the ground levelled out, for the procession had passed into the district of Sphorakion where the great men of the city had their mansions. Yazid had never been here before. On the rare occasions that he went with his wife to the markets of the Augousteion, they took a different way that skirted the wall of the Great Palace. No doubt the route had been carefully chosen by the Romans to show the Egyptians the wealthiest and most impressive parts of the city. The mansions stretched all the way to the wide thoroughfare known as the Mese and the procession turned left along it to reach the Augousteion. The great square had always been a source of wonder to Yazid, especially the tall column that stood at its centre, topped by a statue of an emperor sitting on a horse. He always wondered how the Romans had got it up there. The great domed cathedral of Hagia Sophia loomed over the square and at the far end was their destination, the Brazen Gate, the entrance archway to the Great Palace. Yazid had seen it many times before with its stone emperors and empresses from long ago crowded into niches on its façade and the small church planted precariously on top of it, but he had never been inside.

Since they were expected, the gates had been flung wide and on both sides a detachment of guards armed with axes and shields saluted them as they passed. Inside the gate, there was a spacious hall with a vaulted roof where a larger than life emperor and empress made of little cubes of marble peered down from either side. Yazid though was careful to not to look around him and kept his eyes fixed on the turban of the man in front. The procession made its way up a wide marble staircase, the bearers behind hoisting the litter up above their heads to keep it level. Then unexpectedly they all emerged once more into the summer sunshine. For the truth is that the Great Palace is not just one building but a sprawling jumble of them, set among terraces and gardens on a slope overlooking the Bosporus. The Egyptians were guided round to the left and led towards the closest of the large buildings which Yazid heard one of the guards call the Magnavra. The route led through parterres and avenues of cypress trees and into a wide courtyard. The entrance to the Magnavra was at the far side behind a colonnade and on the steps in front of it a reception committee was waiting, lined up behind a heavy man who was holding a staff and wore a tall silk hat. At an order from the foreman, Yazid and his companion laid down the cedar chest while al-Wuzara emerged from his litter.

The reception committee stepped forward and Yazid tried not to gawp at their gaudy robes. People dressed like that never found their way down to the corner near the gate of St Eugenios so the sight was novel to him. All the Egyptians though were quite used to the splendours of the Fatimid palace in Cairo and stared ahead of them impassively. By now the man with the staff, whom Yazid took to be the chamberlain, was in conversation with al-Wuzara, leaving gaps every now and then for Jacob to render his words into Arabic. He was telling the ambassador about the protocol for an audience with the emperor and Yazid listened to what he said.

'You will process down the centre of the hall and as you proceed I will walk in front of you and two of my colleagues will escort you, holding your arms: that is our custom. Your men will follow you. As you process, you will observe that the throne of Solomon in the apse at the far end will be empty: that is quite in order. At my signal you will stop and make the obeisance, even though the throne is empty and the crowd present will make their acclamations. When the acclamations cease, you may arise and you will find that their majesties the holy emperors will be seated before you. You may then make your presentation during and after which their majesties will remain seated. The Emperor Basil will ask you some questions about your mission and then at my signal,' he banged his staff on the ground three times to demonstrate, 'the audience will be over. You will withdraw backwards, not turning your backs on the emperors.'

Al-Wuzara said that this was all as he had expected and Yazid thought so too. He had heard many things about the splendours of imperial receptions: about the golden lions on either side of the throne that were said to move and roar as if by magic and the golden tree from whose branches mechanical birds sang sweetly as if they were alive. So as he helped to pick up the cedar casket once more, he was full of anticipation about the spectacle he was about to see. The procession mounted the steps and moved between the columns. As it entered the cool entrance hall of the Magnavra, a heavy curtain was drawn aside and Yazid could see ahead into the throne room beyond. It was a cavernous hall, lit by small windows that ran all around the base of the dome that surmounted it. Bronze lamps hung from chains on the ceiling to supplement the natural light. There was a great throng of people there but they all moved aside to make a passageway for the chamberlain and the Egyptians who followed behind. Al-Wuzara looked very ungainly with his bulky frame gripped firmly by the rather short men whom Yazid took to be two of the eunuchs who were everywhere in the emperor's court. Ahead the throne was indeed empty as the chamberlain had said it would be. It was much wider than Yazid had expected, with room for two men to sit. He wondered whether that was because there were two emperors but someone later told him it was because the emperor was believed to share the throne with the prophet Jesus. There were two lions made of gold that supported the arm rests as he had heard and the golden tree was there too, at the very back of the hall behind the dais on which the throne stood. But none of the birds moved or made any sound and the lions lay passive and silent.

Then the chamberlain turned and rapped his staff once on the marble pavement. Everyone in the room went down on their knees and bowed their foreheads to the floor. Yazid and his fellow bearers hastily put down their burden and followed suit. Then the crowd stood up and began shouting in words that al-Wuzara did not understand but Yazid did:

'Hail, Basil and Constantine, great emperors of the Romans, most powerful sovereigns, servants of God, may you reign for a hundred years!'

When they had fallen silent, the chamberlain's staff was rapped on the marble again. The Egyptians slowly got to their feet and, looking up they beheld: a god!

Standing before them on the raised dais was a man well above average height with a commanding presence. He had a thick mane grey hair and a matching beard that reached down to his chest. Although he must have been over sixty, one could see that he was powerfully built and that it was muscle, not fat, that filled out his imperial robe. On his head was a crown, from which strings of precious stones dangled and glinted. He was swathed from head to foot in a gorgeous vestment made of silk and spun gold that sparkled in the beams of sunlight that entered the chamber from the windows above. He made Yazid think of that Sultan Muhammad ibn Thailun who ruled over Egypt with justice and mercy in the tales his father used to tell him. So this was the conqueror of the Bulgars!

Al-Wuzara, on the other hand, was not so much overawed as somewhat put out and discomfited by the breach of the very protocol that the chamberlain had so tediously lectured him about. Why was the emperor standing and not seated as they had been told? Seasoned envoy that he was though, he put the thought aside and began his speech:

'Great Emperor of the Romans, I come in peace and friendship from the caliph and commander of the faithful Ali az-Zahir, with these tokens of our esteem and good intent.'

He turned to indicate the gifts and Yazid and the others hastened to unfasten the clasps of the cedar casket. But that was as far as they got for the godlike emperor did not react, not in words anyway. Instead he made a most curious sound, like the bark of a dog, which al-Wuzara strongly suspected to be laughter at his expense. The emperor then turned his back and walked away to a smaller throne at the back of the dais. Throwing himself into it with an audible puff, he began reaching inside the folds of his robe as if searching for something. After some fumbling and more puffing, his hand emerged holding a small knife and he then stretched languidly over to a bowl beside the throne from which he selected a ripe peach. This he began carefully to peel, bestowing no further attention on anything or anyone. Everyone in the Egyptian party stood rooted to the spot, with not the faintest idea of what to do next. Al-Wuzara helplessly looked towards the chamberlain who was by now standing impassively at the left of the dais. His eyes met those of the ambassador and flickered urgently to his left, to the great golden throne in front of which the god had been standing a moment before.

The light in the hall was uneven, for although the summer sunshine was streaming in through the high windows, the beams fell on some spots but left others in deep shadow. The light of the lamps was likewise uncertain and flickering. No beam fell directly on the throne so it was only now that Yazid realised that someone was sitting on it and that he was watching the ambassador intently. As his eyes became accustomed to the gloom, he made out a diminutive figure whose feet scarcely reached the cushion at the throne's foot. His long beard grew in two forks from his cheeks, while his chin was bare, and he was gently turning the grey hairs in his stubby fingers. Unlike the god, he was very plainly dressed with only a purple cloak and one jewelled brooch on his right shoulder to mark his rank. He wore no crown. This then was the famous Emperor Basil, and the god the brother. How very strange that their appearances should be the opposite of the power they were said to wield!

Like the brother, this emperor seemed to pay little heed to the chamberlain's protocol for he too got up and stood looking down at the ambassador from the dais, with his hands on his hips. Hardly a regal posture, thought Yazid. He noticed too that the emperor was rather plump and wondered whether he might not have been better advised to stay sitting, for when he was on his feet it became apparent just how short he was. Most powerful men would have preferred to hide that. These musings were soon dispersed for the emperor had begun to speak and his voice was full of anger.

'It was our deepest wish and bounden duty to welcome you magnificently to our hall but the impiety of your master does not permit it.'

Al-Wuzara was dumbstruck by the tone, even if he did not know the meaning of the words, and he staggered backwards, causing the interpreter to sidestep neatly even as he translated.

The envoy stammered helplessly in an effort to reply but could not get any words to come out. The emperor went on:

'Yesterday, elements of your master's army crossed the border in Syria and marched towards our city of Antioch. Because we have long had a treaty with the caliph of Egypt we had in place no preparations for such a sudden and unprovoked attack. Only just in time were the gates of our castle at Harenc closed or the forces of the caliph might have occupied it. Yet you come here speaking of friendship and asking for the renewal of the treaty? We had thought that the followers of Muhammad respected truth and honour, yet you have shown yourselves to be no better than barbarians. You will leave my hall and return to your lodging. You will remain there under guard, until we have heard from our governor in Antioch that the troops have withdrawn. Such is my will. Let it be done.'

With that he turned and disappeared into some hidden passage behind the throne. The god had vanished too though he had long since been forgotten. The chamberlain's staff crashed to the floor three times and he cried 'The audience is over!' before he too slipped away behind the throne. The crowd in the hall did not disappear though. Every man and woman began bellowing 'Treachery, treachery!,' jabbing their fingers at the Egyptians and closing in on them like angry hornets. Al-Wuzara nearly fell over the cedar casket of gifts as he turned and rushed for the door. Yazid and the others dived for their burden to make it fast for the journey back but then suddenly with one accord decided to leave it where it was and started to run after al-Wuzara. One of the bearers whispered urgently to Yazid:

'Do we have to run backwards?'

By now they were having to force their way through clutching hands that pulled at their clothes and tried to slap their heads. When they had passed through the entrance hall and emerged into the daylight, there was worse to come. Yazid could see al-Wuzara who had reached his litter but the perimeter of the courtyard was lined with soldiers who had drawn their swords. They were wearing metal helmets with visors over their eyes which made them look even more menacing. Yazid now wished that he had never come with the ambassador and feared that he would never see his wife, his children or indeed the mosque or the house by the Sea Walls ever again. But the soldiers did not move. They merely started to tap their swords on their shields, at first softly and then harder and harder until they were making a sound like thunder. This was very threatening but the Egyptians could see that the soldiers had left an opening at the far side through which they could pass. So very deliberately al-Wuzara began to walk towards that point, trying to look dignified as he led the retreat. His servants followed behind him, carrying the litter underarm rather than on their shoulders. Yazid and the bearers followed, then the interpreter, the foreman and Aziz. All the time, the soldiers kept up their rhythm, crash, crash, crash, as their swords hit their shields. The procession passed slowly through the gap and out onto the path towards the Brazen Gate. As they passed between the rows of Cypress trees, al-Wuzara's pace started to pick up. The men behind were much younger and fitter and could easily have overtaken him but they loyally trotted along behind, matching their steps to his. The crashing died away behind them and al-Wuzara hitched up his robe to help him go faster. They hurried down the marble stair and through the Brazen Gate to find themselves once more in the Augousteion, the guard waiting to escort them back to the han and to make prisoners of them. Only now was the litter set down and the curtains drawn aside for al-Wuzara to enter. As he did so, Yazid distinctly heard him hiss to Aziz: 'How could he possibly have heard so soon, after just one day? We are betrayed.'

2

Kainourgion (958-63)

In the deepest recesses of the Great Palace, there are three round-arched stone windows that look out on the blue line of the Bosporus and the first fields of Asia beyond. No one admires the view, though, for the room that they give light to is always kept locked. In the winter months, it is left shuttered and unheated. In spring, the shutters are taken down and the dust removed but then it is sealed up again. It can stay like that for decades. Only when the doctors pronounce that the empress is three months pregnant are the doors thrown open and an army of menials descends. Every inch is meticulously swept and the domed ceiling and the upper walls are repainted with several coats of a mauve that makes a pleasing contrast with the porphyry facing on the lower level. A bed, couch, bath, brazier and all the other necessary furnishings are carried in and, when everything is ready, fresh flowers are brought in daily to be strewn on the floor. When the labour pains begin, the empress is carried the short distance down the corridor and laid on the bed. That way, when it is all over, the child can be said to have been born in the purple. It was in that room that I came into the world.

My grandfather, Emperor Constantine VII, the fourth emperor of the Macedonian dynasty, was still on the throne then. My parents were his son Romanos and his daughter-in-law, Theophano. A few weeks after my birth, I was christened in the cathedral of Hagia Sophia, which stands on the other side of the square called the Augousteion from the Great Palace. One of my godparents was the celebrated Nikephoros Phokas, who at that time held the office of domestic of the east, and commanded our armies against the Saracens. It was in November the following year that my grandfather died and my father succeed him as emperor. It has become the custom in our house to crown the heir to the throne in his father's lifetime to remove any doubts as to the line of succession. So one spring morning, when I was not even two years old, I was paraded across the Augousteion to Hagia Sophia where the patriarch Polyeuktos placed a tiny, gilded crown on my head.

I cannot remember any of those events, of course. My earliest memory is probably of my nurse, Pita, holding me on her lap. I looked up at her face and then at our surroundings, what seemed to me to be an enormous room, lit by windows set high up in one of the four walls. This was the nursery in the Kainourgion which is tucked away in a secluded spot in the inner part of the Great Palace complex, known as the Boukoleon. It had been built by my ancestor Basil I as a residence for himself and his numerous children. At the entrance, there is a wide hall on whose walls Basil, his wife and those same children are immortalised in mosaic. On the floor is a giant mosaic peacock surrounded by four eagles who always looked to me as if they were about to pounce on the gaudy bird and tear it to pieces. The upper floors are accessed by three marble spiral staircases set into the walls, one at either side of the entrance hall and one in the middle. I have often pondered on the thinking behind that layout. Perhaps it was to provide alternative exits in case of a fire. The nursery is on the third and final storey, with adjoining bedchambers. My brother came into the world two years later and I do not recall that event either. When he later joined me in the nursery, though, he was an object of fascination to me because his tiny fingers were smaller replicas of my own. The birth of my sister Anna, I do remember. It was a cold day, in March as I now know, and the underfloor heating was keeping the nursery warm. Pita and the midwife brought in a bundle of wrappings, and pulled them aside for us to see a face. She looked like a frog: little bulging eyes tightly shut and pouting lips that were blowing tiny bubbles.

Of my father and mother, I have few memories from that time. They did not reside in the Kainourgion but in another part of the Boukoleon and we had nothing that might be described as a family life. I dimly remember sitting with them in the gallery of Hagia Sophia while the liturgy went on below and walking with them through a long dark passage to suddenly emerge into bright sunshine in the royal box at the Hippodrome. That must have been, I think, when my godfather, Nikephoros Phokas, returned from the conquest of Crete in the summer of 961. I am told that I was with my parents a few months after that at the funeral of my paternal grandmother, Helena, in the church of the Holy Apostles but that occasion I cannot recall independently. Likewise I cannot remember Constantine going through the same ceremony of coronation as I had the following spring, but I certainly did later ask Pita why he needed to be crowned too. It seemed like a debasement of the currency.

My mother made regular visits to the nursery but they were whirlwind affairs. She would suddenly rush in with her silk robes billowing around her crying 'Where are my babies?' She would gather Constantine and me up, one on each arm, planting frenzied kisses with her wide mouth while her jewellery poked and scratched us. I can even now smell her exotic, heady scent and see those heavily painted eyes. She would then set us down and survey us longingly before retreating backwards through the door amidst a welter of endearments. My father came rather less frequently. All I remember is his pale, thin, young face smiling down at us. I once reached up to try to touch his curly black beard but he gently moved out of my reach. He died only two days after Anna was born but those events are not connected in my memory. I just recollect standing with my mother next to a wooden box and her saying: 'Father Anthony will lift you up'. Up I went and there was my father lying with his eyes closed. The monk leaned forward with me and I was told to kiss him. I did so but he was all cold.

I have numerous memories which I realise must be from the summer of 963, in the months following my father's death. The figure who looms largest is Pita. I recall one sunny morning, when I was out with her in the small garden that fronts the Kainourgion. I decided to run along a low stone wall that bordered some flowers beds, not realising that the damp moss that covered it was so slippery. I ended up on my back on the soggy ground, covered in mud. She picked me up herself and took me inside to plunge me in a bath. She need not have done so, as the task could easily have been delegated to someone in the fleet of servants under her command. She spent a great deal of time with Constantine on her lap and me playing around her feet. But for me she did something special, for which I have always been very grateful. She would whisper to me in a speech that was different from that used by everyone else. Her family were Armenians from Sebasteia and it was from her that I picked up the rudiments of the language. I wonder now whether my mother would have approved, had she known. Pita certainly took the precaution of switching to Greek if any of the other servants were within earshot. I have no doubt that she was envied for her position and there would have been no shortage of rivals who would have been willing to exploit anything to her discredit so that they could supplant her. The Great Palace is like that. It is not only the emperor who has always to be looking over his shoulder.

There was something else that Pita gave me. It was the small figure of a soldier, about three inches high, roughly carved by someone in her family from dark wood. She said that he was a Rus, meaning one of the Russians who live on the other side of the Black Sea. I took her at her word and called him Arus. Princes get given endless presents but very few that they actually want.

After Pita, my most regular adult visitor of those months was my aunt Theodora, my father's sister. She would play with me on the nursery floor, even though her weight made it a considerable challenge to get down there and an even greater one to get up again. She always used to wear her hair up in a sort of top knot and it used to wobble as she leaned over. When she was not there and Pita was busy, Constantine was my only companion. He started crawling and walking very quickly but he still had not started speaking when he was three. That made him a frustrating playmate. When we went outside, I tried to involve him in various species of chasing games around in the shrubberies and along the stone-paved paths. When I laboriously explained the rules of a game to him, he would just stare back so it was impossible to know whether he had understood or not. If hiding was involved, he always left bits of himself sticking out so I had to pretend not to see him which was hardly satisfactory. I complained to Pita but she said I must make allowances because he was young. So I gave up and instead imitated Pita, talking to him in baby language, wiping his face and hauling him out of harm's way when he was about to do something dangerous.

During this time, we often went to church with Pita, outside Sundays and festivals when we went with our mother. Our nurse favoured the little chapel of St Barbara, I think because it was small and intimate, unlike Hagia Sophia, St Stephen's or the New Church. She was particularly devoted to an icon of the Virgin there which hung at the centre of the iconostasis in front of the altar. All three of us would kneel down in front on it, on cushions that the servants brought, and she would whisper to me, explaining how the Virgin was pointing to the Child that she held, indicating the way, the truth and the life. I listened but I could not help running my eyes along the lines of icons. Most of the saints looked so sad and preoccupied that I could not believe they would have time to listen to my prayers. One of the icons though was different. It showed a beardless young man with light brown hair. I pulled Pita's sleeve and asked who he was:

'That's St Demetrius, a soldier who was martyred for not denying his faith in Jesus.'

He had such a friendly, open face that I decided that I would address my prayers to him as he was bound to listen.

During those summer months, our mother visited less frequently and she seemed different somehow. I remember her taking me in her arms and saying how busy she was because she was looking after everything until I was grown up enough to be emperor. She often talked about someone called Lord Bringas the Chamberlain who was also looking after everything as well. Once she brought him with her. He was a grave man with a pale complexion and a smooth chin who wore a tall, almost conical hat. He had very dark, rather bushy eyebrows. There is a dim memory of being in the Magnavra, my mother seated on the throne of Solomon, wearing her crown, with the strings of jewels hanging down from it: I am not sure that I had seen her in it before. I was at her side on a smaller seat. The hall was crowded and lines of people came up and prostrated themselves in front of us. For the occasion, I had to wear a completely new silk robe, a small cap and around my waist a purple stole. The robe was hot and heavy, the sleeves were far too long and its collar itched. I wished I could be like St

Demetrius who wore just a long white tunic with a square opening for his neck.

✱ ✱ ✱

Having come this far, I am having second thoughts and wondering why I am writing this. In doing so, I am breaking a lifetime's habit of concealing my innermost thoughts, hence the precaution of using the Armenian language to protect myself at least from casual prying eyes. It was after my visit to Hebdomon in 1018 that I resolved to try to make sense of what happened by writing it down. So many things took place when I was young that I only understood later and there were others which I am only just starting to comprehend. That is why I am going to try to record events as I saw them at the time and not as I perceive them now. I am going to start by describing an incident that I have not spoken about to anyone for more than sixty years. In fact, I have scarcely revisited it in my own mind during that time.

It was an August day, so we had been taken out early into the garden and then to the Hippodrome where we were placed on small ponies and walked around the central spine of the stadium for a couple of laps. That might have been the first occasion that I noticed the gigantic statue of Hercules there. His slumped posture struck me as odd, given the heroic deeds that Pita had told me about. I asked the grooms about it but they did not know the answer. Arriving back at the Kainourgion, we were given some bread and olives to eat and then sent to our rooms for a rest during the hottest part of the day. It was after a few hours that I noticed that something was wrong. No one came to rouse us and I became aware that there was an unaccustomed hush outside the window. I came out of my room into the nursery to find that Pita and the other servants had vanished but Constantine was there, sitting contentedly on the floor and playing with some wooden bricks.

I went over to the door that gave onto the corridor and put my ear to it. Not a sound. The door was a heavy one, carved with geometric patterns and with a latch of ivory and metal. I had never touched either the door or the handle before as they seemed part of the world of adults in which I had no right to be. I looked back to see that Constantine was still sitting there with his thumb in his mouth, piling up the bricks with his other hand. I reached up and pulled down the latch and the door opened inwards a crack. There was no one out there. I walked into the corridor expecting Pita to appear at any moment to shoo me back inside again. I took a few steps along the cool marble floor but still nothing happened. Wondering just how far I could go, I padded down to a shuttered window at the end of the corridor and stood on tiptoe to see if I could peer through the slats but I could see nothing. I looked back to the nursery door. Constantine had by now become curious and was looking out with his thumb still in his mouth and a wooden brick in his hand. It was then that a sound floated up the marble spiral staircase, that made me freeze with terror. Someone was weeping but disturbingly it was an adult, a thing that I had never heard before. When the shock had worn off, I scuttled back to the nursery. We retreated into a corner and waited.

After a while, we heard footsteps in the corridor. They were definitely those of men. The door opened and Bringas looked in. We gaped back at his unsmiling, bushy-browed gaze. He looked different but I had no idea why. I could not have known then that having heard an adult weeping, I now saw one afraid. He stood back and said to someone outside: 'Take them both.' Two large men came into the nursery and lifted Constantine and me onto their shoulders. We were borne out into the corridor where two other men waited with Bringas and the group then turned to descend by the nearest staircase. The smell of the man who held me on his shoulder is with me still: a mixture of leather and sweat. I gazed curiously at the hair in his ears and felt my own to find out if I had it too. Then there was a scream.

Down the corridor, Pita had just reached the top of the far stairwell. She came running down the corridor, shouting to the men to put the children down. Bringas had already started down the stairs, closely followed by the man who held Constantine. The two men with hands free moved forward to intercept Pita who clawed and pulled at them. Bringas had stopped on the stairs and he yelled up:

'We are taking them to safety in Hagia Sophia, can't you see that? Do you really want Phokas to get his hands on them?'

The man behind him said: 'We haven't got time for this!'

They started off again down the stairs and the man carrying me followed. My view of what happened next was restricted because I was leaning over the man's shoulder. As he went down the steps my view became the blank wall of the stairwell. But I did have a momentary glimpse of what happened above. Pita was still trying to grapple with the two men and was now shouting in Armenian rather than Greek. One of them suddenly lost patience. He did not shove her off or slap her, he bunched his fist and punched her full in the face. It was the sort of blow that I have seen men trading in boxing bouts at military camps, only this time it was directed against a stout middle-aged woman who was barely five foot tall. She flew backwards, a spurt of blood shot from her mouth and she disappeared below the balustrade. Then the scene was lost to view as we were taken down the stairs and out across the hall. Through the small garden we went and then along the seemingly endless succession of porticoes and courtyards that leads out of the Boukoleon and into the more public parts of the Great Palace. We reached the Brazen Gate and from the top of the marble stairs we could see that it was deserted and quite open to the square beyond.

'God is with us!,' said Bringas.

We launched out into the void, needing only to cross the Augousteion to reach the sanctuary of Hagia Sophia on the far side of the square. As we bumped along I was looking back over my bearer's shoulder and I noticed a line of men running into the square from the Hippodrome side. They were clearly soldiers but not like any I had seen before, not like the guards in the palace. They wore helmets with slits for their eyes, long chain armour that came to their knees and their swords were drawn. They ran in a line, arcing round to cut us off from the entrance to the church. Bringas and his men had seen them too and knew the game was up. We were hastily set down and while Bringas sprinted for the church his men scattered in other directions. I stood there dazed, looking at Constantine at whose feet a small puddle was starting to form, the vast bulk of Hagia Sophia looming over him. I grabbed his hand and, since running seemed to be the order of the day, I put my head down and started back towards the Brazen Gate, glancing over my shoulder to see if we were pursued.

Most of us, I am sure, have walked or run without looking where we are going and collided with something. It feels as if the laws of nature have suddenly changed and the air has become solid. In this case, it was not so much solid as soft and enfolding. I had run straight into someone wearing a long silk robe. I pulled my head free of the fabric and my eyes panned up the seemingly endless tower of blue embroidery to reach a face. It was youngish, clean shaven, framed by thin brown hair and a double chin that was accentuated because its owner was looking down at me. The lips moved:

'Your Majesty is safe now. I am Nothos.'

He withdrew his arms from his sleeves and scooped Constantine up to his side, heedless of soiling his gown. Then he held his hand down to me. After so much terror, I suddenly felt a wave of calm and reassurance. I placed my hand trustingly inside his enormous paw and together the three of us made our way back towards the Brazen Gate.

* * *

I am not sure what happened immediately after that. I certainly remember asking the servants what had happened to Pita but no one would answer and then our mother came to see us. She rushed in with all the extravagant affection that she had neglected over the past few months. She squeezed us and kissed us and told us how worried she had been. She was followed slowly into the room by Nothos who, I noticed, was now sporting the tall chamberlain's hat, and by Anthony, the very thin monk who had lifted me up to kiss my dead father. The conversation went something like this. I first asked was where Pita was, at which my mother looked completely blank and from her position kneeling on the floor with us, she turned her head up to Nothos. He squatted down and whispered something in her ear.

'Oh,' she said, 'well, it would seem that this nurse had an accident and hit her head.' Nothos whispered again.

'And she died.' I began to wail. 'But it'll be alright, darling,' she forged on, unprepared for my emotional reaction to the demise of an underling. 'Mummy will give her family some gold coins and,' she added brightly, 'that'll make it better.'

'Will the coins bring her back?,' I asked. My mother froze open mouthed, not quite sure what to say next. She was rescued by Nothos.

'Not all the gold coins in the treasury will do that, Majesty, but perhaps we can help her people in their sadness.' I am not sure that those were his exact words but that was the kind of thing he would have said. I never did find out exactly what had happened to Pita or to her family even though I made enquiries in later years. Presumably her assailant lost his temper and lashed out, not meaning to kill. I hope he felt remorse for what he did. He was certainly never brought to justice.

'There you see,' said a grateful Theophano. Then she went on, 'Now I have to tell you that the Lord Bringas turned out to be a very bad man. Mummy thought she could trust him to look after you both just like your poor father would have done, had he lived. But look what he did, trying to take you from the nursery with those horrid men to help him. So he's been sent away as a punishment and he'll never be allowed back. He'll never be able to frighten you again like he did yesterday. Instead your godfather is coming, Lord Nikephoros Phokas, and he'll look after everything.'

While I digested this, there was some talk with Nothos and Anthony about my mother going to Petrion. I did not know what or where Petrion was but it sounds like our word for "stone." I remembered Pita telling me the story of Perseus and the Gorgon and I thought my mother was going to be turned to stone and would die. I started crying again and was assured that she was not going far and would soon be back. Then she was gone.

At some point after that, perhaps even later the same day, the servants started dressing us up because "the Lord Emperor Nikephoros" wanted to see the purple-born emperors. I was surprised to hear him referred to like that but everything had moved so fast that I had given up asking questions. The next few hours were spent in dread and anxiety for the arrival of this mysterious figure. Even at that tender age, I was aware of the possibility that this new emperor might present some kind of threat to us. His arrival was heralded by a stamping and a crashing from the corridor. It came from armoured men marching up all three spiral staircases simultaneously and then lining up along the walls. Someone shouted: 'Make way for the Emperor Nikephoros!' and that was followed by a resounding clang as the soldiers struck their shields with their swords. Constantine and I cowered back against the wall, our eyes on the doorway where our visitor would appear.

When he did so we shrank still further because we had never encountered anyone quite like him. For a start, Nikephoros had not donned the court dress that we were accustomed to. He had come straight from the stables, and was clad in riding breeches and a black leather jerkin: a distinct smell of horse wafted across the room. His head was covered in a mass of black hair pushed back from his forehead. His grey-flecked beard was straggling and unkempt and grew only underneath his chin and not on his cheeks at all. His body looked all out of proportion. The upper part was stooped but broad and clearly powerful and the hairy arms that protruded from the jerkin were muscled and tanned. Yet the torso was supported by two spindly legs that appeared all the more slender from being encased in the riding breeches. They were mirrored by his scrawny neck which somehow held up his large head. At the time though, I probably did not notice all that, only the horse smell and the most disturbing feature of all: the small, piercing coal-black eyes under bushy black brows. As he leaned forward with his stoop, they seemed to burn into us while we stared back in terror.

If that nightmare vision were not enough, two almost identical figures had marched into the room behind him, although they were dressed more appropriately for the occasion. One was ancient, the thick hair and beard completely white, and there was a jagged scar that ran from the hairline, across the left eye and far down his cheek. The other was clearly younger but had the same stoop and ungainly body as the other two. All three were now scanning us with identical eyes. Behind them Nothos glided in followed by a rather short and plump man with receding hair and a neatly trimmed beard in the usual palace attire of a patterned silk robe.

'Majesties,' Nothos said to us, 'this is our emperor, Lord Nikephoros. This,' he indicated the older, scarred replica, 'is his father Lord Bardas Phokas. This is his brother, Lord Leo Phokas,' pointing to the plump man, and then indicating the younger replica, 'and this is his nephew, Lord Bardas who is the son of Lord Leo.'

I doubt if I took any of that in at the time. I was just staring in fascinated horror at the vision in front of me.

3

'Ha!,' said Nikephoros. How appropriate that the first word we heard him utter was his favourite interjection. He turned to Nothos: 'Which one is which?'

The chamberlain made the introductions and that was as far as the interview went. Nikephoros made no attempt to engage us in conversation. He merely glanced around the room, took a look at Constantine, then pointed at me.

'This is no place for the older boy. Needs to move to somewhere else. Start his education. Chamberlain, see to it.'

He turned on his heel. The two Bardases moved aside to let him pass and then followed him through the door. His brother Leo gave us a kindly smile and departed as well. We were left alone with Nothos towering over us, benign and reassuring, although I have no recollection of what he said. I shall return to him later.

✳ ✳ ✳

Those were very confusing days. Just as she had promised, my mother was back within a few weeks, only to announce that she would be marrying that same alarming Nikephoros. We were told that he was now our stepfather and that we should love him just as we had our real father. The ceremony took place late in September in the so-called New Church within the Great Palace. Constantine and I had to follow our mother to the altar and stand through the long droning of the nuptial liturgy. By the time of the marriage, I had been moved out of the nursery and installed downstairs in the Kainourgion in the suite of rooms that had for time immemorial been reserved for the heir to the throne. I was very pleased to have my importance marked in this way but I soon found the new environment to be a rather lonely one. There was no one to replace Pita, just a cohort of servants who would dress, wash and feed me. They seemed to be different people every day. I never learned their names and when I asked them they merely smiled and said that

I did not want to know about them. I realise now that this was what they had been told to say and I know too who it was that gave those instructions but I do not want to get ahead of myself.

A few days after the move, I suddenly ran upstairs to the nursery to see Constantine before the servants could stop me. I pushed open the door but found that it was completely deserted. The floor had been swept and everything put away. In Constantine's bedroom, the bed was bare and the chest empty. Someone caught up with me and explained that Constantine had gone with my mother and little Anna across the Bosporus to Hiereia where there was a small summer palace. They would be staying there for the time being. So the only relative that I saw in the months after my mother remarried was my aunt Theodora. Her apartment was in the section of the Boukoleon set aside for women only but my tender years allowed me entry and it became established that I should dine with her once a week. She had a generous suite of rooms but they felt cramped because they were cluttered with furniture and all kinds of miscellaneous objects. She acquired voraciously and discarded nothing: lumps of translucent sea coral, illustrated psalters, porcelain bowls, ivory diptychs and anything else that caught her eye. She had long since run out of storage space for them all and many of these objects lay discarded around the room or piled on the couches: one had to clear a space to sit down. I enjoyed those occasions even though conversations with Theodora were somewhat one-sided. She would always start off with: 'Now I am going to ask you about all the things that you have been doing today' but then go off on some tangent which meant that I never got to tell her about my activities (not that there would have been much to tell).

I had no companions of my own age. I was taken every day to the now autumnal small garden by the Kainourgion. Those who accompanied me kept me in view but left me to entertain myself. Unsatisfactory playmate though Constantine had been, I did start to miss him. For want of anything better, I took to amusing myself. I gathered up the cones that had dropped from the huge umbrella pines and gave them life as soldiers under the command of Arus who I had carefully brought with me from the nursery. There were paving stones on the paths that wound through the trees and they were arranged in a pattern – a large diamond in the centre and a frame of rectangles at the edge. These I turned into castles and palaces, stationing the pine-cone army at strategic points. In this way, I passed many afternoons in the warm October sunshine, until summoned in before the light faded.

It was as October became November that I began to experience strange things, usually after dark when I had been put to bed. There was always an oil lamp burning in my bedchamber and the door was left open to the next room. One servant would sleep across the doorway, another in the room beyond. But their presence did not ward off the horrors. Figures used to rise up out of the walls and run around the ceiling shouting and screaming. Then they would peer and point at me so I would duck under the covers. But after a while the thought that they might be still out there would overwhelm me and I would poke out my head to see. Sometimes they would be gone but sometimes they would still be charging around the walls, ignoring me and intent on some chasing game of their own. Then they would stop and turn to me and I would take cover once more. At some point, I would presumably fall asleep but that was not the end of the visitations. I would find myself standing on the diamond-paved path, looking down a long avenue of trees, their leaves a seasonal red and gold. At the end of the avenue stood a woman and I knew that it was Pita. I would begin to walk towards her, then to run but I never got any closer, then I would fall to the ground and wake up with a start. Looking around I would see the flickering lamp and hear the regular breathing of the servants but by then light was starting to well up behind the shutters as dawn came.

Sometimes, the line between dream and reality became blurred. I have an image of myself, sitting in the garden with the afternoon sun very low in the sky. The servants sometimes used to forget about me and brought me in much later than they should have. I looked up from what I was doing towards the buildings beyond the Kainourgion. There was a figure standing on a balcony and staring out across the Bosporus. With the light failing it was no more than a silhouette but I knew for certain that it was my mother. She must be back from Hiereia, I thought, and tomorrow she would come to see me. But then another, male figure appeared, stood behind her and then placed his arms about her waist. She seemed to lean back against him. Who was this? It certainly was not Nikephoros whose unusual build was recognisable in any light. Then I deduced that the man must be my dead father and that I was dreaming. My mother had not returned and would not come to me tomorrow. As with all dreams, once you know it is one, it come to an end. The figures had vanished, leaving me to the pine-cones, rustling leaves and gathering gloom.

I think that those surreal adventures continued to haunt me during the day because it was around then that I developed a curious habit that I am still not entirely free of. It became a matter of some difficulty for me to enter a room unless I knew first who – or what – was in it. The issue does not really arise these days as wherever I go I am preceded by two guards whom I trust to deal with any eventualities. At that time though I would sidle up to the door post and peer round. For the most part, no one seemed to notice this eccentricity or if they did they were too polite to mention it. The only person who did was my aunt Theodora, who would wave me in impatiently. It was then that I discovered too that I had one of those faces which, when at repose, looks both sullen and apprehensive. Theodora would say: 'Don't worry it may never happen!'

∗ ∗ ∗

Of my newly acquired stepfather, I saw nothing. I used to hear the roar and cheering in the Hippodrome when he appeared in the royal box to preside over a race or to distribute largesse but I was never invited to join him. Only when we were well into Advent did a message arrive to say that I would be expected to dine with him in the Golden Dining Hall over the Yuletide festivities. This came as something of a disagreeable surprise as I had hoped not to have to see him and his alarming family. There was no escape and on Christmas night, I was sealed into the appropriate vestments, had a small round hat tied to my head and was led across the Boukoleon to the hall. It was evidently already full of guests because I could hear the buzz of conversation when we were still some way off. We entered the octagonal hall by the double doors at the opposite end to the apse and dais where Nikephoros sat with his brother Leo and his ghastly father. Silence descended immediately and everyone stood up. I had to waddle self-consciously down the whole length of the octagon, painfully aware of the weight of the robes, with my attendants following behind. It is something I do every day now but I think that that must have been the first time. The guests towered over me like a forest. As they bowed, their scarred and weather-beaten faces moved towards me: they did not look like the kind of people I usually encountered in the corridors of the Great Palace.

'Low provincials, dear,' Aunt Theodora had said on a visit the previous day, 'from Cappadocia.'

I walked up the steps to the dais at the end and my attendants installed me at the end of the table on a large, carved wooden chair from which my feet dangled a foot from the ground. My stepfather and the others did not rise to meet me. His sole comment on my arrival was 'Ha!.' Once I was seated, he rose. He was dressed for the occasion in silk rather than the leather jerkin that he had on when I had first encountered him, although the robe sat on him very awkwardly and looked rather old and faded. It was as if he kept it in a chest somewhere and reluctantly donned it for occasions such as this, gratefully tossing it back when the ordeal was over. To be fair, I do much the same myself. He launched into a speech to welcome the guests and to acknowledge the part that many of them had played in his campaigns. Doubtless he revisited his justifications for occupying the throne which properly belonged to the child on his right but I was not listening. Turning round I gazed at the Pentapyrgion which occupies the lower part of the apse behind the imperial table. It is a kind of gigantic cabinet of curiosities, filled with rare and precious objects that the emperors have brought back from their wars: vases and urns, jewelled daggers and crowns, and the horns of long-dead fabulous beasts. I have added a few choice items to the collection myself since then. My inattention was noticed by the ghastly Bardas and he signalled to one of the servants who gently directed my gaze back to my stepfather. Mercifully, the speech was brief. Nikephoros' favoured mode of expression was the monosyllable and when he did have to give a speech it consisted of a number of clipped sentences that conveyed the necessary information with nothing much to link them. It was soon over and after they had greeted it with entirely unmerited cheers, the guests all sat down and the food was carried in.

A dish was placed in front of me and a small beaker of heavily watered wine. Nikephoros drank only water. I picked up the fork with which I had been taught to skewer my food. Nikephoros used his hands, so did Bardas but Leo prodded away with the fork. Nothing was said for some time. Then Nikephoros turned to me. He did not believe in any preliminaries to open a conversation:

'Your education will begin after Epiphany.'

He returned to his food. I felt I ought to say something so I timidly enquired after my mother and siblings.

'In the Hiereia. Safer there.'

Silence. Bardas leaned across and growled something to his son, who cackled briefly. Suddenly, one of the guests, a gigantic man, jumped to his feet, raised his goblet and exclaimed:

'Hail to Nikephoros! White Death of the Saracens!'

The rest of them all struggled upright and joined the cry. I did not know whether I was supposed to as well for Leo and Bardas were on their feet too. I stayed put. As further toasts followed, I became restless. The hat I had to wear was itchy and it was constantly slipping down to one side and having to be pushed up again. I occupied myself at first by tracing patterns on the ceiling where the oil lamps were casting curious shadows. Then I began to fidget in the chair, slipping down further and further to see if my feet would touch the floor. The ruckus eventually died down and silence reigned once more at our table, in contrast to the cheery and increasingly animated buzz of conversation going on elsewhere in the hall. Then Leo, who was much less forbidding than his brother and father, leaned forward so that I could see his round face beyond Nikephoros and spoke to me.

'That was Theodore Lalakon. He has been with the Lord Emperor at every one of his great battles, carrying his standard and watching his back. He would follow the Emperor into the mouth of hell!'

I nodded understandingly. Nikephoros went on chewing and staring ahead impassively, as if oblivious to the conversation being carried on across him. Undeterred, Leo went on, telling me about how, when he was my age he and Nikephoros had lived in Cappadocia. He turned to Bardas and asked him whether he remembered when the three of them had ridden out of Caesarea to the cave churches when Leo was six. Bardas growled something and Nikephoros said 'Ha!' before launching into some technical detail about the terrain of the region. Bardas added a few words of wisdom, Leo disagreed and I lost any interest that might have been kindled by his friendly attention. A point came when someone whispered in Nikephoros' ear and he said:

'Yes, the boy must go now.'

Relieved, I slipped smartly off my chair and prepared to follow the attendants who were indicating a side door next to the Cabinet of Curiosities but Bardas stopped me. He had risen and his scar looked particularly red and vivid as it sliced down through his face.

'Are you not going to bid goodnight to your stepfather?'

So it was goodnight to stepfather and goodnight to Leo, who had to be addressed as "Lord Count Palatine," and goodnight to Ghastly who had to be called "Lord Caesar." Then I was ushered out. Perhaps it was the watered wine but that night when I was in bed even more figures than usual danced across the walls in the flickering lamplight. One of them was giant who carried a flag and threatened me with his enormous fist. Another was starved and skeletal and had a scar right down the side of his face.

3

Boukoleon (963-9)

When I described the isolation and inarticulate fears that I experienced that autumn, I left out the most important point. It must have been in November, as the colder weather restricted the visits to the small garden, that I started to develop a friendship with the new chamberlain, or rather he developed it with me. I called him Nothos, or rather "Nofos" as I was still having trouble distinguishing the phi sound from the theta. That was how he had introduced himself when we first met in the Augousteion. Even now, I still think of him as Nothos as I never addressed him as anything else. His predecessor Bringas had been a remote and frightening figure. Most other adults either ignored me or were frigidly deferential. The affable Leo Phokas made a few attempts to befriend me but the constant chilling presence of Nikephoros and Ghastly soon stifled them. But by some process of which I now have little recollection, the chamberlain succeeded in winning my complete trust within a few weeks of my mother's remarriage. It began with regular and then daily visits to my apartment and by the time I dined with Nikephoros at Christmas, Nothos had become the centre of my universe: father, mother, friend and teacher all rolled into one.

On the one hand, he was an almost mythical figure that I held in reverence and adulation. He was, I knew, a eunuch although I did not comprehend exactly what the word meant. I assumed it referred just to grown men who had no beards. The smoothness of his face, rather like mine, and the double chin on which it rested fascinated me. Like many of the palace eunuchs, he wore perfume but his was distinct and unique. I have never encountered its like, so I assume that he had it specially formulated somewhere. Not that there was anything effete about him. I later learned that he had commanded a detachment of troops under Leo Phokas during the eastern campaign in the year I was born and he later took part in the 971 invasion of Bulgaria. Rather the scent was another way in which he was marked out from the common run of men. On his visits, it would fill the room, announcing that Nothos was there and that enjoyable and exciting things were about to happen.

There were all kinds of other fascinating traits, such as his enormous hands that were covered in rings. Sometimes he would place them flat on a table in front of me and get me to pull off the rings one by one. He would then explain what each was made of, what stone was in the mounting and what images were carved on the stone. My favourite featured St Basil of Caesarea picked out in enamel on a gold lozenge. When all the rings were off, then we would slowly put them all on again, one by one. There was his tall hat, the one that only a chamberlain was allowed to wear. He would take it off and put it on the chest during visits and I would go and look at it and trace the intricate woven patterns on it with my finger. Then there was his bulk, so broad, tall and imposing, perfectly proportioned from head to toe. I watched him once when we were out in the garden sitting on a wall. It must have been April or May by then as the horse chestnut tree was covered in white candles. He stood up, gently took a low branch in his hand and conveyed the flower to his nose to savour its scent. Then suddenly he let go of the branch and slammed his hand, wrapped in his sleeve, down on the wall. I was startled and looked down as he removed his hand. Underneath were the remains of a poisonous recluse spider.

Yet while he was a figure of awe and veneration, Nothos was also the only person apart from Theodora who would play with me. He would pick me up and sit me on his shoulders so that my head nearly touched the ceiling. He brought fascinating things for me. One was a small wooden model of the type of warship we call a dromon. I set it on the floor but then left it there when something else caught my attention. As I went to find it again, there was a sickening crunch and I looked down to see that I had trodden on it. 'Oh dear,' said Nothos, 'it will have to go to dock.' He took it away with him when he left and it never came back. Sunk, I suspect, with all hands.

Then again, he was also my teacher and my guide. We would sit on one of the marble benches in the long Boukoleon corridors or, once the weather turned to snow, in one of the state rooms that were warmed by underfloor pipes. I would ask him things, now that I was of an age to be curious.

'Nofos, why have the leaves on the trees gone brown?'

'Because winter is coming and they are going to fall. New ones will come in the spring.'

'Nofos, who is that man on the horse on top of the column that I can see from the window?'

'That is Emperor Justinian, Majesty, who built the Great Church.'

'Nofos, where do the stars go during the day?'

'They are still there, Majesty, but the splendour of the sun outshines them.'

'Nofos, why is Nikephoros emperor when he was not born in the purple?'

'Because His Majesty is much too young to rule, so the Lord Nikephoros rules in his place for the time being. You and he are emperors together. Look.'

He opened his huge palm to reveal a gold coin, the one that we call the Nomisma. On it were two crowned figures on either side of a cross which they were holding firmly. He told me that the bearded one on the right was Nikephoros and that I was the one on the left, without a beard.

'But won't Nikephoros want his son to be emperor later?'

'He has no son living, Majesty. There was one but he died in an accident a year ago. It is you who will be emperor later.'

I thought for a moment of that horrible nephew but accepted the reassurance. On some days, he would stay longer and take me on what he called "an expedition" around the Great Palace. We would wind through seemingly endless courtyards and cloistered walkways until we reached something that he knew I would like. He showed me the Horologion, a great white clock that uses water to measure the hours, and the courtyard known as the Triconch which has an upper and a lower portico around it and fountain and pool in the middle. Why is it that children are so fascinated by bodies of water? He took me to the palace workshops where goldsmiths were hammering, jewellers were cutting and enamellers engraving. He showed me the great reliquary he was having made for the monastery of St Basil. One summer morning we paced across the wide open atrium that leads to the chapel of the Holy Virgin of Pharos. The atrium is open to the sky and the sun shines directly onto the brilliant white marble paving and walls so that you have the impression of moving through celestial light. At the far side the doorway is filled with metal grille to keep most visitors at a distance. For us though, it glided noiselessly to one side as we approached and we moved into what seemed the utter blackness of the interior. Then I saw in the candlelight a priest holding a cushion on which I was told rested the Crown of Thorns, the very same one that had been placed on the head of Our Saviour when he suffered crucifixion. Nothos said that if I looked carefully I would be able to see blood on some of the thorns. It was too much dim to be sure but I said that I could.

One of my favourite places was the one called *Chrysis Cheiros* in the language of the Romans: the Portico of the Golden Hand. It is a horseshoe-shaped space, open to the sky, with a columned portico that runs all the way round it, situated halfway between the Brazen Gate and the entrance to the Boukoleon. The main attraction for me was that the portico had two levels that both link to the network of corridors that run through the palace. I could run up the staircase at one end, go right around the upper level, down the staircase at the other and then double back to end up where I had started. At the top of the horseshoe, a colossal marble hand stands on a plinth, its finger pointing upwards to the sky. I asked Nothos why it was white and not gold and was told that it had once been covered in gold leaf when it had been part of a gigantic statue of Emperor Constantine the Great. It had been placed there to remind us to always direct our thoughts to heaven.

There was one last thing that Nothos did that no one else had ever done, not even Pita. He listened to what I said and having listened, he remembered. I must have told him about being taken to the chapel of St Barbara and seeing the friendly icon of St Demetrius. A few weeks later I found a small replica of it on my bed, the same brown hair, the same welcoming eyes. I put it on the little table by the bed and that night the nocturnal visitors stayed away. In fact, they vanished completely once Nothos started visiting regularly. It was only on long lonely days, when business called him away, that they rose up to haunt me.

✳ ✳ ✳

There was a whole series of banquets throughout the Christmas season all of which I was required to attend. They were all punctuated by shouts of praise for Nikephoros and muttered conversations between the Phokas family members on our table. It was a few days later that my elementary schooling began. It was decided to entrust it to Father Anthony who was my mother's confessor so I assume that he must have been her choice. I had met him before. First when he had lifted me up to kiss my father's corpse and later when he had accompanied Theophano as she went off to Petrion following Nikephoros' takeover. He now held the office of Synkellos, a kind of deputy to Patriarch Polyeuktos but before that he had been a monk at the monastery of St John Stoudios which is situated in the far southwest of Constantinople. That would have secured the approval of Nikephoros for my stepfather was a great admirer of the monastic vocation. It was a good choice. Father Anthony's emaciated frame may have made him look rather austere and unsympathetic but he was kindly enough and entirely at his ease being given a responsibility that would have overawed many bishops. He almost never gave me a title, preferring "my dear." We met in the specially designated school room in the Kainourgion that had been set up by the founder of our dynasty, Emperor Basil I, so that the celebrated patriarch Photios could teach his children there. There were some fifteen desks and stools, small ones at the front and larger ones at the back. The desks lifted up to provide a space to store writing tablet and stylus. I kept Arus in mine too. We began with the alphabet which I almost knew already and then began to read short sentences.

I cannot pretend that I was a particularly apt pupil. Reading and writing did not come naturally to me but Father Anthony was one of the most patient men I have known. I can still see his black, silky hair and beard bent over the page as he urged me to try again or asked whether I remembered that when an alpha and an upsilon were together they made a special sound. It must have been several years before we finally started to read the Gospel of Mark and even then I could only manage a few lines before getting lost. Eventually I got the hang of it and as time went on I did start to read in my own time, purely for pleasure, though the books I chose were not those Father Anthony would have recommended. When I was eleven he gave me the life of St Nicholas of Sion to read. Apparently this Nicholas could read better than his teacher by the age of seven. I drew the conclusion that I would not have liked him very much and I put the book aside.

Matters became more difficult when I was expected to write. I instinctively picked up the stylus with my left hand and, although Father Anthony would gently transfer it to my right, it still somehow ended up in the left again. He gave up in the end. I suspect that he consulted higher authority and was told to let me do it my way. So that was fine until after a few years I was expected to write with paper and ink rather than on a wax tablet. As I wrote, my hand would smudge the wet ink and make the whole thing unreadable. I was not cut out to be a scribe, nor to be a literary emperor like my grandfather, Constantine VII.

When the days grew longer, the Great Palace became a hive of frenzied activity and the servants told me that the emperor was going to war. Naturally, I asked Nothos all about it when he next visited.

'The Lord Emperor Nikephoros is travelling to the eastern frontier of the Roman state, Majesty, to make war on the Saracens. The Romans once owned all the land to the east as far as Egypt but the Saracens pushed us back behind the Taurus mountains in Asia Minor. Now the Emperor wants to advance beyond that border and take back some of the territory that was once ours, especially Tarsus and the province of Cilicia.'

I asked whether his departure meant that my mother, brother and sister would be returning to the Great Palace.

'Why no, Majesty. They will be accompanying the Emperor to the east. It is only right that a wife should be at her husband's side and she will need your brother and sister to support her during the long days when your stepfather is dealing with military affairs.'

'So will I be going as well?'

'His Majesty is too important to be sent away from Constantinople. There are many vital duties to be fulfilled here in the absence of the Lord Emperor.'

'But I thought I wasn't going to be emperor until I'm grown up.'

'You are an emperor already, Majesty, even if you do not carry the full burden.' He paused, bowed his head and put his finger to his lips as if gathering his thoughts to announce something of vital importance. 'That means you must be very careful in the way that you act towards others. To take one example, you cannot speak to other children and make them your friends. Do you know why not?'

There had never been any opportunity for me to do so but since he had raised the issue, I was curious to know why. I tilted my head back: that's how we say no.

'If you are particular friends with another boy, his family will believe that they stand in special favour with you and will try to exploit that to their advantage. Other families will feel excluded and will become your enemies, possibility even supporting rebels and usurpers. No, Majesty, you must be distant from all but the friend of all, then you will be the enemy of none. Indeed it is not just with other children that you must observe this rule but with everyone.'

It was on a blustery day in March that Nikephoros set out. He was to cross first to Chalcedon on the imperial galley that is always moored at readiness in in the small harbour of Boukoleon. The harbour is enclosed by two stone moles, one of which has at the end a bronze statue of a lion fighting an ox, and is reached by a set of stone steps that runs down from the

Great Palace. I remember watching from a window as he stalked down that staircase and passed between the two stone lions that stand where the steps meet the wharf. Two regiments of troops awaited him at Chalcedon and Theophano, Constantine and Anna were to travel there from Hiereia to join him. Leo and Bardas senior were at the harbour to see him off but they were staying behind to keep an eye on things here.

The summer passed but the emperor did not return to Constantinople at the end of the campaigning season. It was decided instead that he would spend the winter at Caesarea with the army so that he could more easily renew the campaign in the spring. My mother, brother and sister stayed with him. In their absence, the pattern of my life was set. My days were occupied by lessons with Father Anthony, daily visits from Nothos, occasional ones from Leo Phokas and weekly dinners with Aunt Theodora. Old Bardas, I was relieved to discover, had retired to his family's mansion down near the harbour of Sophia and seldom came to his apartment in the Great Palace. There was, however, something new. In Nikephoros' absence, I was now called upon to play the emperor's part in an endless round of ceremonies and Church festivals. I distinctly remember Ascension day in what must have been 965. I was dressed in a very heavy vestment which was weighed down with gold thread and bangles while an equally weighty crown was fastened onto my head. They physically heaved me onto a docile pony, which itself was burdened down with a jewelled bridle and had silk ribbons tied to its tail and legs. I was then led out of the Brazen Gate, Nothos and Leo Phokas riding behind. As I clutched the pommel of the saddle to prevent myself toppling off to left or right, we plodded across the Augousteion, onto the long straight Mese, through the forums of Constantine and Theodosius, ever onwards. It began to dawn on me that this was to be a long journey, something that had not been made clear when I was told that I was going "to the spring." So I clutched still harder and the effort of staying in the saddle was not helped by the attentive gaze of a crowd that lined the streets and squares, all dressed in their best for the holiday. We finally reached the Land Wall and to my astonishment we carried on through an open gate. I began to fear that the trek would never end and that we would continue until we fell off the edge of the earth. In fact, our destination was only a little further on and still within sight of the walls: the church of the Virgin of the Life-giving Spring. A reception committee of clergy and civic dignitaries met us there, swinging censors and singing hymns, and they escorted my pony into the courtyard. I was dismounted and marched up a spiral staircase at the side of the church to a small room. There I was mercifully relieved of the casket-coat and put in a flowing white robe instead which was much more comfortable. In that I presided over a long communion service from my box at the back of the church and then over a lunch in an adjoining hall for some forty guests, all doubtless carefully selected as supporters of the Phokas family.

Later in the year, I was at the palace of Hiereia for the vintage festival. I had to ride with the aged Patriarch Polyeuktos to a nearby vineyard, once again in a hot and heavy outfit. At the gate of the vineyard a kind of rustic bower had been set up made of branches and vines. Inside the bower was a marble table piled with bunches of grapes. I had to get off my pony and go to this table and after the patriarch had said a prayer, I had to hand out bunches of grapes to all the assembled local dignitaries. They then shouted various acclamations such as 'Unutterable joy has come to the world.' Perhaps it had but it passed me by as I sweltered in the heat. Experiences like that are, I think, why I am so impatient of ceremonial to this day. Luckily I can now delegate most of these duties to my brother.

✳ ✳ ✳

Between ceremonies, I was allowed to roam by myself in the palace gardens while my flock of attendants sat nearby chatting in the sunshine. I found a particular mulberry tree with low branches that I could climb. At first, the attendants clucked and scolded at this activity, fearful that I would fall and that they would get the blame. I thought it strange that they were so concerned about that when no one had worried in the least that I might topple off the pony on Ascension day when I was weighted down with gold thread. But when they saw that I could climb perfectly well (I was now seven), they relaxed and returned to their talk. The tree was not very high (it is still there in fact) but it gave me the impression of being on top of the world. It opened up a view across the Bosporus to Asia much better than I could get from ground level and once I was on my branch, nobody knew I was there. Generally people avoided that section of the garden if they saw that the emperor was around but now they came and went, blithely unaware that I was watching them from the foliage above. I liked that.

It was a day in early summer, not long after the Ascension day torture, around nine, when I had been taken out before the sun rose too high and before my scheduled attendance in Hagia Sophia in the late afternoon. I was watching a ship making its way north along the Bosporus and making bets with myself whether it would put in at the Golden Horn or continue north to St Mamas or Sosthenion. Footsteps sounded below and, looking down, I saw two figures walking along the path that led directly beneath me. They were in deep and animated conversation and one of them, a tall, dark-haired young man with a beaklike nose, was bent forward slightly. That was because his companion, who was around the same age but had blond, receding hair, was rather short. I could not hear the words but as they got closer I realised that they were speaking Armenian. Its very tones took me back to the nursery and to

Pita's voice that I had almost forgotten. When they were directly beneath me, the fair man said something that I understood:

'We must take the galley across to Chalcedon today if we are not to miss the attack on Tarsus. Besides, I miss her so much, it hurts.'

I suppose I wanted to show off, both my understanding of Armenian and my cleverness in concealing myself without their knowing I was there. That was why I broke the rule that Nothos had given me and shouted down to them in Armenian:

'I can see Chalcedon from here!'

When they looked up startled, I intended to jump down and land triumphantly in front of them. When I looked though I saw that the distance to the ground was daunting, so I swung and scrabbled until eventually I stood before them. The effect was not nearly as dramatic as I had hoped but they did seem rather disconcerted. They bowed deeply in confusion, apologising in Greek that had they known that I was present and all the rest.

'Majesty,' said the short fair one, 'I am John Tzimiskes, the nephew of the Lord Emperor Nikephoros: my mother is his sister. I serve as domestic of the east. This gentleman is Roupenios, a commander in our army. So Your Majesty speaks Armenian?'

I reeled off a few phrases that Pita was fond of using. Roupenios instinctively corrected the mispronunciations and then at once apologised for doing so.

'Not at all,' said John, 'How will His Majesty learn unless someone corrects him? We shall address you henceforth in Armenian so that you become perfect and your many subjects who speak that tongue will love you for it.'

'Are you going to the wars?'

'The Lord Emperor is advancing towards Tarsus but he will have to take Mopsuestia first. We have been in Constantinople for a few days to deliver messages and arrange supplies but we

must return now to be at his side. That is why we must go soon
to the harbour to cross the strait.'

Even if he was part of the Phokas gang, John seemed affable
enough. His blue eyes were merry and kind and I was fascinated
by his beard which was red at the top and blond at the bottom.
Then he asked:

'Did your Majesty hear us saying anything else, apart from
about crossing on the galley?'

'You said you missed your wife,' I said, proudly showing off
what I had understood.

He looked relieved and confirmed that he did indeed miss
her. Then made their excuses about having to get to the galley.
They hurried away and somehow I did not want to climb up the
tree again. Later I asked Nothos about John Tzimiskes. He told
me that his wife was called Maria and she lived in
Constantinople. So I thought that I must have misunderstood
and that perhaps he had meant that he would miss her once he
was back in the east. My Armenian was evidently not that good
after all.

✳ ✳ ✳

In the autumn of 965, Nikephoros returned to the capital in
triumph. He had taken both Mopsuestia and Tarsus during the
summer campaign and the gates of both cities accompanied him
back as trophies. In a rare display of extravagance, he had them
gilded and put on public display, one outside the Golden Gate
in the Land Walls and the other on the acropolis near the
Orphanage. Nothos, Leo and I rode to meet him at the Golden
Gate but although races and shows were laid on in the
Hippodrome to celebrate the victory, I was not invited to sit in
the royal box. Now that the real emperor was back, I no longer
had to take a leading role in ceremonies, to my great relief.

My mother returned with him and she rushed to see me,
proclaiming how she had missed me dreadfully in that cold dark

castle in Cappadocia. Constantine and Anna were not with her. My brother had, apparently, taken to army life very naturally. He would go straight down to the camp every day to watch the soldiers while they drilled and cleaned their equipment so after a while they invited him to come and sit at their campfires and to share their meals. He became a kind of military mascot. They found a little pony for him to trot around on and the smith forged him a miniature helmet and mail coat. So when the time came to return, it was agreed that he should stay behind in Caesarea in the household of Nikephoros' uncle Constantine Maleinos. This Maleinos was a veteran of the wars against the Saracens who had fought alongside old Bardas back in the day. It was decided to leave Anna in the Maleinos household too. Nikephoros wanted her to learn the frugal and virtuous ways of the provinces and not be corrupted by the luxury of the capital.

'You have to remember that about your stepfather, dear. He is a very religious man. He has no time for rich food or wine or fine clothes. Or anything else for that matter.'

I am not sure that she said that last bit and even if she had, I would not have understood. Doubtless it was widely noticed in Constantinople though that when Nikephoros returned to the east the following spring, Theophano stayed behind. I just assumed it was because she did not like the castle. The old pattern of rushed visits was resumed. She would sometimes come into my bedroom during the night and sit on my bed to talk but then she would disappear for weeks. Nikephoros did not return until March of 967 after a successful, although not spectacular, foray into Syria. A few weeks later, Nothos told me that my brother and sister would be coming back to Constantinople later in the year.

I was intensely excited at the thought of their arrival and of having not one but two companions at last. For weeks, I daydreamed about how it would be when the three of us were reunited. We would love each other and be boon companions but there would be no doubt about my precedence and authority. I would instruct Constantine and pass on my accumulated wisdom: 'What sound does alpha make when it is with upsilon? The stars are still there during the day, it is just that the splendour of the sun outshines them.' Our little sister would look up to me as a glorious hero, capable of anything, even of climbing the highest mulberry tree. So intent was I on these reveries that I scarcely noticed what was happening in Constantinople during the early summer. Unusually hot winds had blown for weeks, destroying many of the crops in Thrace and western Asia Minor, and the poorer citizens found that they could not afford to buy food. Crowds would gather in the Augousteion and clamour angrily against Nikephoros, who did not seem overly concerned. At least, nobody seemed to blame me.

When Constantine and Anna did finally reach Constantinople, there was no welcoming ceremony probably because it was feared that it might spark unrest in the streets. They arrived by night in the Boukoleon harbour and were hustled up the steps into the palace. It was only three days later that Nothos told me that they were reinstalled upstairs in the Kainourgion and that I could pay a visit straight away. We went together and I ran up the spiral staircase excitedly while Nothos ambled along after me. I was told that they were in another room from the one that we had occupied as infants so I raced down the corridor and burst in.

It was a comfortable sitting room with a wooden floor and couches along the walls. Kneeling on the floor together were a boy and a girl, intent on some game they had devised using the knucklebones that adults gamble with, according to some set of rules of their own. He was obviously Constantine to judge from his curly blond hair but that was as far as recognition went. They looked up. Nothos was still some way behind, strolling along the corridor at his own pace. Anna pointed at me: 'Who's he?' Constantine rose slowly but that did not lessen the shock.

He was as tall as I was, for all that he was seven and I was nine. Nothos appeared in the doorway.

'Majesty, here are your brother and sister, well recovered I see from their long journey from Caesarea.'

I was speechless and Constantine did not have anything to say either. He merely regarded me quizzically as if I was the last thing he expected. I looked at Anna who was still sitting on the floor glaring with mute hostility. Finally Constantine broke the ice.

'I've got a pony. They brought him with us from Caesarea. Lord Maleinos gave him to me. He's called Dorkon. He's a gelding. Have you got one?'

I considered for a moment, remembering the tiresome plod to the Holy Spring. Presumably that counted, so I nodded. But that just got me in deeper because then Constantine demanded to know my pony's name. I considered again. No one had indicated to me that the docile nag on which I had been balanced had anything to distinguish him from the herd of his fellows in the stable. So I announced that he did not have a name. Constantine's eyes widened and for the first time in my life I heard him give his extraordinary laugh: 'Arf! Arf! Arf!' like the bark of a dog which he had somehow or other picked up in Caesarea.

'How can it be your pony if it hasn't got a name? I bet you don't even know if it's a gelding or a mare!'

Nothos came to the rescue and suggested that we should go with Constantine to the stables so that he show us Dorkon. So we left Anna with the nurse and set off with Constantine chattering incessantly all the way there, telling us about camp life, the Maleinos household in Caesarea and his numerous equestrian exploits. I made a few interjections in the rare gaps, asking him if he remembered Pita. He looked at me blankly and genuinely had not the remotest idea who I was talking about. I let it drop. The stables are close to the palace's extensive polo ground and once we were there, Constantine insisted on

Dorkon being led out and saddled up so that he could ride around and show him off to us. As we stood at the edge of the polo field, returning Constantine's waves and obediently watching when he told us to, I asked Nothos why he was so big.

'He is not so very big. It is merely that Your Majesty is rather small for his age. Boys grow at different speeds and just like grown men, some are tall and some are short. As you see, I am a tall man and perhaps your brother will be too. You may grow later and catch up or you may always be quite short. But every inch of you is an emperor.'

As ever Nothos had reassured me but I remained apprehensive. As the two of us were walking back to the Boukoleon I ran on ahead again, until I reached the Triconch courtyard. I leant over the pool to see my reflection, still holding Constantine's gold head, blue eyes and peerless skin in my mind's eye. Staring back at me was a round and frowning visage topped with a mop of black hair. The eyebrows were dark and the skin spotted, the complete opposite of my brother's. I had thought siblings were supposed to look like each other. Straightening up I saw my plump figure and I thought of Constantine leaping effortlessly onto Dorkon's back. I knew for sure that with him back, nothing would ever be the same again. In spite of the icon of St Demetrius and the day spent with Nothos, my nocturnal visitors returned and during the day unknown rooms held even more terrors than before.

✳ ✳ ✳

Now that Constantine was once more in the Great Palace, he too had to play his part. There were some special occasions when our presence was called for and we both had to follow after our stepfather in processions. Nikephoros was naturally the main centre of attention but I noticed that when we passed by in his wake, the gaze of the crowd was on Constantine, not on me. I partly liked that as it shielded me from attention but also I partly resented it. It was the same with the servants. They were there instantaneously when Constantine wanted something. I had to find them and demand it. The other thing that amazed me was the speed with which Constantine built up a huge circle of acquaintance in the palace. He used to a spend large part of the day at the stables talking endlessly about the merits of this or that beast to the favoured officers who were allowed to keep their horses there, to their sons and to the grooms and stable boys. I could only assume that Nothos' injunction about not talking to anyone applied only to me and not to him. When he was not at the stables, he was in one of the kitchens where the cooks and scullions made a great pet of him. He loved food and ate prodigiously although it never had the slightest effect on his lithe figure (nor does it still). He was fascinated by the preparation and cooking of it too. So he used to help out in the kitchen until Nothos found out and told him not to. Before long everyone knew and loved him while I was an unknown. I almost never spoke to anyone. So it was that within a week of his arrival, I was completely under my brother's shadow.

That did have some benefits. Constantine soon knew everything that was going on, much of it culled from gossip in the stables and kitchens, and could pass it on to me. I learned a great deal late one summer's afternoon when we sat on a wall by the polo ground. Constantine was throwing a ball into the air and catching it and swinging his legs restlessly throughout the conversation. He found it impossible to sit still.

'Everyone really hates Nikephoros here.'

I certainly had never been partial to the man but it came as a shock to learn that grown-ups did not like him either. I pressed him to say more.

'He only likes his soldiers and couldn't care less about anyone else. He's put all the taxes up so he can give them more money and buy them armour. He brought some of them back with him from Caesarea and they robbed some houses. The people that owned them all complained but he wouldn't listen. He just said that things like that happen sometimes and they've just got to put up with it. So a few weeks ago when he was riding through the streets, some women got onto the roof of their house and threw stones at him! Arf, arf, arf!'

Then, more soberly:

'And they say rude things about him and mum.'

As I digested this, he abruptly changed the subject:

'Why do you call him Nothos? That's not his name. He's Basil like you. They only call him Nothos because his pa wasn't married to his ma! Arf, arf, arf!'

He was right. In our language, Nothos means "illegitimate" and it was a kind of nickname that the chamberlain had acquired. I suppose that he had introduced himself to me in that way to avoid any confusion over our Christian names. He might also have surmised that chamberlain, which is *parakoimomenos* in the language of the Romans, would be something of a challenge. I think I must have known that Nothos was not his real name or have had some inkling of it. What came as a shock was the revelation that a child might come to two people who were not married to each other. Why would God give a child in those circumstances? I turned to Constantine for illumination but already his attention was fixed on some more interesting companion who was waving to him from the far side of the polo field. Without a word, he slipped off the wall and was gone.

The only place where I had a slight edge over him was the schoolroom. Constantine was an even worse pupil for Father Anthony than I was. To be honest, I don't think he ever really learned to read. On the other hand, he did write better than I did because he held the pen in the correct hand. Before long he had perfected a flourishing signature: "Constantine, in God, emperor of the Romans" which was all the writing he would ever be called upon to produce. In adult eyes at least, I had the advantage that I was never naughty. It simply never occurred to me to disobey the injunctions of Nothos and Father Anthony or to do anything much on my own initiative – except in my head. Constantine was endlessly in trouble. Like me, he had been given an apartment in the Kainourgion but if required to stay in it by bad weather or to wait to be robed up for a procession, he inevitably ended up damaging something. He decided to light a fire inside a wooden cabinet, just to see what it looked like and came close to setting the whole building alight. It was soon realised that it was best to have him out of doors during the day when he was not in the school room or involved in ceremonial duties. But even when he was at the stables, riding and immersing himself in all things equine, he still managed to cause trouble. One day, without permission, he took Nikephoros' horse out of its stable and leapt on its back: God only knows how he got up there. It was a great prancing stallion and, seeing the open polo field, it immediately took off at speed. The pair parted company as it raced past the viewing stand. Constantine was completely unhurt and Nothos saw to it that Nikephoros never found out. It was decreed that he should spend a day in prison in the Kainourgion: there is a room there that Basil I had installed there for that specific purpose. Corporal punishment was never meted out, for nobody in their right mind hits an emperor. True, in later life he may laugh, clap you on the back and say how much he deserved it. But why take the risk?

The only person who seemed to prefer me to my brother was Nothos. He never visited him in the way he did me nor did they ever have the long involved conversations that we did. By now, my relationship with Nothos had changed slightly. Once I started playing a ceremonial role, there were no more shoulder rides. Instead, he started to talk to me as if I were an adult, which I found very flattering. That feeling became stronger when I found out more about him. It was one morning when I was due to take part in a procession to Hagia Sophia later in the day. I cannot remember exactly what the occasion was. Nothos arrived and greeted me brightly whereupon I began to complain about the prospect of another five-hours of tedium.

'It's all very well for you,' I said petulantly, 'Your father wasn't an emperor!'

'Ah, but you see Majesty, he was.'

Whereupon he gave me the first of many history lessons. My grandfather, Constantine VII had, like me, been only a child when his father died in 912. And like me, he had seen a military man seize power to rule in his stead, in his case the admiral of the fleet, Romanos Lekapenos. This Romanos had ruled as emperor from 920 to 944. He was already married at the time of his accession and had a large family but after his wife died in 924, he sought consolation in the arms of a Russian woman who had come to Constantinople with the traders from Kiev who visited every year. Nothos, or Basil Lekapenos to give him his real name, was the product of that liaison.

'That means, Majesty, that we are kinsmen. Your grandmother Helena, the daughter of that first Emperor Romanos, who married Constantine VII, was my half-sister. So I am your great uncle.'

'Does this mean you are an emperor too?'

'I can never be an emperor, Majesty, because I am a eunuch. Our law forbids it.'

He told me how Emperor Romanos, not wanting to jeopardise his legitimate sons' claim to the throne, had decided to have him castrated. He had been gazing from the window as he spoke, but now he paused, looked me in the eye and read my mind.

'I have no recollection of it being done.'

I know that this sounds appalling to outsiders but it is not unusual in our state for families which have been blessed with several sons to have one deprived of his manhood, doing it when the child is still very small and will have no memory of it. That way he has a chance to embark on a career in the Great Palace and to become one of the administrators, overseers and masters of ceremonial that effectively run the place. They are trusted more than whole men precisely because they cannot occupy the throne and as they have no wives or children, they can dedicate themselves single-mindedly to the service of the state. In Nothos' case, it was indeed a blessing for he was to have the most illustrious career of any of Romanos I's offspring. He had been in high office for over twenty years at that point, apart from a brief hiatus during my father's reign when he had been elbowed aside by Joseph Bringas.

I distinctly remember that I treasured that conversation for years afterwards. That was partly because I was flattered and grateful to him for his candour in telling me about his life and in explaining what "illegitimate" and "eunuch" meant. At the time, though, the important thing was that it was me, and not Constantine, in whom he had chosen to confide. In return, I wanted to please him by showing that his trust in me was not misplaced and that I would always follow his advice. I even started to imitate his mannerisms such his way of bowing his head and putting his finger to his lips before speaking. It is a useful tactic to gain time to think and I still find myself doing it. I was his echo and I wanted to be his image, to look like him when I grew up. That ambition was not fulfilled as I never reached even average height, but at the end of the day he was my Nothos, not Constantine's, and for that, more than anything else, I adored him.

4

Philopation (969)

wo years passed. Nikephoros spent more time in Constantinople now and left much of the campaigning to his subordinates. His presence did not endear him to the people of the city though and for all that he was the hero of the war against the Saracens, he lived in mortal fear of an uprising. He took the precaution of building a defensive wall around the Boukoleon section of the Great Palace. I watched it going up from my window. His presence meant that we were occasionally favoured with a visitation in the Kainourgion schoolroom.

I particularly remember one of these that must have taken place in September as we had just resumed lessons after the summer break. There was the usual crashing and banging in the corridor that heralded Nikephoros' advent and the door flew open. He stalked in with a posse of hangers-on behind him: his brother Leo, the domestic John Tzimiskes, the nephew whom I had met in the garden, and his other nephew, Ghastly

Junior Bardas. By then, Anna had joined us in the schoolroom with Father Anthony, so the three of us stood respectfully as we had been taught, our hands hidden in the sleeves of our silk robes. Just as Nikephoros did not believe in preliminaries or small talk, he likewise did not consider conversation to be a two-way process. He simply pointed at me and barked:

'Who is the greatest of the Fathers of our Church?'

Now that I was eleven, I was sorely tempted to reply that it was a matter of personal opinion but I discerned the game that he was playing and thought it best to go along with it.

'Basil!'

He indicated Constantine:

'Who was the first emperor of our faith?'

'Constantine!'

Then to Anna:

'Who was the mother of the Holy Virgin?'

'Anna!'

'Ha! See to it that you imitate their holiness!'

Without another word, he turned and strode out, followed by nephew Bardas. Leo and Tzimiskes lingered for a few seconds and looked apologetic before they slipped out too. Father Anthony, who had been completely ignored, signalled for us to sit down and we carried on as if nothing had happened.

Abrupt though Nikephoros' manner was, I now realise that he had been trying to be affable. When he wanted, he could be extraordinarily unpleasant. Anecdotes of his scathing treatment of foreign ambassadors filtered back to me, usually through Constantine. He had told the envoys of the tsar of Bulgaria that their master was a "leather-chewer who wore a leather jerkin." His sarcasm was deadly. When an Italian bishop arrived to propose that the king of Germany's son marry his stepdaughter Anna, he casually asked where the king was from. When told that he hailed from Saxony, he remarked that he did not recall ever having read about such a place in the Bible or the great works of classical literature. All in all, we got off fairly lightly.

Outside the schoolroom, I was still completely overshadowed by my brother. He had become the centre of a cohort of boys of varying ages who formed teams to compete against each other at polo. Constantine's team was called the Reds and since everyone wanted to join it and he had the pick of the players, it always won. At an early stage, he had asked whether I would like to play, without offering a place on his team, I should add. I declined, knowing perfectly well that my decorous plods through the streets on ceremonial occasions were a completely different experience from the furious pursuits in the polo matches. The other participants were all shaped like Constantine, not like me, and besides, every now and then one of them would take a tumble and suffer some injury or other. The whole thing looked very unpalatable to me so I remained on the side-lines.

My isolation did not go unnoticed. My mother, Aunt Theodora and Father Anthony all took me aside and said that, while they understood my reticence, I really ought to join in more. An emperor could not stand completely aloof: he had to be there among his subjects. I suppose that I could have objected that they were directly contradicting the advice I had been given by Nothos but it somehow would have seemed disloyal. Someone, Theodora I think, suggested that I join one of the October hunts. It would, she urged, be so very different from all that ceremonial riding. Unlike the polo, the hunts were not dominated by reckless boys, for everyone took part, so I would be able to attach myself to the older members of the party and keep pace with them. So I allowed myself to be persuaded. How could I have known what it was all going to lead to?

* * *

Imperial hunts depart from Blachernae, that incongruous bulge at the north western end of the Land Walls. There is a small palace there which is really more of a hunting lodge, a place to stay before and after a day spent chasing deer, wild asses and other game in the woodland known as Philopation that lies beyond the walls. It does serve another purpose. When foreign envoys visit the emperor of the Romans and when they seek some advantage from him, they vie with each other to bring magnificent gifts of kinds that have never been seen before, especially animals that thrive in their part of the world but are unknown to us. These are housed in a menagerie at Blachernae so that the roar of lions and the trumpeting of elephants greeted us as we disembarked. We had travelled by ship from the harbour of Boukoleon and up the Golden Horn, probably because Nikephoros was reluctant to have his head broken by a stone as he trotted through the streets.

The party consisted of Nikephoros, Constantine and me, Bardas Junior and a number of young men from military families whose fathers had served under Nikephoros at one point or another. One of them was Eustathios Maleinos, son of the man in whose house at Caesarea Constantine had spent so much time. We attended a special liturgy in the church of the Virgin, before the pre-hunt dinner, and then we were up and ready at first light the next day, to make the most of the dwindling Autumn daylight. We were all expected to wear identical cloaks with a hood for some reason. Nikephoros alone was exempt from that particular dress code. As we walked our horses out of the Kalligaria gate, the sun was hanging over Chalcedon, warming our backs and revealing the plane trees through the morning mist. Then we mounted and rode out into Philopation.

Leading the way, Nikephoros was on the magnificent beast that Constantine had attempted to ride that time. It was far too big for him so that he looked rather absurd but he certainly knew how to handle it. Constantine was on Dorkon but he would not keep him for much longer. By now he was taller than I was and he looked enviously at the eighteen-year-old Maleinos who was on a shiny black beast of sixteen hands. I had been provided with a gelding called Digger from the Blachernae stable, a pony which the grooms had promised me was obedient and docile. Constantine and the older hunters all carried spears but no one offered me one, which was just as well. We reached a clearing in the trees where the rest of the huntsmen were waiting. Goblets of wine were handed out as we sat and waited for what seemed an age. The groom who had been assigned to accompany me fussed around, checking my girth and advising me not to hold the pommel of the saddle. I began to daydream, as I tended to do, gazing into the dark depths of the forest. Suddenly, the atmosphere changed. I saw Digger's ears prick up and his body tense between my legs. Looking around, I could see no reason for the change, though the other animals had reacted in the same way, prompting their riders to gather up their reins and throw aside their goblets. A horn was blown and, with a jerk that nearly knocked me backwards, Digger was off in pursuit of the pack. I had expected to have some control over what the animal did: to kick with my ankles when it was time to go and to pull on the reins to stop. In an instant, I now realised that anything I did was irrelevant. Digger was now possessed by the ancient instincts of his ancestors and would be obedient to those and those alone.

We tore across the clearing and I saw the horses in front of me vanishing into the wood. That was where I would be going very shortly and to my horror I saw that many of the trees had low branches which Digger would fit under but I would not. Just in time, I dropped forward, letting go of the reins and clinging to the hair of his mane. By now, my allegedly docile mount was in full gallop weaving through the trees in a plucky attempt to keep up with the other horses, most of which were a lot larger than he was. I glanced behind me: the groom was cantering along apparently unconcerned. Looking forward again, I could just discern Constantine. He was evidently enjoying himself, to judge by the succession of disjointed "arfs" that were carried back on the wind rushing past my ears. I decided to straighten up but kept hold of the mane and the pommel and scanned ahead for any more low branches. Then we burst into another clearing and came to a halt.

I was shaking. The experience of being completely out of control had unnerved me. I wondered whether there was any way to get out of the rest of the hunt. Perhaps I could go to Nikephoros, complain of feeling unwell and ask to be escorted back to Blachernae. As I pondered the options, I looked down and saw that the ground was much closer than it should be. The next moment I found that I was sitting on the grass having slid naturally off the saddle. Digger, who was sweating profusely after the headlong chase, had felt an irresistible urge to roll in the dirt to relieve his hot and itching back, after depositing me, gently and harmlessly on the ground. I stood up and watched in bemusement until a voice bellowed:

'Ha! What idiot allowed that animal to roll without taking the saddle off first?'

The groom came scrambling out of the undergrowth where he had been answering a call of nature and hastily removed Digger's saddle. But the pony then refused resolutely to roll again so the saddle went back on and I was cajoled into mounting once more. Nikephoros rode up and surveyed me coldly, then turned and ignored me. Eustathios Maleinos then trotted up to him.

'Majesty, your younger stepson would make a magnificent cavalryman, but not the older one!'

He had not seen me behind Nikephoros' horse and rode off unaware that I had heard. Nikephoros also moved away. I whispered urgently to the groom that I might want to drop out of the hunt at this point but he glanced behind fearfully and said that the Lord Emperor would not like that as we were now far from Blachernae. Even as he spoke, the horn sounded and we were off again, although this time mercifully at the trot. At this pace we went on for some miles with me trailing behind the main body and completely ignorant of what we were doing or where we were going.

By then I was beginning to think that I might survive the hunt after all. Just trotting along an easily discernible track was something I could cope with well enough. Then there was a crashing in the trees on my left and a brown bear lurched into the space between me and the rest of the riders. The poor creature evidently thought that it had found an escape route, only to encounter me. As it went up on its hind legs, Digger likewise reared up in terror and the groom's horse shied and plunged violently too. The bear, equally terrified, then turned round and loped back to the undergrowth but Digger was off. He turned tail and headed back the way we had come while the groom desperately fought to control his own plunging mount. As I careered away, I could hear the other hunters whooping gleefully as they spurred in pursuit of the bear. Of course, I should have reined Digger in, patted his neck and reassured him that the bear was gone. But I just clung on instead, hoping that he would run all the way back to Blachernae: someone had told me that horses instinctively know the way home. Before long though I became aware that the landscape was looking very unfamiliar. We were charging along a wooded ridge and, through the trees, I could make out that the land dropped away in a steep slope: my terror was that Digger was going to gallop down that and that I would pitch forward over his head and be trampled under his hooves. So I just clung on. At that point I was startled to hear someone speaking to me from very close behind.

'Majesty, are you in difficulties?'

Like an imbecile, rather than admitting that I had no control whatsoever over the situation, I blithely answered:

'All is well.'

We rode on. I was tempted to glance back to ascertain whether the owner of the voice was still there or whether he in fact existed at all but I feared that I might fall off if I did. I felt that he was there, but of course natural deference meant that he could not contradict my fatuous reply. After a few minutes, he did speak again.

'Your pony is getting tired. It will stop very soon.'

He was quite right. In a small glade, not slowing to a trot then a walk but just pulling up abruptly, Digger ended his flight and immediately dropped his head to start cropping the grass that grew under a gap in the tree canopy. I slid from the saddle to the ground and saw that the disembodied voice belonged to a youth of about sixteen with black hair and a pale complexion mounted on a piebald mare: I had seen him earlier among the riders on the hunt. He too dismounted, bowed and apparently concluded that the easiest thing would be to see to my pony. Leaving his own to graze, he took off Digger's saddle and taking a handful of grass, he started to rub him down. This rubbing had a marvellous effect. The startled look vanished from the pony's eyes and he stopped moving in a jerky, nervy way. He even had another roll. My companion seemed to be one of those people who knew what to do. The problem with emperors is they cannot do anything because it is all done for them. I decided to just leave him to it.

One thing he could not do though was to work out where we were. I deduced that when I saw him squinting up at the sky attempting to gauge the direction of the sun. It must have been around midday by then and quite warm for October, with scarcely a cloud in the sky. The rest of the party would be repairing to the Philopation hunting lodge at some point to take refreshment but where that was, I had no idea as I had never been there. I asked if we were lost.

'Oh no. Well, yes, at the moment but we just need to wait a bit. When the sun starts to go down we will know that is west and if we go in the opposite direction we will get to the Land Walls. Besides, they are sure to come looking for us.'

That sounded like good sense to me, so I sat down and leant against an ancient beech whose trunk had a useful fold about the size of my back. The ponies pulled away at the grass and the black-haired youth busied himself with the tack. I closed my eyes and slept for a while. When I woke up, he was sitting nearby, holding a leather water flask which he offered to me and I gratefully took. Then the novelty of my situation dawned on me. I had never been like this before: alone with a person I did not know yet who was not a servant. It made me feel very awkward until I looked at him and realised that he felt exactly the same. In fact it was worse for him, as he had probably never been this close to royalty. Although he seemed so capable, it really was up to me to make the first move. So I did what I had heard Nothos and Leo Phokas do and asked him about himself. He said that his name was Nikephoros Ouranos. He was from the Taurus Mountains in Asia Minor. His father had accompanied Nikephoros on the Cretan expedition in 960 and on the recent Cilician campaigns. He had been brought to Constantinople to complete his education and had been invited on the hunt because of the high esteem in which Emperor Nikephoros held his father.

While we were talking, the shadows had been lengthening in the glade and we could now see that the sun had moved to a position just above the trees. It was plain now which way was west so we got ready to go. Ouranos saddled up his own horse completely forgetting that I had no idea how to do mine but he quickly rushed to cover his mistake and soon got me mounted. As we rode, we followed what seemed to be paths wherever we could but sometimes there was no obvious trail in the direction we wanted to go. So then we would forge a tortuous path through the undergrowth, getting scratched and pricked as we went. To start with I had expected that the Land Walls would loom up before us at any moment but as the weary traipse went on I began to grow despondent. So did Ouranos and he started to apologise, although it was in no way his fault. It must have been about six o'clock and the day was starting to wane when we found ourselves on yet another wooded ridge but this time with an unexpected sight: the sea. It could only have been the Marmara. We had no idea that we had come so far and that we had ended up travelling south rather than east. We were probably no nearer the Land Walls than we had been when we were in the glade. Then, as we emerged into a clearing that gave a better view of the land between us and the sea, Ouranos suddenly brightened and pointed.

'Look, there is a castle on that headland! I bet it's Strongylon. We are not going to reach the Land Walls before nightfall but we can easily make it there.'

I had a better idea: we should make for Hebdomon.

It is a small port, seven miles outside the Golden Gate at the southern end of Constantinople's Land Walls. It has a couple of a couple of fine churches, a broad exercise cum parade ground for the troops and a harbour which is sometimes used by emperors and generals returning from Asia. Nikephoros had disembarked there in 963 when he arrived to oust Bringas and marry my mother and again in 965 after his victory at Tarsus. More to the point, there is a small imperial villa there, left over from the days when Hebdomon was a summer retreat. It had long since been superseded by Hiereia but the villa was kept on and was occasionally used to lodge favoured guests. I proposed now to Ouranos that we should ride there and seek shelter.

It was already twilight when we rode down the main (and only) street. There were few people around and those that were paid us no attention. Strangers were always coming and going in Hebdomon, thanks to its harbour. At the far end we rode up a winding path towards the villa until we came to a wall with a pair of doors. Ouranos dismounted and hammered on them. As he did so, I noticed that ivy was growing up the wall and had penetrated underneath the tiles that topped it, pushing some of them up and cracking them. The plaster had fallen away in several places and a new coat of whitewash was long overdue. I began to wonder whether the place had not been entirely abandoned. Certainly there was no response to Ouranos' now frenzied knocking. He had given up and turned to spread his hands despairingly when a small grill opened in one of the doors and a frail elderly voice called out:

'There is nothing here. If you are on official business, then it is to Strongylon you must go!'

I have to say, Ouranos was superb in a situation that he can never have planned for or encountered before in his sixteen years.

'The Emperor is here and demands admission!'

The doors did not open so I got off and walked over to the aperture where I could be seen. I must have presented a sorry sight. My face was streaked with dirt from having been pressed down into Digger's mane. The cloak and hood, new on that morning, were in shreds, ripped apart by overhanging brambles. So I reached inside my tunic and fished out the small purple stole that emperors always carry for situations such as this. It was dyed with the deep shade that is made from one particular kind of sea mollusc; thousands of them are needed to make the tiniest amount. Only those of imperial rank are allowed to wear it. As I held it before the grill, there came the clunk of bolts being hastily drawn and of keys being turned in rusty locks before the doors were heaved open. On the threshold appeared an ancient man with thin and wispy white hair and scarcely a tooth in his head who dropped to his knees and kissed the ground before my feet.

'Praise be to the Virgin and all the Saints, Majesty, that you have come. We have waited so long that I thought to go to the grave before I ever looked on your face. But,' he added in his curious archaic accent as he struggled to his feet, 'please enter both. Catia, Catia, the emperor is here, the son of Romanos!' A stout elderly woman emerged into the dark hallway and sank to her knees and launched into fervent prayer. Then she looked up and ventured:

'Is His Majesty the older or the younger?'

'I am Basil, the elder.'

We were ushered in the short hallway which led to an open courtyard where there had once been a pond, now dry and full of dead leaves. Our host introduced himself:

'I am Philemon, Majesty, the caretaker of this place and this is my wife,' Catia bobbed again. 'We shall make a room ready for your lordships but please come into the salon'. He indicated a door to one side of the courtyard, but in the gathering dusk nothing of what lay inside could be seen. I hesitated. Protocol dictated that I go in first but now, after the demands of the day and gripped by my recurrent fear, I could not move and stood rooted to the spot. How long this impasse would have gone on is anyone's guess but fortunately Catia now bustled up with an oil lamp and I was able to walk in in her wake. As she stripped the dust sheets off the couches, I sat down and looked up at the walls which were covered with old paintings of men and women reclining in rustic settings.

'We will send to the town, Majesty, and have a boy go to Strongylon to tell the garrison commander you are here. We will get help in to prepare some food and a bath. Only, forgive me Majesty, we have a difficulty.'

I looked up quizzically. It must be remembered that I was not accustomed to difficulties. Everything generally just happened.

'Since your stepfather took over, Majesty, we have received our allowance only very irregularly and for the last year we have had nothing. We have had to let all the other servants go and my wife and I can scarcely live ourselves.'

I looked down at my hand at the gold ring that my mother had given me on my tenth name day. It had a portrait of Christ in jasper and an inscription in tiny letters: "Lord, help thy servant Basil, emperor of the Romans." I took it off and handed it to Philemon. Catia fell to her knees once more and the caretaker's face was suffused with joy.

'I will go at once, Majesty. With this, all will be made right.'

Catia pottered off to find water and Ouranos, who had stood in embarrassment during this performance, slipped out to see to the ponies, leading them round to the long-disused stables at the rear. That was how I first came to Hebdomon.

$$* * *$$

I woke up very early the next day. Another room across the courtyard had been hastily prepared as sleeping quarters and in the motes of light that filtered through the shutters I could see Ouranos still asleep in the other bed. I had insisted that he be in the room with me. I had never slept alone before and the danger of nocturnal visitations was all the greater in a strange room. After we had eaten some bread and cheese, water had been laboriously heated and poured into a copper for a bath, which I certainly needed. Ouranos had been prevailed upon to go in after me as he needed it too. Then I had slept the whole night without a single visitor, until the fingers of sunlight awoke me.

Since it looked like being another bright day, I decided to explore this new place and crept out into the courtyard where a light wind was rustling the dead leaves in the pond. I noticed now that it had a fountain at the centre and that the water would once have spurted from a jug held by a woman clad in flowing drapery. At the back of the courtyard was a pair of latticed doors. Peering through them I saw that they led to a garden so opened them to be confronted with a spectacular view across the Marmara to Chalcedon and to the mountains of

Bithynia, with the castle of Strongylon standing out on a headland to the left. The garden itself did not seem much at first: just a large rectangle of overgrown flower beds and cracked paths. Some parts were clearly being used to provide sustenance for Philemon and Catia. There were lemon and apple trees, a vegetable plot and a herb garden but they did not interest me much. Then I became aware that the garden was in fact much more extensive than it seemed. On the left hand side of the dull rectangle was a wide area which had been completely taken over by a dense undergrowth beneath shrubs and trees. Even so, a winding path could still be discerned, leading invitingly into its depths.

Strangely, pushing through undergrowth here at my own pace was much more enjoyable than it had been in Philopation, especially as I did not have to worry about Digger at the same time. The path led into a twilit world of weed-choked ponds, little hillocks and valleys and stone benches with curiously carved pedestals. There was a gigantic column of red porphyry, lying on its side amidst the greenery as if hurled there by an angry giant: it must have been at least as big as the one in the Forum of Constantine. It completely blocked the way, so I had to clamber over it to get any further. By now, I was nearly at the end of the path. I could make out a wall ahead and presumably beyond that would be a rocky cliff which sloped down to the beach and the sea. I could hear the sound of waves lapping on the beach but there was also a trickling sound coming from somewhere. Turning a corner, I found a stone face set in a wall. It had horns, pointed ears and a riot of curly hair and beard. A steady stream of water poured from its gaping mouth into a stone bowl. I wondered why the bowl never overflowed. Moving on, I came to an archway and beyond that was a sunken enclosure about four-feet high and faced with marble slabs. In it sat four men of stone, their arms clasped in fraternal embrace, their faces and bodies covered in moss and lichen. They wore no crowns but I assumed that they must be emperors who had ruled a long time ago. There was nothing to tell me, though I noticed there were some inscriptions set into the wall. Some of the letters were familiar from the lessons with Father Anthony, others looked very strange and the language was not Greek.

Any child, I am sure, loves exploring and "discovering" places that are perfectly well-known to their elders. That was not quite the fascination that the Hebdomon garden held for me. Although emperors are in theory powerful and wealthy, in practice they own nothing. Their property is public property as are even their persons and their time. Their days are divided up and parcelled out for the benefit of others. Wherever I went in the Great Palace, there was always someone hovering somewhere, waiting to take me away to do something that I did not want to do. Here I was free. True, a messenger was doubtless already on his way from Strongylon to report my whereabouts. But for the time being, Hebdomon was freedom.

It could hardly last. A voice was calling me and I realised that it was Philemon, terrified that he had lost me. So I came out to join him. He was full of apologies for the garden: it had been so long since anyone from the Great Palace had been there. As a boy he remembered when the tsar of Bulgaria had stayed with his new wife, the granddaughter of Emperor Romanos I. But that was back in 927. Since then there had been no one. Emperor Nikephoros had gone straight from the harbour to the Golden Gate on the two occasions that he had passed through. They had always kept the place spick and span just in case but then the payments dried up, so that everything had gone to wrack and ruin.

By then a message had been sent back by the commander at Strongylon asking if I would stay in residence until he could contact the Great Palace for instructions. So I spent the rest of the day in the villa and all the next. For most of that time, I wandered in the garden with Ouranos. By now, Nothos' rule was well and truly broken. In spite of the gap in our ages and the problem of who I was, it was a strange relief to talk to someone young and not to have to make the effort to be adult to please Nothos. When I vented my dislike of Ghastly Bardas, he was initially reticent, as his family were proteges of the Phokas clan. But he could not resist laughing a little when I mimicked Nikephoros' clipped and laconic tones. But that was as far as he went. It dawned on me that just as he knew what to do with horses, so he also understood the realities of the world he lived in.

At mid-morning on the third day, one of the boys who had been hired in the town on the collateral of my ring came running into the courtyard to say that horsemen were riding up the hill. We climbed the staircase that gave access to the walkway above the front doors and I was surprised to see that it was a troop of twelve kataphracts in full armour. Their horses were armoured too as if about to go into battle but the riders had fluttering plumes on their helmets and those are only used on ceremonial occasions. Their visors were down, so that they projected an intimidating blank stare. They drew up in front of the villa as Philemon heaved open the doors, and their leader dismounted and removed his helmet. I recognised him as Roupenios, the Armenian officer who had been with Tzimiskes during that encounter in the garden. He handed over a letter and Philemon examined the seal first and then opened it to read, holding it at arm's length. He could read very well I later discovered. When he proclaimed that all was in order, Roupenios spoke:

'The Lady Theophano asks me to thank you for the care you have extended to her son and sends this token of her regard. It is but a down payment on the recognition that will follow.'

He handed over a bag what I assume was gold coins. I had descended to the entrance by this time and Roupenios went down on one knee the moment he saw me. One of his men led forward a small pony which I mounted without difficulty: my experiences at Philopation had greatly improved my horsemanship. Ouranos had rushed to the stables to retrieve our ponies and he now joined us, leading one and riding the other. Philemon hastened to my side and pressed my ring back into my hand: the mere sight of it had been enough to unleash a flood of credit. Catia waved from the doorway. Then we set off: Roupenios taking the lead, me on the pony behind, Ouranos after me on the Piebald with Digger on a leading rein and the kataphracts in a protective ring around us. We trotted through the town where the main street was thronged with curious onlookers and past the wide parade ground which could be seen behind a line of walnut trees. Roupenios called back to me:

'We will enter by the Golden Gate, Majesty. I hope that this is the first of many times.'

Emperors returning from a victorious campaign always re-enter Constantinople through that gate, although the main one, of course, and not the small postern that we used. So the words were prophetic in a way though I doubt the thought would even have crossed his mind at the time.

It was a curious feeling to return to the apartment in the Kainourgion. Everything was exactly as I had left it when I had set out for Blachernae but it felt that I had been away for years rather than for four days. My mother was there within half an hour, with extravagant protestations about how she thought she had lost me forever, how it must have been perfectly frightful for me to be lost, what a nice young man that Nikephoros Ouranos was and he really must be invited to the palace soon. This went on for some time, until there was some crashing and the door opened to reveal my stepfather who looked even grimmer than usual. Bardas Junior was behind him but no one else. By now, I was old enough to have worked out that the relations between my mother and Nikephoros did not amount to rapturous conjugal bliss. I could appreciate that the arrangement was politically convenient and required neither a display nor cultivation of affection on either side. I had scarcely ever so much as seen them together, apart from at church services. Even so, I was hardly expecting what followed.

'What do you want, you piece of Anatolian shit?'

The conqueror of Crete and Tarsus shifted uneasily and mumbled something. Theophano's voice rose into a scream.

'How dare you take my boy out on a dangerous nag with nobody but a turd-tossing stable hand to look after him? He is a real emperor, born in the purple in this very palace and not in a miserable Cappadocian cave full of goats like you were!'

In the midst of this tirade, as if to emphasise her point, she seized hold of me and squeezed me to her body. In doing so, she put her arm over my nose and mouth so that I struggled to breathe, and had to wriggle and pull at her arm to get some air.

'You and your friends just went back to Blachernae as if nothing had happened. It was a sixteen-year-old who rescued him and took him to Hebdomon. And when they got there, they found our villa in ruins and the caretakers half-starved because you'd been too stingy to fork out for the maintenance.'

Some exaggeration there but it was justified in the circumstances.

'I suppose you hoped he'd die so that there'd be one less rival for you. Well, you had better understand this: if you lay one finger on his head, then neither your wall nor all your soldiers will protect you in this city. So why don't you go back to the goats and be done with it?'

He had listened impassively to this torrent of words, not attempting to interrupt or to offer any justification. He allowed the fury to die down and then said in a flat tone:

'Madam, I came to tell you that my father has passed away. We are going now to escort his body to our house at the harbour of Sophia where it will be laid out for viewing. We shall be absent for some days.'

With that he turned and left, while his nephew shot a glance of pure hate at us before following after.

'Well', said Theophano, sinking down and sitting on the floor after her exertion, 'About time. He was at least a hundred anyway.'

We looked at each other and started to giggle, just as I had with Ouranos in the garden at Hebdomon. I realise now that she was really not very old then, not even thirty. We were just a couple of children, laughing at our elders and betters. It was because of this incident that I first started to feel some genuine affection for the mother who for most of my childhood had only ever been an occasional visitor. It also made me thaw a little towards Nikephoros. I would not say that I ever got to like him, it was just that I began to perceive that, contrary to appearances, he was a human being and as vulnerable as the rest of us. His helplessness before my mother's fury first made me see that and the impression was confirmed on All Saints' day a few weeks later. There was a dinner in the Golden Dining Hall and, as usual, I was on the top table with Nikephoros and Leo. Constantine was now sitting in the seat that Old Bardas had once occupied, energetically shovelling food into his face. Nikephoros was still in mourning for his father and took only bread and water. He turned to me:

'Antioch is ours. News came a few days ago.'

I will say one thing about Nikephoros: he never talked down to me. In fact, he spoke to an eleven-year-old child as if he were his chief adviser on foreign affairs. Because he always delivered his comments in a monotone, it was impossible to gauge what kind of answer he was expecting but this seemed to be good news as it was an important city. I had read about it in the Book of Acts with Father Anthony and I knew that it had been a Roman city before the Saracens took it. So I hazarded an observation that this was an event to be celebrated. He looked at me sharply:

'It's a disaster,' he growled, 'Now we've got to defend a narrow salient sticking out into Syria. It'll be a permanent bone of contention between us and the Fatimids of Egypt. If we'd left it alone they'd have no reason to trouble us and would keep themselves occupied warring against Baghdad. Disaster.'

It was the longest speech that he had ever made to me. There was more to come.

'D'you think I wanted to be emperor? I'd have done anything to get out of it. That Bringas forced my hand. One day I'm going to abdicate, become a monk.'

The word "abdicate" was new to me but I marked it down for future use. Nikephoros relapsed into silence, as if exhausted by the effort of producing four, clipped sentences. He turned his head away to stare out into the hall, so that his sharp, austere profile, with its shaggy beard below the chin, was outlined against the whitewashed wall. The conversation was at an end but it seems incredible to me now that he was so open when there was no need to be. There was no dissimulation in him. What you saw was what he was. What he said was what he thought. That is something very rare in the court of the Romans. It is rare because it is extremely dangerous.

* * *

One dark and very chilly evening in December, Nothos came to my apartment as arranged. Over recent months he had been making these visits regularly, specifically to discuss current affairs. This was, he said, to prepare me for my future role. Recently we had talked about Antioch and he had been impressed that I appreciated the potential difficulties of defending it. Tonight, though, he did not look quite himself.

'I hope His Majesty will excuse me on this occasion: I am not quite well.'

I was surprised. Nothos was never ill: I have never known anyone with so unfailingly robust a constitution. He certainly did not look under the weather and his fleshy cheeks were as rosy as ever but he was undoubtedly worried and concerned.

'A passing indisposition, Majesty, nothing that a few days' rest will not cure.'

With that he bowed out backwards. I thought nothing further of it. Children have little concern for the ailments of others. Outside it began to snow heavily, the thick flakes carpeting the Augousteion and causing a muffled hush to descend on the city.

The next day, Constantine and I were scheduled to read with Father Anthony in the morning and attend an advent liturgy in the New Church in the afternoon. Where Anna was, I cannot recall. I do distinctly remember that the text we were going through was the *Life of St Porphyrios of Gaza*: we had reached the point where the saintly bishop was travelling to Constantinople to implore the emperor's permission to destroy the pagan temple of Marneion. Constantine was already in the schoolroom when I arrived. The windows looked out on the gardens and the polo ground but because of the season, they had been closed with glazed wooden panels. It was a gloomy, overcast day so little sunlight came in but I knew that Constantine was yearning to be beyond the window at the polo ground which was covered in snow. The door opened and Father Anthony stood in the frame.

Normally he would bustle in cheerily: 'Now, my dears, where did we leave the good bishop of Gaza when last we met?' Today, he just stood there and we saw that tears were streaming out of his eyes, past his nose and into his beard. Some of them were dripping onto the floor.

'My dears, I have the worst news in the world for you. Your beloved stepfather, the Emperor Nikephoros, is dead.'

Sudden death, though not uncommon, never loses its power to shock but for children, for whom time moves slowly, it is even more devastating. Unappealing though my stepfather was, he had been around almost as long as I could remember, a fixed certainty that had now been swept abruptly away. Father Anthony moved to his desk, slumped heavily down into the chair and went on:

'He is with the saints, as a man of purest virtue. He had only contempt for the fleeting vanities of this world. He was the friend and protector of holy men and sought to imitate them in his own life. He scorned dainty food and intoxicating wine. At night he refused to lie on silk sheets in the imperial bedchamber but wrapped himself in a cloak upon the floor.'

All this seemed to have been culled from the very saints' lives that we read in our morning sessions and seemed at first sight to bear little resemblance to the gruff personage I had known for the past six years. But then I remembered the last conversation that I had had with him and his avowed longing to become a monk. Constantine took advantage of a gap in the eulogy to blurt out:

'What did he die of?'

While posed with his usual lack of diplomatic finesse, the question struck me as a reasonable one. I had glimpsed Nikephoros from an upstairs window the previous day, striding across a courtyard with his attendants, barking commands as he went. He had looked perfectly well then. Father Anthony now rose, went over to Constantine and put his hand on his arm.

'My dear, I have to tell that your stepfather has been cruelly murdered. It would seem that some ruffians gained entry to the palace during the night and broke into his bedchamber.'

'But how could they get past the wall and the sentinels? And what about the guard outside his room?'

These questions came from Constantine. I was just sitting and staring at Father Anthony.

'The chamberlain will investigate these things, I am sure.'

At this point, I roused myself and put in:

'When will he be laid out?'

After all, the last time this had happened I had kissed my father's cold corpse in its coffin before the funeral procession.

'The funeral of the Lord Emperor has already taken place. I presided over the obsequies myself. He lies among Your Majesties' forebears in the mausoleum of the Holy Apostles.'

'Already?'

By now Father Anthony was starting look rather uneasy, rattled by our direct questioning. He retreated hastily to his desk.

'But at a time like this we must pray. Let us go to the church of St Stephen and beseech the mercy of the saints for our departed emperor.'

He hustled us out of the room, down the stairs and out into the courtyard. A bitter wind was blowing in from the Bosporus and servants pattered after us, fixing fur hats on our heads and throwing cloaks around our shoulders. Father Anthony strode on purposefully, ignoring our questions and was visibly relieved when we entered the church and its hushed interior silenced us. He walked up to the iconostasis, threw himself onto the floor in front of it and lay there with his arms stretched out on either side. We remained on our feet but my brother could not stand still or keep quiet for long:

'I'm glad he's dead. I didn't like him.'

'Shut up. It's a church. Anyway, you are supposed to say good things about dead people.'

'Like what?'

There was a certain unanswerable logic in that so I relapsed into silence. Constantine kept glancing at me, then said:

'Does this mean you'll really be emperor now?'

'I'm praying.'

'No, you're not.'

How long Father Anthony would have left us there I have no idea. To this day, I am convinced that he would have lain on the floor all day if necessary to escape from our pointed questions. Fortunately someone, I never found out who it was, sent a minor official to extract us from the church and escort us back to the Kainourgion. We were told that the afternoon liturgy had been cancelled and that we were both to stay in my apartment until called for. A couple of guards were posted on the door. I thought a lot about Father Anthony. It was not so much that he had obviously been lying about something: I had long since discovered that adults did that. It was that he had done it so badly.

* * *

The afternoon passed very slowly. There was nothing much to do except play dice and backgammon and Constantine gradually began to get on my nerves. But I was also very apprehensive. As dusk began to fall and the lamps were lit, it occurred to me that if "ruffians," as Father Anthony had called them, had been able to enter the palace to murder Nikephoros, what was to prevent the same thing happening to us? The guards posted outside were lean veterans who would be able to protect us but then they could also potentially be our assassins. Every time the door opened I felt a shudder of dread. Constantine had no such fears but he could not remember what had happened the last time an emperor died. Around six, food was brought in and with it was Nikephoros Ouranos. He had been fetched to keep us company. Needless to say, Constantine already knew him as he was one of the polo players and before long they were happily engaged in horse speak. He dined with us and in due course we all spent the night in that apartment. Thank goodness that he came.

The three of us discussed the situation endlessly. Undoubtedly a summons would be issued sooner or later but by whom? The three of us had no idea who was in charge now. Ouranos had been collected from his family's house by a palace servant but no indication had been given as to who ordered the fetching. It was not until well into the afternoon of the next day that someone came to the apartment, and the summons was for me alone. I was led out of the Kainourgion and across the Boukoleon to the line of residences that backed onto Nikephoros' recently completed wall: I realise now that we were very close to the bedroom in which Nikephoros had allegedly died. We walked down a corridor and I was shown into what looked like a private apartment. There were hangings on the walls, comfortable couches, vases in niches, a painted screen in the corner: the kind of thing that could be found in most of the apartments. What was surprising was who was there. Nothos, I expected. He was standing at the far end, with his hands in his sleeves. But oddly enough, seated on a couch in the centre of the room was that John Tzimiskes that I had met in the garden. Roupenios was standing behind him along with a tall and imposing man whom I had never seen before. They and Nothos bowed as I entered but John neither bowed nor got up. He hailed me gravely in Armenian and waved me onto a couch, then said:

'But we must speak Greek for the benefit of the chamberlain.'

That was a delicate way of putting it. I doubt that my baby-Armenian would have been up to the discussion that followed. Nothos stepped forward: they had obviously rehearsed the scene among themselves beforehand and agreed who was to say what.

'I hope that you are fully recovered, chamberlain,' I asked demurely.

For one moment, he looked lost, but he recovered and assured me that his illness only had lasted for one night and had been cured by a good rest. In fact, he looked in rather worse shape now than he had when I had last seen him, for he had a black eye and the left side of his face was marked with scratches and bruises. He went on:

'Thank you for coming to see us, Majesty. I believe that you know the Lord John and Captain Roupenios. This other gentleman is Bardas Skleros: the Lord John's late wife was his sister.'

Why he or Tzimiskes should be there was still a mystery to me.

'As you know, Majesty, your stepfather, the uncle of the Lord John here, was regrettably murdered the night before last in his bedchamber. We have apprehended the culprits. They appear to be former soldiers who had some kind of a grudge against the emperor. Of course we are all shocked and horrified at what has happened but we should also thank God for his mercy. After all, it might have been worse. These assassins might have gone to Your Majesty's apartment.'

He paused and looked around the room at this point. There were murmurs of concern and approbation. Then he cleared his throat. You could tell that he was coming to the difficult part and that he was steeling himself for the distasteful task ahead.

'We subjected the culprits to close questioning as to how they gained admittance to the palace, in spite of the gates to the Boukoleon being locked and the usual guards being posted. What we discovered will shock and disturb Your Majesty as much as it did us. It would appear that they were allowed in by Your Majesty's mother. She apparently arranged for them to be hoisted up one by one through an open window. She also saw to it that the door to the Emperor's bedchamber was unlocked.'

'No,' I said.

They all looked at each other. Nothos went on:

'Please believe me, Majesty, when I tell you that we did not credit it either but we were confronted by evidence that could not be refuted.'

My reaction had been instinctive. I felt that I had to defend Theophano but my mind flashed back to that last encounter with Nikephoros and her bitter tirade. I was so bewildered that I did not know what to say. So I started shouting:

'It's not true. Father Anthony was lying, I know he was. That is why he took us to the church so he wouldn't have to talk to us. Nikephoros isn't dead. He wanted to become a monk, he told me so. He's not dead, he's abrogated!'

There was a moment's silence before Nothos put in:

'I believe that His Majesty means "abdicated."'

It was John Tzimiskes who moved to calm me.

'I am sorry but you must face the facts. The Emperor Nikephoros is dead: I saw his corpse myself. You must accept what we have had to conclude: that your mother is a woman of violent passions who had come to hate my uncle. She seems to have urged these men to kill him and to have arranged an opportunity for them to do so, which makes her as guilty as them.'

I sank back in the couch, because I had no words with which to continue mu outburst. I had to admit that there was some plausibility in what John said. I asked if I could see her.

'She is no longer in the city, Majesty,' said Nothos, 'and even if she were it would not be safe for you. Before she was taken away she attacked me when I confronted her with her guilt: you can see the scars on my face.'

'Where has she gone?'

'To an island a long way off, Majesty, to be with some pious nuns who will teach her to curb her passions.'

'So who will be the senior emperor then?'

'The Lord John has graciously consented to undertake the burden of that office and to become the guardian of Your Majesty, and of your brother and sister.'

By now I was looking around, scanning one face then another but these men were not like Father Anthony: nothing could be read there. It was all too much too fast. First, my mother branded a criminal, now the amiable soldier John Tzimiskes promoted to be emperor of the Romans. It still did not seem quite right but Nothos could see that I was weakening.

'How long have we known each other, Majesty? Since the day that Bringas tried to abduct you and your brother. Since then, have I not watched over you and guarded you, even when your mother never bothered to visit you for weeks or months on end? Do you think that I would lie to you now?'

And that was that. I believed it all because Nothos told me so. When Christmas day came, Constantine and I were once more in Hagia Sophia to watch as Patriarch Polyeuktos placed a crown on the head of Emperor John. It was as if Nikephoros had never existed and he was scarcely ever mentioned again. The only official acknowledgement of his six-year reign was the rhyming epitaph that some poet was hired to write and which was then carved onto the tomb. It extolled his courage and his victories but there was a mocking edge to it:

He who chose but little in the night to sleep,
By his wife was slain, as if he were a sheep.

There was no mention of Father Anthony's "ruffians." Instead, my mother's sole culpability was set in stone for ever and for all to see.

5

The Caretaker
and the Spy (1020)

When Yazid was fifteen, one of the worst storms that anyone could remember blew in from the Black Sea. The wind howled down from the north for three days and nights in December, whistling round the domes of the churches and whipping the waters of the Bosporus into a boiling fury. No one dared take to the water even to cross to Chalcedon or Chrysopolis and the ships stayed at anchor in the harbour, bobbing crazily on the swell. The column in the Forum of Constantine swayed ominously but by some miracle its statue did not fall. The people of the city kept to their houses and avoided the streets, for the wind caught up tiles from the roofs and then dashed them to the ground so that passers-by were in grave danger of being struck down.

On the first morning after the wind had died down, Yazid went with his father Mahmud through the Gate of St Eugenios to see if there had been any damage to the mosque. There was still a strong breeze and the foreshore was littered with flotsam thrown up by the waves: ragged figures were gathering it up in armfuls to take home as fuel. The mosque was in an odd place on the far side of the Sea Walls. It had been put there to keep it out of the way as not all Christians were happy to have infidels worshipping in their city. That did mean though that it was very close to the water and there was nothing apart from the headland of Galata to shield it from the north wind. Mahmud and Yazid were relieved to see that, in spite of its exposed position, the building had got off lightly. The only damage seemed to be on the low dome, where some of the tiles had been swept off and Mahmud decided that he needed to make good the damage now, before it started to rain and water got in. So with Yazid holding the bottom of the ladder, he clambered up with his tools on his back and began to make his way round the parapet at the base of the dome to reach the far side where the damage was, for the ground was too uneven on that side to place the ladder. But he did not see that the wind had flung bits of seaweed up onto the parapet, so that when he placed his foot on some of it, his leg shot forward. As he fell, he turned and tried to clutch at the parapet but it was no use and he plummeted to the ground. When Yazid reached him, he was on his side and crying out in pain.

Some of the people on the beach came and they lifted Mahmud and carried him to the mosque porch, although that made him cry out all the more. Yazid ran back to the house by the wall and told his mother and the neighbours and they all hurried to see. The sailmaker who lived down the street said that Mahmud might have broken his leg and it would need to be set. There was a woman who set bones further along the wall but everyone said it would be better to go to a hospital. There was one in the Orphanage on the Acropolis where the monks and nuns treated all who had need, without any payment and for the love of God alone. So they put together a makeshift stretcher and lay Mahmud on it as carefully as they could. They carried him, with Yazid's mother walking alongside, up the steep hill to the Acropolis where the gates of Tarsus stood, brought back from the east by Emperor Nikephoros many years before. It was said that they had once been covered in gold but that had long gone, worn away, stolen or both. The Orphanage was like a city which covered the Acropolis. There was a home for children who had lost their parents but also a soup kitchen for the poor, a home for the elderly, an asylum for the insane and, at the far side, a hospital. When Mahmud and party arrived, they were directed to a portico where the sick and injured were lying with their friends and relations around them, swathed in blankets to keep out the cold. Someone will come soon, they were told, to have a look and to see whether Mahmud should be admitted to the hospital or treated there. So they waited. By now, it was mid-morning and a priest came with two boys who sang and swung an incense censor. The priest held a small icon of the Virgin which he gave the waiting patients to kiss. Mahmud kissed it too because she was the mother of a prophet after all.

It was around midday that a monk came and looked at Mahmud's leg and said that the thigh bone had been broken. He added that he wished that they had not moved him as it would make the setting more difficult: they should have left him on the beach and sent someone to fetch help. But there was good news as well because no bone was protruding, so the job could be done there and then. The monk despatched the boy who assisted him to collect the wooden splints and lengths of cloth, while he measured with his hands to find the right place for the setting. When he had laid the splints and bound them loosely, he asked two of the larger neighbours to take hold of Mahmud's arms, and pulled firmly on the leg while the boy tightened the splints. Mahmud yelled with pain and Yazid's mother cried but at last it was over and the monk said he had done his best to make sure that the leg healed well. He turned to Yazid because he realised that he spoke Greek better than his mother, and gave him instructions on how the leg was to be positioned and when to loosen the splints. He told him that he must come back in two weeks' time to find a monk who would return with him to make sure that everything was progressing as it should.

They carried Mahmud home and did everything they were told. His father lay in his bed for weeks on end with his leg straight out and Yazid became the caretaker of the mosque. There was not much to do, for at that time of year there were no merchants in the han and it would not be until April that the galleys arrived from Alexandria. There was not even an imam for he had gone back to Cairo in September and there would not be a new one until the spring, so the only prayers that were said were Yazid's own. The only work was replacing those few tiles on the dome and generally keeping an eye on things.

Yazid told his father this to cheer him up but even so Mahmud worried. He now told his son that over the past few years, the payments from Egypt for the upkeep of the mosque had become irregular. They were always late and the amount sent often fell far short of what had been agreed and what was necessary. When the money had run low the previous summer, the merchants had rallied round and provided what was needed for the mosque and some extra to help Mahmud feed his family. But there were no merchants now and Mahmud said they might never come back. Last summer they had said that there was trouble in Cairo. The caliph had gone mad and had executed many innocent men. He had even knocked down the Church of the Holy Sepulchre in Jerusalem and so risked war with the Emperor of the Romans. If that came to pass, what would happen to the mosque in Constantinople? Yazid did not know but he was young and optimistic and he felt sure that something would turn up.

By the time February came, though, he was not so sure. Mahmud was still on his bed. As the monk had warned, the leg had not set well and he could not walk on it because he was a big man and his weight bore down on it very painfully. There was very little food or money left although as it was Lent, most of the neighbours were going short too. Yazid swept and cleaned, he did all the routine winter maintenance jobs that Mahmud would have done but he did not know how long he could devote himself to those tasks. Sooner or later, he would need to find other work. He thought of perhaps applying to the shipbuilders and stevedores at the docks further up the Golden Horn. They always needed willing hands to carry planks, unload barrels or caulk the sides of newly-built vessels.

One evening, as he locked up the mosque, he resolved that tomorrow he would make his way along the walkway that ran along the base of the sea walls and ask at each of the wharves whether they were hiring hands. Then, as he turned, he noticed a man sitting in the porch. He had his back to the wall and had his very long, thin legs stretched out in front of him as he stared vacantly across the water to Galata. Yazid did not like the look of him at first. Men would sometimes use the porch to drink cheap wine and then to relieve themselves against the wall, though they seldom lingered when the gate was due to close. This one had a thin, pinched face, straggling black hair and a short beard and he wore a long brown coat of cheap cloth. He did not look like one of the respectable artisans who plied their trade along the harbour, rather more like one of the unsavoury characters who always cluster around ports. He did not turn his head when Yazid came out but just continued staring. But he did speak:

'Are you the one they call the infidel?'

Yazid was taken aback. It was not by the question itself that surprised him but the language in which it was asked: Arabic rather than Greek. The strange man was certainly not an Arab for he spoke with an accent very different from that of Mahmud and the merchants. Nor did he look anything like them in his long brown coat. He went on, without waiting for an answer to his question:

'Funny building this. It seems to face the wrong way, like. You'd think it would face right at the other side of the Horn, not be sideways to it.'

He had not waited for an answer, Yazid decided, because he already knew it. He was right too about the mosque. Yazid had learned from his father why it was aligned the way it was. The site outside the walls was very constricted so they had to put it sideways to the wall to make the best use of the space. Two experts had been brought in from Cairo to determine the best spot for the mihrab but their estimates differed by several feet. In the end, the architect split the difference and put it somewhere in the middle.

'You must have a very interesting life here,' the man went on, 'Visitors from all over the world, exotic locations in the east.'

He had still been staring out across the Golden Horn as he said that but now he turned to the caretaker.

'You must hear quite a few things as well. Interesting things.'

Yazid admitted that it was so but dusk was falling and soon the gate would be closing, and he advised the stranger that it would not be pleasant to be locked out on this side. The man rose to his feet.

'I don't need to worry about that. I can come and go as I please. You see, I work for the Governor of the City, the one that they call the Eparch. We have to make sure that everything works well. That there's water in the cisterns, food in the markets, order in the streets. All that kind of thing.'

Looking at the cadaverous figure in the long brown coat, Yazid felt it unlikely that he really was an inspector of aqueducts. But what was he? Not that it mattered for Yazid now wanted just to end this conversation and go home. It was cold and it would be dark soon. But the man persisted.

'Do you know what the most important thing we need to make the city run well? Go on, guess.'

Yazid was young, the man was older. He found it impossible to break away without being rude. So he tried to answer the question and volunteered that skilful labourers might be what was required. Perhaps this man could tell him where labour was needed so that he could earn enough to keep his mother and father. But to his disappointment, the thin man shook his lank hair.

'Information. That's what we need. We need to know things so then we can respond and make sure we have planned for what's going to happen in the future. But it is hard to find and so it is really valuable. That's where you come in. All those merchants from Egypt and Syria, they must have a lot to say about what is going on back home.'

Yazid said that he agreed but he really wanted to get away. He started walking towards the gate and the thin man went with him. He asked the thin man why the city governor would wish to know about what was happening so far away. The answer came back:

'It's because trade is important to this city. The governor charges customs duties on everything the merchants bring in and take out. He wants to know if anything is happening out east that might stop the merchants coming or might stop our merchants going there. So we'd like to know about what they say, especially if anyone says anything about Antioch, right?'

He took Yazid's hand and pressed something into it. Yazid could feel that it was a coin.

'My name is Angelos. I'll come to this same place about once every month in the spring and summer. Store what they say in your head and keep it ready for me. If you do that there'll be more rewards for you, depending how good the stuff you tell us is. But one thing: don't tell your mum and dad about me or about our arrangement. If you do, the merchants will find out and they'll want to sell their information to us direct and you'll lose out. In fact, don't tell anyone. You got all that?'

Yazid nodded mutely. Angelos turned to go but then stopped:

'One last thing – I nearly forgot. If you hear something that you think is very important and it's a long time before my next visit or it's winter, then stick a stone in there.'

They had passed through the gate and Angelos was pointing to a small niche in the wall on the left-hand side, about four feet from the ground. He then backed way, turned and was absorbed into the shadows of the gathering dusk.

Afterwards Yazid wondered whether he had not dreamt the encounter but the coin was real enough: it was a gold one, newly minted with a picture of the Emperors Basil and Constantine holding a cross. He gave to his mother, saying that he had earned it by doing casual work over the past month in the shipyard and had now been paid. The next morning, she went to the baker and grocer and paid off their debt, for in their kindness they had allowed her to take food on credit. At first he doubted whether Angelos would ever come back and wondered whether he ought not go to the docks and shipyards anyway. But when the spring came and the galleys from Alexandria arrived, there was Angelos one evening sitting in the porch, staring across to Galata. He was pleased with what Yazid had to say and there were more gold coins.

From then on, Yazid's life became much easier. He did not have to work in the docks and he could employ a servant girl to help his mother and to sit with his father when she was out. And when late the following year, Mahmud's heart gave out, Yazid could offer a wake for the neighbours to come and view the corpse and provide a decent burial in the small cemetery for Muslims on the slope of the Acropolis. Soon after, news came that there was a new caliph in Cairo and from then on the funds for the mosque started arriving more regularly. So Yazid found that he and his mother were now quite comfortable. He was able to marry the Roman girl that he had always liked, though he had to promise not to circumcise any male children. Angelos kept coming and he always seemed happy with what Yazid had to tell him. But the caretaker never felt the need to summon the thin man with a pebble in the niche. At least not until his interview with Sayyid al-Wuzara.

6

Paideia (970-4)

By early January, the Great Palace was a very different place. The new Emperor John may have been a Phokas on his mother's side but on his father's he was an Armenian. He had no time for the swarm of hangers-on that Nikephoros had brought to Constantinople with him.

Scores of faces that I had become accustomed to vanished overnight, having been sent trudging back to Cappadocia. The Phokas mansion down by the harbour of Sophia was closed up and abandoned. Those who had received appointments in the provinces from Nikephoros were now relieved of them. His unpleasant nephew Bardas lost the post of duke of Chaldea and that Eustathios Maleinos, whom I had encountered on the Philopation ride, was dismissed as governor of newly-conquered Antioch. I asked Nothos about Nikephoros' brother

Leo, the only one of the Phokas tribe who had ever struck me a remotely human.

'The Lord Count Palatine, Majesty, has been deeply saddened by the loss of his brother. He has decided to withdraw from the city to seek seclusion elsewhere.'

John's adherents flooded into the Great Palace: Armenian could now often be heard in the corridors and I was able to practice regularly. His brother-in-law Skleros replaced him as domestic of the east but one thing remained exactly the same: Nothos was still chamberlain.

There was one outstanding constitutional matter. While a sudden change of rulers is not uncommon in our state, it has to be justified and it has to be made legitimate, especially if the new incumbent has not been born in the purple. Nikephoros had surmounted that barrier by marrying my mother. Nothos' father Romanos Lekapenos already had a wife so instead he had married his daughter to my grandfather Constantine VII. John Tzimiskes had recently become a widower so the way was open for him to ally himself with my family. My sister Anna was too young for the role so a few months after his takeover, John announced that he was engaged to be married to my aunt Theodora. You can imagine Constantine's reaction:

'Tzimiskes marrying dowdy old Theodora with her wobbly topknot! Arf, arf, arf!'

We were taken on a visit to the future empress shortly after the announcement. For some reason, I had supposed that she would look different but she was exactly the same, in the same cluttered apartment in the women's section of the Boukoleon that she had occupied for decades. As ever she commenced talking as soon as we arrived and continued to do so without interruption until it was time for us to leave. I tried to look interested, while Constantine concentrated on the bowl of sweetmeats on the low table in front of us. She was prattling on about how being empress would make little difference to her and how she would stay in the same apartment. Then she said:

'Of course, there won't be *relations...*'

She glanced at us furtively to see whether we had understood. I had not and Constantine was too busy with the bowl. Over the last year, my understanding of politics had advanced considerably so that I was probably quite precocious in that respect. When it came to other aspects of human life though, my isolated existence had left me completely ignorant. I need to put that down here, so that what comes later makes sense.

After Epiphany, Constantine, Anna and I resumed our lessons with Father Anthony. The atmosphere was no longer the same somehow. Our teacher was furtive and embarrassed for he knew that we had detected his evasion and possible mendacity over Nikephoros' death. There was another reason why I now disliked the lessons: I did not get on with Anna. Why that should have been, I cannot be certain but I do not think that she had ever accepted the idea that she had two brothers after first believing that she only had one. She went out of her way to drive a wedge between Constantine and me. They would always be in the schoolroom before me, whispering together, and they would fall silent the moment I came in. One day that happened and I ignored them and sat down. I got out my tablet and pretended to read what I had written down last time. Then a tiny voice squeaked from the back of the room:

'Basil, help me, Basil! She's hurting me!'

Anna was standing behind the rows of desks brandishing Constantine's little knife. Then she held something up: it was Arus, with one of his arms cut off. He had been left and forgotten in the desk for some years.

'Please, Basil, rescue me before she hurts me again!'

I should have ignored her. I should have turned back to my tablet as if nothing was happening and waited until Father Anthony came. But no, I jumped to my feet and tried to snatch Arus from her hand but she dodged round the desks, shrieking in mock terror, and taunted me from the other side:

'Please, please, Basil…'

Constantine was convulsed with strangled guffaws:

'He even gets bullied by a girl! Arf, arf, arf!'

The chase went on until I seized Anna's arm. At the same moment, the door opened and Father Anthony was standing there. We went back to our desks. He looked at me reproachfully:

'My dear, I am grieved to see you treat your sister so.'

When we were packing up for the day, I saw that Arus was lying on the floor, minus his legs and remaining arm. I pretended not to have seen and left him there. By the next lesson, he was gone, doubtless cleaned up by the servants. It was probably the right thing to do but then I despised myself for giving up so easily my last physical link to Pita and those days in the nursery. That was why, when Nothos told me that I was to have a different teacher from Constantine and Anna, I was only too pleased.

'Majesty, it is time for you to embark on the *Enkyklios Paideia*. This is where you will no longer read sacred texts but secular ones. The language will be that of the ancients, more difficult but more pure. We have two teachers for you. One is a learned grammarian, who will instruct you on style and language. The other will guide you on history and statecraft. That second teacher will be me.'

From then on I ceased to attend Father Anthony's lessons. Emperor John was to make him patriarch of Constantinople two years later.

In preparation for our history and statecraft sessions, Nothos gave me the Chronicle of Theophanes Confessor and its Continuation and I used to become deeply absorbed in them in my own time. My favourite period was the reign of my ancestor Basil I and the story of how he had restored the eastern frontier after years of defeats at the hands of the Saracens. Sometimes I went to the palace library in the Magnavra and had a look at some of the other chronicles, like that of Nikephoros of Phrygia.

I noticed that each chronicle reported the same incident in a different way.

All that reading proved very useful when the summer approached and I put in to action the plan that I had nurtured ever since I had got back to the Great Palace in the autumn. I proposed to Nothos that I should spend the summer in Hebdomon. Bureaucrats love precedents, so I pointed out to him that it had been the practice for the entire court to do this in ancient times as Theophanes Confessor records under the year 548/9.

'His Majesty is well-informed. I wonder whether your Aunt Theodora might not wish to join you there as she prepares for her marriage to the Lord John?'

I quickly conceded that and then requested that Nikephoros Ouranos should be allowed to come too, given that I owed him so much for rescuing me in the Philopation. Nothos looked doubtful.

'Ouranos? Surely they were protégés of the Phokas family?'

'They were minor clients but Ouranos is now training to be a kataphract in the army of the Lord Emperor John.' See how at age twelve I even talked like Nothos. Then I added pertly: 'Besides, Great Uncle, were you not yourself an ally of the Phokas clan? Didn't you join forces with Nikephoros' father Bardas to drive your half-brothers into exile in 959? And didn't you...'

I stopped. His eyes had become cold and hard. Then mercifully they softened.

'Already His Majesty has learned that allegiances shift in the course of political life. Let Ouranos go with you to Hebdomon.'

But I knew that I had angered him and I resolved never to mention his past again.

✳ ✳ ✳

Somewhat to my surprise, Aunt Theodora was enthusiastic about the prospect of spending the summer at Hebdomon. I am fairly sure that she had not been out of the Great Palace, apart from attending services in Hagia Sophia, for decades. Unfortunately she communicated the plan to Anna who announced that she wanted to come as well. The three of us sailed from Boukoleon in early July and were met at Hebdomon harbour by a litter to carry Theodora up the hill. She had become even larger by that time and would never have made it any other way. There was a litter for Anna too and I walked alongside. At the villa, Philemon and Catia were at the door to welcome us. They led us into the courtyard where the pond was now filled and water trickled from the mysterious woman's pitcher. Emperor John had spared no expense in having the place renovated for the comfort of his bride to be. The outer walls had been crisply whitewashed, the inner ones repainted throughout. The figures on the walls of the salon had been touched up so that they looked unbelievably lifelike. The garden had been weeded and replanted, although I was glad to see that the overgrown shrubbery at the side had been left as it was. There was even a new icehouse in a shady corner. John had had it stocked with blocks of compacted snow cut from the peak of Mount Olympus in Bithynia so that we could have cool drinks on even the hottest day.

As I had hoped, at Hebdomon I felt free. Of course, there were numbers of guards and attendants. With a consort-to-be in residence that was inevitable. But the guards contented themselves with patrolling the perimeter and the limited space in the villa meant that there were not hordes of under-employed attendants as there were in the Great Palace. So I was not followed around and spied on constantly. I had brought with me a couple of chronicles from the Magnavra library and I would take one of these in the afternoons along the path through the shrubbery, over the pillar and past the satyr fountain: I had made enquiries about the hairy, horned head. I would settle down on the plinth in the sunken enclosure, under the four lichened emperors, and read. It was perfectly cool, even when the sun was high, and I could pretend that nobody knew that I was there.

Aunt Theodora used to emerge at mid-morning and install herself on a couch that was placed every day on the terrace overlooking the garden and the sea beyond. A silk awning would be spread over it to keep off the sun and a servant would stand by with a plume of peacock feathers to fan her. Anna and I would sit on either side of the couch, listen to her ramblings and, if we got the chance, talk to her, although not to each other. It was on one of these occasions that Theodora abruptly fell silent. She was going to broach the unmentionable subject and I feel sure that someone had primed her to do so. After taking a deep breath, she went on:

'Darlings, I have to say that I never liked your mother. Romanos was besotted with her, you see. His first marriage was to a Frankish princess. It was arranged: something about securing our lands in Italy. But she died after a few years and that was when he started courting Theophano. She wasn't suitable at all. Her father was quite well off but he was in trade: some kind of wine merchant. But your grandfather gave in and let Romanos go ahead.'

She paused. For Theodora this was a remarkably succinct and direct speech. Anna said nothing and neither did I. Our aunt went on:

'I know that it seems hard to say this, children, but it would be better just to forget about your mother, after what she did. Not everyone liked Nikephoros and he was a difficult man, that I grant you. But to go and do that to him, that can't be defended. So she is better off in the convent...'

She was looking out to sea as she said that, from which I deduced that Theophano must be on one of the island convents in the Marmara.

'I have sometimes thought about entering a convent but I can't now that I have accepted the Emperor John's proposal. There is a nice one not far from the Petrion palace that I thought about. Perhaps when I'm older...'

And off she went into a rambling soliloquy which neither Anna nor I interrupted. The idea of my mother as a murderess just did not seem right to me. There could be no doubt that she had hated Nikephoros: I had seen the evidence with my own eyes. But would she really have aided and abetted some common soldiers in a plot to kill him? Yet Nothos had told me so and now Theodora was confirming it. I looked up to see Anna shooting a venomous glance at me across the couch and forgot about the murder issue for the time being.

Constantine may have been crass, loutish and occasionally revolting but I could get on with him. With Anna, I had no connection whatsoever. Fortunately we did not need to encounter each other too much. We could even attend different Sunday liturgies. Hebdomon has two churches, one dedicated to St John the Evangelist and the other to St John the Baptist. For us all to go to one would be to rob the other of its congregation as everyone would flock to get a sight of us. So we split up. Theodora and Anna went to the Baptist as the more important church: it houses the Baptist's head that was struck off and presented on a platter to Salome. I used to go to the Evangelist where I presided from the gallery with Philemon and Catia as my attendants. None of the icons there spoke to me particularly, so I used to take along the small one that Nothos had given me and directed my prayers to St Demetrius instead, thanking him for preserving me from the company of my sister.

Ouranos joined us after a few days. They gave him a lodging in the barracks on the far side of the parade ground and he dined with us at the villa every few days. Theodora declared him to be charming and even Anna became something like a human being in his presence. It was arranged that he and I should ride together early every morning. He had been provided with a new horse and he undertook to find one that would suit me. He came up with a chestnut-brown mare called Willow. She was nothing like the beast he rode on, a placid, amiable, knock-kneed creature. For some reason I came to feel at one with her in a way that I never had with all the other ponies onto which I had been reluctantly hoisted. She seemed somehow to want me to be on her back. I remember exactly when it was that I first felt that. Ouranos had set off at a canter across the parade ground and I was watching him in admiration. My mounted bodyguard was behind me waiting patiently. Ever since the Philopation episode he or one of his comrades accompanied me whenever I was out. Then I made a decision. I signalled with my heels for Willow to pursue Ouranos and off we went. We had no chance of catching up with him but as I sped along, something funny happened. I suddenly felt exhilarated and I looked down at the shadow that was keeping pace with me. Usually, I cringed when I saw my reflection or shadow but now I thought it looked very fine. I had merged with Willow and the two of us were gliding effortlessly along the grass, matching the contours of the ground. That was the moment that I lost my fear of horses and these days I like to be in the saddle whenever I appear in public as I cut a much more impressive figure. I have Ouranos to thank for that, as well as Willow. It was during that first stay at Hebdomon too that the bad dreams stopped once and for all.

I should set down here that Nikephoros Ouranos had become a figure of fascination to me just as Nothos was. Part of it was the adulation that children heap on their slightly older contemporaries who have acquired some of the attributes of adulthood yet are still obviously young. Ouranos was a married man and had been since he was fourteen. It was one of those matches that had been decided when the couple were still in their infancy. Her family held land in the foothills of the Taurus range that adjoined that of Ouranos' father so it made sense for them to merge the families and the estate. At present, Ouranos and his wife lived in his parents' house south of the Great Palace. Come the autumn he would be a fully trained kataphract and ready to serve in Emperor John's army. But there was more to it than that. It was the way that he always knew what to do, rubbing down Digger, choosing Willow and reassuring Constantine and me the day after Nikephoros died. He was everything that I was not.

In early September we returned to Constantinople and two months later, John and Theodora were married. The ceremony itself was rather muted and, like that of Nikephoros and Theophano, it was staged in the New Church within the Great Palace rather than in Hagia Sophia. Afterwards, the happy couple appeared in the royal box in the Hippodrome and scattered largesse to a huge crowd, relieved to discover that the marriage had turned out to be very popular. With the formalities completed, Theodora returned to her apartment and John re-joined his army to initiate preparations for next year's Bulgarian campaign. They participated in ceremonies as a couple when required and sometimes would meet to discuss matters in Theodora's apartment. They remained the best of friends. As a marriage of convenience, it was made in heaven.

On my return, I discovered that both Constantine and I were to be given new apartments in the building that stretched alongside Nikephoros' wall. Shortly after I had moved in, the new arrangements for my education began. I was to be taught once more in the schoolroom, while Father Anthony, Constantine and Anna were moved elsewhere. That was because my guardian had decreed that I should not be taught alone. It would be good for me, he said, to rub shoulders with youths of my own age from carefully selected families. The criterion of selection was adherence to John and his relatives of the Skleros family, not academic ability. To be honest, I doubt whether any of those chosen would have progressed beyond elementary education had they not been selected for their families' political credentials. Some were my age, some older. I sat at the front with the other twelve-year-olds, the rest behind me in order of age up to the sixteen-year-olds in the back row.

The learned grammarian that Nothos had promised was a certain Leontios Diaphantes. He had a huge bald cranium, fringed with uncombed black hair that stuck out wildly, and balanced on a thin neck and scrawny body. He would often balance this unwieldy head on the tips of his fingers with his elbows on the desk, as if the burden of his intellect was too much for his neck alone. He certainly lived up to Nothos' praise for no one could fault his knowledge of the ancient Greek classics. He was so imbued with their language and style that he often spoke in the same idiom, if he thought that anyone might understand. But he made no secret of his distaste for having to teach of group of such unsuitable pupils. Presumably he accepted the tedious post because of its political benefits and doubtless generous salary.

Lessons with Diaphantes were not very engaging occasions. We began with Plutarch's *Life of Julius Caesar*. You would have thought that this was just the kind of thing that would spark the interest of a roomful of teenagers, with the tale of Caesar's revenge on the pirates coming during our very first session. Sadly Diaphantes was not in the business of making anything interesting. In an unvarying routine, a grubby copy of the text accompanied him to the classroom. We took it in turns to read out loud from it in a monotone, stumbling over the names, until he raised a finger and the book would be passed to the next student. The reader would stop when he reached a word that he did not understand and Diaphantes would survey the room to see if anyone could supply a meaning. We were never able to do so but he would never do anything as helpful as succinctly defining what the word meant. Instead, he would give a lengthy and largely incomprehensible lecture on its derivation and variants, and only then would the reading proceed. As you can imagine, since none of us had encountered Greek writing like this before, there were frequent stops and very slow progress was made through the text. The story of Caesar vanished under a welter of finickity explanations and after the first half an hour I was acutely aware of a collective yearning for escape welling up in the rows behind me.

There would be some relief when Diaphantes complained of one of his frequent headaches, brought on, no doubt, by the weight of his prodigious intellect. He would then give us some task to do in order to spare himself the burden of speaking. While we were thus occupied, he would lean back in his chair, close his eyes and place his fingertips on his forehead. He always carried with him a small silver box in which he kept some white tablets. Every now and then he would pop one between the pink, pursed lips that protruded from his beard. To this day, I have no idea what the tablets were or contained. The task that he set was what he called composition. We were expected to produce two sentences of dialogue, related to the text. What, for example, would Caesar have said to Vercingetorix when he surrendered? What would Mark Antony have said to Caesar when he was departing for the Senate House? We were supposed to use the language of Plutarch but our efforts were pitiable and elicited only cutting contempt from our teacher. I, of course, was never asked to read out my dialogue: it would not have done to expose an emperor's efforts as derisory. Eventually the noonday bell would be sounded by a servant outside and we would be free.

I much preferred my lessons with Nothos, as it was just me and him and effectively a continuation of the casual conversations that we had been having for years. We did not read whole books but collections of sayings culled from them and copied years ago into a leather-bound codex. Some of them seemed to me to be remarkably sensible, like the remark of Diogenes Laertius that wealth is the sinews of state affairs. We often discussed some of the concise sayings recorded in Leo VI's *Handbook of Tactics* and I recall Nothos reading out this one:

'We enjoin upon you to lead a guileless life in every other respect, but with the sole exception of the stratagems of war.'

When I asked what it meant, he explained:

'The morality that we should follow in our everyday lives is not that which should be applied in times of war. Let me give you an example. Imagine you are facing a powerful enemy force. Your army is strong and you think you can be victorious. But you know that there is traitor in the enemy camp and that on your instructions he will murder their general. Which course would you take?'

'The battle is more honourable. The other course is shameful.'

'But think about it. If you took the first course, even if you won, thousands would die on both sides. And you might lose. With the alternative, only one man dies and thousands return safe to their mothers, their children and their wives. By violating the injunction that we should not kill and by dispensing with the idea that it is honourable to settle matters face to face in battle, you would actually save lives.'

To this day I have wondered why he pointed that text out to me. Was he advocating it as a guide to policy? Or subtly pointing out the ways in which those in power justify their underhand actions? Or simply enjoying himself by confusing an innocent child? At the time though, I just basked in his wisdom.

✳ ✳ ✳

During this first year, I did not interact in any way with the other boys in the class, either during lessons or outside them. On the first day, they had all been lined up and presented to me by Nothos, all on best behaviour and doubtless with the exhortations of their families about what an honour it was ringing in their ears. Five minutes later I had forgotten all their names. None of them dared to speak to me and I would not have known what to say to them if they had. I had only spoken to Ouranos because I had been placed in a position where there was no alternative and in any case, none of my classmates looked as if they were anything like him. So at the beginning of the class we would sit and wait for Diaphantes in awkward silence. At the end, I would leave first, join the servant who was waiting outside and return to my apartment while they all filed out silently.

In the second year, the atmosphere in the class changed completely with the arrival of Constantine. With him came three others to make up the numbers: he and they occupied the first row, and I moved one back. Those on the last row departed for inglorious careers in the army. As I sat down, I noticed that at the end of his row, Constantine had got his knife out, the one that Anna had borrowed to maul Arus, and was showing it to the boy in the next seat. The ones behind then started leaning forward to see. He already knew some of the older ones from the polo field and within five minutes all the rest were captivated with him. When Diaphantes arrived and wished to begin, he had some difficulty establishing silence.

We began. It was still Plutarch but this time the *Life of Cicero*. The usual routine again. Diaphantes was at least enough of a teacher to have the boys at the back read first so that the new ones could get the hang of it. Now although Plutarch wrote in Greek, the ancient Romans he describes in some of his biographies lived in Italy and spoke the Latin language. Their names were Latin too. To us modern Romans, who speak Greek, Latin has a harsh and barbaric sound, which is why so few of us learn it. As the boy at the back read, he came to just such a name and Constantine gave a supressed but audible snort. There was a moment of silence as the reader hesitated. Diaphantes' lips pursed tighter.

'Proceed.'

The stilted recitation continued. The book was passed to the next reader who stumbled on the long name of a barbarian tribe. Constantine laughed out loud this time, while the rest sniggered. Diaphantes simply ignored the titters and went on regardless until eventually we were released by the bell.

The pattern for the future was set. Constantine would audibly puff, snort and sigh throughout the session and his gang of sycophants would snigger behind their tablets. After a few weeks though, they were disappointed to discover that Diaphantes had learned to select texts that contained no foreign words. So they developed a new tactic to make the lessons bearable, which involved playing on Diaphantes' fathomless vanity. Someone would stand up and ask him to expound the etymology of a particular word, mimicking his archaic manner of speaking:

'O learned Lord Diaphantes, enlighten us about *rabdos*.'

He invariably took the bait, unaware or unconcerned that he was being secretly mocked. He would fish a tablet out of the silver box, drop it in his mouth and press the tips of his fingers together.

'Ah yes, *rabdos*, the rod or wand, from which we derive *rabdophoreo*, "I carry a rod" and *rabdodia*, "a bundle of rods." Thence we arrive at the metaphorical derivations. I take as an example *rabdosis*, the fluting on a column that resembles rods.'

And so it would go on. We had no interest in rods but as long as Diaphantes droned on, we were safe from having to read out the day's text or scratch out our painful compositions. He would usually conclude with something along these lines:

'A more detailed exposition will be found in my treatise on the style of Euripides, a copy of which has been lodged in the library of the Magnavra.'

As if he really thought we would all rush there to pore lovingly over his words. Then the noonday bell would ring and our ordeal, and his, was over. The tactic was very effective and had the advantage that it could be used over and over again with the same result. Even Constantine realised though that it was inadvisable for the same student to ask every time. So one day, as we were walking to the school room together, he broached the subject with me. We had just entered the Kainourgion and were passing the peacock mosaic when he said:

'Why don't you ever say anything in class?'

'I do. Sometimes.'

'Well look, the others think it was about time you got Diaphantes onto one of his red herrings. Ask him about a word.'

'I can't think of one.'

He raised his eyes despairingly to heaven. I should have smelt a rat at that point. After all, we never usually went to the schoolroom together, setting off separately with our servants as soon as we were ready. Today though he had come early to my apartment to collect me and had dismissed the servants.

'Do I have to do everything for you? Hang on, I'll try to think of one.'

He pondered for a while and then came up with a word, which he made me repeat several times until I had it perfectly.

'But think of your own next time!'

In the schoolroom, the same deadly routine was enacted and after an hour Constantine was drumming his fingers and looking across at me expectantly. When a reader had finished his piece and the book was being passed, I stood up:

'O learned Lord Diaphantes, enlighten us about...'

A deathly hush descended on the room, while Constantine turned his head away to smother his guffaw. Diaphantes was staring at me fixedly, although I noticed that his eyes flickered momentarily towards Constantine. Perhaps he had worked out that I had been put up to this. The word that my brother had given me was not a classical one but a demotic insult that one might hear bandied around in the alleys near the Droungarios

Gate. It denotes a man who has some of the attributes and behaviour of a woman. Eventually, Diaphantes spoke:

'I shall despatch an epistle to your guardian.'

Despatch it he did although it was not until years later that I read the letter, having extracted it from the archives.

Leontios Diaphantes, Master of the Palace School, to John, Christ-loving Emperor and Autocrat of the Romans, greeting.

The learned Xenophon remarked that the growth of virtue is assisted by education yet it pains me to report that I see no evidence of the veracity of his dictum in the two princes whom you have entrusted to my care. The elder not only lacks virtue but any discernible talent. He is not a scholar, for his Greek inclines to the barbaric. He will not make a soldier, for he fears even his own shadow. If he were not heir to your Majesty's throne, it is difficult to imagine what he could usefully contribute. Perhaps he might enter the Church, although he shows no inclination towards piety. He might pass as a bishop provided that he had scribes to write for him, priests to chant the liturgy for him and monks to pray for him. Had he been born outside palace circles, one cannot imagine into what craft he might have been apprenticed, for his manual dexterity is in proportion to his limited intellectual capacity. His writing is illegible. As for the younger boy, I understand that he is not without some aptitude in the banaustic arts and I would advise that his energies, which are considerable, be channelled in that direction.

Perhaps his tone was understandable as we had sorely tried him, even though it was inadvertent in my case. I do not think that that is the whole story here though. To have written so pointedly, Diaphantes must have made a political choice. He had seen no future for Constantine and me and so had hitched his chariot firmly to that of Emperor John and his brother-in-law, Bardas Skleros. Their family would provide the emperors of the future.

$$* * *$$

As in previous years, I never really spoke to any of my fellow students in Diaphantes' class. I would sit stiffly in the seat at the far end of the second row that none of them would ever have dreamt of occupying. Their prattle in the minutes before the session began went on around me and I just filtered it out. Perhaps if I had listened I would have been saved from the embarrassing incident that had prompted Diaphantes' letter. But as the autumn went on, I started to notice the boy in front of me. There was nothing remarkable about him. He was not one of the muscled polo gods who used to hang around with Constantine at the stables. He was rather short like me, perhaps a bit dumpy. He had mousey brown hair, that looked as if it had been cropped short but had then grown again, rapidly and unevenly. Tufts of it stuck out as did his ears. It was his awkward demeanour that caught my attention, his jerky movements and the rather gauche way in which he held himself. When he arrived, he would carefully take his tablet and stylus from a leather bag and position them precisely on the desk in from on him. Then within seconds he would manage to knock one or other or both onto the floor. When the proceedings began, he would gaze with knitted brows at Diaphantes, evidently straining to make sense of the erudite language. I could see that beneath the desk, he would place one sandal on the other and work it gently to and fro. When it was his turn to read, he would bend over the book, tracing the words with his finger, doubtless adding to the grubbiness. As he painfully made out the words, his tunic, which was slightly too big for him, would droop over one shoulder and he would pull it back. On Diaphantes' signal, he would straighten up with relief and pass the book to his neighbour. All this I watched every day and came even to look forward to.

A few weeks after I had first noticed him, Diaphantes arrived with a new book for us to study.

'Pupils,' that was his favourite term for us, 'today we shall depart from the pure Attic and study the form that is designated Ionian. It is employed by the historian Herodotus. We shall peruse his account of Cleisthenes the Athenian, although I shall not require composition in this idiom.'

The book was handed to one of the students in the middle row who crept through his passage stopping virtually every three words for guidance. Diaphantes would then make some completely unenlightening observation such as:

'Here we see a prime difference between the Attic and Ionian. Proceed.'

The book moved inexorably from reader to reader. I had my turn and Constantine remained quiet: Diaphantes had chosen a passage that was free of foreign names. The book reached the new students in the first row and passed to the one in front of me. Nervously he took it and began to read, conscious of all eyes being on him, tracing the lines with his finger. Diaphantes kept testily correcting his pronunciation. The boy droned on:

'Cleisthenes first inquired the country and lineage of each; then he kept them with him for a year, testing their manliness and temper and upbringing and manner of life; this he did by consorting with them alone and in company.'

'ARF, ARF, ARF!!!!!'

Following Constantine's lead, the other boys did not this time suppress their laughter but roared their heads off. The cause of the explosion was this. Our language is an ancient one and over the centuries some words have changed their meaning. The one that Herodotus used for "consorting," has now come to mean "copulating." Only three of those present did not join in the merriment. Diaphantes was sitting rigid and disapproving waiting for the row to subside. I was too absorbed in watching the reader's reaction. The reader himself was glancing around him anxiously, his face having turned a shade that I can only describe as vermillion. Then Diaphantes began rapping on his desk and some form of order was restored. He signalled for the book to go to the next reader but he offered no indication as to why Herodotus had used such a word. Nor did he extend any kind of reassurance to the crestfallen reader who must have thought that he had committed some unforgiveable breach of etiquette and was about to be flung into the deepest dungeon of the Boukoleon. I cannot think why the man chose that passage in the first place. Intellectuals never fail to amaze me: so cultured, so knowledgeable and yet lacking even the most basic common sense.

I did not sleep well that night. The old nocturnal visitations had now ceased but the vision of the hapless reader, flushed and embarrassed amid the mayhem, kept floating before my eyes. The oddest thing was that just thinking about him was as compelling as staring at him and I was perplexed as to why he was filling my head. I missed my mother's occasional visits then as I thought that this might have been the kind of thing that I could have asked her about. The next morning, I resolved that the first step would be to find out his name. I must have been introduced to him at the first class but I had no recollection of it. In normal circumstances, it would have been easy: I would merely have had to wait until Diaphantes called on him to read the text. But our learned teacher never used names, he merely pointed. I doubt he knew what any of us were called apart from Constantine and me. As it happened, though, I was due that day to meet with Nothos for one of our statecraft sessions and I saw my opportunity to get what I wanted. By then, I was enough of a politician to take a concealed route to the ultimate goal so I did not merely demand to be told the name. Instead, when we were seated I asked Nothos about one of the sayings we had read earlier. It was about one of the ancients, Xenophon I think, who knew the names of all the soldiers in his army. I asked how that was possible.

'Like most things, Majesty, it can be done by an act of will. If you repeat the name out loud when the person is introduced to you it helps to fix it in the mind, as it does if you make an effort to recall it later. If writing materials are to hand, it is useful to make a note, though I doubt Xenophon would have had that luxury on his long march.'

I asked why one should bother to remember names.

'It is of the utmost importance, Majesty – recall a man's name on the second meeting and he will love and serve you forever.'

I nodded earnestly and said that this was a skill that I needed to acquire to fulfil my future role. I would start with the students in the grammar class whose names I had been given but immediately forgotten. Was there by any chance a list? Nothos looked impressed:

'Yes indeed there is. We would never let anyone close to the person of Your Majesty and that of your brother without careful scrutiny.'

The list was delivered that evening, with Nothos' leaden chamberlain's seal attached. I perused the names but they meant nothing.

The next day we were back in the school room. Diaphantes had yet to arrive so there was chaos with boys shouting and throwing things, and Constantine at the centre of the maelstrom. The main topic of conversation was how we were to get through the next three hours of dreary pedantry. Someone at the back shouted out:

'Hey, Spondyles, why don't you read out some more dirty words?'

In the front row, he turned bright red and looked round shyly. So that was it: he was the Demetrius Spondyles on the list. And now I had discovered that, it seemed to me that he did look rather like that icon of St Demetrius in the chapel of St Barbara, a miniature version of which stood by my bed. That got me thinking that the pleasure I derived from staring at him must be something spiritual and religious.

Sunday came, and that meant attending the liturgy in Hagia Sophia. The emperor himself is present on these occasions when he is resident in Constantinople but John was there much less than Nikephoros had been in his last years. That October he was on the eastern frontier, raiding into Mesopotamia and capturing Nisibis. So it was just Theodora, Constantine, Anna and I in the imperial gallery. Father Anthony had not yet become patriarch but as synkellos he had the job of deciding who gave the weekly homilies. He tended to choose preachers from his own Stoudios monastery, and that Sunday a young monk called Symeon stood in the pulpit. His text was from St Paul's first letter to the Thessalonians: "Pray without ceasing." I cannot honestly say that I was paying much attention. I accept the teachings of the Church and revere the holy icons but abstruse points of theology are beyond me. But then Symeon said something that made me sit up and take notice:

'It is in this continuous prayer, that we become caught up in the mystery of God. We can, if only in a very small way, transcend our sinful human natures. We can take on, infinitesimally, some small part of the essence of God. We can have a tiny foretaste of the transfixing ecstasy that we shall experience when we see Him face to face. We undergo a foretaste of *theosis*.'

I have left that last word untranslated. Literally it means "deification" but our theologians use it to mean that union with God that is the ultimate aim of the Christian life. But I did not know that then. All I heard was the word along with the phrase "transfixing ecstasy." That was it! That was what I had felt in the schoolroom when Spondyles had read Herodotus and I had been possessed by it ever since. I leant over the balustrade and looked down at the preacher. He raised his eyes to mine, doubtless flattered to see that the young emperor was drinking in his words with such rapt attention. Now I think about it, a few decades later he made a pest of himself and he had to be exiled to Asia, but at this point I was intensely grateful to him and I left the church with his words ringing in my ears. It was a beautiful and holy thing, I told myself, my theosis.

So it was that throughout that autumn and winter of 972-3, I endured Diaphantes' teaching and sat behind Spondyles. I found out more about him through the usual indirect method. I asked Nothos first about two other names on the list he had sent me, who their fathers were and how they had been chosen to be my classmates. Then I asked about Spondyles. It turned out that his father had been killed during Nikephoros' reconquest of Crete and it had been John Tzimiskes who visited his widow to break the news, for Spondyles senior had been a junior officer under his direct command. John had promised to do all in his power to ensure that her son was given every chance in life and, as emperor, he had added Demetrius' name to the list for the dubious benefit of Diaphantes' pedagogy.

I did not address a single word to him during that time, though I wanted to and I racked my brains to find some means to initiate a conversation. Perhaps I could drop my tablet and ask some question when he picked it up and handed it to me. Perhaps I could intervene with some pithy remark in a conversation that he was having with his neighbour. These very thoughts were going through my head one morning when he arrived after the rest of us. My eyes went straight to him and on meeting my gaze, he at once went bright red, bobbed in a little bow and rushed to his seat. Then I knew it was impossible.

He would go rigid and absurdly deferential if I addressed him, bewildered and full of dread to have been singled out.

Unfortunately for him, his worst fear was soon to be realised. Diaphantes had now decided that we were to read a portion of Arrian's account of the campaigns of Alexander the Great. For composition we were set two sentences on "What would Alexander have said when he found the king of Persia?" I had prepared my two and was rather proud of them but I knew by now that I would never be called upon. Constantine was well aware of that too so he had prepared absolutely nothing and his tablet lay defiantly empty on his desk. Diaphantes surveyed the room and pointed to Spondyles. He rose hesitantly, for Diaphantes insisted that we stand to read our sentences. He began to read and inevitably the sentences were dreadful, a ghastly concoction of words he did not understand, padded out with a few that he did:

'How lamentable, o monarch, is thy recurrence on stones…'

Diaphantes placed his head on his fingertips, as if to support it against the crushing weight of this barbaric and loutish ignorance.

'With all thy power illiterated, without thy crown and horse…'

'Stop!,' cried Diaphantes, although a more exact translation would be something like 'Let cease the flow of thy discourse!'

Spondyles looked up as did we all. For those at the back and Constantine, the lesson had suddenly become interesting.

'What was it, pray, that the recumbent king lacked?' Diaphantes' tone was one of sweet reasonableness.

Spondyles thought that our teacher had merely not heard and was asking him to repeat so he dropped his head to his tablet and resumed:

'Without thy crown and horse richly comparisoned…'

'No, no, no! Upon what beast did the king of Persia ride, pray?'

Spondyles gaped. He did not have the remotest idea what the man was talking about and looked close to tears. He was completely unaware that he had committed what for Diaphantes was the unforgiveable sin: he had inserted a demotic word in a sentence that was supposed to be in Attic Greek. For 'horse' he had used a word that was what we all would have said down at the stables but which jarred in the ears of anyone steeped in the classics.

'That is a term used by stable boys and muck spreaders,' spat Diaphantes with snide contempt. He had doubtless sized up the lowly social standing of his victim with a practised eye and knew that he could act with impunity. 'The divine Arrian would never have allowed such a word to escape from the prison of his teeth! *Hippos* is the correct word in Attic, you moron. Sit!'

Spondyles flopped back into his chair and bent over his tablet. He remained like that for the rest of the class. It passed uneventfully enough, for Constantine and his cronies had had their fun for the day. The noonday bell rang and Diaphantes was out of the door before we were. The moment it shut behind him a hail of pinecones, doubtless kept in pockets for just such an eventuality, descended on Spondyles and on the students on either side of him.

'Hippos! Hippos!'

He turned round, reddened and then smiled slowly. From that point, there was no going back. He was as compelling to me as Nothos or Ouranos, regardless of the vast gulf between him and them.

7

Hebdomon (975)

Y ou will achieve frequent victories against your enemies without actual war by making use of money,' read Nothos, 'When they have other enemies lying in wait for them somewhere, an offer of money should be persuasive in getting this people to wage war on your adversaries.'

Nothos paused and shut the book: it was Leo VI's *Handbook of Tactics.*

'How does Your Majesty regard this injunction of your illustrious predecessor?'

'I suppose he meant that it is better to spend money than sacrifice Roman lives?'

'Quite so, Majesty. Whenever we are confronted with a powerful foe, we can be sure that they themselves have other enemies and we make contact with them. This is what Emperor Nikephoros did in 967 when he paid the ruler of the Russians to attack the Bulgars.'

'But the tactic hardly worked well! The Russians did the job but then they grabbed Bulgaria for themselves. Emperor John had to invade three years ago and defeat the Russians in the field.'

'Your Majesty is quite correct. No tactic is fool proof. But it is always best to consider other options before resorting to military force.'

I was now seventeen and my time in the schoolroom had come to an end. At that age, intellectually gifted students would already have moved on to the highest level of education in the Magnavra palace. Diaphantes had made it clear in his letter that these higher studies were not an option for me and for once I entirely agreed with him. In fact, they are not really appropriate for any emperor, only for bureaucrats and senior clergy. Instead I was to continue to have lessons on statecraft not only with Nothos but with other officials so that I was familiar with all the departments of state.

By now I was much more politically aware. It had all begun when I asked Nothos for of a list my classmates. Thereafter I expanded the bare names by adding details. I discovered, for example, that the two cronies who sniggered at Constantine's every feeble jest were brothers, Leo and Theognostos Melissenos. Leo was about my age and had been there in the front row with me before Constantine had joined us: he had been quiet as a mouse then. Theognostos was Constantine's age and a kind of mirror image of him, both in looks and character. They had known him long before they had been drafted into the schoolroom, from hanging around the stables. But I learned something even more useful. I had always assumed that everyone adored Constantine and wanted to be in his gang but that was not the case. From the first day, there had been in my row a boy with black, tightly curled hair who I now discovered was called Stephen Kontostephanos. He was known to the others as Impy for he was even shorter than Spondyles and he did look rather like some minor demon. I began to notice that he did not join in with the sycophantic titters and deduced that he was deeply hostile towards the Melissenos brothers, although I never found out exactly why. It was probably one of those feuds that are rife among families originating in Asia Minor. Usually someone stole a goat several centuries ago and they have been at daggers drawn ever since. I made a note of that. It might come in handy later and I began to acquire a sense of who was aligned with who.

After listing my schoolmates, I took to inserting the names of people as I met them, filling in a few details as and when they became available. Needless to say, I had quite a few notes on Father Anthony, Ouranos and Diaphantes but I also jotted down people I had met only once or twice. These pages I had bound together in notebooks with blank ones inserted so that I could add further details and names in the right place. I might well have got bored with this task sooner or later, had I not one day been given a demonstration of just how useful those jottings could be. My ceremonial task after the schoolroom one afternoon had been to review troops recently returned from the Mesopotamian campaign: John was still out in the east at that time. They paraded through the Hippodrome, several elite regiments that we call the Tagmata. I watched from the imperial box and afterwards descended to ground level to inspect a line of soldiers who had distinguished themselves. We walked along the ranks and a Count Palatine told me the name of each and what he had done to deserve this honour. Now I would not pretend that I remembered all the names but when we got to a fellow with his arm in a sling, I stopped and asked him about how he got the wound. I had been told that I should do that in a few cases: not so many as to delay the parade, or so few as to make it look like favouritism. Some months later, I was crossing the Augousteion with John and Theodora: it was the Dormition of the Virgin, one of those festivals when the emperor attends a liturgy in Hagia Sophia and a big crowd turns out to see him. Soldiers lined the route to keep the throng back. They were all John's men who would return with him to the east a few weeks later. I saw that one of them was the man who had had his arm in a sling and, as I drew level, I stopped and asked him whether he was fully recovered. The effect was astonishing. His mouth literally fell open before he remembered himself, snapped it shut and assured me that he was quite well. At that moment, he would gladly have given his life for me. Come to think of it, he did: he was one of those who did not come back from Trajan's Gate in 986. As we carried on and entered the church, John was looking at me curiously. Constantine was easy to work out but he was wondering about me, that I knew.

My last year in the schoolroom had been a very happy one. For a start, Diaphantes was no longer our teacher. Emperor John had rewarded him for his endurance by making him Logothete of the Drome, one of the higher administrative posts. In his place, we had a younger man named Symeon Metaphrastes and everything went a lot better. Another improvement was that Constantine was not there. John had evidently read Diaphantes' letter and my brother had been enrolled for military training instead, which he thoroughly enjoyed. I did for a time worry that Anna might join us but she had no desire to take her education further. Once she was 12, she was provided with an apartment of her own in the Women's Quarters and she became very religious. She attended church at least once a day and filled her room with icons of all the saints that had ever lived. She used every possible occasion to prove that I was in some way her moral inferior. She once came into my apartment when I was reading Theophanes and eating a bowl of figs. After a few moments, she demanded to know why I had not offered her a fig and passed some remark about how greedy I was. I held out the bowl to her and she raised her hands in horror and asked whether I had forgotten that it was Advent and that she was fasting. Even the most harmless throwaway remark would be twisted into evidence of my utter depravity. We were once in the imperial box at the Hippodrome. John had laid on a show for the crowd: wild animals, tightrope walking, mock battles: the kind of thing that always goes down well. An elephant was brought in, led by a man wearing a sheepskin jacket. I observed that he looked like he might be a Vlach. She retorted loudly, so that John and Theodora could hear:

'So what if he is a Vlach? We are all God's creatures.'

Given she was now at an age where girls of noble families have their marriages arranged, I asked Nothos whether she would be betrothed soon. He responded with great frankness. John did not dare to betroth her for whoever she married would have a claim on the throne that trumped his. I had not thought of that.

To return to my schooling, with no Diaphantes, Constantine or Anna, I rather enjoyed that last year of ancient literature. There were no new students either. We all sat demurely and gave Metaphrastes no trouble. He in turn was encouraging and genial, gave us Homer to read and never asked us to compose sentences. Instead we used to learn sections by heart and I can still remember quite a few of them. Even better, Spondyles was still there. After that first year, he had disappeared for the summer and I had wondered whether I might not forget him. In fact, I made a conscious effort to do so, convinced that he would not return in September. I told myself that he was just an abstraction in my mind, a kind of fantasy remote from any real individual, and that I ought to think about something more rewarding. But he did return in September, and every September after that, and I felt the same exhilaration as before. I always made sure that I was behind him but again I never spoke to him. The closest I came was on an occasion when we were reading about Odysseus and the nymph Calypso. Whereas Diaphantes never used to stir from his desk during the lesson,

Metaphrastes used to walk around the room and rather than making us read in order would choose someone at random. From the back of the room, he chose Spondyles. The book was passed forward from hand to hand and placed in front of him and he goggled helplessly. I leant forward, stretched out my arm and pointed out the place. He turned gratefully, only to see it was me and drop his eyes. I did not mind but I now had to think what I was going to do once the classes came to an end and I was faced with the prospect of never seeing him again. A plan began to form in my mind.

* * *

It was one rainy March day in the spring of 975, that I was called to a meeting with Nothos and John Tzimiskes to decide my future. My guardian was at that point preparing to set out on what was arguably to become his most celebrated military expedition, although some might prefer his 971 Bulgarian campaign. It was at this meeting that it was decided that my education should come to an end and that I should concentrate on studying the mechanics of government with Nothos and others. With that business out of the way, I made my move. I reminded them that I had spent the last few summers at Hebdomon with my aunt and sister and proposed that this year I should do so in a rather different way. Theodora and Anna could reside at Hiereia instead and I would go to Hebdomon with Constantine and a group of young men of our own age. We could use the parade ground there, which was much bigger than the polo ground at the palace, for sports and military exercises and it would help me to prepare for the military aspects of the emperor's role. John and Nothos looked at each other: I doubt they had ever seriously considered that I would have a military role. It was John who spoke:

'You will need to have someone of experience there to lead the military training.'

'Yes, uncle, I have thought of that. I would like the kataphract Nikephoros Ouranos to fulfil that role. He served with distinction in the last two Mesopotamian campaigns. Could he be spared from the next one to teach us what he knows at Hebdomon?'

Somewhat to my surprise, John agreed and suggested that Constantine and I should compile a list of twenty names each of potential participants and submit them to the chamberlain's office where they could be vetted for suitability. Constantine loved the idea and quickly had his list ready, although he had to get someone else to write it for him. On mine, I carefully hid Spondyles' name among the others and went through three days of tortured anxiety in case Nothos said that someone so obscure was not worthy of joining the summer court at Hebdomon. As it turned out, he raised not a single objection to my list. Two names were scratched from Constantine's because, as Nothos put it, their parents' political activities in the past made it inadvisable for them to be in close proximity to the emperors. He substituted two names of his own. One was an obvious political choice: Romanos Skleros, the son of Emperor John's brother-in-law. The other was a complete unknown called Kalokyris Delphinas: I assumed he had been chosen precisely because he was unimportant and innocuous. The arrangements were made and at the beginning of June, Constantine and I rode with a small suite to Hebdomon and moved into the villa with Philemon and Catia. The rest of the 'court' followed over the next few days and were lodged in the barracks by the parade ground.

* * *

When I first saw Spondyles among the boys milling around outside the barracks, I felt immensely pleased with myself. Not only did he look exactly the same and exerted the same quite inexplicable fascination, but I had engineered an entire summer

with him close by. Just as satisfying was my reunion with
Ouranos who arrived on a white charger escorted by two
comrades. He had just become a father for the third time and he
now had a thick black beard and noticeably broader shoulders.
He would have no difficulty putting the fear of God into
Constantine and his gang. Leo and Theognostos Melissenos
were the core of his clique and that Delphinas, who had been
added to the list by Nothos, soon gravitated there. They shared
the same rather basic sense of humour. When Constantine
barked, Delphinas would add his own cackle in a kind of hideous
descant. He was a tall and scrawny youth, a bit older than me.
A weedy moustache covered his upper lip, above his slightly
protruding teeth. Around the four of them, the weaker
personalities revolved like the planets going round the earth.

Early on the first day, Ouranos lined the boys up,
Constantine and I standing on either side of him, and
announced that they would need to choose captains and teams.
This came as a shock to me. In making my plans, I had thought
only about seeing Spondyles again and had not worked exactly
what role I was going to play in the planned activities. The
same thought had evidently occurred to Constantine who
immediately piped up:

'That's not fair: who's going to choose him?'

He was pointing at me. Most of those assembled looked
away or at the ground. The Melissenos brothers snorted with
supressed giggles, delighted that someone could say out loud
exactly what they had been thinking. Delphinas sniggered, a
sound like "Yee, hee." Once again Ouranos rescued me:

'The older emperor will not participate, he will preside. He
will make judgments and award prizes.'

The selection went ahead without me. Inevitably
Constantine was voted one of the captains. The other was Impy
Kontostephanos who, in spite of his small stature, had a
stentorian voice that could be clearly heard across the parade
ground. The Melissenos brothers naturally ended up in

Constantine's team, as did Delphinas. Romanos Skleros, on the other hand, was inseparable from Impy and became his second-in-command. After the more prominent and sporty individuals had been snapped up, it was down to the no hopers and Spondyles was one of the last two to be chosen. I was pleased to see that he ended up with Impy by default when Constantine reluctantly chose the other one. Once the choices had been made, with the clannishness of male adolescents, they all became fiercely loyal to their team. On Sundays, Constantine and company went to the Baptist, Impy's team to the Evangelist. Needless to say, I went there too with Philemon and Catia.

While my exclusion from the teams was welcome, it did mean that I was on the margins of the daily activities. Ouranos insisted on an early start and organised different sports every day: running, wrestling, discus and archery contests predominated during the first week. I would take up a position at the side of the parade ground, in the shade of the line of walnut trees to watch. Ouranos gave me various tasks involving refereeing and adjudicating to keep me included. I could have enjoyed this routine but Constantine was not going to give up that easily. He did everything he could to undermine me in front of the others. Whenever I spoke, he would cast an sardonic glance over to Delphinas and the brothers and I am sure that the four of them derided me mercilessly when I was not around. The sports themselves bored me as did the sight of Constantine showing off endlessly.

There was only one thing that I wanted to see and I constantly strained my eyes to pick put the diminutive figure in the distance. When I had found him, I kept my eyes on him. Looking back on it, I can say that I have never known anyone who expended so much energy and enthusiasm with so little result. In wrestling, he would be hurled to the ground within seconds but would leap back to his feet and be ready for more. In jumping, his size told against him but he would still try to vault across an impossibly high hurdle with predictable results. In discus, he would hurl the thing high up into the air but when it came down it had not travelled very far at all.

When midday came and it was too hot for any more contests, Constantine and his friends would rush to the pond at the far end of the parade ground, hurl off their clothes and leap in. I could not expose my person in that way so I sat to one side as, I noticed, did Spondyles and several others. There was one area of physical development though where I did have the edge. They were at the stage where they were constantly scanning each other's chins to detect the first stirrings of a beard. As I am dark, I had quite a lot of facial hair for my age, although it has always tended to be thicker on the cheeks than on the chin. Impy was similarly blessed and every day grew to look more and more like the satyr fountain in the garden of the villa. Constantine and the brothers had nothing. I was rather proud of my beard and I think that is why later, when it grew long enough, I developed the habit of stroking it and folding around my fingers. At Hebdomon, it gave me a kind of authority in my presiding role.

At the beginning of the second week, Ouranos decreed that the equestrian events were to begin, although there was some doubt as to whether there would be enough horses to go round. He and I had purchased three extra ones from a nearby farm and we managed by grouping contestants into threes, each taking a turn on the same mount. It was this rationing that finally gave me my chance. The sport of the day was jumping and boys without a mount had to wait around for much of the morning until it was their turn. Similarly, as only one horse could negotiate the course at a time, those who were mounted and waiting their turn to compete, would ride around to warm their horse up. I saw Spondyles get into the saddle and canter off across the parade ground in the direction of the town centre. On impulse I spurred Willow after him with my bodyguard in pursuit. Spondyles had reined in and was turning for the canter back when he was confronted by the sight of me riding up with a burly man on a black horse behind me.

'Come on,' I said, 'I want to show you something.'

I set off towards the villa and, although he looked back towards the jumping contest momentarily, he trotted along after me. We clattered down the street that led past the harbour and turned into the grassy meadow that stretched alongside wall of the villa garden. Although the villa itself had been renovated since my first visit, many sections of the wall were still broken down and I was very glad of that. When we reached the right place, we stopped and dismounted, leaving the horses with the guard, and we crawled through a hole into the garden. I led the way through the undergrowth to the sunken enclosure and the four lichened emperors. He asked who they were.

'Emperors from long ago who spoke a different language, look.'

I showed him the inscriptions on the walls. Suddenly he remembered himself and launched into a speech beginning with "Sir:" they had been told that they were to call us that during their stay. It was something about expressing his great appreciation for the honour I had done him in inviting him to Hebdomon. All doubtless dinned into him by his mother and carefully rehearsed. I imagined them on the threshold of their house, her brushing the dandruff from his shoulders and priming him on every word. I knew that I must not laugh, so listened gravely, then told him that he was most welcome and that I hoped he would enjoy his stay. Almost immediately afterwards, a voice floated over the wall:

'Spondyles, you dirty cheat, it's my turn for the horse!'

Would I never be left alone?

'Stay where you are!,' I told him, taken by surprise at the commanding tone of my own voice. Having come this far. I was not going to be baulked.

I ducked through the hole to find two indignant boys looking uncertainly at the black horse and the big man leaning against the wall. They were out of breath from having run all the way from the parade ground and one of them was bent over with his hands on his knees, recovering from a stitch. I asked whose turn it was for the horse and one of them raised his hand as if I were a teacher.

'Then you take it and you can have Willow: you can both keep them for the rest of the morning.'

They looked as if they could not believe their luck and rushed to grab the bridles before I could change my mind. I went back through the hole. He was still there. He had sat down on the pediment under the statues and was leaning forward with his forearms resting on his thighs. He had placed one sandal on the other. I sat down quickly to forestall him from getting up. I wanted to stop being commanding and to go back to being just one of his classmates. So I began:

'Do you ever think about what you're going to do? I mean after this summer and then after that?'

As if by magic, the constraint suddenly dropped away and he started to speak. For the first time I heard his normal voice in continuous flow, not snatches overheard in the classroom or the strangled monotone in which he had made his rehearsed speech. And he was speaking Demotic, not reading out Attic or Homeric Greek. I realised then that he had a light Thracian accent, which gave a faint burr to everything he said. It all came out in bits and pieces, in no particular order. This is broadly what he said.

He had never met his father as he was not born until after Nikephoros' expedition to Crete had departed. After his father had been killed, his widowed mother lived on her pension in Psamathia, a respectable but rather remote district over towards the Golden Gate. Although it is inside the city walls, much of the area is given over to wheat fields, market gardens and vineyards. The owner of the house next door owned a vineyard and Spondyles used to work there in the late summer to supplement the pension. So come this September he would be cutting the grapes and treading them in a vat. It must be understood that this was all very novel to me. I had just assumed that he and his mother lived the same kind of life that I did and the news that he had to work for a living came as a revelation. During the autumn and spring, he had attended the school in the Great Palace, making the long trek there and back again twice a week. What on earth, I wondered, had been the point of him perusing Plutarch with Diaphantes? But I knew the answer really: he was there to make up numbers and would have been paid to attend.

For a moment, it looked as if he was about to dry up, so I prompted by asking whether he would always want to work in the vineyard. He confessed that his ambition was to be a soldier, even though his lack of height would prevent him from entering the more prestigious regiments. Then he coloured again. I asked what the matter was. Apparently, the vineyard owner next door had seven children. As he was an only child, Spondyles played with them and especially with the smallest daughter who was about a year younger than he was and was called Efi. That is short for Euphemia, he explained, as if I would never have come across such a foreshortening in my rarefied existence. About six months ago, sitting on the wall of the vineyard, they had decided that they should get married as soon as they were old enough. They told Efi's father who said that he was quite happy to give them his blessing but insisted that his prospective son-in-law must be able to support his daughter. Seasonal work in the vineyard simply was not enough. That was why he wanted to follow his father's profession.

He came to a halt abruptly, taking me by surprise because I had been sitting there quite happily listening to him. By now the morning was well advanced and the heat was penetrating even the shady enclosure. I asked him if he was thirsty and led him under the archway to the wall where the water gushed from the blank stone mouth of the satyr. We held out our cupped hands and caught it. Our eyes met as we drank. Behind him a swarm of midges was dancing deliriously in a mote of sunshine that was streaming through a gap in the trees. He straightened up and a light breeze blew in from the sea, ruffling lock of his hair into his eyes, and he pushed it back with his hands, then pulled the neck of his tunic to one side. There was a drowsy buzzing all around us. He was waiting deferentially for me to tell him what to do next.

'We need to get back,' I said, 'Ouranos will be wondering why Alypios is hogging your horse and why someone other than me is riding on Willow!'

Emperors cannot slip away or if they do they are soon found but that was not why I ended the encounter. The fact was that we had arrived at perfection. I could not believe that I had heard him speak uninterrupted and for so long. Inwardly, I was hugging myself with joy. There was no question of my being jealous of his romantic attachment or disappointed that more had not happened by the fountain. Quite the contrary. I was overjoyed that I had at last discovered how I could help him and I could scarcely breathe for the exhilaration of it. It had all been exquisite theosis. We ducked out of the hole in the wall and set off on foot back along the meadow towards the harbour street, the guard leading his black horse behind us. When we reached the parade ground we could discern in the distance that the jumping contest was coming to an end. I told him he had better run on ahead and I watched him go as I plodded over towards Ouranos. He just walked away without once looking back, a tiny figure in the vastness of the parade ground.

✳ ✳ ✳

Throughout my life I have enjoyed remarkably good health but I did succumb to camp fever on a couple of occasions in Bulgaria during the 990s. For several days, I was in a twilight world where my febrile dreams merged with the reality of my tent and my anxious attendants. That pretty much describes the state I was in at Hebdomon throughout July and August. Every morning I would preside over the games, beaming beatifically as I dropped a handkerchief to signal the off or handed the olive branch to the winner. While the contests were on, I would ride around on Willow, rejoicing that the old demon of horse-fear was dead, letting the breeze waft across my face and even letting go the reins and holding out my arms wide, my knees gripping her flanks. In the afternoons, I would lie in the shuttered darkness of my room and dream of a perfect world where there were no processions and ceremonial and I would not be shy of jumping in the pond with everyone else. In the late afternoons we would emerge and I would watch the wrestling and the jumping before we would all sit on the raised ridge that ran around the periphery of the parade ground. Slowly the sun would go down, the air would cool and the stars would come out and I would sit and listen to all their chatter, never joining in, and staying as far from Constantine and Delphinas as I could. One evening Ouranos stood up and pointed to the sky. There, hanging in the firmament, was a star brighter than all the others. I had never seen one like it before as it had a kind of beard sticking out behind it. Why God might have put a new star in the sky was the topic of conversation for the rest of the evening and for several evenings after that. For me, it was obvious why it was there: it was all part of the theosis.

Although I did not speak to Spondyles directly again, I constantly had my eye on him or had him in my mind. I pondered matters endlessly, resolving that I would have to do something for him: find him a post in the army so that he could marry. Then I heard his name being shouted. It was early evening and we were all out sitting on the ridge. The line of walnut trees was behind us and a debate had begun as to which of their branches Spondyles would or would not be able to touch. After various opinions had been canvassed, he got to his feet and ran over to put them to the test. He stood, silhouetted against the red sky, reaching up with one hand, the other arm held curiously rigid against his body while he shouted for them to look and see that he could indeed touch the branch. At that moment, the thought struck me that I was completely and utterly happy and that I wanted this moment to last forever.

It was when Spondyles had gone back to the group, that another thought came to me. This happiness could not and would not last. In another year, I would be eighteen and old enough to rule in my own right. The very idea appalled me. What kind of a life would it be, carrying the full burden of the imperial office, like my stepfather and now my uncle? I remembered that last conversation with Nikephoros when he had told me that he had never wanted to be emperor. Only now did I appreciate what he meant. There was some comfort in the knowledge that I would probably never really be emperor in more than name. John Tzimiskes was young and likely to rule for many years and his nephew Romanos Skleros was probably being groomed to take over after him. But then again was it really an option for me to spend my entire life as a ghost emperor? Could those who held power really afford to permit the continued existence of an adult who had a better claim than they did?

It might have been that same evening or another, that a strange ominous atmosphere began to creep in. I became aware that beakers of wine were starting to circulate as we sat under the walnut trees. They appeared as if by magic, for no servants were present, aside from my and Constantine's guards who were standing at a respectful distance. I took a beaker and tasted it: thick, dark and sweet. So I knocked back the contents and then heedlessly accepted several refills. When I rose to my feet to go back to the villa, I found that I was decidedly unsteady and I ended up puking in the ditch at the end of the parade ground. My guard looked on sardonically. Emperors are not even allowed to throw up in privacy.

I paid for my over-indulgence the next day but so did many of the others. Some of them had never drunk the stuff in their lives before and they did not emerge from the barracks. Spondyles was nowhere to be seen. Constantine, Delphinas and the Melissenos brothers, of course, showed no ill effects even though they had drunk quite a lot. I was sitting on the ridge watching Constantine charging around at full pelt in a three-aside polo bout, when Ouranos came and sat next to me. He asked whether I knew where the wine had come from last night and then went on:

'It was good quality, from Crete I should think. One of the sweet ones - a perfect choice for a bunch of adolescents. I asked Philemon about it and he said he had a few jars of the local white in the cellar but nothing imported and expensive like this. There are six more large jars of it in the barracks so it would have needed a cart to bring them in.'

For some reason, I thought for a moment that Delphinas might be behind the wine but then I dismissed the idea. I did not know for certain but I doubted very much that he was from a rich family. A mansion in Sphorakion and a few thousand acres out in the province of Boukellarion bestow a patina that Delphinas conspicuously lacked. Constantine was a possibility but we carried no money of our own: the servants took care of all that. Ouranos went on, saying that he did not understand how the women got there either. I confessed that I had not noticed any women, apart from Catia.

'They are prostitutes, Majesty. Someone has been collecting them up in the city and bringing them here after dark: they must have brought them along the road in a carriage. Like the wine, they are the expensive sort. Do you think I ought to say something about it?'

I was flattered that he looked to me for guidance and I surprised myself by rising to the occasion. Given that whoever was behind this had considerable resources at their disposal, I advised, it would not be prudent to make waves. He should just look away. He was relieved and grateful.

'Thank you, Majesty,' he said, 'You are a true emperor.' I was still not sure that I wanted to be a true emperor.

Some days later the wine reappeared at dusk. I took a beaker and sat with my back to a walnut tree, sipping slowly because I had learned my lesson and knew not to quench my thirst with a Cretan red. Then a discernible tremor of excitement rippled up around me. Several individuals got up and started walking quickly across the parade ground to the barracks. I noticed that two figures were standing at the bottom of the ridge conversing excitedly and occasionally glancing up at me. Although I could not make out their features, I knew that it was Delphinas and Constantine. Then Constantine walked up the ridge to me, leaving Delphinas staring after him.

'There's one for you, you know.' He said it grudgingly, as if regretting the criminal waste. I stared into my beaker and shook my head. Constantine looked back at Delphinas and then tried to insist, grabbing my arm and trying to pull me to my feet. He had the strength to drag me to the barracks if he had wanted to.

'Come on, we've got to make a man of you!'

I shook him off but he would not take no for an answer, so there was nothing else for it but to take a leaf from my sister's book.

'It's sinful.'

'Oh hark at the holy one! Well, why don't you just go off and be a monk then?' With that he stomped back to Delphinas and the pair of them disappeared off to the barracks. I stayed at the tree and the breeze brought me snatches of the fevered chatter going on around me. It would seem that the women were offering a wide range of services to suit all tastes, from voyeurism for the shy virgins up to satisfying the voracious demands of my brother. They had evidently been paid for the evening, not by the hour.

By late August, the gathering at Hebdomon had started to run down. Some of the party had left early, needed by their families for something or other. One day, I missed Spondyles and discovered from Ouranos that he had asked to go back to Psamathia as he was needed in the vineyard. He had left early in the morning to trudge back along the Egnatian Way to the Golden Gate. Thereafter the place seemed lustreless to me. I was glad when, in early September, a galley put in at the harbour to take us back to the Boukoleon. Philemon and Catia came down to wave us off and I hugged them and told them I would be back next year. I was already planning it, hoping to find some way to enable Spondyles to stay longer and for Constantine not to come at all. None of it ever happened. I did not return to Hebdomon at all for over forty years and I never saw Philemon and Catia again.

In Constantinople, both the palace and the streets were buzzing with news of the exploits of Emperor John in Syria. He had invaded Fatimid territory and met virtually no opposition, so he cruised from city to city extorting money and holy relics of the saints in exchange for sparing them from capture and sack. Damascus gave him 60,000 Dinars, Beirut an icon of the crucifixion of Christ which had once bled real blood. He had moved south into Palestine and even looked close at one point to capturing the Holy City of Jerusalem. As his supply lines were over-extended, though, he wisely withdrew and I was later to solve the problem of Jerusalem in a very different way.

Now that I was away from Hebdomon and Spondyles was no longer in front of my eyes every day, I was able to start thinking about the questions I had asked myself during the long evenings under the walnut trees. Within a day or two, I had come to a decision. I would relinquish my birth right, stand aside and allow John, Romanos Skleros, Constantine or whoever to sort it out among themselves. All I would ask would be to live as a private citizen in the villa at Hebdomon. Once there, I would find some way to have Spondyles join me, with his wife-to-be if that was what he wanted. Now that I was resolved, the first step would be to communicate it to my guide and mentor Nothos. Our meetings to discuss affairs of state had resumed and we were sitting during the late afternoon on a marble bench in one of the long corridors that overlook the harbour of Boukoleon. We had been discussing a passage in one of the books of tactics which stresses the importance of an emperor never appearing downcast even when he has received bad news. That seemed like sensible advice but perhaps easier said than done. Nothos then gave me a lecture on how most people take their estimate of the state of affairs from what they read on their emperor's countenance.

While he was speaking, I felt a welling up in my chest. When he finished, something caught in my throat and I gasped out without any preamble:

'Nothos, I want to abdicate.' He looked concerned but said nothing. 'Theophanes says that Emperor Diocletian abdicated and went to live in a palace somewhere. Nikephoros told me he wanted to do that, only he would be a monk. He would have done it if he hadn't been murdered. I want to go and live in Hebdomon, like a private citizen. Emperor John, and you and Constantine, you can all rule instead of me.'

I had no doubt that Nothos would have arguments to counter me. He put his finger to his lips, bowed his head for a moment, then looked up and said:

'Majesty, Diocletian and Nikephoros were not born in the purple. They were generals who donned the purple in later life, so they could also take it off again. For you, it is part of your being, like your heart and your soul. You cannot set it aside. Next year you will be eighteen and old enough to rule in your own right.'

I was ready for that:

'But Emperor John will be on the throne for a long time yet. Even when he dies, there will be another general who will want to take his place, just like he took Nikephoros' place. There is no need for me.'

'We do need you, Majesty, because you are our purple-born emperor. Yes, Emperor John is ruling now but remember that we never know what may happen in the future. Consider that.'

This was exactly what I had expected and I was ready for it. The time had come to play my trump card. I had to tell him what I had not dared breathe a word about to anyone. I had to tell him about Spondyles. My mouth went dry.

'Nothos, there is something that you must know…'

But he was not listening. He was pointing out of the arched window to where the bearded star was now visible in the darkening sky, hanging ominously over the harbour of Boukoleon. He mused softly, almost as if talking to himself:

'Some say that the appearance of such a star betokens a change of rulers, though no one really knows why God should put it in the sky. Perhaps He just wants to remind us how brief and uncertain our lives are.'

The moment had passed. I was certain now that I would not, could not and should not tell him. Had I done so, who knows what would have happened, for better or for worse? But he would not let me. He would not listen. That is why I hold myself guiltless of everything that followed.

8

The Caretaker
and Nobody (1024)

After Yazid put the stone in the niche at the Gate of St Eugenios, Angelos came very quickly. In fact, he was sitting on the porch with his long legs stretched out on the very evening after the disastrous visit to the Magnavra. As had become their custom, he did not look at Yazid or speak to him but merely got up and strolled away along the walkway at the base of the Sea Walls towards the wharves and jetties beyond. Yazid waited for a short time and then he followed along in the same direction. He found Angelos sitting on a coil of rope by a wooden pier where men were loading barrels onto a ship and calling out to each other in a foreign language. He sat down beside him and told him all about his interview with al-Wuzara: how the Egyptian envoy was suspicious of his interpreter, how some great matter might hang on that and on how al-Wuzara thought he might have been betrayed. But he did not tell Angelos about how he had gone to the palace: he was not sure why not. Angelos thanked him and said he had done well to leave the stone for him as this information was clearly very important. He needed to tell the city governor about it and he would come back and see Yazid soon.

In fact, he came the very next day and was on the porch at the same time, just as Yazid came out and locked the door. He walked away but this time he did not head for the wharves and jetties but went through the gate and turned right into the street. Yazid followed at a distance wondering why the route had been changed. The street was crowded because the sun was quite low now and people had emerged from their homes to enjoy the pleasant breeze. But then Angelos turned left into a narrow lane that led uphill towards the acropolis and this one was virtually deserted, apart from two men who were dismounting from a covered mule cart. Angelos walked on past the cart and Yazid followed but as he did so one of the men came behind him and threw a sack over his head. With his companion, he lifted Yazid up and threw him into the back of the cart. Yazid could feel them get in after him and they placed their heavy hands on him to stop him moving. Someone had got onto the driver's seat and whipped the mule into motion so that they clattered off through the streets.

Yazid was very uncomfortable on the floor of the cart and his shoulder hurt from being thrown in. The bumping as the wheels passed over the cobbles caused his head to keep banging on the wooden boards. He thought about his mother, his wife and his daughters and he prayed to God the compassionate, the merciful that no harm should come to them. His chief dread though was what would happen when they arrived at wherever it was they were taking him. When the cart stopped, Yazid was dragged out, set on his feet and taken through a doorway. He knew they were inside because the light filtering through the sack grew dim. They hustled him up a stone spiral staircase, so fast that he missed his footing and would have fallen if they had not borne him up. They took him along what felt like a constricted passage, as he kept bumping against the wall, and through a door. Then the sack was pulled off his head.

He was in a small, whitewashed room and Angelos was walking away from him letting the sack drop to the floor. There was a small square window but it was closed with a wooden shutter and the only light came from two small oil lamps on a table. The only other objects to be seen in the room were a wooden bench in the middle and a bronze plaque about a foot square that was leaning up in the corner. On it were the words: "Office of the Wine Steward." Behind the table sat an elderly man who looked like a priest. He wore the sort of black robe that priests wear and he had tied his long white hair behind his head in the way that priests did. But Yazid looked at his face, which was covered in a network of lines, and into his eyes which were fixed upon him and he knew that he was not a priest. Another man was standing, leaning against the wall with his arms folded. He was completely bald with a black beard on his chin and upper lip. Angelos indicated the wooden bench for Yazid to sit. He pointed to the bald man and said in Greek:

'This is Matthew. He is going to ask you some questions.'

Matthew propelled himself forward from the wall and began to circle round the bench.

'Hello, Izid. How's the family? My friend Angelos has told me a lot about you and all the good work you've been doing. And there's this other friend of mine, he's been talking to me about you. Says he saw you the other day.'

Pause.

'What we want to know, Izid, is why you haven't been honest with us. You went to the palace, didn't you? Don't pretend you didn't, because we know you did. Do you think we are so stupid that we wouldn't recognise you just because you stuck a turban on your head? So why did you go there in disguise? And why didn't you tell Angelos that you'd been there? You thought he wouldn't be interested? Wouldn't care that you'd gone in disguise and stood fifteen feet away from the holy emperors? So why did you go?'

Yazid gave a gasp and managed to stammer out something liked 'asked me.'

'Oh I see! I get it now. So it was like this was it? "Oh please Mr Caretaker, could you give us a hand carrying this heavy box? We're one man short because poor old Ali Baba here, he's got the lumbago something rotten. Ooh, very painful it is! Much obliged and next time you're in Cairo, why don't you pop round and meet the wife." Like that?'

Yazid sobbed again. The man at the table stared at him.

'Nothing like that, was it? Shall I tell you what happened? We think you were down by the water in the synagogue with your mates from Egypt and they all said: "Hey Izid, here we all are with the same religion, so why don't you give us a hand and come and spy on the Christians. You can really help us as you speak such good Greek. You do that and our god will be really pleased with you." Was it like that?'

Pause.

'No, it wasn't like that either. That's pretty bad but it was even worse, wasn't it? You didn't even do it for your religion. You did it because you are a dirty, greedy little bugger.'

Pause.

'Greedy little bugger thought: "I'm onto a good thing here. I've got the caliph of Egypt sending me dinars for the synagogue. I've got the city governor handing me cash to tell him about what I hear from the merchants. And now here is another sucker who'll grease my palm, so I get paid three times over." And they did pay you, didn't they? Didn't they?'

Wretched, Yazid stared at the floor and nodded his head.

'Do you know what happens to greedy little buggers? Do I have to tell you? You go down to that synagogue of yours on the morning after a big storm and the beach is all covered in wood and bits and pieces, isn't it? And sometimes there's a dead body or two as well. Someone went out in a boat and didn't get back in port fast enough when the sea got up. But sometimes the sea is calm as a millpond, not a cloud in the sky but there is still someone dead on the beach. Might be a man, might be a woman. Might be a little old lady, might be a little girl. We can do anything to anyone.'

Pause.

'But don't worry! We're not going to do that. Do you know why? Because we can't be bothered. Why go to all that trouble for one greedy little bugger? All we need to do is to send a message to the caliph in Cairo. He's our best mate because he's got a treaty with our emperor: "Hey, caliph old son, here's a bit of a friendly heads up for you: you've got a nark in that synagogue of yours up here in Constantinople." And what would happen then?'

Yazid clasped his arms around himself and sobbed, rocking gently to and fro. The man at the table raised a finger and Matthew went back to the wall. He spoke:

'Yazid, are you working for the Fatimids? Be honest and tell us if you are. We want to know because it could be useful to us. And in any case, we will find out sooner or later.'

Unable to wait any longer, Yazid spoke and the words came in a torrent. He was not working for the caliph. The ambassador had asked him to come to the palace and he could not refuse: it would have made him suspicious, if he had. After speaking to the envoy, he went straight back and put the stone in the wall to warn Angelos. But they went to the palace first thing the very next day so there was no time to ask Angelos if it was alright. When he came in the evening, Yazid thought it was not worth telling him about going to the palace as it was all over and nothing had happened anyway. The interpreter had done his job well: there were no mistranslations or bits left out. He need not have gone at all. He wished he had not gone. He fell silent. Matthew, Angelos and the priest looked at each other. Yazid scanned the face of each of them in turn. And then

Matthew knelt down before him and taking his head gently in his hands, he kissed him on his forehead. The man with the white hair, although he was not a priest, he blessed Yazid and forgave him all his sins. Then Angelos took him by the arm and apologetically put the sack back on his head because he must not know where he had been. He led him down to the street and carefully helped him into the cart. Together they rode back to the Sea Walls.

As they rode, Yazid no longer minded the bumping and the discomfort, as he knew that he was going home. He even plucked up courage to speak to Angelos and to ask him who the man in a black robe with white hair had been: was he the city governor that Angelos worked for? Angelos' voice came back through the sack: 'Nobody like that was there, Yazid. Only you, me and Matthew.'

9

Lausiakos (975-6)

G o out, emperor, the Emperor of Emperors and the Lord of Lords summons you!' Three times Patriarch Anthony said this, circling around the wooden box that stood on a bier in the centre of the hall known as Dekanneakoubita. Literally it means "the Nineteen Couches," another of the spacious banqueting-cum-reception rooms of the Great Palace. I was standing on the dais down at the far end, underneath the apse where there was a mosaic portrait of Nikephoros and Theophano kneeling on either side of the Virgin and Child. Theodora was beside me, Constantine and Anna were a few steps back. Nothos, Diaphantes and other officials stood to one side. Emperor John was there too. He was lying in the wooden box, a crown on his head, his arms crossed over an icon of the Virgin and Child. Great care had been taken to comb and arrange his two-tone beard and he looked very peaceful, as if he had just fallen asleep.

For two days he had lain in state in the Hall of the Nineteen Couches and officials, dignitaries and soldiers had filed past to pay their respects. Now the time had come to convey him to his last resting place.

'Go out, emperor, the Emperor of Emperors and the Lord of Lords summons you!'

Six men stepped forward to hoist the coffin onto their shoulders. They were all soldiers who had served under John. One of them was Roupenios. They carried their burden out of the hall and into the portico that led to the Brazen Gate. Theodora and I followed, Constantine and Anna behind us, shadowed by a long line of mourners. It was a bitterly cold January day and a sharp wind was whipping around the columns of the portico. In the normal run of things the procession would leave the Great Palace and make its way up the Mese to the church of the Holy Apostles, the traditional place of interment for emperors. John, however, had not been born in the purple and he had provided a convenient alternative by bestowing his patronage on the tiny church of the Saviour that sits on top of the Brazen Gate. He had lodged there all the holy relics that he had brought back from his campaigns in the east and had the whole place rebuilt, extended and redecorated. So it was up the spiral staircase to this sanctuary that the coffin was borne. Most of the mourners remained below for even though John had made the church larger, it still could not possibly have accommodated such a crowd. Only Theodora and I were watching as the pall bearers lowered the coffin into the Sarcophagus, removed the crown from John's head and pulled the heavy lid across to seal it forever.

John had returned to Constantinople from his triumphant Syrian campaign at the end of December, just a few months after my abortive attempt to offer my abdication. He had been visibly unwell and was huddled under a cloak as he edged painfully up the steps from the Boukoleon harbour, supported by Roupenios and another of his officers. In less than a fortnight, he was dead, the victim, it was said, of camp fever picked up on the march home. Nothos had come to see me the day before John died. By that time, the emperor had made his confession and it was looking ever more unlikely that he would live. My great uncle came straight to the point:

'Majesty, while we should continue to pray for the recovery of the Lord John, we must ask ourselves what we should do if those prayers are not answered.'

Throughout the autumn and over the Christmas festival, I had been constantly on the lookout for another opportunity to discuss my abdication with him. Somehow, the right moment had never seemed to present itself. Perhaps this was it, for Nothos had fallen silent and was gazing at me earnestly as if waiting for me to speak.

'As I remember when the same thing happened unexpectedly seven years ago,' I said sulkily, 'you and my uncle had me locked up until you had made arrangements for the next emperor. Is that what you are going to do this time, if he dies? To give yourself time to find a replacement?'

'You were but a child then, Majesty, and we had to act on your behalf, to take the decisions that you could not. But now, even though you have not yet quite reached your eighteenth birthday, you have already shown such sagacity and discernment that your youth is no longer a reason for you not to be advanced to supreme power.'

It took a moment for his exact meaning to sink in.

'Are you saying that I will be senior emperor? That I will not be in anyone's shadow anymore?'

'That is exactly what I am saying, Majesty.'

The turn of events was so swift and so unexpected, that the thought of confessing all and demanding to abdicate was swept clean out of my mind. I just sat back and let matters take their course.

* * *

There was no need for a coronation as I had already been crowned in Hagia Sophia when I was two. So instead, the day after John's funeral a modified version of the ceremony for the investiture of a Caesar was held in the Nineteen Couches. I sat with Constantine on thrones that had been set up on the dais. The room was filled with all those worthies who collectively make up the senate. I remember reading in Plutarch that back in the time of the early Romans, this was a legislative body. These days it is purely honorific and is packed with appointees of the reigning emperor. So most of those present owed their appointments to John, with a few survivors from Nikephoros' time. All were anxious to find out what their position would be now. There were also representatives of the army and the civic guilds.

Behind us on the dais were the great men of Church and State. Patriarch Anthony and the archbishops of Nikomedeia and Adrianople represented the former. Nothos as chamberlain, Diaphantes as Logothete of the Drome and a crowd of other officials represented the administrative machinery of the Great Palace. It was Patriarch Anthony who began the proceedings, stepping forward and intoning:

'In the peace of the Lord, let us make supplication!'

I stood, turned to the east and gave the response:

'Lord have mercy.'

After the prayers, Constantine and I took off our crowns, handed them to the patriarch and sat back down. He kissed them, moved behind our thrones and replaced them on our heads. A roar went up from the crowd:

'Most fortunate! Most fortunate! Most fortunate! Many years for the emperors, Basil and Constantine! Many years for the great emperors, divinely appointed emperors!'

After the acclamations, I rose to speak, which is what they had all been waiting for. I began by lamenting the loss of the great emperor John, my uncle and my guardian, who had been victorious so often against the enemies of the Romans. I thanked the senate, clergy, army and people for the loyalty and support that they had shown to him and assured them that I would live up to their faith in me. Turning to Nothos, I thanked him for having stood by me during my formative years, for inculcating the elements of statecraft into me and preparing me so assiduously for this day. I expressed the hope that he would consent to remain by my side to offer me the benefit of his wisdom and experience. Then I came to what everybody was waiting for and I said exactly what they all wanted to hear: I confirmed all appointments that had been made during the reigns of my stepfather and uncle, whether administrative, military, clerical or purely honorary. An audible susurration of relief rippled through the hall: there would be no repeat of the cull of 969.

From that day, my life was transformed out of all recognition. Most governmental business takes place in a hall called the Lausiakos. It is really just a long colonnaded corridor with meeting rooms and offices opening off it. I now took over the office that was, Nothos told me, traditionally used by the emperor, although neither Nikephoros nor John had ever gone there when they were in Constantinople. It had two adjoining rooms with connecting doors, one of which was occupied by an elderly eunuch as spare and angular as Nothos was plump and rounded. He was one of the three officials in the Great Palace who then held the office of Keeper of the Inkstand. We would meet in my office every morning and he would lay out the agenda for the day. For the first two hours or so I would have to sign documents: rescripts, letters, treaties, privileges and just about everything else. The Keeper would stand looking over my shoulder as I signed, holding a pot of the special purple ink that only emperors use. For some reason, it was not permitted for the pot to sit on the desk so that I could dip my pen in it as the need arose. No, the Keeper had to retain tight hold of it, lowering it to the desk when I needed to dip and then withdrawing it protectively. I soon found that an emperor's existence is completely hedged around with pointless restrictions like that. I began to see why Nikephoros and John had spent so much time away from the Great Palace.

On most days, I would preside over the council of ministers. These meetings usually take place in the Blue Council Room at the end of the long corridor of the Lausiakos. During the summer months, its open windows look out onto a courtyard which has a Judas tree in the centre. During the winter, frames filled with squares of opaque glass are inserted but natural light also comes in from the ceiling where very thin sheets of alabaster allow it to percolate through. Even so, the three oil lamps that hang from the ceiling all have to be lit. A long table occupies the centre of the room and I took the place of honour at one end. The regular attenders were Nothos, Diaphantes and archbishop Stephen of Nikomedeia. The latter was a very useful worldly prelate. I doubt he had ever set foot in Nikomedeia but he could be trusted to get difficult things done. Other officials attended as the need arose so that there were usually eight to ten men around the table at any one time. Scribes and secretaries lined the wall and my Keeper would stand behind my chair.

Afternoons were usually devoted to activities outside the Lausiakos. Once a week, I would sit on the throne of Solomon in the Magnavra Hall to receive petitions. The petitioners would assemble outside the Brazen Gate several hours before the session was due to begin. They knew that only a certain number of them would be allowed in so it was essential to get a position near the wall. Some people even camped out overnight, while relatives and friends ferried food and drink or occupied their place while they went to answer nature's call. About an hour before the ceremony, the guards would emerge from the small doorway that was cut into the iron grille and start hauling in petitioners at random. The crowd would surge forward as those at the back tried to increase their chances of being pulled in. Unseemly tussles would break out as someone would grab hold of a petitioner who had chosen by the guards and try to drag them back so that they could take their place. At least half if not more of the petitioners were women and they pushed and shoved even harder than the men. Then the sergeant in charge would decide that there were enough for one day and the soldiers would retreat back inside the gate. A wail of disappointment would go up from those left behind who would have to return next week and the one after that, perhaps never being pulled in. The lucky few were taken to the Magnavra courtyard where they were formed into a line and marched into the hall in pairs. When each pair reached steps to the throne, they dropped to their knees before me and touched their foreheads to the floor before rising and handing their scrolled petitions to the two officials on either side of the throne. There are stalls out in the Augousteion where you can get these things written for a small fee. Needless to say, I never actually read any of them so I asked Nothos what the point of the exercise was.

'It is of great importance, Majesty. Your people have to believe that their emperor cares for the welfare of each individual since God has put him on the earth for that purpose. To see him face to face as he receives their petition means a great deal to them. Of course, it is impossible to respond to every case and many are no doubt specious anyway. Nevertheless, the office of the Logothete looks at a random sample every week. If it finds a case of manifest injustice that can be rectified without any political repercussions, it does so. We make sure that this is widely reported so that the people will bless the emperor for his justice and mercy.'

'And the rest of the petitions?'

'They are used to stoke the central heating furnaces.'

So I suppose that I had advanced to the kind of ceremonial occasion that did have a political point to it. I used now to preside over banquets in the Golden Dining Hall, just as Nikephoros had, making a speech and receiving the acclamations. Tasks such as leading processions on holy days and handing out bunches of grapes were now largely devolved to Constantine, who I have to say performed them with singular ill-grace.

* * *

In those heady first few weeks as senior emperor, I had not forgotten Spondyles. In fact I had been wondering what he was doing during the winter, with no more visits to the schoolroom and the vineyard dormant until the spring. So when the Keeper asked me what appointments I would be making, I had a list already prepared. This was the moment I had been hoping for when I could do everything I wanted for him but my political instincts were well-tuned now. To bring him into the palace, to invest him with a lucrative sinecure, to mark him out as a "favourite:" that would be fatal. He would at once become a magnet for false friends and a target for jealous enemies and the very artlessness that I found so endearing would be destroyed. So I did what I had done for the stay in Hebdomon and hid him in plain sight. At the top of the list that I handed to the Keeper were the names of Ouranos and Roupenios who were to become Counts Palatine. I knew that eyebrows would be raised at both, one a mere cavalryman, the other an Armenian, but I just had to dig my heels in. Below them came a line of very unexceptional names for Strator. This is a rather vague office. Originally the strators had been no more than grooms in the imperial stables but as time went by they came to fulfil any function the emperor thought fit. So I appointed a number strators with the proviso that they were to form part of the palace guard and act as my riding companions when called upon. Among them were the short and peppery Impy Kontostephanos, George Alypios, one of the boys who had come looking for the shared horse on the day that I had talked to Spondyles at the fountain, and Spondyles himself. In this way, I planned that he would obtain the salary and the army post that he wanted but without his being brought to anyone's notice. The Keeper took the list between thumb and forefinger and perused it at arm's length.

'His Majesty has taken care to present his appointments in good order. But on one detail I must remonstrate with him.'

Oh God, he knows.

'His Majesty has written the list out in his own hand. There are three scribes now assigned to His Majesty to whom he need only dictate.'

It was a circumspect way of pointing out that the list was illegible. The scribes occupied the other room that connected with my office, so one of them was called in and a fair copy made. The appointments went through without a hitch and within a few weeks I was at the ceremony where the new office holders were invested. It took place in the Magnavra rather than the Nineteen Couches as these are semi-public events to which the families of the appointees are invited. Unlike the petitioners, the appointees enter in single file but they bow to the floor long before they reach the throne. Then they come forward the rest of the way and kneel in front the throne, kissing the feet and the knees of the emperor. By that time, the emperor has been handed the stole and he rises to place it over the outstretched arms of the appointee. Ouranos and Roupenios came forward for their Count Palatine's stoles. I said a few words to each, then it was the turn of the more lowly strators. As Spondyles approached, it struck me that he did not look quite right somehow in a strator's robe. It did not suit him and I hoped that he would not wear it often. I was overjoyed that we had reached this moment but my acting abilities were by now so finely honed that I went through the motions with him in exactly the same way as I had with the others. Some remark was called for so I asked casually:

'So Spondyles, you will be marrying now?'
It seemed incredible to me that he was obviously taken aback that I had remembered what he had said to me at Hebdomon. But his face lit up in gratitude and said that he would indeed be wed that coming May. I nodded and he followed the directions of the waiting official to move away. Impy was approaching and bowing down to the floor.

I left it at that for the time being. About a month before his wedding, I gave orders that married quarters were to be made available for the Strator Spondyles and his wife in the apartments alongside the stables and the polo ground. I was surprised at how easy it had all been. The next steps would be to arrange for a few rides with him and then to make plans for Hebdomon in the summer. I honestly believed for those first few months that I could be the senior emperor and still live in my comfortable dream world.

* * *

The awakening came gradually during that spring. It was in early March, I think, that the Keeper brought in an armful of documents for my signature, none of them, he assured me, of any great importance. I scanned each cursorily before I signed: most were the renewal of tax exemptions for monasteries. Then I stopped at a document mentioning the name of Bardas Skleros, the late emperor's brother-in-law. This one I read in full, ignoring the Keeper who stood at my shoulder with his pot, ready to sprinkle sand on the wet ink. It announced Skleros' appointment as duke of Mesopotamia, "the better to guard the approaches to our realm." I asked to see the chamberlain.

Nothos came quickly. He had a suite of offices similar to mine on the other side of the corridor, so he only had to step across. I asked him why Skleros, a fine soldier, was being demoted from domestic in the east to duke of Mesopotamia. Might this not cause resentment and provoke him to rebellion? Besides, should

I not have been consulted before the decision was made. I did not remember it being raised in council.

'In normal circumstances, I would agree with Your Majesty on both points, but you must consider the situation as it is now. Here in the capital, no one questions your right to be senior emperor. Out in the provinces, people have grown used to a soldier taking command in Constantinople and think that this is how it will always be. They are asking who is going to replace the late Lord John in that role. Whoever has control of the army of the east, they will look upon that man as a potential emperor. And if, like Skleros, he is related to the previous emperor then his claim is all the stronger. Provincials do not all cherish the purple-born emperors in the way that we do. That is why we cannot afford to let Skleros retain control of the eastern army. Your Majesty was not consulted because it was a matter of some urgency and I knew that you would scrutinise the document when it arrived on your desk. You have only to withhold your signature, if you think that I have acted improperly.'

I saw his point and felt ashamed that I had doubted him. I took up the pen and signed. The Keeper shook the sand. But I still felt uneasy and voiced my fear that Skleros would rebel as soon as the messenger handed him the letter.

'We do have a useful leash with which to restrain him, Majesty. His son Romanos is still in Constantinople and if necessary we can use him as a hostage.'

But Skleros outwitted us. Somehow Romanos managed to get out of Constantinople and travelled out to Mesopotamia to join his father. That July, the army of the east proclaimed Skleros emperor and he began to move westwards, augmenting his forces with contingents sent by the Saracen emirs across the border. That was when my dreams vanished in a puff of smoke. As Nothos explained, there was now no question of my going to Hebdomon. It would have been suicidal to be outside the capital at this juncture, since possession of Constantinople is a trump card when there is any contest for the throne. So instead, I spent the summer in an endless succession of crisis meetings in the Blue Council Room, discussing the situation with grim-faced army officers. The main difficulty was that Skleros controlled the bulk of the army of the east so we had nothing to send against him at this juncture. In the end all that was resolved was to send the archbishop of Nikomedeia to Skleros' camp to negotiate. He achieved nothing. Skleros sent back a message saying that once a man had put on the purple, it was impossible to take it off and that, if we did not accept him as emperor, he would come to Constantinople and take the throne by force.

For many weeks, the pressure of these events drove Spondyles completely out of my mind. Thankfully, by the early autumn I had come to the realisation that since the world of politics is one of permanent crisis, life has to go on and space has to be made for living it. I let it be known that I would be taking daily early morning rides on the polo field. A rota should be drawn up among the strators as to who should accompany me.

By now, Willow had been put out to pasture and her place had been taken by a black stallion and it was on him that I set out on the first ride in early September, accompanied by the first name on the list, Impy Kontostephanos. That outing was rather instructive. In the course of the conversation, I learned that Impy was in a state of perpetual rage against the whole world which he believed was against him on account of his size and lowly origins, apart from me who had recognised his worth and made him strator. It struck me that that might be useful someday. The next companion was George Alypios who has to be one of the dullest individuals that I have ever encountered. After him I had to endure two of John's residual appointees until the day came for Spondyles to accompany me.

It was in mid-September, a misty sunny morning, and I could make out his figure as I approached the stables with my two guards behind me. As he got nearer, I saw that he looked different but I was not quite sure why. Then I realised that he was kitted out in a very new-looking green tunic which reached down to his knees, red woollen hose and leather boots, all perfectly cut to his size. He had been imprinted in my memory the way he was, in his ill-fitting clothes at Hebdomon. I chided myself for my stupidity: did I really think that I could bring him here and that he would stay just the same? It would have been made very clear to him that he would have to be properly attired for the honour of riding with the emperor and he would have been directed to an appropriate tailor. I thought he was slightly taller too and, as he must have been sixteen by now, his beard was starting to grow, albeit hesitantly. I strode up to him and announced, just as I had to the others, that he could stop using titles for the duration of the ride. He should just talk to me normally and tell me about his life and his family. Right on cue he protested that his life was far too unremarkable to be of interest but I insisted: these are the details that emperors never hear and it would be a soothing distraction from affairs of state. So we moved towards the horses, and of course he tripped up on something and nearly fell over. Once we had set off across the polo ground, he started prattling just as he had at Hebdomon. First he thanked me fervently in his Thracian burr for making his life so perfect, for allowing him to live here and for letting him join the guard. He would always be at my service for anything that I asked of him. Then he recounted how the vineyard owner had suddenly decided that he was the ideal son-in-law after all. He and Efi had been married in the church of the monastery of Euthymios in Psamathia. All the neighbours had come as well as quite a few people that he only vaguely knew and some that he had never even set eyes on before. They all insisted that they had always been his dearest friends. The little church had been packed.

We walked, we trotted, we cantered, we jumped and the ride passed in a breathless rush. My head was reeling when I got back to my apartment. I told the servants to wash me quickly as I had an appointment with the chamberlain very shortly. Then, cleaned up and in a court gown I strode across to the Lausiakos with two attendants and gathered up a couple of scribes as I went. Even so, by the time I reached Nothos' office, I thought I was late and so I just threw open the door and walked in. Then I saw him as I had never seen him before. He was not sitting at his desk on the far side but was standing with his back to the door. He was apparently dictating separate letters to three scribes while simultaneously barking commands at a number of officials. I just caught the tail end: 'Tell them that if they don't get their act together, I'll be down there in person to bang their noses on the nearest stone wall!' Then he became aware that everyone was staring at the door. He spun round and immediately bowed as did all the others. They were mainly low ranking, although there was one Magistros present. There was also an elderly man in a black robe who had no insignia. Nothos straightened up.

'Majesty, forgive our informality. We thought that it was in the afternoon that we were to meet.'

He was absolutely right. The ride with Spondyles had so excited me that I had in my head somehow transformed the later meeting into an imminent engagement. I backed out of the room, saying yes, that was quite in order or something like that. I regained my own office to find the Keeper waiting patiently with his documents, his pot and his sand. I sat down, dipped the pen and began to sign. What I was agreeing to, I had no idea because my mind was still whirling. Spondyles' voice did that to me. Even so, there was something else nagging at the back of my mind and eventually I managed to pin down what it was.

'Keeper, correct me if I am wrong but a Magistros wears a white tunic embroidered in gold I believe? And a Count Palatine a red tunic and belt?'

'His Majesty has studied the Lists of Precedence with great assiduity.'

'So who wears a plain black gown with no other distinguishing mark?'

As I had expected, he hesitated.

'That office is not in the Lists of Precedence, Majesty. It is a lowly one and its holder reports only to the Logothete of the Drome.'

So what, I wondered, was he doing in the office of the Chamberlain?

$$* * *$$

I think that it is worth setting down clearly at this point exactly what my relations with Nothos were after some eight months as senior emperor. Inevitably our relationship had changed. I was no longer his pupil. The statecraft sessions were at an end and he was now my chief minister and adviser. We met in the council and, at least once a week, he would step over to my office to discuss some particular issue. But he was also my relative, almost as closely akin to me as my aunt Theodora. So I regularly dined with him, just as I did with her. While I ate with Theodora in her apartment, Nothos always insisted that we took our meals in one of the great halls, usually the Nineteen Couches. So the pair of us would sit at a table in the middle of the hall, I at the head and he at the side. A bevy of servants would wait on us, far too many really, while others would bring the dishes across from the cookhouse. The meals with Theodora sometimes included Constantine and Anna but with Nothos it was only ever him and me. There were no meaningful conversations on those occasions. The presence of lines of servants behind our chairs precluded that. But I am sure that Nothos valued them precisely because they marked him out as more than a mere office holder.

Let it be set down here that I knew perfectly well that he was an emperor in all but name. When I had entered his office at the wrong moment and had seen him in action for the first time, bursting with energy as he carried out five tasks at once, I had not discovered anything that I did not know already. He had been the power behind the throne for decades, even under Nikephoros and John. How else would everything have been kept in order in Constantinople while they were away on campaign? I was uneasily aware too that there were entire areas of government that I was not competent to handle and I tacitly left them to him. As he had pointed out in the case of the Skleros demotion, in theory I had a say in everything he did because the documents needed my signature. In practice though, many departments of state accepted his seal, his signature or even his spoken word without requiring further authority. It had been like that for so long now that nobody thought to question it, especially as it all worked perfectly well.

The events that had followed the death of John Tzimiskes had only served to reinforce my conviction that Nothos was my greatest friend and ally. After all, he could easily have summoned Skleros to Constantinople to make him senior emperor. I had even once suspected that he was colluding with Skleros to make his son Romanos John's heir. Instead, he had handed me my birth right and in doing so he had placed his career and possibly his life on the line. If Skleros were take Constantinople and install himself as emperor, then the worse that might happen to me would be relegation to the purely ceremonial role that I had already occupied for most of my life. But Nothos could expect no mercy from the man he had demoted and side-lined. The very least that I could do for him in return was to accept his wise guidance and allow him to rule as he always had. I was content with my limited role and in my mind I revived the dream of retiring to Hebdomon with Spondyles.

Then, almost overnight, my attitude to Nothos was to change completely. It would be a radical turning point in my life and the circumstances that prompted it were not political but personal. I never talked about this openly with anyone, not even to Ouranos: he only ever knew a part. Even in my own mind, I never really articulated it in full. That is why I am going to write it all down next.

10

Apostoleion (976-83)

Towards the end of September of the year that John died, I looked at the rota and discovered to my dismay that my riding companion was to be the Strator Kalokyris Delphinas. Apparently, he had been appointed in the last months before John died. I began to regret my circumspection in not allowing myself to be seen showing particular favour to Spondyles. Still there was no help for it and I turned up at the stables to find Delphinas waiting there. Since the previous summer he had acquiring a straggly beard to go with his moustache. As we set off, I made a few conventional remarks and then relapsed into silence, hoping that my companion would take the hint. For a time he did but then, after we had circled the field at a canter and slowed to a walk, he abruptly put in:

'I know what it is that Your Majesty desires.'

I nearly fell off my horse, then turned to him and blushed which he coolly noted and took as confirmation. He glanced behind him to ensure that the guards were out of earshot. That was why he had chosen this moment.

'There are many men who love other men. But it is hard for us. We have to live life behind a mask, hiding what we feel, locking it away inside ourselves.'

I wondered how he had found out, in spite of all my precautions. Perhaps he had seen my eyes following Spondyles at Hebdomon, then noted his promotion and made the connection. I felt an overwhelming relief, as I am told that some murderers do when they finally confess their crimes after years of deception. All was now laid bare and the struggle was over. I wondered too why I had been so suspicious of Delphinas. True, his closeness to my brother suggested a poor choice of friends, but I felt bad now that I had held his unprepossessing appearance against him, as others held mine against me. After all, the attempt to push me into the arms of a prostitute at Hebdomon was probably sincerely meant as a favour. By now, our horses were walking back towards the stables. Delphinas resumed:

'I can take you to a place where all constraints can be set aside. Where you can say what you want to say and do what you want to do.'

Difficult though it is to admit, it was my honest belief that he was offering to take me to meet Spondyles. We would be together in some magical place like the satyr fountain where there would no longer be any barrier between us and no need for pretence or dissimulation, where we could talk and enjoy each other's company as equals. Before I knew it, I had surrendered to him. I had agreed to make a nocturnal foray into the city with him and no one else in two nights' time. It did occur to me that I might be taking a risk but I was past caring. The opportunity to resolve matters might not come again.

Delphinas had chosen a pleasantly warm night when a huge harvest moon was hanging over the Golden Horn. The only way I could escape without someone trailing after me was to bribe the servants, promising them that I would be back in the early hours and asking them not to report my absence. We met at about 11, wearing cloaks and hoods as a disguise and agreeing that for the evening if we needed to use names, he would be Paul and I would be Saul. We left the palace not through the Brazen Gate, but from a side door that was opened and closed behind us by one of his friends. The door gives onto the alleyway that leads alongside the Hippodrome and into the Augousteion. We crossed that open space hurriedly with our hoods up and then plunged into the maze of streets to the north of the Mese. The moon provided plenty of light even in the streets but we carried dark lanterns just in case. I confess that I was in a fever pitch of excitement, as I had never done anything like this before. The narrow byways were completely new to me since my forays from the Great Palace were always along the main streets. As it was a warm night, the shutters of the tenement windows were open and I could get a glimpse of the people inside. I remember a woman sitting at a table sewing in the light of a smoky lamp, frowning as if at some distasteful thought.

We moved northwards until the vast bulk of the church of the Holy Apostles loomed up on the skyline. Delphinas slowed his pace and whispered that we were nearly there. I strained my eyes through the gloom to try to catch sight of Spondyles and I saw that there were a number of young men waiting around by the columns of the portico which surrounds the courtyard in front of the church. As we walked towards them, I observed at once that none of them was him. One was tall and muscular and was leaning nonchalantly on a column watching our approach. Close by was a thin, willowy figure with a very white face who was pacing around restlessly. There were others: the more I looked the more I saw. They would emerge from the portico, walk around for a bit and then disappear back into the darkness. Delphinas whispered urgently:

'Which one do you like?'

I looked at him in puzzlement. This was not right. It was not what I had hoped for. I stood there not sure what I should do. Then I heard a noise coming from inside the portico, a confused purl of shuffling and groaning. To this day, I have no idea what possessed me or why I did what I did but I mounted the steps to the portico and uncovered my dark lantern. For a split second its beam flashed over a scene of shocked faces and bared buttocks before pandemonium broke loose.

'It's the watch! Run!'

Figures scattered in all directions, heaving up their clothing as they went. One barged into me and sent the lantern spinning out of my hand. For a few seconds I stood there then I joined the general exodus, stumbling unsteadily down the steps though I had no idea where I was going. A voice called urgently behind me:

'Saul! Saul!'

Those of us who are brought up reading the Christian scriptures get to know them by heart and words and phrases from them constantly come to mind. So that was partly why I stopped, turned and shouted as in the Book of Acts:

'Why do you persecute me?'

But I meant it. My eyes were full of tears of rage and frustration that I had allowed myself to be gulled into thinking that my longing could ever be resolved. Why could he not have just left me alone? I turned and ran to put a distance between us, but even in those days I could not keep up that pace for long. After checking that no one had come after me, I stopped in a doorway to decide what to do next. As I did so, a bank of cloud moved across the face of the moon and the light was extinguished. It occurred to me how vulnerable I was, alone, lost and unarmed in a dark street. Then I saw a slight glow above the rooftops to my right and I realised that it must be the Mese which is always lit by torches at night: that was where I would head. I was very relieved when the narrow back street gave onto the main thoroughfare but then another problem presented itself. Even at this late hour, there were plenty of people about and someone among them might recognise me. So I pulled my hood over my head and marched out to join the anxious faces. No one gave a second glance to a young man in a cloak heading purposefully towards the Forum of Theodosius. The square itself was quite crowded and I had to come close to passers-by at times but again no one looked at me. They were not going anywhere. Merely walking up and down, arm in arm, greeting friends, seeing and being seen. I understand that this is the custom in the great Forums in the summer and early autumn evenings. There were some who were obviously foreign visitors and they were gazing up in wonder at the tall column at the centre. Then I was out and hurrying on through the Forum of Constantine and then into the Augousteion.

I could have returned through the small door by which we had left. I had only to give the agreed signal and Delphinas' friend would have let me in. But I wanted nothing further to do with him or his associates. So I walked directly across the Augousteion towards the Brazen Gate. Six flaring torches lined the façade, casting flickering shadows on the imperial statues in their niches. The gate was open but the iron grille had been lowered and the only way in was via the small doorway. Two soldiers were on guard on either side of it. As I got nearer, they decided that they did not like the look of this hooded figure that was marching straight towards them and they took their spears in both hands, ready to bar my way. I undid the clasp of my cloak, letting it fall to the ground, and as I did so the light from the torches above the entrance fell on my face. The men fell back, one of them shouting "The emperor, the emperor!" I passed them through the doorway, looking neither to left nor right. Under the vaulted ceiling and up the marble steps I went, passing the guardroom where a crowd of soldiers was loitering. For the second time that evening my unexpected appearance caused chaos. Dicing tables were overturned as men leapt to their feet, frantically throwing on their leather surcoats, grabbing their weapons, and coming to attention. As I forged on through the covered walkways that lead to the Boukoleon, I was followed by cries of "The emperor is unattended!" and a crowd of followers coalesced in my wake. I strode across the upper portico of the Golden Hand, the white finger pointing accusingly. When I finally reached the gate in Nikephoros' wall around the Boukoleon, I stopped, turned and addressed the throng:

'Good people, we have startled you by our unexpected arrival. We are safe and well and have returned to the Boukoleon. We thank you for your concern and ask you now to go to your rest.'

With that I turned, nodded to the guard and entered the Boukoleon. The night's adventure was over.

* * *

I did not sleep much and the next morning I was in the Lausiakos at an absurdly early hour. As I awaited the arrival of the Keeper, I went over the events of last night in my mind, sometimes cursing Delphinas, sometimes blaming myself. I felt particularly bad about the havoc I had caused in the portico of the Holy Apostles so when the morning's signings were over, I asked the Keeper to have the commander of the night watch come to see me. A summons had to be sent to the city governor's office and it was not until the late afternoon that I was told that he was waiting in the anteroom of the Lausiakos. He was a heavy set man in his fifties, very obviously a former soldier. I asked him where he had served and he told me that as a young man he had been on John Kourkouas' campaign to Edessa. Then I enquired whether he was aware of the nocturnal activities at the church of the Holy Apostles. He did not answer directly:

'Does Your Majesty want a stop to be put to them?'

'On the contrary, I want them to be left in peace. They cause no harm to anyone.'

His face cleared: 'That is good to hear, Majesty, as we have for a long time been following the very same directive from the Lord Chamberlain.'

'The Lord Chamberlain is our most trusted and able adviser and we rely on his wisdom in all things. But I see from your face that there is something else. Please speak freely.'

'Only to say, Majesty, that the Lord Chamberlain particularly requested that our men should still patrol the area and if they saw anyone that they recognised they were to let me know and I was to pass the name to the office of the Logothete of the Drome.'

It has to be remembered that during this interview the Keeper was standing behind me, noting everything. So I just said:

'Yes, that is quite in order, commander. Thank you for your time, you may go.'

It was shortly afterwards that Nothos himself appeared, full of grave concern about my sudden appearance at the Brazen Gate. I reassured him that all was well. I had decided to go out of the palace alone, after reading how my ancestor Leo VI used to wander the city after dark in disguise to satisfy himself that the night-watchmen were performing their duties conscientiously. In the same way, I wanted to see the city as it really was rather than when it was decked out specially for my visit. But then I had got lost and had been unable to relocate the door I had left by.

'His Majesty's concern for his subjects is commendable. But you must understand the anxiety that you can cause among those to whom your welfare is entrusted. Were anything to befall you, they would be held responsible and therefore it is your duty, for their sakes, not to put yourself in danger.'

At that moment, I felt very contrite and as ever overwhelmed by his knowledge and his wisdom. Once again I was on the point of confessing all, of telling him how and why I had gone out with Delphinas. But again, he left no space for me to do so before he intoned softly:

'It is twice now that we thought we had lost you. But at least the Holy Apostles is not as far away as Hebdomon.'

For a few days afterwards, my main dread was that I might encounter Delphinas or even be forced to endure another morning ride with him. That was soon allayed though. His name vanished from the rota and he from the Great Palace. I later discovered that he had been posted to the furthest outpost of the realm in southern Italy when the confirmation of his appointment as governor of Bari landed on my desk. I signed it without demur. That should have been the end of the matter. But it was not.

Another preoccupation was growing in my mind. I kept coming back to Nothos' words to me the day after the nocturnal adventure. How was it that, even though I had given no precise details about my movements, he had known that I had been at the Apostles? Perhaps I had been spotted by a watchman and the information passed back. Yet could it have reached his ears by the late afternoon of the next day? Anyway, would I have been recognised under my hood? No one gave me a second glance as I walked all the way from the Apostles to the Augousteion. It was not until I threw off the cloak at the Brazen Gate that the soldiers realised who I was. No, there was, I had to face it, a much more likely explanation. Nothos had been told by the only other witness of my presence there, Kalokyris Delphinas.

But that was hardly satisfactory either. Why would a humble strator inform the most powerful minister of state that he had taken the emperor on a clandestine jaunt to a place notorious for activities that were proscribed in both Church and secular law? I knew the answer even as I posed the question. Nothos had known about the expedition even before it took place. In fact, he had planned it and had ordered Delphinas to lure me into it. One by one the pieces of the puzzle fell into place. It had been Nothos who had added Delphinas' name to the list for Hebdomon after finding some pretext to scratch out two of Constantine's choices. His job was doubtless to report back on Constantine and my vices, to encourage them and to pander to them, with a view to reducing us to a pair of self-indulgent drones who would never challenge Nothos' hold on power. He had done his job well. He had arranged for the Cretan wine and the street walkers to be brought in and had doubtless reported back to his master that Constantine was shaping up very nicely. Promotion to strator was the promised reward: the appointment had been made in the last months of John's life when he was away in the east, so it had obviously been pushed through by Nothos.

But there had been one loose end. Delphinas had had to report that he had not succeeded in working out what attracted me. After the first time, I had shown little desire to drink myself into a stupor and on that other evening on the ridge by the parade ground, I had resolutely refused to go to the barracks. Clearly my tastes lay elsewhere and the trip to Apostles had been dreamt up by Nothos to see whether they lay in that direction. Once that was uncovered, then I, like Constantine, could be kept out of the way, happy in the pursuit of my desires.

That much was clear but I knew that there was much more. This careful manipulation had not started with the summer in Hebdomon. It had been going on all my life. I felt certain now that, after Nikephoros had taken over, it was Nothos who had advised the new emperor that my mother, brother and sister would be safer at Hiereia but that I should stay in the Great Palace. I could almost hear his voice reassuring Nikephoros: if a rumour went around that some harm had come to the purple-born emperors and a crowd gathered in the Augousteion, little Basil could be displayed from the Brazen Gate to defuse the situation. Sensible advice but it meant that I was left all alone in the Kainourgion. He had seen to it that it was he and only he who ever saw me regularly, even arranging for the servants to be changed every few weeks so that I did not get to know them. Even as he carried me on his shoulders, he was making a careful assessment of just how useful I would be to him. But he foresaw a difficulty. As I grew older, I would make friends of my own age. Those friends would have parents and families who could use their sons' connection with the emperor to boost their influence at court, spawning rivals to his monopoly. So he gave orders to the servants that I was to play alone in the palace gardens. If I ever ranged further afield, it was with him, and so the bond between us was strengthened. He had even got me to believe that I should never speak to anyone else.

It was only to be expected that there would be obstacles to his plans. One cropped up when Emperor John noticed, or perhaps Theodora told him, that I lived a rather isolated existence. John had insisted that my secondary education should be undertaken with other students and that could have led to my making unwelcome contacts. Nothos easily overcame the difficulty. He deftly ensured that my fellow students were, like Spondyles, from families that were both loyal to Tzimiskes and of no importance. It was Nothos who had told me that he was John's choice. Now I doubted that. He was so perfect: utterly obscure and his widowed mother deeply grateful for the honour. All the rest of Diaphantes' pupils were from much the same background. Doubtless they were told that they must not address me. At that stage, Nothos must have been more worried by Constantine who simply could not avoid gathering a gang of friends about him. That, I think, is why the Melissenos brothers were there to lure him down the path of vice. Nothos really should have known that no luring was necessary.

Why did I mind? Why should the realisation that his power extended to manipulating my dreams and desires make any difference? I had been perfectly content in the past to accept Nothos' control over every aspect of government. This might have been a good moment to broach the abdication plan again and pave the way for me to live in peace at Hebdomon along with Spondyles and his family. But I knew now with utter certainty that I was not going to do that. Something had changed. Having tasted power, even the watered down version that Nothos had graciously allowed me since John's death, I could no longer accept my relegation. There was something else. My great uncle had deliberately kept me isolated and alone to fulfil his lust for power. I thought of those long hours in the schoolroom when I could not speak to Spondyles because I had been told that I should not make a friend of anyone. It was then that I first experienced a new emotion. It was not the dislike that I felt for Diaphantes and Delphinas or the annoyance that my brother and sister provoked in me. It was not just that I stopped adoring Nothos. I had come to hate him.

Even as I brooded in resentment, something else occurred to me. I had discovered that there were limits to his knowledge and wisdom. I could see now that he had made mistakes, albeit small ones, and that meant that he was not invulnerable. He had unguardedly mentioned my being at the Apostles when I had not told him I had been there and so revealed his involvement. The year before, when I sat with him overlooking the harbour of Boukoleon, with the bearded star was still hanging in the sky, and had begged him to let me abdicate, I had been at the point of telling him everything. I was about to deliver to him the key that would have kept him in power for ever but he did not have the patience to listen. Lastly, he had allowed me to go on that hunt in Philopation. Thanks to that, I had someone to whom I could now turn.

It was about a week after the Apostles expedition that I summoned two servants first thing one morning.

'Give my compliments to the Strator Alypios and my regrets that I will not be able to ride with him today. And you, go to the Count Palatine Ouranos and say that I wish to meet him at the stables as soon as possible.'

In the light of the revelations of the past few days, I needed to talk to someone and I needed an ally. Ouranos was the only person I could think of. As we rode away from the stables, I did what Delphinas had done and looked back to make sure that the mounted guards were not too close. I then apologised for the abrupt summons and for meeting him in this way, out in the open. It had occurred to me that my apartments and the office in the Lausiakos might not be entirely private. Quite apart from eavesdropping servants, I had heard that vents could be built into walls with a tube to carry the sound of voices to another room. I launched into my explanation. Obviously, I was not going to tell Ouranos about the trip to the Holy Apostles. Instead I asked him whether he or others were aware of the role that the Chamberlain played in the governance of the state. Naturally, he was guarded:

'Everyone knows, Majesty, how the Lord Chamberlain keeps all aspects of government under his supervision, as he did under your stepfather and uncle.'

'And do you think that everyone is happy with that state of affairs?'

'No one could reach the position that the Chamberlain has without making at least some enemies.'

'Who would you say that those enemies are?'

'I'm sure Your Majesty knows better than I do. But naturally they don't think much of him in Caesarea, where he is blamed for ending the influence of the Phokas family.'

'And?'

He hesitated. He was not sure what I was fishing for and feared to expose himself by delivering information that I did not want to hear. I would have to come out into the open.

'Ouranos, over recent days I have come to wonder whether the Chamberlain's influence is entirely to the benefit of the state.'

He gave an audible sigh of relief and it was his turn to look behind him.

'For years, Majesty, there have been those who have chafed at the power wielded by the Chamberlain, but as long as you seemed to revere and trust him, there was nothing we could do. The only way to oppose him would have been to join the rebellion of Skleros and nobody in Constantinople wants to do that. Now that your eyes have been opened, many will rally to your side.'

That was how the alliance was made. The first step was to move Ouranos to a more senior position from which he would have constant access to me. I could not move too fast for fear of arousing suspicion so it was not until late October that I turned to my Keeper as we finished the business of the morning and informed him that I had some good news. He was to be promoted to Protospatharios, a dignity that involved no duties apart from the collection of an annual salary of 72 gold pieces. He was overwhelmed and confessed that his arthritis had been making his long periods of standing behind my chair rather a trial to him. My new Keeper was, of course, Ouranos. On the day that he took up his duties, he arrived in the Lausiakos office looking as if he had been a palace bureaucrat all his life. His robe and hat fitted perfectly, his black beard and hair were trimmed and oiled. It was hard to believe that he had experienced the rigours of John's Mesopotamian campaign and that, in all probability, he had killed men. I could not imagine, though, that he had participated in those excesses that soldiers consider to be their right when a town or village is captured. To my still rather naïve mind, he seemed to embody both strength and virtue: with such a man at my side, I would be able to do anything.

So Ouranos now stood behind me with the inkpot but we took care that during routine business hours in the Lausiakos we never spoke of anything but trivialities. Discussion of the next moves was done elsewhere and we varied the locations.

Sometimes we would go to the Triconch courtyard and sit on the edge of the fountain so that our words could not be heard for the trickling water. Sometimes I would visit Ouranos in his house, which was in one of the streets south of the Hippodrome: his wife would discreetly retire upstairs. Or we would ride out together: a hunting trip to Philopation was a good way to have an extended discussion. Our next priority, Ouranos urged, was gradually to take control of as many positions of influence as we could. We went for the captaincy of the palace guard first as Ouranos knew that it would not be difficult. Nothos was not popular among the men but I was, largely thanks to my remembering the names of some of them. Those lists had proved to be very useful and since becoming senior emperor I had delegated to my scribes the task of keeping them up to date. So in early January we made our move. It was announced that the current commander of the guards was to be dismissed. During my snap inspection on my return from the Apostles, I had noticed a deplorable and inexcusable slackness at the Brazen Gate. As his replacement, I chose Impy Kontostephanos.

Ideally the next office to fill would have been that of Logothete of the Drome but that was hardly feasible at this stage. It was still held by Diaphantes who was a close adherent of Nothos. To unseat him would be an open declaration of war. So Ouranos suggested that we take Roupenios into our confidence. I was reluctant at first. Although I had made him a Count Palatine, I wondered whether he might not have residual links to Nothos, given that the Chamberlain had helped to make an emperor of his friend and patron John Tzimiskes. An interview with Roupenios allayed my doubts. It turned out that he had grave doubts as to whether John's death had been a natural one. The emperor had been in the peak of health when they travelled back from Antioch, flushed with the success of the Syrian campaign and full of plans to renew it in the spring. When the army reached Bithynia, Tzimiskes and his immediate entourage had lodged at the house of a man called Romanos Lekapenos, a kinsman of the Chamberlain. It was while he was there that the emperor started showing symptoms of illness, with boils breaking out on his shoulders and blood coming from his eyes. Roupenios was convinced that John had been poisoned on the orders of the Chamberlain. Whether it was true or not was neither here nor there. He and many other soldiers who had served under John believed it and would do anything to harm the Chamberlain. So I promoted him to Protonotarios with the specific role of deputy to the Logothete of the Drome. That way he could keep an eye on Diaphantes and report back to us.

Then there was the Archives office. It occurred to Ouranos, Roupenios and me almost simultaneously that the more information we had about what had been going on over the past fourteen years, the stronger we would be. Ouranos suggested that we should have someone we trusted placed in the archives with a view to making a systematic search for interesting documents. The perfect candidate was dull George Alypios who was delighted with the new job and had no idea about the political agenda behind it. We asked that, in the course of his everyday duties, he should check everything from the period 963 to the present and make a note of its contents. We knew that it would take some time for him to come up with anything, for the archives are vast. They are kept in vaults beneath the northern seating area of the Hippodrome, and stretch for hundreds of yards on several levels. Nevertheless, he fulfilled the task admirably, supplying us with monthly lists of documents, most of which were of no interest whatsoever. There were one or two useful ones though, like that letter that Diaphantes had written to John about my poor educational performance. These could be stored up for the future.

Our success in taking control of these offices was offset by loss of another. The patriarch of Constantinople is the only person who can summon the emperor to see him rather than begging for an audience in the Great Palace, and so when in February I received word from Father Anthony that he wished to see me I rode out with two attendants to the patriarchal residence which stands behind Hagia Sophia. He received me in a bare and rather cold reception room on the first floor. The only colour came from an icon of the Virgin on the far wall, in front of which a candle burned in a bracket. The light came from bronze lamps that hung from the ceiling, the insufficient heat from a brazier in the corner. We sat facing each other on wooden chairs and Father Anthony looked gaunter and thinner than ever. He indicated a sealed letter on a small table nearby.

'I wish to give Your Majesty my resignation from the office of ecumenical patriarch as I am deeply unworthy of it.'

To my ears that sounded absurd. Anthony had a reputation for self-denying sanctity and he donated most of his salary to the poor. He tipped back his head.

'My dear, you do not understand. I obtained this office through a grievous sin that I committed at the very time that I was teaching you and your brother when the Lord Nikephoros was emperor.'

'Father Anthony,' I had never been able to call him "All-Holiness," 'I cannot believe that you have anything for which to reproach yourself. It may well be what you call a sin in yourself, would be everyday behaviour in most men.'

He tipped back his head again and pointed to the letter, saying that it was all set down there. I got up, took the letter from the table, leant down and kissed his ring and then I left. By taking the letter, I had accepted the resignation but I did not announce it publicly. Father Anthony retired to the monastery of Satyros and I did nothing about making a new appointment. I hoped that he would change his mind and come back and then be our ally against Nothos. That was why I did not open the letter: I just put it in the wooden chest in my apartment, where I kept my completed lists and other papers, and soon forgot about it. To this day, I wonder what would have happened if I had read it then.

It will have been noticed that one associate of mine played no role in any of this. I now bitterly regretted that I had ever bought Demetrius Spondyles into the palace. I had attempted to own and possess him, rather than just watch over and do good for him. Not only had I inadvertently changed him, I had also placed him in danger. There was no certainty as to how the rivalry with Nothos might end. If I went down, all those associated with me would fall too and who knows what would become of them. Why had I not left him in Psamathia, bought him a vineyard of his own, set him up with a little house and let him be what he was? There was now nothing else for it: I would have to distance myself from him for the time being.

The rides continued, though less regularly now. Towards the end of one outing with Spondyles, I turned and asked whether I could visit his home one day. He burbled something about great honour and the rest of it and it was settled that we would go there after the next ride. When the day came, a rather fresh one in early April, we walked back from the stables to his home which was on the ground floor of a whitewashed tenement block occupied by officers of the guard and their families. There was a pomegranate tree outside and a small herb garden. A rough stone bench stood to one side of the door. When we went in, it was obvious that the place had been scrubbed and scoured for weeks in preparation for my arrival. The floor tiles were spotless and I could see my reflection in the glazed pottery bowls that were lined up along a wooden shelf. In one corner a collection of icons glowed in the light of a votive candle, and a ladder led up to the room above. His tiny wife was there and so was his wizened mother, to whom my arrival was something akin to a materialisation of the Archangel Gabriel.

They asked whether I had received the gift of grapes from the vineyard in Psamathia that they had sent to the palace. They had been delicious, I said, knowing perfectly well that they would have been whisked away to be inspected for spiders and scorpions before being given to the servants to eat, a note have been made of the provenance in case of ill effects. I accepted some bread dipped in oil, and thanked the mother for the sacrifice her husband had made for my father on the Cretan campaign.

Then it was time to go. I insisted that Spondyles should not walk back with me to the stables and I re-joined my waiting guards. When we were some distance away, I looked back. Spondyles and Euphemia were sitting on the stone bench, hand in hand. They reminded me of a copper coin I had found once in the Kainourgion garden when I was playing alone after Constantine was taken to Hiereia. It was badly worn but you could make out on the back an emperor and an empress sitting side by side, just as they were. They looked like children, which is what they still were. A few days later, I announced that I would be taking no more morning rides.

✳ ✳ ✳

It was a few months afterwards that that we scored our first solid success in our campaign to wrest the initiative from Nothos. An unexpected piece of business had landed on my desk: a formal request, drawn up by one of the palace scribes, for my consent as head of the family to my brother's marriage. The lady in question was Helena, the sister of the dull George Alypios who was burrowing away in the archives. So from my point of view it was ideal. The family was respectable but not too influential or powerful. Quite apart from that, the pair of them were perfectly suited to each other. She was tall and slender, strikingly good looking and very down-to-earth: she would take no nonsense from him. In fact, I was tempted to take her aside and point out that she could do rather better. I said all this to Ouranos, though without the last bit. He agreed but at the same time he gave the hand gesture we had settled on to indicate that further discussion was needed in a secure place. So we went to the Hippodrome which was closed at that hour and walked around the long central spine. No one was about, only the sweepers cleaning up the horse droppings from yesterday's race and they were down at the Augousteion end.

'There could be danger here, Majesty. Sooner or later, the Chamberlain is going to get wind of what we are up to, if he hasn't done so already. When he does, he may start to think of Constantine as a more attractive proposition as emperor than you. After all, next year he turns eighteen and will be entitled to make appointments and to attend council. When he is married, he will probably produce an heir. That will make him look very imperial while at the same time, the Chamberlain knows he can control him as long as the wine and women flow freely. He must have realised by now that you have a mind of your own even if, as I hope, he has not grasped how far things have gone.'

This was a worrying thought, especially as I had never considered my brother as a rival for power. Fortunately, the regrettable features of his character came to our rescue. After we had returned from Hebdomon in 975, Constantine had resumed his military training and shortly after the death of Emperor John, he was attached to a regiment of cavalry. It had been intended to post him to the provinces but the political situation made that impossible. In Asia Minor the army was under the control of Skleros while the Balkans were increasingly unstable because of the revolt of the Bulgars. We could not risk him being captured and used as a political pawn. So he stayed in Constantinople and made a nuisance of himself with the Melissenos brothers. Here was a man who had everything. A beautiful fiancée, food and wine in abundance and a limitlessly supply of whores whenever he wanted them. But that was not enough. He had also to experience the paltry pleasures of those who are born into the world with nothing. One night, he and the Melissenos brothers decided to dress up in workers' clothes and pay a visit to the taverns of Perama, a district down by the Golden Horn inhabited by sailors, dockers and fishermen. After a few beakers of appalling wine, Constantine became raucous and objectionable, as he always did but he forgot one thing: the deference which he took for granted would evaporate if no one knew who he was. He had just let out a loud guffaw at the expense of one of the other patrons when a meaty fist slammed into his face. He was up in a second and the three of them slugged it out with all comers for several minutes before a shout went up that the watch was coming. Everyone scattered but not Constantine who stood his ground and fended off the watchmen with a chair leg. He was finally overpowered and thrown in a nearby lockup. It was well into the next morning before he could persuade his jailors to notify the office of the Logothete and ask that someone be sent to identify him.

It all had to be smoothed over. The damage to the tavern was paid for, the watchmen handsomely tipped, their commander assured that he had earned the emperor's undying gratitude. I was indeed very grateful as I could now resolve the matter of the marriage. Constantine was summoned to my office in the Lausiakos. I also asked Nothos and Ouranos to be present and they stood behind my desk as we waited for Constantine to arrive. When he finally turned up, he plonked himself down in a chair and said:

'I've been a naughty boy, haven't I? Arf, arf arf!'

'Brother, I will come directly to the point. On the table are two documents, one for me to sign and one for you. The one for me is my consent to your marriage. The one for you is a renunciation of all the privileges of your rank and birth apart from those that are purely ceremonial and honorary. My signing the first is contingent on your signing the second. In the event of your signing, no news of your escapade in Perama will be passed to the family of your fiancée. The scribe will now read you the document.'

Constantine's mouth fell open and on this occasion there was nothing available for him to put in it. The scribe stepped up to the table, took the document and began to read:

"I, Constantine, faithful emperor of the Romans, renounce, foreswear and abjure forever all privileges, powers and emoluments of that rank..." and so it went on until

> saving only that I be known by the style, title and appellation of emperor of the Romans, that I wear the purple buskins and other dress appropriate to the said rank, that on ceremonial occasions I be escorted by an honour guard of no more than six persons... etc.

The scribe folded the document. Silence, then:
'You bastard.'

An improvement on some of the names he had called me over the years, I thought. Then came a flood of expostulation, threat, self-justification and complaint directed first to Nothos, then to me. We both stared back at him stonily. Then he had no more to say. He slouched forward, took the pen and placed it at the point helpfully indicated by the scribe. I took my pen and signed my consent to his marriage. He turned to leave but he did manage to have the last word:

'You know what the trouble with you is, my dear brother? You're just not normal!'

I waited for his barking laugh. It never came.

By now Ouranos and I were exultant. It was all going so well. We had inserted our friends and allies into strategic places and neutralised a potential threat without Nothos so much as raising an eyebrow. We began to plan our next steps. But it was all to go disastrously wrong. Ashamed as I am to admit it, even after a lifetime's acquaintance, I had failed to grasp what kind of a man I was dealing with. He knew perfectly what was going on but he gave no discernible reaction. He had quietly accepted the promotions of Ouranos, Roupenios and Kontostephanos and had raised no objection when Constantine was demoted. He attended council in his usual jovial way, speaking little, deferring to me at all times. When news came that Father Anthony has passed away, still in the monastery of Satyros, Nothos ostentatiously left the appointment of the new patriarch to me. When I selected the dull and unremarkable Nicholas Chrysoberges, he fulsomely congratulated me on my excellent choice. In short, he provided no pretext whatever for me to move against him. Meanwhile he prepared his counterstroke.

For months now the main topic on the agenda at the council meetings had been the latest movements of Skleros and his army. It was well over a year now since his proclamation as emperor and he was nowhere near Constantinople, although he had moved westward as far as Phrygia. In the normal run of things, revolts that do not take the capital after a few months fizzle out and die, the supporters melt away and someone betrays the would-be emperor to the loyalist troops combing the country. But that did not happen in this case. It would seem that Skleros enjoyed solid support from provincials who deeply distrusted the eunuchs and bureaucrats in Constantinople. So in the autumn of 977, we sent a force to the region, providing its commander with plenty of gold to lure the rebel's supporters away. He had some success but his army ended up being torn to pieces by Skleros at Rhageas and he was taken prisoner. With the opposition removed, Skleros resumed his westward advance. By early January, he was in Nicaea, a little more than a hundred miles from the capital.

The arrival of this news prompted groans of despair around the council table and we all prepared to listen very carefully when Nothos announced that he would like to propose a solution. Diaphantes brought out his little silver box and popped a tablet into his mouth.

'Gentlemen. The time has come for us to admit that we are dealing with no ordinary rebel. Skleros is a soldier of consummate skill as he proved during the Bulgarian campaign of Emperor John. He commands the same respect and loyalty that his late brother-in-law did. We cannot expect to stop him by despatching a few levies to stand between him and the capital. He can only be brought to heel by a commander of a similar calibre who enjoys a similar reputation. We have such a man but the Roman state has been deprived of his services for many years. He is Bardas Phokas, the nephew of the late Emperor Nikephoros.'

There was a gasp from some of those present. Perhaps I was one of them. I had largely forgotten about Nikephoros' surly nephew. I had not seen him since that evening eight years before when I had returned from Hebdomon and my mother had screamed at Nikephoros. I vividly remembered the bitter look that he had shot at us as he left. Nothos went on:

'Bardas is currently living in exile on the island of Chios. I propose that he be restored to favour and placed in command of an army to confront Skleros.'

There simply was no other option so we all acceded to Nothos' proposal. It was an odd feeling to receive Bardas in the Magnavra throne room a few months later. As he walked down the aisle towards me, I observed that those eight years had turned his hair grey and made him into a mirror image of Nikephoros. When he halted before the throne and went down on his knees, I fully expected him to greet me with his uncle's "Ha!." It turned out that he had a rather better speaking voice, articulating entire sentences rather than Nikephoros' strangled phrases, but he still was not one for small talk. So we got the business over and done with quickly. I handed him his commission as domestic of the east and wished him Godspeed.

His arrival on the scene did not turn the tide overnight. He was heavily outnumbered by the rebel army and for the first year or so, Skleros came off best whenever the two titans clashed. Then in the spring of 979, they collided halfway between Ankara and Caesarea. To start with Skleros looked likely to prevail and his troops began to push Bardas' off the field. But then Skleros received an injury to the head: some say it was inflicted by Bardas himself. Whatever the truth of that, Skleros was lowered from the saddle by his attendants and laid down on the ground to recover. But they forgot about his horse. Unnerved by the mayhem, it bolted and charged though the ranks. Skleros' soldiers, recognising it and seeing it riderless, drew the obvious conclusion that their leader had fallen. They turned and fled. At a stroke, Skleros' bid for the throne was over.

Naturally, I rejoiced with everyone else and I could hardly fail to express my gratitude to Nothos for his foresight in proposing this solution. I did so at the council meeting and afterwards invited him to my office so that I could do so again more informally. He bowed gravely in acknowledgement.

'As ever, it is my pleasure to be of service to Your Majesty. It is my duty though to alert you to the possible drawbacks of our policy here. It would not have been possible just to recall Bardas from exile without rehabilitating the rest of his family. The Phokas have returned to Constantinople. Their house by the Harbour of Sophia has been reopened and reoccupied. The Count Palatine Leo, brother of the late Emperor Nikephoros, will shortly arrive there.'

Even then I did not see the drift. Nothos put his finger to his lips, looked at the floor and then went on.

'Majesty, this is awkward but I feel that you should be informed. When the Lord Bardas departed for the east, I went with him to the galley in the harbour of Boukoleon. I was surprised to discover that he cherishes no friendly feelings towards Your Majesty. He seems to feel that Your Majesty was hostile towards his late uncle and had been indoctrinated to be so by the Empress Theophano. He had at first been reluctant to accept our commission as he thought it hypocritical to fight for the cause of one so opposed to his family. Fortunately I was able to persuade him that the interests of the Roman state should take precedence over personal feelings. But I would counsel His Majesty, and the Keeper Ouranos, not to make any rash moves that might be interpreted as hostile. In such circumstances, I might not be able to restrain the domestic of the east.'

It was a blow so masterly, delivered with such finesse, that even now I am lost in admiration as I describe it. The man was an artist. He did not need to spell it out further. It was to Nothos and to him alone that the Phokas family owed their restoration to grace and it was from him that they would take their orders. Any more acts of insubordination on my part and Bardas would be in the Augousteion with his cohorts behind him. My impudent challenge had been crushed as comprehensively as that of Skleros. Nor had Nothos finished with me yet.

In his report on the battle and its aftermath, Bardas wrote that Skleros had escaped from the field and was believed to have sought asylum in the territory of the Abbasid Caliphate. That was confirmed a few months later when news arrived that a Saracen envoy had entered our territory and was travelling towards Constantinople. When he reached Chrysopolis, he presented his credentials to the town's governor and requested to be ferried over to the city. We scrutinised the credentials in the Blue Council Room. The envoy had been sent by the Buyid emir, Adud ad-Daula, who currently controlled both Baghdad and the caliphate and he wished to discuss the fate of Skleros who was being held at Adud's court.

'This envoy must be brought over at once,' I said, 'directly into the harbour of Boukoleon. Then he can be interviewed in the first instance by the Chamberlain. We must be careful where he is lodged. We do not want him making contact with any residual supporters of the rebel.'

Nothos intervened.

'I suggest, Majesty, that the envoy might be lodged at the house of the Keeper Ouranos.'

'And why there particularly, Chamberlain?'

'But surely you know, Majesty? The Keeper is originally from the eastern frontier and speaks fluent Arabic. He will be able to ensure that nothing passes between the envoy and any third parties. Indeed, it will essential for us to have the Keeper at the heart of our negotiations.'

I twisted round to look at Ouranos. He had never mentioned that he spoke Arabic. He stammered uneasily and admitted that what the Chamberlain said was true. So the envoy was lodged in Ouranos' house and my Keeper played a leading part in the discussions that followed. It soon emerged that Adud's main concern was to use Skleros as a bargaining chip to protect Mesopotamia from the kind of raids that Emperor John had mounted in the middle years of his reign and which Bardas Phokas was champing at the bit to resume. I was not unsympathetic as I saw no reason to give Bardas the opportunity to cover himself with glory and I had a stroke of luck when Nothos fell ill. He vanished from the scene for several weeks and that left the way open for Ouranos and I to sketch out the terms of a ten-year truce with the envoy. By the time Nothos recovered, the whole thing was settled and he was clearly annoyed that the business had been taken out of his hands. For the time being, I thought that I had scored one over him.

When the time came for the envoy to depart, Ouranos was the only possible choice to accompany him as our representative. It was now the spring of 982 and I saw him off from the harbour of Boukoleon. He assured me that he would be back by the feast of the Dormition in August. The journey was not so long and at that time of year the passes through the Taurus mountains would be free from snow. But August came and went and so too did Christmas and Epiphany, but Ouranos did not return. I gave orders for enquiries to be made among the merchants who arrived from Baghdad in the spring as to whether anyone had heard about the fate of a Roman ambassador. Eventually it was discovered that Ouranos was a prisoner in Baghdad. I hoped that some message would come, if only a demand for a ransom or a concession in return for his release. None came.

It was Diaphantes who explained to me what had happened, although he did so in his usual pretentious fashion. I was standing in the corridor that overlooks the Boukoleon harbour: the one that I had sat in with Nothos when we looked at the bearded star. I was gazing out to sea and Diaphantes, as he passed, guessed that I was thinking about Ouranos. He stopped:

'I believe that His Majesty has imbibed the nectar of the poet.'

That was his way of observing that I had read Homer. He had an extraordinary talent for evincing loathing and contempt under a sheen of icy correctness. He had never forgiven me for my inadvertent insult nor I him for his treatment of Spondyles.

'Then doubtless he will bethink himself of the missive which King Proetus vouched safe to Bellerophon to deliver to the king of Lycia.'

With a smirk, he glided away. The sealed tablet that Proetus gave to Bellerophon requested that the recipient kill the bearer. Nothos had doubtless given Ouranos something similar, hidden away among a pile of other dispatches and credentials. It would have called in some favour and assured the Buyid emir that the best way to keep Bardas Phokas and his army on the Roman side of the border would be to place Ouranos under lock and key. It had not been enough merely to ally himself with Bardas,

Nothos had also to remove my main ally and support. He himself never said anything: he would never be so crass as to gloat as Diaphantes had done. We continued to dine together once a week and would occasionally discuss affairs in private in my office. He merely sometimes caught my eye with a sad, pained look. There was no hate or malice in it. Quite the reverse. His eyes seemed to say: 'Did you really think that you could have opposed me, who cherished you and guarded you from infancy?' If he had said it to me out loud, I would have agreed with him. I surrendered. I had been completely outclassed and my inferiority to him had been starkly and brutally exposed.

It was in this time of despondency that I began to think about Spondyles again. The sheer pressure of events had pushed him out of my mind, just as I had pushed him out of my life. I had sometimes ridden in the polo field and had come and gone from the stables but I never came across him. Nor did I ever see him at ceremonies. That did not surprise me particularly. As a strator his role in the guards was largely honorary, so he would not routinely attend ceremonies or undertake other duties. In any case, the Great Palace is a vast world of its own where people who work all their lives in one part are complete strangers in another. It now seemed appropriate to seek him out. Not only did I have plenty of time on my hands but given the totality of my defeat, there no longer seemed any point in distancing myself.

So one bright morning I rode over to the tenement beyond the stables with my guards behind me. As I approached I could see that the pomegranate tree was beginning to grow its leaves and red flowers and that the stone bench was there too: I almost expected to find him and Euphemia still sitting on it just as I had left them. The door of the apartment was open and a little child of two or three came running out: that was as it should be, I thought. As I halted and got down from my horse, Euphemia emerged from the house to steer the child back in. She looked to have a rather fuller figure than I remembered and her voice sounded different when she looked up, saw me and shouted:

'Ianni, Ianni, it's the emperor!'

Several faces appeared in the windows above and a tall muscular man with a black beard looked out of the door, only to duck back in and then re-emerge hastily buttoning a tunic. The woman bowed hastily, grabbed the child and ran inside. She was not Spondyles' wife at all. I felt like I did when I was six and had glimpsed Nothos across a crowded hall, run across, taken his hand and then raised my eyes to see another man's face looking down at me. Ianni had come to attention in front of me.

'Guardsman, I am looking for the Strator Spondyles who once lived in this apartment. Can you tell me where he has moved to?'

'I don't know any strator of that name, Majesty. We have lived here for eighteen months now and a guardsman called Soterikos had his family had it before us.'

'I see. How many children do you have?'

'Two, Majesty, little Stavroula there, and Michael who's five.'

'Then buy them something from me,' I said, handing him a coin and making a mental note to add him to the list before turning back to my horse. How stupid of me, I thought, to have expected that he would be in the same house just as if no time had passed at all. Doubtless, he would have used his strator's salary to purchase a property somewhere. I resolved to search further in due course but not immediately. The visit to the tenement would have been reported to Nothos and a subsequent spate of enquires would pique his interest. So I just continued my life as his obedient drone and dreamed of the day when I could go riding with Spondyles again. When the new

Keeper brought the documents to my office each morning, I signed them without a second glance. In council, I just went along with whatever Nothos said. Perhaps I would have passed the rest of my reign in that state of apathy, neither exercising any real power nor succeeding in throwing it off entirely and retiring to private life: the worst of both worlds. Perhaps – had I not returned to my apartment late one wet autumn evening from a liturgy in Hagia Sophia to find a letter lying on my bed.

It exuded anonymity. The address "to the Emperor Basil" was in a scribal hand that could have belonged to any member of that numerous professional caste. The paper was of high enough quality to ensure that the writing did not show through but not the most expensive. The seal was a blob of black wax with no impression. Not an official communication then, I thought. Still, I opened it and the stark first line seemed to strike me in the eyes:

"Your mother is in the Petrion."

11

Petrion (983-4)

It is not unusual for letters to appear on the emperor's bed. Someone pays a servant to bribe another servant who pays one of the emperor's attendants to put it there. It can be a useful chain of communication so I have never discouraged it. This particular mysterious missive was not one of the normal rather opaque kind for it included detailed instructions on how, when and where I was to pay a visit to my mother whom I had not seen for nearly fourteen years.

The Petrion was once, I believe, the private mansion of a prominent citizen who later became emperor, although I cannot remember which one. So it became an imperial possession and a very fine colonnaded mansion it is. Unfortunately, with the passage of time, the neighbourhood in which it stands has gone downhill and the rich and well connected have long since moved to Sphorakion or to the airy quarters south of the Hippodrome. These days the palace is marooned among seedy and dilapidated tenement blocks and fetid taverns where for a few coppers you can drink yourself into oblivion on adulterated wine. That is why it is so useful to us. It is where we house whatever it is we do not wish to be seen. Rooms are set aside there for the emperor's mistresses: Constantine had at least three at that point to my certain knowledge. My mother had gone there when Nikephoros had taken over in 963 to wait and see how things might work out. Now apparently she was back there and I had only found out in this rather cloak and dagger way.

It could have been a trap, designed to lure me out of the safety of the Great Palace but I took the chance. I had been told to go after dark with just two guards to a doorway off the alley at the back of the building. We found the door unlocked but the very sight of it awakened my old fears of what might lie on the other side. One of the guards went before me and looked in to see if all was clear: after all an assassin might have been lurking there. Reassured, I entered and climbed up a stone spiral staircase, holding up the lantern that I had been warned that I would need. When I reached the first floor, a door was standing open. The staircase spiralled on upwards into the darkness but as instructed I stepped into the lighted room. It had been cosily fitted up, with brightly painted walls and cushion-strewn couches, although they were looking rather old and scuffed. In fact I think that it had been one of those reserved for concubines, hence the direct access from the back door, even though it had probably not been the scene of much imperial lovemaking in recent years. The faded but gaudy decoration made Theophano look very incongruous. She was sitting bolt upright on one of the couches, dressed in the grey habit of a nun. Her head was completely encased in a close-fitting cowl with only her face showing. She still had the large eyes and lips but all the vitality and passion were gone. She got up slowly and walked over to me. There was no extravagant display of affection, no throwing of her arms around me as she had used to. She just laid her hand on my chest and said:

'I didn't think you'd come. I thought you'd washed your hands of me.'

'Nobody told me where you were. I had no idea you were back in Constantinople.'

'I was brought back when Skleros started his revolt. They could not risk him getting his hands on me and marrying me to give himself a claim on the throne. Before that I was in a convent on an island in the Marmara, Prokonnesos.'

She had by this time moved back to the couch and slumped down wearily. Her hand went up to her cowl.

'Do you know, in all those years in the convent, I never took the vow. They shouted at me, begged me, threatened me but I never did. Do you know why I wear this? It's because I've got almost no hair: I picked up scabies on Prokonnesos. They could have sent me to one of those nunneries up and down the Bosporus. They specialise in looking after widows and women whose lives have gone wrong. You get your own room and a private bathroom. But no, they had to send me to a rock in the middle of the Marmara, run by fanatics. Why did they have to torture me as well as punish me? Even when they brought me back to keep me out of Skleros' clutches, they locked me in a miserable place miles from the centre of town.'

'How do you come to be here then?'

She did not answer immediately. Instead she scanned my face as if seeking some clue there as to how she should answer.

'I seem to have some friends after all. They have given me an apartment here. Officially, I am still in the convent.'

I am rather ashamed to admit that at that point I burst out petulantly:

'It made no difference to me when they sent you away. I never saw you anyway. After you married Nikephoros, you went off with him to Asia and left me all alone. Even when you did come back I hardly saw you.'

She looked at the floor.

'You are right. I don't deny it. I adored you and your brother and sister but you have to understand what happened. I was fourteen when I married your father. He had taken a fancy to me after his Frankish wife died and I could hardly say no. Your grandmother on your father's side was furious. She said that Romanos had married beneath him. She wouldn't even allow my parents in the Great Palace. So after you were born I took you to their house. They were over the moon as you can imagine. They walked around with you in their arms, saying that you were their very own little emperor. Everyone was overjoyed in the palace too: by producing a purple-born heir to the throne, I had silenced all my enemies. But then I did something incredibly stupid.

'It was when Nikephoros came to Constantinople after his sack of Aleppo. Romanos and I reviewed the troops and met his officers. I came face to face with one of them and just like that I was lost. I couldn't keep my eyes off him and he felt the same about me. It was like a mania. He was married so the whole thing was utterly mad and unbelievably dangerous but we did it anyway.'

She looked around the room.

'We even met here a couple of times. I would do anything to be with him, even neglecting my own children. That is why I went away to Asia, just to be with him. You wouldn't understand.'

I did not correct her on that. Then a thought occurred to her and she relented:

'But you knew him. Perhaps you can conceive something of what I felt for him.'

She scanned me again, noting my look of puzzlement. 'You really don't know, do you? You always were such a baby. He was John Tzimiskes.'

I was silent for a moment as this sank in. In a way, I suppose I had known. After all, I had seen them together on the balcony: it had not been a dream at all. I had overheard Tzimiskes talking about her to Roupenios in the palace garden the first time we met. Then I burst out with:

'So am I my father's son?'

'You are. And Constantine and Anna are Romanos's too. I saw John so seldom in those days, before Nikephoros came to Constantinople.'

For one moment, I had thought I had found the explanation for the gulf between me and my siblings.

'So when we were children, when you used to come to the nursery to see us, you were regularly seeing John at the same time?'

'You condemn me then.'

'No, I am merely trying to ascertain the facts. How can I condemn you for seeking happiness? But because you were always with him, I was abandoned.'

'I wanted to take you when we went to Cappadocia but they would only let me have Constantine and Anna.'

'I was left with no friends except Nothos.'

Her eyes flashed in the way they had the evening she had confronted Nikephoros after my return from Hebdomon.

'Friend?' Then she considered. 'He doesn't know you are here, does he?'

I quickly reassured her that neither Nothos nor anyone else knew about my visit, then I changed tack.

'He and John told me you were involved in the murder of Nikephoros. That you let the assassins into the palace and made sure that the door to his bedchamber was unlocked. Is that true?'

'Of course it's true', she snapped. 'But it's not the whole story.'

✳ ✳ ✳

Over the next few weeks, I made repeated visits to the Petrion. My guards evidently imagined that I was going there on the same errand as Constantine and once or twice I caught them exchanging knowing glances. I suspect that this might have been the origin of the later rumour that during my youth I "indulged in the pleasures of love." I actually spent the evenings sitting side by side with Theophano on one of the couches, trying to piece together the sequence of events that had shaped my childhood.

'Lekapenos, Nothos as you call him, is the most dangerous man in this city. Never let him know who or what it is you love.'

I did not mention that I had already arrived at that conclusion and acted on it.

'He found out about John Tzimiskes. That was what destroyed me.'

Heavy rain was falling in the streets outside as we had this conversation. I thought of the guards huddled in a doorway, awaiting my return.

'He had been chamberlain under your grandfather. That was his reward for bringing in the Phokas family and ousting his own Lekapenos half-brothers in 945. But your father distrusted him. Romanos was feckless in many ways but he had good political instincts. He could see that Lekapenos was eaten up with ambition and could never forget that he was the son of an emperor. So as soon as his reign began, he appointed a new chamberlain, another eunuch called Joseph Bringas. It was a brilliant choice. Bringas was every bit as able as Lekapenos but without an accident of birth to make him think that he was something special. But then Romanos got ill. He was young and a bit wild and he drank too much. He'd been out hunting in Philopation and was not at all well when he came back. He developed a fever and died before any of us had realised there was any danger.

'I was just getting over the birth of your sister: she came two days before your father went. We did what is always done when the emperor dies and his son is too young to rule. We formed a council of regency to govern the state until you were old enough. I headed it and the other members were Bringas, the Patriarch Polyeuktos, one of the keepers and a logothete. We were well aware that there was a danger that Nikephoros Phokas might try to seize power, so we were very careful not to give him any pretext to march on Constantinople.

'That was when your Nothos made his move. He came to me and bluntly told me that he knew that I had a lover and that I had been unfaithful to your father. We thought we'd been so very discreet but he had found out somehow. After he'd allowed the shock of discovery to sink in, he turned on that charm of his. He said he had no plans to expose us but quite the opposite: he wanted to bring us together. He told me about the plan he had made to bring Nikephoros to Constantinople and have him proclaimed emperor. John would come too: he assured me of that. With Bringas out of the way, no one would object to John divorcing his wife and marrying me. I didn't fall for it right away. I insisted that I could not support him if your and Constantine's rights were going to be harmed in any way. "Don't worry," he said, "Nikephoros has no children living so Basil will still inherit the throne in due course." So I joined him in the plot. Nikephoros brought his army into Constantinople but Bringas tried to save himself by grabbing you and Constantine from the nursery. He wanted to take you to sanctuary in Hagia Sophia and use you as a bargaining chip.

211

He certainly didn't want to hurt either of you but apparently there was a scuffle on the stairs and some servant got hit. She died later, I think. Anyway, you know the rest. The soldiers stopped him in the Augousteion and you were taken back to the nursery.

'So Nikephoros was crowned emperor and Lekapenos was reappointed chamberlain, just as he had planned. I came here, as agreed, to wait for John. How could I have been so stupid? I was very young and hadn't a clue about politics. If I had, I'd have seen at once that, as a usurper, Nikephoros would have to link himself to your family in some way to make sure that he did not get toppled by someone else. He demanded me, knowing perfectly well how dangerous it would be if I married another soldier. Lekapenos must have been aware all along that there was never any chance of me being with John but he had strung me along so that he could be chamberlain again. For a brief moment there was hope. Patriarch Polyeuktos announced that because Nikephoros was your godfather, he could not marry me because he was a sort of relative. Lekapenos soon dealt with that. He got Nikephoros' father, that wizened old Bardas, to swear an oath that it was he who was your godfather not his son. So the patriarch relented. They actually took me from here under guard and just about pushed me to the altar at the point of a sword. In the church, looked back at the procession and saw you and Constantine standing there and I wanted to run back, catch you both up in my arms and run out. But I didn't. I married that old Cappadocian goat.

'For the first few weeks I was in despair. The very sight of Nikephoros disgusted me and I dreaded the day when he'd demand his lawful rights. But then it began to dawn on me that my situation was a lot better than I'd thought. Nikephoros never came to my room. Since the death of his wife, he'd been abstaining from just about everything. He'd long since given up on screwing.'

The crudity contrasted strangely with her sombre attire.

'So I was able to be with John again very shortly after the wedding. Nikephoros decided that it would be better if I stayed in Hiereia with Constantine and Anna in case there was unrest in the city. That made it very easy for us. John could be ferried over by night and back early the next morning. Sometimes I even came across to him and we made love in the Boukoleon. The autumn and winter after Nikephoros' accession were one of the best times of my life.'

I thought of myself at that same time, wandering in the empty garden by day and haunted by frightening visions at night but I did not say anything.

'In the spring, Nikephoros announced that he'd be crossing to Asia Minor to begin the Tarsus campaign. Naturally, John would be travelling with him and so I insisted on going too, along with Constantine and Anna. Those were good times as well although I missed the city and you, of course. But after he had taken Tarsus, Nikephoros spent less and less time on campaign which meant that I had to leave John and return with him. Someone was feeding information to the emperor that was making him paranoid that there was a plot against him. Maybe he had an inkling of what was going on between John and me because he had John relieved of his command and sent back to his estates. That was the autumn of 969. I was desperate by then and full of terror that I would never see John again. I hated Nikephoros: that was when he nearly lost you on that ridiculous hunt in Philopation.'

She paused here because the most difficult part of her story was yet to come.

'I was so desperate that I did something very, very foolish. I went to the Chamberlain. You would have thought that I'd learned my lesson after the first time but I was wild with desire to see John again. And Lekapenos said, in that way he has, that he would arrange it all. He would let me know in due course what he needed me to do. He acted as if this was some big favour that he was doing me but he had his own reasons for wanting Nikephoros dead. He'd thought his soldier-emperor would spend all his time of the frontier, leaving him to run things in Constantinople. But now Nikephoros was permanently in the Great Palace, making laws that were aggravating everyone, the Church, the bureaucrats, the people. Only the soldiers liked him. So I was doing the chamberlain a favour, not the other way round. But I was too besotted to see that then.

'It was one December night that he sent a message to me, asking me to leave the women's quarters and come to him in the Lausiakos. When I arrived he gave me the best news in all the world. John was in Chrysopolis and it was only the narrow strait that separated us. He had brought with him a group of close friends and they had a boat to ferry them across to the harbour of Boukoleon the following night. There were two tasks that they needed me to carry out. One was to make sure that the door of Nikephoros' bedchamber was unlocked. The other was to find some way of getting John and his friends into the Boukoleon. They could hardly stroll brazenly up the stone steps from the harbour while any other entrance had been sealed off by the wall that Nikephoros had built. I told Lekapenos not to worry, I would arrange it.

'I took aside two of my favourite waiting women, Anastasia and Theodote. They could be trusted as they had been with me ever since I arrived in the palace as a young bride. I told them that during the evening we would need some men to do some heavy lifting and so they contacted their families outside the Great Palace. Six of their brothers and cousins turned up the next morning, bringing with them a large basket like the one tradesmen use to carry their wares to market and a long rope. During the morning we did a survey of the windows overlooking Nikephoros' wall and found one that was perfect: John and his friends would be able to disembark in the Boukoleon harbour and work their way round the wall to be directly below in next to no time. I distributed the gold then and there as I told the men that they'd have to leave as soon as the lifting job was done and head for the harbour where a boat would ferry them to the Golden Horn. After that, we had only to wait.'

She winced at this point and I asked what was wrong. She said it was only one of the pains she got sometimes. She went on:

'It was at around midnight, when snow had started to come down quite heavily, that we received the signal from below. We let down the basket and the first of John's party lay down in it. The men then heaved him up, hand over hand. John was the last to come up and we fell into each other's arms the moment his foot touched the floor. I remember brushing the snowflakes off his head and shoulders. One of John's friends interrupted us and reminded us that the night's work was yet to be done so I led them along the corridor and pointed out which was Nikephoros' room. I then withdrew round the corner and waited. Seconds later one of them reappeared with a face like death and whispered that Nikephoros was not in the room. The bed was empty and had not been slept in that night. He was convinced that the plan had been betrayed. But then another of them rushed back and said Nikephoros was there. He was sleeping on the floor on the far side of the bed, wrapped in just a rough woollen blanket. I think he did this as part of his preparations for becoming a monk.

'So I was left alone again in the dark. I had assumed that they would run him through then and there while he was asleep but they did not do that. Their voices floated back along the corridor. They'd woken him up and were hurling abuse at him. Then I heard his screams of pain as they started kicking him then hacking at him with their swords.

He kept on crying out: "Mother of God, help me!." I couldn't bear it so I held my hands over my ears and ran off down the corridor.'

✱ ✱ ✱

I think that it must have been on separate visits that we went over the murder of Nikephoros and its aftermath. I know that she became very distraught when describing the actual killing and I had to soothe her and calm her down. It was only on another occasion that I could finally put the question that I was desperate to ask:

'So why didn't John marry you and make you his empress once he had disposed of Nikephoros?'

'He fully intended to, that I don't doubt. His wife had died the previous autumn so he was free. The morning after the whole horrible business, he sent a servant into the women's quarters asking me to stay there until matters were arranged. By that time, they'd taken Nikephoros' body away and buried it in the Holy Apostles. Next they needed to have John crowned emperor in Hagia Sophia and then the wedding would follow on from that. He and the Chamberlain went to Patriarch Polyeuktos to tell him that Nikephoros was dead and that to provide an emperor, John must be married to me and crowned. They spun him a story that a group of men with a grudge had killed Nikephoros and that John had had nothing to do with it. That was when it all started to go wrong. Old Polyeuktos was no fool. He knew perfectly well what had happened. But he also knew that with Nikephoros dead, John would have to be crowned or else there would be civil war as all the other generals piled in to grab the throne. So he agreed to crown John on two conditions. First, John had to abandon some law that Nikephoros wanted to pass which gave the emperor control of the election of bishops. Second, he had to ditch me.

Polyeuktos, like your paternal grandmother, had never approved of Romanos marrying someone whose father was in trade. Now he took his chance to get rid of me. John could have stood up to him. He could have deposed Polyeuktos and brought in a new patriarch. But no, he caved in and did as he was told.

'He did not even have the guts to tell me himself. He got someone else to do his dirty work for him. Your Nothos sent me a message saying that all was arranged and could I come to the Chamberlain's office in the Lausiakos so that he could give me the details. So I set off with Anastasia and Theodote. The events of that night had been horrible but they were over now and I thought that all was going according to plan. We passed the place where John and his friends had been hoisted up. There was nothing to show that anything unusual had taken place that. That boded well, I thought. Everything had been carefully tidied up.

He was alone in the room when we got there and he told my women to stay outside. Then he sat down at his desk and leant back in his chair like the great man he is. He did not make the slightest effort to soften the news or to make it easier for me – just airily announced that John was soon to be crowned but I would not be crowned with him. Instead, next year, he would be marrying my ugly sister-in-law. I knew then in a devastating, crushing instant that I would never see John again when only seconds before I'd believed we'd finally be together for the rest of our lives. What did the chamberlain expect me to do? Swoon gracefully onto a couch? Before I knew what I was doing, I was across the room and up on the desk from where I launched myself at him. He fell back with me on top of him and I started pummelling and scratching his face. Two scribes rushed in from the next room and tried to drag me off him but Anastasia and Theodote ran in through the other door and started to fight them. We held our own and gave as good as we got!

'It all ended, of course, when some guards came crashing in. Fool that I was, I thought they'd would respectfully come to attention and await my orders. That's what I was used to. Instead, they didn't hesitate for a moment: they'd been waiting outside ready to arrest me. One of them locked his arm around my neck, others grabbed me by the arms and legs. My women they swept aside as they carried me out of the door. Down the corridors we went, three of them lugging me under their arms like a rolled-up carpet. We passed servants sweeping and dusting: some of them I knew by sight. They just carried on with what they were doing, as if an empress being borne off bodily happened every other day. The next thing I knew I was on my way down the steps to the harbour. They took me onto a galley and locked me in the cabin below. The door had a little grille in it and through it I could see the face of the guardsman. He was young, not so very much older than you were then, so I pleaded with him to let me see my children one last time before I was taken away. But of course he couldn't. So I screamed and shouted but no one could hear, or rather they chose not to. In any case, it can only have been after about an hour or so that the crew pushed away from the quay and set sail for Prokonnesos.'

She stopped and looked at me pleadingly.

'You don't happen to know what became of Anastasia and Theodote?'

I did not but I could guess. They would have fared better than she did, their silence purchased with gold. But I could hardly say that.

'Nikephoros was murdered, I do not deny that, and if I was not exactly one of his murderers, I was certainly an accessory. But why were those involved treated so differently? John was rewarded by becoming emperor.

Lekapenos was rewarded by remaining as chamberlain. John's friends were arrested for the crime and sent into exile. But that only meant that they went to their homes in Asia with a lot more money than they had had before. Only one of the guilty parties was truly punished and guess which one that was? The woman!'

* * *

During those months when I was making regular visits to the Petrion and listening to Theophano's revelations, I was constantly asking myself what it all amounted to. I was not shocked to discover that Nothos and John Tzimiskes were responsible for Nikephoros' death but then my mind went back to that interview with them two days later in which they had sanctimoniously placed the blame on Theophano and I was incensed by their hypocrisy. Even so, it did occur to me to wonder how much of my mother's unsubstantiated testimony I could accept. I tried to place her account of events alongside my own memories: Nothos coming to announce that he felt unwell and that he would retire to bed, the marks on his face when I next saw him. They certainly tallied with what she had said. I thought about how I had heard that Nikephoros was dead. It was Father Anthony who had told Constantine and me when he came to the schoolroom. He had been very evasive and even then I suspected that he was covering something up. Then I remembered my last meeting with him in the patriarchal residence when he had handed me his letter of resignation over what he had referred to as a "grievous sin." I had never opened it because I had hoped that he would change his mind. After he had died, I had completely forgotten about it and it did not occur to me to look for it when I appointed his successor. Now I went to the wooden chest in my apartment and fished it out. The patriarchal seal was still intact so I broke it and read. First came the formal renunciation of the office of Ecumenical Patriarch and then this:

I take this step because I was an accessory to and a beneficiary of the murder of the late Lord Emperor Nikephoros. I had admired him to start with. He was a deeply spiritual man, the friend of monks, and he was indifferent to all worldly pomp and vanity. But after a few years in power he changed. He came to care about nothing but his soldiers and was intent on extorting ever more money to pay for his wars. When he had squeezed the taxpayers dry, he turned on the Church. He passed a law forbidding any new gifts of land to be made to monasteries because he did not want them to gain tax exemption. Then that autumn, the one when the Lord Emperor Basil was lost in Philopation, he announced that he was going to make all appointments of bishops subject to his approval. We all knew that his motive was to keep sees vacant for a year or two so that he could take the revenues. I was appalled and so was his late All-Holiness Polyeuktos.

One cold December day, when the first flakes of snow were starting to fall, I was in the office downstairs that I then used in my capacity as Synkellos. A distant kinsman of mine, who is a monk at a house in Bithynia, paid me a visit. We were discussing the proposed law and suddenly he burst out that the emperor would receive his punishment for his impiety that very night. I asked him what he meant but he quickly corrected himself and assured me that it was just that his anger had got the better of him. He had meant on the Day of Judgment. In spite of his retraction, after he had gone, I was very worried about what he said and I felt that I should do something. I took a piece of expensive paper and wrote on it "Protect yourself, o emperor, for no small danger is being prepared for you this night." I closed it with a blank seal and gave it to a servant, ordering him to pay a child to carry it across the Augousteion to the Brazen Gate and give it to the guard. I felt certain that the quality of paper and the script would ensure that it reached at least a Keeper. That was all I could do.

It was about an hour after midnight that I was woken by a servant who said that there were men from the palace at the door wanting to see me and that they were most insistent. They said that the Emperor was calling for a priest and that only I would do. I rose and went out to them. I did not know who they were but they had with them one of the waiting women of the Lady Theophano whom I recognised because she used to come with her mistress when she received the sacrament in the Pharos chapel. They also showed me a ring of the Emperor Nikephoros that I knew. So I agreed to go with them and we crunched our way across the snow to the Brazen Gate. They took me to the Boukoleon and up to Nikephoros' bedchamber. I went into the room but no one was there. The bed had not even been slept in. I looked back and they told me that he was on the other side of the bed. I took a lamp, leaned over and saw an awful sight. At first it appeared to be a pile of meat such as you see on a butcher's slab, except that parts of it were wrapped in a blanket. Then I realised that I was looking at a human body and that the mess sticking out of the blanket was what remained of its head. I staggered back, retching but one of the men caught me by the shoulders and hissed: "Say whatever prayers you must, priest."

I fell to my knees and started to implore God to have mercy on the soul of Nikephoros, emperor of the Romans, but after a minute, the men dragged me aside and brought a wooden box into the room. They used shovels to heap the remains into it. It was not very big – about the right size for a large dog but they got everything in by compacting it down with the shovels. They carried it through the deserted corridors to a side door, the one that gives onto the alley by the Hippodrome and put it onto one of those push carts that fruit sellers use. We trundled it across the Augousteion and along the Mese until we reached the Holy Apostles. They unloaded it from the cart and carried it into the mausoleum, which was already open for us, and they dropped it into an empty sarcophagus. Then they told me to say the words. I recited as much of the liturgy as I could remember but it had been many years since I had presided at a funeral. I do remember saying "Go out, o emperor," three times.

I confess then that the Emperor Nikephoros did not receive the funeral sacrament that was his due but that is not the sin for which I must lay down my office. That misdeed I will confess now. As the men took the box out of the bedchamber, I followed them and I glanced back along the corridor. There were two figures silhouetted against the window at the far end. At first, I had no idea who they were but as a cloud moved away from the moon I recognised them: they were the Domestic Tzimiskes, who later became Emperor

John, and the Lord Chamberlain Lekapenos. The next day, I was summoned to the palace and shown into a room with the Chamberlain, Tzimiskes, Bardas Skleros, an Armenian officer and a man dressed in a black robe without a stole whose name was not given. They told me that I had done my duty as a priest extremely well and that I would be rewarded. The patriarch Polyeuktos was very old and would soon need to be replaced and, if not at the next opportunity, then at the one after that I would be so favoured. In the meantime, I must tell nobody what I had seen that night. In my weakness and vanity, I allowed myself to be swayed by these blandishments, may God forgive me, and I kept silent.

✳ ✳ ✳

I was with my mother in the Petrion again. This time we were talking about the present, not the past. By now she was a grandmother for the first of Constantine and Helena's daughters had been born. I was trying to work out what would be the best way to organise a visit by Constantine and Anna who still did not know that she was in Constantinople. It would be tricky. The more people who knew of Theophano's whereabouts the more likely it would be to reach the ears of Nothos. There was something else I needed to know.

'Who was it who brought you here? And who was it who sent me a letter with instructions on how to find you?'

'I can't tell you that. They say that when you are ready to find out, you will do so.'

That left me feeling frustrated. I now had in my possession evidence which, if it were used intelligently, had the potential to bring Nothos down. But I felt so alone without Ouranos. I longed for allies. I hoped that Theophano would change her mind and let me know who my mysterious well-wisher was but she gave me no comfort:

'I hear you've been standing up to Lekapenos once or twice. That's a dangerous game but you've been safe up to now. Why do you think that is?'

'I'm the purple-born emperor. He is a eunuch and he can only rule through me.'

'Nonsense. He could have you put out of the way any time he liked. But he doesn't. You know why? Because he loves you. You're the only person or thing in this world that he cares for: the son he never could have.'

I did not want to hear that so I made my excuses and left. That is something that I regret. A few evenings later, it was April by now, I was presiding over a banquet for army officers in the Golden Dining Hall when a servant handed me a note. It just said: "Come to me." There was no signature: that would have given everything away had the note been intercepted. I was not sorry for the excuse to leave, nor I expect were the diners. Such occasions are dull affairs and the absence of the emperor allows them to be much more raucous and fun. So I stood up, called for silence, gave my regrets, wished them all a good appetite and left. At the Petrion, I went up the spiral staircase and found a lamp burning but the room seemed to be empty. Then I saw that there was a bed in the far corner, partially hidden by the cushioned couches. Theophano lay on it, quite dead. Her eyes were open and staring up at the ceiling, her lips slightly drawn back from the teeth. I felt on my hand for the ring, the one she had given me and which I had later lent to Philemon, and intoned out loud:

'Lord, help thy servant, Theophano, empress of the Romans.'

Then I turned and walked away, down the staircase and out into the street.

* * *

I was standing on the diamond-paved path, looking down the long avenue of trees, their leaves autumnal red and gold. At the end of the avenue stood a figure that I knew. It was Pita. I began to walk towards her and then to run. But as I got nearer, I realised that it was not Pita at all. It was Nikephoros. I was standing right in front of him and I saw that it was not him in person but the mosaic portrait that had been put up in the apse of the Hall of the Nineteen Couches. I was somehow standing face to face with him and I could see the Virgin and Child and Theophano to my left. The mosaic Nikephoros began to speak:

'D'you think I wanted to be emperor…'

But he never finished because a sword crashed into his face sending mosaic cubes and splinters showering in all directions.

'It will be alright, darling,' spoke the mosaic Theophano, 'Mummy will give him some gold coins.'

I did not want to hear any more so I turned away but I found myself enmeshed in a heavy curtain of what felt like embroidered brocade. I struggled for a moment and then looked up. Nothos' smooth face was looking down at me.

'Your Majesty is safe now.'

He stretched out his hand to me but it was bunched into a fist. I prised open the fingers one by one to find a small icon. I thought it might be St Demetrius but all I could see were two amorphous figures sitting side by side.

12

Dekanneakoubita (984-5)

P etitions day. I was seated on the throne of Solomon in the Magnavra. I nodded graciously to each pair of petitioners who came forward but my mind was elsewhere. It had been some time since I had visited Spondyles' tenement and found it occupied by someone else. Although I had waited before looking further, I kept hoping that I would glimpse him in the crowd at ceremonies. So on this occasion too I had scanned the faces of the guards present but he was not among them. I gazed out into the assembled throng, but he was not there either as far as I could see. The next pair come forward and I nodded again. Then my thoughts moved to the golden tree on my right with its metallic birds. Apparently it had a mechanism that could make the birds sing but no one had ever seen it working. The lions under the arms of the throne could be made to roar too. Perhaps I should see if they could be repaired and got back into working order. The two petitioners had handed their scrolls to the attendants and the next pair were on the way: a very small, elderly woman and a florid middle-aged man. They were making their bows and I prepared the gracious nod for when they rose. Suddenly the woman's face was within an inch of mine, her toothless mouth working as she hissed:

'Son of Romanos! Why do you let the murderer go unpunished? Speak to the one you saw, the one in black!'

She was seized at once and dragged away. The other petitioners at the back of the hall awaiting their turn looked on in horror. They obviously dreaded that the session would be terminated and they would have to go through months of waiting all over again.

'Let the petitioning proceed,' I said.

Afterwards I asked about the woman and was told that she was mad. She had been taken to the asylum at the orphanage. I did not believe a word of it. Her words were not insane ravings. They were a message.

* * *

It must have been about ten days after I had found Theophano dead that Nothos glided into my office, closely followed by Diaphantes, whose bald head was hidden under his logothete's hat while strands of wiry black hair protruded on either side.

'Majesty, we have sad news for you. We have been informed by the abbess of the Prokonnesos convent that your mother has died there. It would seem that her passing was swift and painless. We would like to offer our deepest condolences for your loss.'

Diaphantes then put in:

'I understand that towards the end the late empress evinced manifestations of remorse for her previous conduct.

Chamberlain, with your permission I shall convey the melancholy intelligence to His Majesty's siblings.'

His deliberate insult in asking Nothos rather than me for leave did not go unnoticed but my powers of dissimulation were so well advanced by now that I did not react to it nor to the lie that my mother had died on the island. Once the logothete was out of the room, I merely rose from my desk, walked to the window and looked out. There was no doubt about it, I thought. Nothos genuinely had no idea that I was aware that Theophano had been brought back to the city and that I had been visiting her in the Petrion. A discernible crack had opened up in his flawless web of control. That was why I answered as I did:

'Great Uncle, I last saw my mother when I was eleven. Even before she was sent away, she seldom came to see me and I scarcely knew her. So let her rest in peace on the island. You were always both mother and father to me and that is why I have come to the decision I have. I would like you to accept the office of Caesar. You yourself could never and would never propose this but we can agree, I am sure, that it is in the interests of the state.'

The Caesar is effectively a deputy emperor so that the office is the second highest in the state. It had been vacant since the last incumbent, old Bardas, had died in 969. Nothos gravely placed his hand on his chest and bowed:

'Majesty, I am overwhelmed. Not so much because of the honour itself but because it bears witness to our complete reconciliation.'

'I thought that our name day on the second of January would be the best time for the investiture. I will initiate preparations but I am not going to make a public announcement at this stage. In fact, I would rather wait until after the ceremony. We both understand the jealousy and resentment in some quarters to which it might give rise.'

So that was settled. It was a trap of course and I needed some time to set it, hence the wait until January. The revelations of his involvement in the death of Nikephoros had given me the potential to ruin him but I needed allies if I wanted to avoid a repeat of the debacle that had occurred the last time that I challenged him. He had defeated me partly by realigning himself with the Phokas clan and partly by activating a network of undercover contacts to which I had no access. I intended to use the time between then and January to seize control of those two prime assets.

$$* * *$$

The first step which I had to take was the most ambitious and dangerous one: I intended to act on the words of the old woman in the Magnavra. One morning, I arrived in the Lausiakos and told the Keeper that the documents would have to wait and gave instructions for the Protonotarios Roupenios and Commander Kontostephanos to wait on me. When they came, I told them that the guard room in the Brazen Gate was to be cleared for an interview. I would need them both to be there as witnesses and I might need the commander's sword. Impy visibly brightened up at that. When all was ready we went across and I asked Impy to send two guards to bring the Logothete of the Drome.

To his credit, Diaphantes looked remarkably calm and collected when he arrived at the guardroom between two of Impy's men.

'I attend in obedience to His Majesty's ordinance,' He looked around disdainfully, 'I had not expected such stygian surroundings. May I ask why, like Odysseus, I have descended into Hades?'

'Logothete, I will be brief. Your office accepts the reports of an official who wears a black robe with no other distinguishing insignia. I wish to speak to that official.'

'Your Majesty must be mistaken. To my recollection, no such official is listed in the Books of Precedence.'

'I never said that he was listed, merely that he reports to your office. I am your emperor and I repeat my command.'

He spread his hands.

'But how can I comply with His Majesty's command when its fulfilment is impossible?'

'Logothete, if you do not produce this official you will be disobeying a direct order. That is high treason and I will instruct the Commander of the Guard summarily to execute you.'

Impy put his hand to his sword, drawing it partly out of its scabbard: he had no fond memories of the schoolroom either. You have to admire Diaphantes in a way though. Even when faced with the threat of imminent death, he could still produce a perfect optative conditional:

'Majesty, were such an official to exist, he would scarcely be housed in the Great Palace.'

'And yet he comes to the Great Palace. I and others have seen him here.'

'Were such a man to exist, he would need to enter by one of the more sequestered gates and would only wish to be seen in rooms to which ingress would not involve extensive perambulations through public corridors.'

Two can play at this game, I thought.

'Were such a man to exist, Logothete, he would present himself today at two in the afternoon at the entrance by the Hippodrome wall. Assure him that measures will be taken to ensure discretion. That is all, you may go.'

When he was at the door, I added:

'And Logothete, you are not to mention this interview to anyone, not even to the Chamberlain himself. If you do, I cannot answer for the consequences. I am an emperor and expect to be obeyed but even I sometimes cannot hold back some of the guards who have no love for those who teach in schoolrooms.'

✳ ✳ ✳

That afternoon, Impy and two of his men were ready by the Hippodrome portal. Roupenios and I went to the nearby Nineteen Couches Hall to wait. I had chosen the place because I could be sure that we would not be overheard for if we stood in the centre of the hall we would have a clear view all round and there were no hiding places. I had anyone hanging around cleared out and had the hall searched to make sure. Then I sent everyone away, including Roupenios, explaining that it would be safer for him if he did not hear what was about to be discussed. I was left alone in the echoing space, waiting for a man who did not exist. The mosaics of Nikephoros and Theophano gazed down sightlessly from the apse. For a moment I did begin to wonder whether I was mistaken and the whole thing was in fact a figment of my imagination. Then I saw the double doors at the far end of the hall open and the man in the black robe crossed the threshold.

As he walked slowly towards me, I saw that he was quite old, perhaps seventy. He had cropped grey hair and a rather straggly beard. A nondescript figure, who might be taken for a minor scribe or deacon, but certainly not for anyone of importance. He made the bow with some difficulty.

'Now that I am meeting you for the first time,' I said, 'you must tell me what to call you. I do not even know the name of your office.'

He told me his name, which I will not record but said that those who worked for him generally called him Outis. That was also what his predecessor had been called and no doubt the next in line would inherit the epithet. I chuckled at that. The word means "nobody:" in the *Odyssey*, Odysseus tells the Cyclops Polyphemus that his name is Outis. Then Outis went on:

'Although we are speaking for the first time now, Majesty, I feel that I know you well. I have watched over you and followed after you for years. We knew you were in Hebdomon long before the messenger from Strongylon reached the palace: one of our men saw you as you rode down the street towards the villa. I was there in the church of St Stephen when the late ecumenical patriarch took you and your brother there, the morning after the death of Emperor Nikephoros. I was in the shadows on the far side, so you did not see me.'

Something approaching a smile passed momentarily over his chilly countenance: professional pride perhaps? I wanted to show him that I knew more than he realised and that I had information from other sources:

'Two days after you saw us in St Stephen's, you were in the room with the Chamberlain and John Tzimiskes when they interviewed the Patriarch Anthony and me, although I did not see you there either.'

'His Majesty is well informed. They made me sit behind a painted screen as they thought I might frighten you.'

'Where is your department based?'

'We operate from the Petrion, Majesty, as we find it more discreet.'

'The woman who spoke to me during the petitioning in the Magnavra – was she sent by you?'

'She is one of my best operatives. She can infiltrate almost anywhere.'

These preliminaries aside, I got down to business.

'There are certain questions that I have to ask you.'

'I cannot put my people in danger, Majesty, nor reveal their identities.'

'That is not something I would ask or expect of you. But you must tell me: Was it you who arranged for a letter to be left on my bed telling me that my mother was at the Petrion?'

'Who signed the letter, Majesty?'

Nobody had signed it and so I had my answer.

'Why did you send it?'

Again, he did not answer directly. By now I had worked out that he seldom did. Instead, he made this observation:

'His Majesty will understand that I am but a servant. All my life, I have served the state and the purple-born emperors. As long as the emperors were children, I took my orders from those who wielded power on their behalf. First the Lady Theophano and the Lord Chamberlain Bringas, then the Emperors Nikephoros and John and then from the Lord Chamberlain Lekapenos.'

'Did you continue to receive orders from the Chamberlain even after I had reached my majority?'

'Why yes, Majesty, because they were issued in your name.'

'How did you know that your orders were from me?'

'They were transmitted from the office of the Logothete of the Drome, Majesty, as has always been the custom.'

'Quite so. Did you deliver your reports to the Logothete?'

'No, Majesty. The Logothete's office acted merely as a go-between to relay communications to and from the Chamberlain. We believed that he acted on your behalf and that you had the greatest confidence in him.'

I was about to press him on my first question when I realised that he was going to answer, in his own way and in his own time.

'Your Majesty is quite right to raise this point of where our orders came from. A time came when we were no longer satisfied that the Chamberlain was acting on your behalf or in your interest.'

'When was that?'

'It was about two years ago. We received orders to activate one of our operatives at the court in Baghdad. Their task was to spread a rumour about a Roman envoy who was shortly to visit. The envoy would claim that his mission was to gain custody of one Bardas Skleros, a rebel against the emperor who had taken refuge there and to negotiate a truce that would put an end to Roman raids into Mesopotamia. The operative was to put it about that the envoy was in fact going to promise Skleros his freedom and the command of the Roman army in the east to lead against the caliphate. The story reached the ears of the Buyid emir and he had the envoy and his baggage searched. They found a letter promising Skleros a full pardon if he returned and they took that as confirmation of the story. The envoy was thrown into prison. I believe that he is still there.'

So there was no Bellerophon letter. It was just like Diaphantes to discern a literary parallel where none existed. Outis went on:

'Word came to us that this envoy was a close friend and confidant of Your Majesty. That you had known him for many years and that you had advanced him to the office of Keeper of the Inkstand. We learned too that he had served with distinction as a cavalryman in two of the campaigns of the late Lord Emperor John. We realised then that the Chamberlain was no longer acting on your behalf but his own. We regret greatly now that the Lord Keeper Ouranos is suffering unjust imprisonment because of our actions.'

'As I regret ever having sent him. Please continue.'

'We felt that the only thing we could do would be to place Your Majesty in possession of certain information of which you might not be aware. Then you would be able to arrive at your own decision on how best to proceed. By that time, your mother had been back in Constantinople for some years and was residing in a small convent near the Land Walls. We could see that neither you, nor any other member of your family was aware of this. The abbess was only too happy to allow us to remove her from there: it would appear that the Lady Theophano had no religious vocation and was at times a disruptive influence. We also received the abbess' assurance that she would maintain the fiction that your mother was still in the convent, if enquiries came from the Chamberlain's office. We still filed regular, though now largely fictitious, reports on your mother's activities at the convent. We took her to the Petrion as it would be the most convenient place and a great deal more comfortable. Then we got the letter to you.'

'I always expected the Chamberlain to find out about my visits.'

'But how would he, Majesty, unless we told him? He had ordered us to record all your movements but on evenings when you were in the Petrion, we had you in the library or visiting your aunt.'

'How did my mother die?'

'Of natural causes, Majesty. A physician examined her shortly after she came to the Petrion and found that she had a growth inside her stomach. She knew she was dying, even when she met you for the first time.'

'She never mentioned it. Where is she buried?'

'We took her to the convent of St Euphemia that is down the hill from the Petrion rather than return her to the one near the Land Walls. The Chamberlain was happy enough with our report that she was dead. He made no further enquiries.'

'I am grateful to you, Outis. If I had not spoken to her, I would never have understood what happened to me as a child. You have done your duty and you can now return to being a servant, as you say. From now on all reports will come to me or to my delegate the Protonotarios Roupenios. Your orders likewise will come directly from me. To establish their authenticity they will be accompanied by a code word, which will be changed regularly.' I gave him something off the top of my head for the time being. 'Any orders that are received by any other route, including any from the office of the Logothete, are to be referred directly to me. How am I to reach you in future?'

'Messengers to the Petrion must ask for the Office of the Wine Steward, Majesty.'

'One last thing. Is there any point in my asking to see your records?'

'There are no records, Majesty. We submit our reports in writing but we never keep copies ourselves. If they are preserved, they would be in the office of the Chamberlain.'

'The reports that you submit are not what I had in mind. It is my understanding that your office receives reports from the watch regarding church attendance.'

'Is His Majesty referring to any particular church?'

'The Holy Apostles.'

He made a gesture with the head that was neither a yes nor a no but effectively gave me my answer.

'Burn them.'

* * *

The interview with Outis had freed me from any anxiety that Nothos would be able to use the intelligence network to stop me as he had last time. There remained the fear that if I did oust him, he would mobilise his Phokas allies to come to his rescue. Even though Outis had assured me that I was not longer being tracked, I moved carefully as I prepared to counter this last threat. Going unnoticed by night was one thing. An emperor leaving the Great Palace in broad daylight is much more difficult to conceal and would be remarked upon by many more people that just Outis and his department. So I gave out that I intended to visit the monastery of St John Stoudios, as emperors do from time to time, and I ordered that the galley be made ready on the appointed day. When that day came, I sent a messenger by horse to tell the abbot that I had been prevented from coming by business at the palace but even so I descended to the harbour and we set sail. Ahead of me, another horseman rode south to announce me at my real destination and my galley put in at the Harbour of Sophia.

So here I was, I thought as I walked up the front steps of the Phokas mansion, in the lair of the enemy at last. It is a similar building to the Petrion, with a long colonnade at the top of the steps. I could almost imagine old Ghastly Bardas stalking along it, looking down on me disapprovingly. The area around it though was completely different from the shabby Petrion quarter. It was on a long gracious street which was lined with mansions on one side only so that they would have an unimpeded view south to the sea. They varied in size. I was uneasily aware that not so far away stood a smaller one belonging to Ouranos where his wife sat hoping and waiting for his return. My only consolation was that my business in the largest and grandest of the houses might ultimately bring him back.

As we walked up the steps, the double doors behind the colonnade swung open. My men were well trained. Two of them went before me and entered first. They formed up at attention in the hallway inside while I followed. The butler and the domestic staff were lined up to bow as I came in. A man who introduced himself as the secretary stepped forward to lead me through to the reception room where two chairs had been placed facing each other. In the far one was sitting an old man who was still just about recognisable as Nikephoros' brother, Leo. He struggled to his feet and as I came up to him I saw that his eyelids were closed, red and seared. I signalled to his attendant to help him sit down. As we did so, his and my people formed a line around the walls. I began:

'Lord Count Palatine, I am sorry to see that you have lost your sight.'

'It was carried out on the orders of your uncle, the Emperor John, Majesty. After my exile, I was accused of plotting to put my son Bardas on the throne. I make no apology for that. He would make as great an emperor as my brother was. I have learned to live with it. I cannot see the view from the front of the house but I now feel the sea breeze on my face much more acutely than I did. And my secretary reads to me.'

Looking at this ruin of a man, I found it hard to believe that he was the same one who had tried to be friendly and had made the effort to speak to me at that first Christmas dinner with Nikephoros and Ghastly Bardas in the Golden Dining Hall.

'Certainly, I am pleased to see that you are back in your house once more.'

'We are grateful to Your Majesty and to the Chamberlain and with my son Bardas once again in command of the eastern army, our frontier there is secure.'

'You will understand, Count Palatine, that as a child I felt no friendly feelings towards your brother. He was a usurper, who occupied a throne to which he had no claim, to the prejudice of my and my brother's rights.'

'He never meant you any harm, Majesty. He fully intended to pass the throne back to you in due course. In the meantime, he brought victory and glory to the Roman state. These men,' he waved his hand around the room, 'are ex-soldiers who followed him into battle. They can testify to his worth. Lalakon, tell him.'

A giant of a man stepped forward, past his prime and slightly stooped, but still a towering figure.

'I carried his standard on Crete, at Aleppo and at Tarsus, Majesty. He wasn't like other generals who live in luxury when on they're on campaign and leave their men to rough it. He ate exactly what we ate and drank what we drank. If a wall or fortified position had to be built, he'd carry the first stone block up to the site himself and we'd come after him with ours. We'd follow him up the hill just as we'd follow him into the jaws of hell.'

It dawned on me that I had seen the man before. He was probably the one who had stood up and proposed the toast at that first Christmas banquet. He retired back to the wall. I said what was expected:

'I hear what you are all saying. I know that the Lord Nikephoros planned to resign from the throne and become a monk: he told me so himself only a few days before his death. I now regret his loss and the manner of his passing.'

'Regret it?,' snapped Leo, who had momentarily forgotten who he was talking to. 'How do you think I feel? I'd been working in the palace that day and I'd planned to come back here in the evening. But then the snow started to come down so I thought I'd stay the night in my apartment in the Boukoleon. I gathered a few Cappadocians and after supper we played dice. Never in my life have I been as lucky as I was then. Win after win I threw. Then a Keeper came in with a letter which he said was addressed to the emperor and had been handed in by a child at the Brazen Gate. As the Emperor had retired to bed the Keeper thought it best to give it to me. I took it and could see that it was not a just petition because it was written on expensive paper and was sealed although the seal had no device on it. I promised to take care of it but the moment the Keeper had gone, I stuffed it under the cushion I was sitting on and we went on with the game. We all drank a lot and it wasn't until the early hours that we parted and went to bed. I had not been there very long when a servant came in and started shaking me saying that Nikephoros was dead and that men were running through the palace saying that my nephew John Tzimiskes was emperor. The rest you know. I only remembered the letter when I was already a prisoner in my apartment with soldiers posted outside the door. I retrieved it from under the cushion and even now I can recall its rather curious phrasing: "Protect yourself, o emperor, for no small danger is being prepared for you this night." Then they took me away. All our troubles stem from that night and my decision to carry on playing dice rather than go to the aid of my brother.'

'Count Palatine, surely your own guilt is nothing as compared to that of others.'

'Of course, I hate and despise Tzimiskes and I hope he burns in hell. They peddled some story that he wasn't there and that it was some of his over-zealous friends who just happened to get into the palace and kill my brother, the emperor. Nobody believed that. Tzimiskes had been with us on all the great campaigns. Been promoted, decorated, fed, cossetted and given everything he could possibly want. In return, that was what he did.'

He was getting very worked up now and began to cough violently. A young woman hurried forward to give him some water, a granddaughter perhaps. When he had recovered, and had leaned back in his chair, I resumed.

'And my mother, Count Palatine?'

'I will say nothing of your mother, Majesty, except that since she was punished in this life, I hope that she escapes retribution in the next.'

The moment had come. I spoke very slowly and deliberately now.

'What if I were to tell you and these good people that another of the murderers of your brother is alive and unpunished and still holds high office?'

The atmosphere all at once became tense and expectant. Lalakon stepped forward, only to be gently pulled back by one of his comrades.

'I will spin you no tales. I will simply put the evidence before you. This is a letter that I was given by the late Ecumenical Patriarch Anthony. It bears his signature and has his seal attached. I suggest that your secretary should read it out loud.'

I held up the letter. The secretary came over, took it and began to read. When he had finished, there was silence. Then Leo gasped out:

'The Chamberlain was there? He told me he was unwell.'

'As he did me. I spoke to my mother before she died. She told me that it was the Chamberlain who arranged for John to be brought from his estates with his friends to Constantinople. He was as deeply involved as any of them.'

The men around the wall started shouting angrily but Leo lifted his hand and they calmed down.

'Why are you here, Majesty?'

'To do what emperors have a bounden duty to do: to administer God's law and to punish the guilty. For that I need your help and two things in particular. I want a guarantee that when the Chamberlain is removed from office, your son Bardas will not march on the capital with the army of the east. Second, I will need some assistance at a small ceremony that I am planning in January.'

'You shall have both,' said Leo.

And so it was settled. Perhaps there are those who might say that I was a hypocrite to pose as the avenger of Nikephoros, a man for whom I had held scant affection and who had illegally occupied my throne. All I can say is that such people must know very little about politics.

* * *

With Outis and Leo Phokas now on my side, the trap could be set. I gave orders for preparations to be made for the investiture of the Caesar on the feast of St Basil of Caesarea in January, keeping it a secret as I had told Nothos I would. As the weeks went by though, I found myself prey to misgivings. Surely he must have realised that something was wrong. He said and did nothing to indicate that he harboured any suspicion and he was as jovial as ever at our intimate dinners. He would not have noticed any difference in the flow of information from the Petrion because I had instructed Outis to pass most of it on to him, after certain parts had been extracted. The messages that reached him indicated that all was well and that I was as much under his control as ever. He would have had good grounds for believing that by removing Ouranos, he had put an end to my little rebellion and clipped my wings forever. Or perhaps, an insistent voice kept telling me, he knew perfectly well what I was up to and was merely biding his time, waiting for the moment to strike as he had on the last occasion.

That was why I continued to probe for weaknesses that I could use against him. In mid-December, I thought for a moment that I had found one. The Keeper told me that the archivist wished to see me. I groaned inwardly. I did not feel up to an interminable hour with George Alypios on what he had grubbed up from the shelves under the Hippodrome. But I appreciated his loyalty, doggedly persevering at the task that Ouranos and I had set him some years before, so I agreed to see him. When he arrived I mused on how different he looked now from that boy who had run all the way from the parade ground to claim his turn on the horse. He had a neat, square beard and long fingers that seemed to have been specially designed for turning the pages of documents and indicating particular words and lines in them. He wore the black archivist's robe, the colour was doubtless prescribed so as not to show the dirt, with a dark green sash. His hair was covered with a cap that came down over his ears, likewise useful protection against all that dust. In giving him the job in the archives I had created him and, I think, made him happy. He never attempted to make any political capital out of his sister's marriage to Constantine. He merely laboured on, day after day, year after year, in those sepulchral vaults.

As always, he had compiled a list of possibly interesting documents. He was one of those people who has to go through things in order, rather than cutting straight to the most important parts. So half an hour had gone by before he intoned:

'Tax cadastre of the province of Opsikion, 963 to 980. The latter is the latest year available Majesty, as the cadastres are not sent to the archives immediately from the tax office at the end of the financial year. These ones are particularly illuminating as they can be cross referenced with the register of tax exemptions.'

'Why,' I asked wearily, 'might one wish to do that?'

'It's rather intriguing actually,' said George reproachfully, 'The major landowner in the province has recently received tax exemption for all his properties. It means that the majority of the land pays no tax.'

Now I was all attention. He had brought over examples of both the cadastres and the exemption registers, and he pushed them across the table. He was right. The land had been entered in the exemption register as monastic property and so not liable for tax. In the cadastre it was given as private land but it was still exempt. All of it was the property of Basil Lekapenos, chamberlain.

'So the chamberlain has been defrauding the treasury of tax?,' I asked carefully.

'One might think that,' answered the meticulous George, 'but one must also collate with the register of monastic donations. It would appear that the chamberlain has donated all of his land in Asia Minor to the monastery of St Basil near the Form of Theodosius.'

It was Nothos' generosity that had intrigued George, not any financial irregularity, and so the possibility of another charge evaporated. That should have alerted me to what was really going on but although I did wonder for a moment why he should have given all his land away, I soon forgot about it as the day drew near.

By tradition, the investiture of a Caesar always takes place in the Hall of the Nineteen Couches. The audience is usually composed of members of the senate, senior army officers and high office holders from the palace administration. On this occasion they were all former soldiers who had served under Nikephoros, their wives, sons and daughters. Many of them, like the standard-bearer Lalakon, had been present when I had revealed Nothos' guilt to Leo. They were all provided with appropriate attire for the occasion. I stood on the dais at the far end, with the apse mosaic of Nikephoros and Theophano above me. Behind me were Roupenios and a eunuch who held a cushion with the Caesar's crown on it to preserve the illusion. I had prevailed on Constantine to attend as well, assuring him the night before that Nothos was not really going to be made Caesar and that the proceedings would be rather more lively than the usual palace ceremonies. The patriarch, Nicholas Chrysoberges and the Logothete Diaphantes had to be there too, though neither had any idea what was about to happen. Impy was outside with a squad of guards.

For weeks beforehand, I had gone over in my mind how the ceremony would play out. Nothos would enter the hall, flanked by a Magistros and a Praepositos, exactly as the books of precedence prescribe: he would have instantly noticed the slightest deviation. I imagined him marching confidently down the aisle between the crowd, nodding his head to left and right affably and, with the complacency of unchallenged power, not even noticing that most of those present were completely unknown to him. He would reach the dais and I would begin my speech. I expected him to incline his head graciously and give a slight wave of the hand in completely insincere self-deprecation without the slightest inkling of what was coming.

But on the day, it was not like that at all. He entered with his head bowed and his hands hidden in his sleeves. He remained with his eyes on the floor until he and the two supporters had halted in front of us. After they had completed the customary full obeisance, Nothos kissed Constantine's and my feet, knees and hands and then straightened up. As he did so, I caught his scent, the one he had always worn as long as I could remember. Smell has a power to transport us back into the past and for one moment I was again in the Kainourgion. He had worn well over the years. His thin hair was grey but he was far from bald and still perfectly proportioned. As he rose from his bow, we came almost face to face, even though I was standing on the dais for he was so much taller than me. I looked into his eyes, hoping to read there pride, guilt, complacency or contempt. I detected none of those things. Instead, there was a kind of softness, perhaps with a hint of sadness or resignation. With a wave of my hand, I gave the signal to proceed. The patriarch intoned:

'In the peace of the Lord, let us make supplication!'

I gave the response and began the speech, using the prescribed words for the occasion, long since learned by heart in my sessions with Nothos. Then I moved to the citation. 'Chamberlain, you served the state under our grandfather, you served it under our stepfather, you served it under our guardian and uncle and now you have served it under us. Your dedication to the purple-born emperors was so great that you would go to any lengths to protect and cherish them. You raised us like a father and watched over us with constant care.'

His eyes were still fixed on mine. Was he aware that the faces of the people around him were hard, stony and in no way appropriate to my congratulatory words? It was then that I struck:

'So great was that dedication that you even stooped to murder. You were complicit in the plot hatched against my stepfather Nikephoros Phokas whose image looks down on us from the apse. You stood by while armed men entered the room of an unarmed, unguarded and helpless man. You heard his cries and pleas for mercy and you did nothing.'

My words were a signal for servants to come forward and hustle the bewildered Diaphantes and the patriarch out of a side door. Now the veil was off and I had previously imagined what would happen next: Nothos would stand thunderstruck. His great head would lose its rosy colour as the dreadful truth dawned on him. He had left his apartment that morning without a care in the world to receive some flattering recognition but now in a second everything had changed. But it was not like that. He just kept his eyes fixed on mine. His expression did not change at all.

'You told me that you were ill and confined to your room when these events took place. You lied to me, your emperor. I have in my possession a letter with the signature and seal of the late Ecumenical Patriarch Anthony, in which he affirms that he saw you outside the bedchamber of the Emperor Nikephoros shortly after the deed was done.'

I stopped for dramatic effect, then:

'But those are not the worst things you did. To hide your own guilt you placed it elsewhere. True, you laid it on someone who had taken a part in the plot but their guilt was no greater than yours. You escaped unscathed, she endured years of imprisonment and misery. For that person was my mother, the late Empress Theophano.'

By now the crowd was starting to murmur threateningly and was pressing up against him and pulling at his garments. He was totally alone in a sea of enemies. Yet he did not flinch or take his eyes from mine.

'Yes, you were dedicated to the state but most of all you were dedicated to yourself. You used the power and influence that came with your office to line your own coffers. You acquired land in the province of Opsikion and then altered the records to secure tax exemption for them. So while those with one vineyard, a small holding or a vegetable plot, paid their dues to the emperor, you gave nothing.'

It was grossly unfair, of course, because he had given the land away but even emperors need to play the popular card sometimes. A roar went up from the crowd. But as for Nothos, still he did not react or move. He just kept his eyes fixed on mine and made no attempt to defend himself or to counter the unjust accusation.

'I declare that of this moment you are deprived of the office of Chamberlain. Remove the symbols of his office.'

Hands grabbed his staff, snatched the tall hat from his head, tore the brooch from his shoulder and ripped the silk robe and pallium from his back. Others grabbed his hands and began to pull the rings from his fingers one by one. This had all been carefully rehearsed beforehand.

'The one on the fourth finger of his right hand,' I pointed, 'he can keep.'

It was the one with St Basil of Caesarea that I had played with as a child. He just stood there, allowing them to do their worst. I nodded to Lalakon, who had stood to one side, and he now stepped forward. He punched Nothos full in the stomach, causing him to double up in agony and crash like a great tower to the floor. The crowd closed in, frantically kicking and beating him. It was enough: delay any more and he would be torn apart. I signalled to the six guards who were waiting at the back and they marched in, parting the crowd before them and forming a circle around the prostrate victim. They hauled him to his feet and began to drag him from the room, but his legs gave way under him and he sank back onto the floor. So they seized his feet and pulled him backwards and out of the hall. In my imaginings, I had foreseen a last throw of the die, a desperate appeal that he would have known to have had almost no chance whatever of success. He would throw himself before me and beg for mercy, reminding me of our long association: 'Majesty, am I not your Nothos?' And I would point my finger and shout back: 'As of this moment, you are nothing.' But as he had been mute throughout the entire proceedings, he stayed so to the very end.

Once it was over, and all that was left to show what had happened was a small trail of blood that snaked along the white marble slabs, I felt enormous relief. Up to the very last moment I had wondered whether, when brought face to face with my old mentor and teacher, I might not waver. Although his stony-faced passivity had been disconcerting, I had passed the test and shown myself worthy of the purple. And that was not all and it is only right that I should set down the whole truth. I had not just got through the performance of Nothos' disgrace. I had thoroughly enjoyed every minute of it.

***

After the dramatic denunciation in the Magnavra, I was merciful to Nothos. Rather than send him to some God-forsaken spot as he had Theophano, I had chosen St

Theophylact at Sosthenion on the European side of the Bosporus. The air is good there, wafting down from the Black Sea and the monastery has orchards and a garden. Not that I intended him to live there in comfortable seclusion. I made it clear to the abbot there that he must be made to take monastic vows. He was to participate in the life of the community like any other monk, sharing the frugal diet and attending all the offices, day and night. There were to be no visitors. I did not want him holding court there with a view to plotting against me and planning a return to power.

One summer's evening, about seven months after the Magnavra, a messenger arrived at the Brazen Gate bearing a small box. It was passed up the succession of layers that stand between the emperor and the outside world, searched and prodded by numerous hands. Finally the box was placed before me and I opened it to find the ring with the image of St Basil of Caesarea. With it was a note from the abbot at Sosthenion. A few days previously, Nothos had suddenly collapsed during vespers. They had carried him to his cell but he was quite dead even before they got him there. He was buried next day in the monks' cemetery with only an anonymous cross to mark the spot. Turning the ring over in my hand, it seemed to me that Nothos had pulled off one last sleight of hand. He had known all along. Diaphantes must have warned him that I was planning to contact Outis, in spite of Impy's threat. He had guessed that the Caesar ceremony was rigged but he had done nothing because he had also known that he was gravely ill and had not long to live. I remembered how he had taken to his bed during the negotiations with the envoy of the Buyid emir. He had never done that before apart from his feigned illness the night before the murder of Nikephoros. It must have been the beginning of the malady that ultimately killed him. That was why he had gifted all his land to the monastery. I had to face the galling knowledge that he had let me win. Where was the triumph in that? I opened a chest, threw in the ring and slammed it shut.

13

The Ambassador
and the Emperor (1024)

A l-Wuzara awoke and stared up at the whitewashed ceiling. Then he groaned. He had been far away in a delicious dream, wandering across the courtyard of the Al-Azhar mosque in the cool of the evening as the call for prayer sounded all around him. Flocks of birds were wheeling around the minarets and friendly faces greeted him with "As-salamu alaykum," asking why he had been away so long and exclaiming how good it was to have him back among them once more. But as he looked up at that ceiling, he knew the truth: he was still a virtual prisoner in an infidel city, confined to this wretched han by the water's edge. He had been languishing there ever since the catastrophic meeting in the Magnavra and it was now September. Soon the autumn would come and there would be no more sailings for Alexandria until the spring. The thought of spending the long winter in this place was too horrible to contemplate. He had heard dispiriting tales about the biting winds that swept down from the north and the heavy falls of snow that would block the streets for days on end. The dismal prospect made him shiver, although the room was warm in the morning sunshine. He turned his head to one side and saw that Aziz was standing by the bed, looking down at him gravely.

'Master, a man from the palace is here. He says that the emperor wishes to speak with you.'

So it was that one hour later, al-Wuzara's litter was making its way once more through the fresh morning streets. Jacob the interpreter walked on one side, Aziz on the other. The soldiers who had stood sentinel for all those weeks marched in front and behind, and the three officials from the palace led the way. They had not gone far before al-Wuzara poked his large head out of the curtains and pointed out to Aziz that they were going in a different direction than they did last time because the way seemed to be flat rather than going up a hill. Aziz told him that it was not to the Great Palace that they were going but to another place. Al-Wuzara retreated behind the curtains and sank back on the cushions, convinced now that they planned to murder him.

He was fully prepared and at peace with God when he felt the litter being set down, and he emerged from the curtains ready to face whatever fate had been written for him. He found himself in front of a large colonnaded mansion, constructed of heavy blocks of dark stone. It was an impressive residence but the dwellings to either side of it were small and shabby and grass grew between the cobbles on the narrow street. A weathered and lichened statue was partially embedded in a wall. He looked behind him and saw a row of dilapidated tenements, from whose windows a few pale faces peered out above lines of washing. Yes, he thought, this is the kind of God-forsaken place that they would bring me to die.

As they walked up the steps and through the colonnade, the double doors of the entrance were opened from the inside and the party found themselves in a wide entrance hall, lined with armed men. My assassins, thought al-Wuzara, but then he saw John the Chamberlain waiting for him in his tall hat and with his staff in his hand. John told him through Jacob that the emperor would meet him in the room on the right and that there was no need for a full obeisance, merely a bow from the waist. After last time, al-Wuzara had little faith in the Chamberlain and his guidance on etiquette but was slightly reassured when Jacob translated an aside that the emperor was sometimes impatient of ceremonial and that he preferred to speak to ambassadors as man to man.

So the ambassador and the Chamberlain entered the next room together, side by side. It was almost as wide as the hall and in the centre of it was a large marble table. The emperor was sitting at the far end and a chair had been placed for al-Wuzara at the other. A line of courtiers and servants were standing along the walls behind the emperor. Al-Wuzara had noticed that the Romans always stood lined up in the presence of the emperor. For all that this one protested his fondness for informality, as a people they were obsessed with rank and hierarchy. It was not like that in Cairo where all men were equal under God, even the caliph. Al-Wuzara made his bow and was motioned by the Chamberlain to sit opposite the emperor. Aziz and Jacob took up their stations behind him.

The room was well lit by a line of windows between pillared arches just below the ceiling. This time, he was able to see the emperor quite clearly, so he noticed that the cloak he was wearing was rather old and worn and, for that matter, none too clean. He realised with a shock that the emperor had dead, expressionless eyes. They reminded al-Wuzara of those of the shark that he had watched being hauled alive onto the quayside at Alexandria when he was a boy. It had thrashed and wriggled but the eyes remained fixed and staring, giving no hint of any pain, thought or emotion. Those eyes, and the forked grey beard that resembled inverted diabolic horns, gave this emperor a decidedly menacing appearance. Al-Wuzara could well believe the story that the caretaker had told him about the emperor blinding thousands of his Bulgar prisoners. A scribe came up with a sealed letter. His hands were shaking as he laid it at the emperor's elbow.

Without any preamble, the emperor began to speak in Greek, stopping after a few sentences to allow Jacob to translate:

'We are concerned, Mr Ambassador, about the thinness of your countenance and we fear that the weeks of confinement may not have agreed well with you. So we have invited you to this place, our Palace of Petrion, rather than to the Great Palace, in order that you may feel more at your ease in these less magnificent surroundings which may be closer to those to which you are accustomed.'

Al-Wuzara judged it prudent to ignore the sly insult and made a few appropriate remarks about it being his honour to attend His Majesty wherever he choose. The emperor's own interpreter stepped forward and whispered in Greek in his ear. The emperor started to speak again. Al-Wuzara tried to look as if he were following the incomprehensible words, but he found it difficult to meet those shark eyes and his own involuntarily wandered to the line of men along the wall who were all wearing identical long gowns, white with a red stripe from the right shoulder to the hip and with generous sleeves in which their hands were hidden. They were young, suave and sleek, their well-cut hair reaching almost to their shoulders, their beards carefully trimmed. Well-connected too, the ambassador surmised, to obtain a post so close to the emperor. As his eye went down the line, though, it suddenly stopped abruptly. One figure looked distinctly out of place. He wore the same gown but, as he was noticeably shorter than the others, it was rather too long for him. An attempt had evidently been made to compel his hair to conform but a stubborn tuft stuck out at an odd angle. His beard straggled hopelessly. He conspicuously lacked the polish normally exuded by the carefully selected attendants of the great and the good. While the others stood motionless and impassive, this one had some difficulty keeping still as the slow conversation went on. He shifted position, the folds of his gown twitching as he placed one foot over the other. Then he noticed that the Chamberlain was glaring at him and he snapped his shoe back on the floor. There it stayed for the rest of the meeting, its owner occasionally glancing furtively at the Chamberlain as if fearing further reproach.

The ambassador's reverie ended when the emperor's monologue stopped. Jacob then translated: 'We regret the sternness with which we have been compelled to treat you and your followers. That was not of our choosing. The fault lies with your master the Caliph who sent you here to negotiate a renewal of the treaty while planning to violate it in Syria. Surely you can see that such actions do not accord with the rules of civilised behaviour. You must agree that on learning of this plot we had no choice but to exercise great caution in our dealings with you! As regards that, you should know that our borders in Syria have recently been reinforced and are secure. Your master would find it difficult to gain any advantage there. Indeed he should look to his own frontiers which I breached with ease shortly before I first made a treaty with his father.'

As he listened to this rendering, al-Wuzara wondered whether the emperor's tone, unlike Jacob's flat one, was in fact deeply sarcastic. One never knew with translations but if that were the case, it would make him even more sinister somehow, exercising some fiendish sardonic wit at the ambassador's expense. It was odd too that he made no mention of the Egyptian invasion in Syria that he had been so angry about last time. The emperor resumed but al-Wuzara noticed that the harsh edge to his voice was beginning to soften, even before Jacob translated:

'But come, we cannot let such trifles be the cause of enmity between us. Your master knows that he needs peace with us so that he can protect himself from the threat from Baghdad. And it is peace that we offering, just as we allow his name to be commemorated in the mosque of the Mitaton. But peace does not fall unbidden from the heavens. It has to be earned or bought or at the very least cajoled if its benefits are to be enjoyed.'

The emperor paused at that point and Jacob translated. Al-Wuzara knew this moment well from his many previous embassies. This was when the emperor was going to spell out what it was he wanted.

'Not long ago, the aunt of your master, the Lady Sitt al-Mulk, who was then regent of Egypt during his minority, sent to us the patriarch of Jerusalem with a message. She regretted the action of her brother, Caliph Hakim, in destroying the Church of the Holy Sepulchre, a sacred shrine built over the site of the Resurrection of our Lord Jesus Christ. On her behalf, the patriarch asked how amends might be made for this and we gave him a friendly message to convey to Cairo. But then we heard the lamentable news that this wise regent had died and no more was said on this matter by the court of the caliph. Instead, plots were made to violate our border in Syria. We could, of course, gather our army and march to Jerusalem next spring if we chose. Our uncle the Lord John did this in the year 975. But we propose the way of peace. For as we allow your master control of the Mitaton, so he must permit us to keep the Holy Sepulchre in our care. He must allow us to rebuild the church, to appoint the clergy who service it and to choose the man who is to be patriarch of Jerusalem. That is our price of peace and we think it a fair one.'

Then John the Paphlagonian came to the table, took the sealed letter from the emperor's elbow and placed it before al-Wuzara. The ambassador saw that it carried the gold seal of Basil II and his brother Constantine. The emperor spoke again, Jacob whispering in Arabic:

'Bear this letter to your master. It lays out our terms in full for a lasting peace between us. Let us pray that the caliph and his counsellors choose the path of life.'

The short man that al-Wuzara had noticed earlier was now walking towards the table carrying two goblets while another attendant followed with an engraved wine flask.

'We know that your religion disapproves of the imbibing of wine but we hope now that you will put aside your scruples and join with us in a cup to mark the end of all enmity. This one comes from our vineyards on the Sea of Marmara, around the port of Ganos.'

Al-Wuzara did put aside his scruples so the wine was poured and the emperor drank first to show that it was safe. Then his shark-eyes, which up to then had gazed on some point in the middle distance beyond al-Wuzara's shoulder, abruptly fixed on to his face :

'Tell me, Mr Ambassador, what role does the vizier fulfil in the court at Cairo?'

'One of great importance, Majesty. He is the chief of the caliph's advisers and his main prop and support. He is especially important in times like the present, when our caliph is young and inexperienced. He looks to the vizier as to a wise father and benefits from his accumulated sagacity.'

'It is nothing like that here,' replied the emperor. 'Our chamberlain is merely a kind of housekeeper. The emperor alone makes decisions based on his own wisdom.'

Al-Wuzara regretted at that moment that John the Paphlagonian was standing behind him and that he could not see his face. He noted that the emperor did not like his chamberlain which was something that would need to be reported in Cairo.

He made an appropriate observation about the emperor's long experience exempting him from the need for a vizier. A few other remarks were passed and then the emperor wished him a safe and pleasant journey back to Egypt. John the

Paphlagonian struck his staff on the ground and the audience was over. The ambassador and his companions withdrew backwards, bowing as they went. It was only when they were once again in the sunshine and walking down the steps of the mansion that an overwhelming sense of relief washed over al-Wuzara. He would, after all, live to see another dawn and soon he would be sailing for home.

14

Abydos (985-9)

Almost the first thing I did after the dismissal of Nothos was to order that my mother be reburied with a ceremony appropriate to her rank. The Patriarch Nicholas quibbled that there was no precedent or order of service for the reburial of an empress. I countered by pointing out that the body of Emperor Michael III had been moved from Chrysopolis to the church of the Holy Apostles in 886 and I ordered that this precedent should be adapted for Theophano. So one blustery March day, a procession with the coffin set out from the convent of St Euphemia. I was waiting for it at the Apostles, along with Constantine and Anna who never knew that I had seen Theophano before her death. It did my heart good to see the patriarch censing the casket and intoning:

'Go out, empress, the Emperor of Emperors and the Lord of Lords summons you!'

My father's sarcophagus was opened and Theophano joined him there at last. I did not think she would have wanted to be with Tzimiskes in the church of the Saviour.

During that same spring, I set about reorganising the way things were run in the Great Palace. I abandoned the office in the Lausiakos and I announced that instead I would sit on the throne in the Nineteen Couches for one hour each day, with a makeshift desk laid over the arms. Documents for my attention would be brought in, a scribe would read each one out and I would listen as long as necessary. Then I would either demand to see it myself or order that it be sent to Constantine for signature. That saved a great deal of time as my left handed scrawl is rather slow. To this day the Keepers and other functionaries crowd and jostle around the throne during signing hour, clutching their pieces of paper, vying with each other to bring their particular documents to my attention. And needless to say, the inkpot is no longer held by a Keeper. It stays firmly on an arm of the throne where I can reach it.

When it came to dictating letters and dispatches, I announced that this task would be fulfilled whenever and wherever was pleasing to me. I tried various rooms in the Lausiakos and elsewhere throughout the palace, yet none of them seemed to suit somehow. In the end, I found that the best way was to walk along the corridors with the scribes following after me armed with their wax tablets to jot down my words in abbreviated form. The fair copy would be brought to me in the Nineteen couches for signing. The Keepers despaired and lamented that this way the phrasing of the dispatches would be terse and inelegant. That, I replied, was exactly the point. Doubtless these arrangements caused endless inconvenience for the bureaucrats but I have never been troubled by regrets about that. One should never make it too easy for those people as it only encourages them to create further unnecessary hurdles.

The next step was to institute a review of all laws and grants that had been made since Nikephoros' coup in 963. About half of the legislation was repealed, mainly when I suspected that it had been framed and promoted by Nothos. I cancelled many of the appointments, pensions and honours that he had awarded to his cronies, although political considerations dictated that some of them be confirmed. I reluctantly allowed Kalokyris Delphinas to stay on as governor of Bari, largely because I could not think of a better way to keep him out of Constantinople. I had land that Nothos had donated to the monastery of St Basil confiscated and the new buildings that he had added to it demolished. That got me a reputation for impiety because I can never resist a jest and I quipped, in front of witnesses, that I was doing the monks a favour by stripping away all distractions from their contemplation of higher things. In my defence, I should point out that among the laws that I repealed was the one that had been brought in during Nikephoros' reign, restricting the amount of land that could be gifted to monasteries and convents.

Then there was the matter of the great offices of state. I found some non-entity to replace Nothos as chamberlain. When it came to the Logothete of the Drome, it should be noted that I did not dismiss Diaphantes out of hand, although he fully deserved it given his slavish attachment to Nothos and Tzimiskes. In fact, I promoted him. I discovered that he had been ordained into minor orders as a deacon. Many intellectuals seek this to provide a second career path in case they cannot get a post in the palace administration. So I raised him to be a bishop, no less. The catch was that his see was Amaseia, a miserable windswept hole on the Anatolian plateau in eastern Asia Minor. It is two hundred miles from the nearest library and I doubt if anyone there has heard of his commentary on Euripides. From there he sent doleful letters to his few friends, couched in impeccable Attic Greek, complaining about the weather and quality of the wine. They were later recopied and collected into a volume as shining examples of prose composition. I expect that future generations of students will have to read them and pen sentences in the same style: "What would Diaphantes have said to the emperor when he made him a bishop?" He ended his days in Amaseia, after sending me a pitiful letter begging to be recalled. It grieves me to say that in this last communication I could not help but notice one or two grammatical infelicities.

It goes without saying that now I was master of the Great Palace, I wanted to have Nikephoros Ouranos and Demetrius Spondyles back at my side as soon as possible. Ouranos I had lined up to replace Diaphantes as Logothete and I was planning to give Spondyles at house in Hebdomon so that I could join him there sometimes in the summer. So that same spring, I despatched an embassy to Baghdad to negotiate the release of Ouranos and started to make enquiries as to Spondyles' whereabouts. My first thought was to send for Kontostephanos to attend me and to ask whether Spondyles had been transferred out of the palace guard. Perhaps I could have phrased the request more tactfully as Impy became defensive and blurted out that he could not know the whereabouts of every man under his command. I pacified him and I think I persuaded him that I had not joined the rest of humanity in a plot to undermine him. I did ask though that a search of the rosters be made to find out where Spondyles had been lodged. The answer was brought a few days later by a junior scribe. The Strator Spondyles had vanished from the rosters about six years ago. I sent someone to the treasury office: the Strator Spondyles had not collected his annual stipend for seven years. It was then that I started to feel apprehensive. Leaving the Great Palace was one thing but neglecting to collect the salary suggested that all was not well. I had no alternative but to put the matter into the hands of Outis, suggesting that the enquiry should begin in Psamathia.

While I was in this limbo regarding Spondyles, news reached me that Ouranos was on his way back to Constantinople. The Buyid Emir had been rather surprised to learn that such a prisoner was being detained and he had released Ouranos the moment that my envoy made my request known. I gave orders that he was to be brought across Anatolia by the fastest possible means, using the post horses that are stabled at intervals along the main route. I could not wait to see him again, to tell him about the changes I had made and to discuss with him the next move. When I heard that his ship was approaching from Chrysopolis, I went down to the Boukoleon harbour, so that I would be the first to greet him. He had been away for over three years so I was expecting him to look different. But I was not prepared for the gaunt and wasted figure that walked down the gangplank. He was still dressed as an Arab and his beard now included quite a few grey hairs. When he replied to my speech of welcome he spoke his own language rather haltingly for he had rarely had the opportunity to use it during his incarceration in Baghdad. There was a moment of awkwardness before I suggested that he should be escorted at once to his wife who was waiting in the house beyond the Hippodrome.

A few days elapsed and then I sent him an invitation to dine with me at the palace. We did so in the Nineteen Couches, just the two of us, as I had used to with Nothos but it soon became obvious to me, and probably to him, that our relationship could ever be the same again. I was relaxed and jovial, he was stiff and deferential: a subject in the presence of his emperor. Various conversational sallies, such as reminding him of our alliance against the chamberlain fell flat. In desperation, I asked him outright to be Logothete of the Drome. Without hesitation he pleaded that he was unworthy of such a high office and begged to be given a military post instead. So I offered him Domestic of the West, only to hear him decline and request the lesser rank of Archon. With as good grace as I could muster, I promised him that and we parted. At first, I had to admit, I was suspicious. Had he been suborned by the emir during his stay in Baghdad? Or had the Phokas clan got to him as he travelled back across their heartlands? So again I turned to Outis and had Ouranos followed. All I got was a dry catalogue of blameless rectitude. The only unusual thing that he did was make regular visits to the church of the Forty Martyrs where he would sometimes spend hours on his knees before the icon of Christ the Saviour, the one that had once miraculously spoken to Emperor Maurice. Only then did I fully appreciate the toll that his experiences in Baghdad had taken. I accepted that he had done quite enough in my service and resolved to leave him in peace. I later managed to persuade him to accept the office of Magistros but he never again involved himself in the palace administration so I saw little of him.

It was while I was receiving the reports on Ouranos that another arrived about Spondyles. These communications always stood out in the pile by virtue of their very innocuousness and their bland seal bearing the emblem of the Wine Steward of Petrion. It is easiest if I give the contents in full.

Report into search for Demetrius Spondyles, Strator, hereinafter known as the Subject.
Proceeded to Psamathia as instructed but initial enquiries unsuccessful. Finally blacksmith working by wall of monastery of Euthymios said he knew of a widow Spondyles buried in graveyard of said monastery about one year ago. Could be Subject's mother. Referred me to a Mrs Loukites, living by monastery of St Mamas. Found Mrs Loukites, married to a corn merchant, two children. Initially reticent until shown seal. Then admitted subject had

been her first husband and that he had been enrolled with guards in Great Palace. Deceased some six years ago. Was custom of Subject and informant to travel to Psamathia in September to assist in harvest at vineyard of informant's father. Subject was missed at noon by other harvesters but search did not commence until after the siesta. Found deceased in remote corner of vineyard. Body taken to St Euthymios. Monks said he must have fallen from ladder and hit his head while also impaling self with knife. Bled to death while unconscious. Age of subject at time of death estimated at about twenty or twenty-one years. Interred in graveyard of said monastery. Mrs Loukites did not go back to palace and did not send word of Subject's death as did not know who to send it to. She says sorry for any inconvenience.

And that was that. His passing summed up in the dry phrases of an official report. I saw no reason to question it or to suspect anyone having brought about his death. Neither Nothos nor Diaphantes nor anyone else for that matter had ever been aware of my regard for him, so carefully had I covered my tracks. In fact, he never knew himself. He just thought I was being kind and generous. No, this was exactly as reported: a stupid, careless mishap. I could picture the scene. In the vineyards of Psamathia, there is not a great deal of space, so they train the vines up on trellises to make the most of it. I could just see him hacking enthusiastically at the grapes on the higher branches without thinking to make sure his ladder was firmly secured on the ground, leaning too far to reach that difficult, out-of-the-way bunch. How very like him that he should have ended his days in such a way: so much enthusiasm, so little to show for it. How ironic it was that the very quality that drew me to him should bring about his end. And how appropriate that once he had fallen, no one even noticed him as his life force seeped away into the soil.

* * *

As far as I can remember, I did not feel the loss of Ouranos and Spondyles at the time. That might have been partly because I had already been forced to do without them for some years. But the fact was that there was simply no time for morbid introspection: at that very moment, I was facing the greatest crisis of my reign, indeed of my life. Before his disgrace, Nothos had been dealing with the major problem of the day: our relations with Bulgaria. Back in 971, John Tzimiskes had subdued the whole country and reincorporated it into the Roman empire but after his death, the Bulgars had risen in revolt led by a man called Samuel. It all started as a bit of local unrest but Nothos was reluctant to commit troops to the region for the main threat seemed to come from Skleros and his revolt in Asia Minor. So the trouble grew and grew. Samuel developed from a local war chief into a national leader and had himself proclaimed Tsar of the Bulgars. Town after town ejected its Roman governor and opened its gates to him. He took over Great Preslav which had been the old capital of Bulgaria and then pushed south over the Balkan Mountains. By the time Nothos was overthrown, he had built up a large and threatening Bulgarian state.

It now fell to me to decide our response. Thanks to Bardas Phokas, the Skleros revolt was over so there was no longer a need to keep large numbers of troops in Asia Minor. The agreement that I had made with Leo Phokas had held good. Bardas did not move west with his army when he heard of Nothos' fall. Like the rest of the Phokas clan he was shocked by the revelation that the Chamberlain had been involved in his uncle's death and was pleased to see that he had been brought to justice. So I now had a choice. I could send Bardas Phokas against Samuel and the Bulgars. The man had proved his mettle by his raids into Abbasid and Fatimid territory and by his crushing of the Skleros revolt, so that unleashing him would be the best way to squash Samuel's pretensions. But there was a danger in doing that. If Bardas were to triumph, he would be placed in the position that his uncle had occupied in 963, as the state's greatest general and as a potential emperor.

That was why I went for the second option: I would lead the army against Samuel myself. After all, I had made a close study of the manuals of military tactics during my education and I had many of Emperor John's veterans, such as Roupenios to advise me. Many of them had taken part in his 971 Bulgarian campaign, so they knew both the terrain and the enemy. That gave me an advantage over Bardas whose experience was largely confined to Asia Minor. So in the spring of 986, I mustered the western army of 17,000 men and marched north through Thrace. I was careful to follow the sage advice of Roupenios and the others. They counselled that it would be safest not to take the whole of the army into the Bulgarian heartland. The passes through the mountains are notorious ambush points and if we found our way blocked at the end of the campaign we would need to be able to call up reinforcements from the south. So I left 2,000 men at Plovdiv under Leo Melissenos, the old crony of Constantine, who had now become a very competent soldier. There they were to await further orders.

The rest of the army forged on and we crossed the mountains without incident. Our first objective was the town of Sofia which we surrounded with a view to starving it into surrender. That was when things started to go wrong. We had not seen Samuel or his army, though we knew that they must be somewhere nearby. Instead, small groups of Bulgars would attack our soldiers as they left the camp to forage. Our supplies started to dwindle alarmingly and I began to doubt whether we would be able to maintain the siege long enough to force the town's surrender. Then one night, Impy Kontostephanos came to my tent. He had by now risen to the rank of domestic in the wave of appointments I had made to clear away those who had been too close to Nothos. I remember the urgent expression on his face as he looked up at me in the lamp light and told me that Leo Melissenos had raised the standard of revolt in Plovdiv. He had taken the 2,000 men that were supposed to be protecting our rear and was marching on Constantinople. That settled it. I ordered the army to break off the siege of Sofia and to withdraw. We fixed on the pass known as Trajan's Gate as our route, hoping that Samuel might go for one of the other passes. Unfortunately, I suspect that he had men watching all of them. They let most of the column go through but then attacked the baggage train which is always the slowest part of any army. The troops at the rear ran forward to escape, causing a bottleneck at the far end of the pass and bringing the march to a halt. Bulgar archers now started to pick the soldiers off from behind rocks on the towering slopes. There was only one thing for it. I shouted in Armenian: "To me! To me!." The elite Armenian regiment that we had with us had been scattered among the crowd of fleeing soldiers but now they coalesced around me and we forced our way through the crowd and out of the pass. That had the effect of clearing the bottle neck and the army streamed out behind us but not before we had suffered heavy casualties and lost the baggage train and my tent.

Wretchedly, we marched back to Plovdiv and as we drew near a group of riders came out of the town to welcome us and to say that the Lord Leo Melissenos was making ready for our arrival. The report of his rebellion had been false. He had remained loyally at his post for the entire summer. Once we were in Plovdiv and I was established in the governor's house, I summoned Impy and told him that his antipathy for Melissenos had led him to believe a baseless rumour and to mislead his emperor. Anyone else would have humbly accepted the reproof, thankful to escape worse punishment. Not so Impy.

He actually argued with me and declared that he had been acting on credible intelligence. That was too much and I lost control of myself. I rushed at him and grabbed him by his satyr's hair and beard and shook him. Then I hurled him onto the floor. But I did not dismiss him and I forgave him in time. The fact was that he was about the only person who would ever dare to tell me the truth to my face.

* * *

The debacle at Trajan's Gate gave the Phokas clan just the pretext they had been waiting for. In spite of the agreement that I had hammered out with Leo and our temporary alliance against Nothos, they remained deeply suspicious of me. When Leo died early in 986, they would not have him buried in Constantinople. Instead they put the body onto a ship in the harbour of Sophia and sailed him down the Aegean and across to Cappadocia where he could rest among his virtuous military forefathers rather than in the corrupt mire of the capital. During the winter after the defeat by the Bulgars, Phokas agents circulated in Asia Minor canvassing support and some even operated in Constantinople itself. Outis brought me regular updates on their activities. We managed to arrest a few but most eluded us.

Finally, in August 987, they were ready to issue their challenge. Bardas went to the house of Eustathios Maleinos in Caesarea where my brother had once spent so many instructive months. There, surrounded by his family and prominent supporters, he was proclaimed emperor of the Romans. Emerging onto a balcony that overlooked the town's main square, he gave an impassioned speech to a huge crowd, many of whom were soldiers and ex-soldiers. Outis later gave me a transcript of the gist of it. Bardas listed the achievements of his ancestors and of his uncle and reminded his listeners of his own recent triumphs on the eastern borders. These he contrasted with the efforts of the "effete princeling" which was how he referred to me. Whereas the great Nikephoros had shared the dangers and hardships faced by his men, I had lived in luxury during the campaign in a vast tent that was now the property of Tsar Samuel. When the army was trapped in the pass at Trajan's Gate, I had ordered my bodyguard to hack a path through my own men so that I could save my skin and then left the rest to die at the hands of the Bulgars. Who was most fitted to rule: a pampered creature that knew no world but the palace or the nephew of Nikephoros who inherited the proud military virtues of the Phokas clan? Needless to say, the speech was greeted with wild euphoria and shouts of "Long live Emperor Bardas!" And he was right – my military record at that point was shabby compared to his.

As soon as I found out that Bardas had been proclaimed, I sent a squad of troops down to the house by the harbour of Sophia. It was deserted. They all must have been forewarned and had left by ship. In the weeks that followed, thousands flocked to his banner. Cappadocians were naturally eager to back the local candidate but he found support in all quarters. Outis was soon bringing me reports that, all over the empire, prominent men were leaving their posts to travel to Bardas' camp. Among them were Leo Melissenos and his brother Theognostos so perhaps Impy had been right after all. He certainly did not miss the opportunity to say: "Told you so!" Another was Nothos' factotum Kalokyris Delphinas who quit his command in Bari and made the long journey by sea. That surprised me. He could easily have stayed put and even if Bardas had won, he probably would have remained in post. Perhaps he had not forgiven me for bringing down his patron. Some of the adherents of John Tzimiskes also joined Bardas and were welcomed in Caesarea. The murder of Nikephoros was forgotten as the soldiers came together against the common enemy: me.

With such a force at his disposal, there was nothing to stand in the usurper's way. While Skleros had taken years to occupy a significant part of Asia Minor, by the end of 988, Bardas had virtually the whole land mass in his hands and his forces were drawing close to the Bosporus. My memories of that year are of a succession of meetings in the Blue Council Room, with dusty messengers being brought up from the Brazen Gate with news of the fall of this or that city or the defection of this or that regiment. Sometimes I could bear it no more and my attention would wander out of the window to the Judas tree that stood in the courtyard. I envied the chattering birds that hopped among its branches without a care in the world and felt somehow resentful that they did not share my fear. Come the winter, most of them would doubtless perish but they, unlike me, were blissfully unaware of their impending doom.

It was in this kind of atmosphere, when the main topic on the streets of Constantinople was how the Emperor Bardas would treat me when he took Constantinople, that the arrival of an embassy from the ruler of Kiev, Vladimir, was announced. We were in the Blue Council Room as the chamberlain relayed their message. Vladimir had captured the town of Cherson, our trading outpost in the Crimea. He was perfectly willing to give it back to us but he made three conditions. We had to pay him four thousand pounds of gold. We had to provide opportunities for Russians to serve for pay in our armed forces. Those were hardly onerous. Lastly, we had to agree to his marriage with my sister Anna. A frisson of horror passed through the council chamber. Longer serving bureaucrats remembered Nikephoros' haughty reply when the king of Germany had proposed that Anna marry his son back in 968. The king of France had recently made the same request and had likewise been rebuffed. Why then should we allow the purple-born daughter of a purple-born emperor to marry a barbarian who was not even a Christian? Everyone looked at me.

'We shall receive the Russian envoys in the Magnavra.'

So it was that the next day, Constantine and I were sitting side by side in the Magnavra facing the four Russian envoys. They had hairy arms like joints of meat that protruded from their sleeveless leather jerkins and long platted hair which they had apparently smeared with rancid butter. I turned to the interpreter and instructed him to ask them how many Russians would come to fight in my armies if we agreed to the terms. The answer was at least three thousand. Such a contingent of formidable Russian troops would be a very useful addition to our dwindling forces in the current crisis. In my mind, I quickly reviewed the advantages of accepting Vladimir's terms. If he did not yield Cherson, we would never be able to recapture it, so that this was the only opportunity to recover the town. The only sticking point was his demand to marry my sister.

'The prince of Kiev must know,' I began, 'that emperors of the Romans are unwilling to ally themselves in marriage to foreigners and especially to those who do not share our religious faith.'

At this point in time, the Russians worshipped the thunder and lightning god Perun, whose silver headed idol resided in a temple on the hill above Kiev. The leader of the envoys replied:

'The Lord Vladimir is willing to change his faith and to lead his people with him. He has been contemplating this change for some time. He thought about adopting the faith of the Muslims but then learned that they prohibit the drinking of liquor. He considered the Jews but then wondered why their god had allowed them to lose their land. He thought about the Christians of the west but there is no joy or spectacle in their religion. He wishes to adopt the Christian faith of Constantinople for when we go into your churches, we encounter such beauty that we know not whether we are on earth or in heaven. Our master would like you to send priests to Kiev to instruct us.'

I pondered again. Anna was now twenty-five and lived a sequestered existence in the women's quarters. She saw no one apart from Aunt Theodora, her chaplain and the servants and came out only to attend church services. Here was a marvellous opportunity for her, not only to help crush a rebellion but also to convert the heathen, although the latter task would not be so difficult when the heathen were lined up at sword point for baptism on the orders of their ruler. There were other considerations too. I gazed at the Russian envoys and assumed that their master looked the same. I remembered the taunts that Anna had directed at me in the schoolroom: how appropriate that her destruction of Arus should lead her into a close encounter with a very real Rus.

I turned to the interpreter:

'Tell the envoys that we accept all three of their master's demands, subject to the restoration of Cherson and his acceptance of the Christian faith.'

The Russian troops arrived in the late autumn of 988 and I reviewed them on the polo field. They came just in time. Bardas was by then nearly at the Marmara and the moment of crisis was fast approaching. He was nothing if not methodical. He knew that he could never take Constantinople by direct assault and hoped instead that his closet supporters inside the city would open the gates to him. His strategy was to make a show of strength, first by occupying all the land facing the capital on the Asian side. He divided his force, sending part of it north to seize Chrysopolis while he himself headed for the Dardanelles. Once he had crossed the strait, he would be able to march up to the Land Walls and enclose the capital in a vice.

I awoke one morning to be told that Bardas' banners could be seen flying from the rooftops of Chrysopolis. The people of the city could see them too and no doubt they drew the intended conclusion. Even now, I tried to negotiate. A messenger was sent to Bardas' commander in Chrysopolis, pleading with him to end the civil strife and withdraw. I received a coolly insolent refusal, along the lines that he was carrying out the instructions of the Lord Emperor Bardas and it was for me to end the conflict by yielding the capital to the rightful ruler. I was taken aback to discover from the messenger that the commander at Chrysopolis was none other than Kalokyris Delphinas. I wonder whether he would have been quite so cocky if he had known about the Russians. I had hoped to keep them back until the main clash with Bardas but I saw now that Chrysopolis would have to be recovered quickly before Delphinas became too well entrenched there.

We rowed over in a fleet of small boats with muffled oars one January night. It was freezing cold but I insisted on going with them. When we drew near to Chrysopolis, it became clear that Delphinas had done nothing to prepare for an attack. His men were all inside, warming themselves by the fire: my reputation for military incompetence had proved an asset. When the Russians landed and fanned out through the town, there was no opposition and it was merely a case of rounding up the garrison. The citizens were very co-operative in identifying those who had donned civilian clothes and tried to melt into the crowd. By the time the sun was up, the lines of prisoners were being marched down to the harbour to be shipped back to Europe. Most would be pardoned and sent off to fight the Bulgars. It was the best kind of victory: a bloodless one.

Delphinas had tried to make a run for it but had not got very far before being recognised and pointed out to my men. By then, my tent had been pitched on the far side of the town and it was there that they brought him before me as I sat outside with Impy behind me. In an attempt at disguise, Delphinas had dressed himself up like a labourer but otherwise he looked much the same as he had on the night of the excursion to the Holy Apostles. I demanded to know why he had thrown in his lot with a traitor and betrayed his lawful sovereign. Even now I can scarcely believe what he did in response. He bowed low, spread his hands wide and whined:

'Saul, Saul, why do you persecute me?'

He straightened up and his gaze met mine as if to say: 'Come on, I know all about you. You are no better than me. We both remember where we went.' He still did not take me seriously: a figure of fun, to be jeered at under the trees at Hebdomon. I expected his jarring laughter to assail my ears at any moment. Yet I controlled my fury. Keeping my eyes fixed on his, I inclined my head over my left shoulder towards Impy.

'Domestic, do you see that oak tree, the one with the low branches? Isn't it a fine one?'

'An excellent specimen, Majesty.'

'Take this traitor to it and hang him.'

Delphinas did not react: I honestly doubt that he believed my words. I turned away and went back into my tent so that no one could see how outraged and upset I was, so I never knew when it dawned on him that he was about to die. When I came out later, he was hanging there, his tongue lolling out of his mouth, swaying gently to and fro in the breeze. It was crude, I admit, for I gave way to anger rather than reflect on what might be appropriate but at least that night at the Apostles was purged for ever.

$$* * *$$

Bardas would never have become the legend that he was if he had allowed himself to be downcast by a minor reverse such as that at Chrysopolis. He responded by laying siege to the town of Abydos on the Dardanelles. He still had a considerable numerical superiority along with his family's unblemished record of invincibility. So in spite of the heartening coup at Chrysopolis and the presence of the Russians, the chances of defeating his revolt looked as remote as ever. It was then that I remembered that discussion that I had once had with Nothos about how winning by killing one man is preferable to victory in battle. That got me wondering whether I could find someone prepared to deal a blow to the very head. With that in mind, I decided to summon Outis to ask if anything could be done. He was pessimistic. Gathering information was one thing, covert assassination quite another. Anyone could do the first, the second required ruthless dedication and a nerve of steel. Such qualities did not come cheap. I authorised him to offer an estate in the Peloponnese and a generous pension for life. Then I returned to making plans for the final military showdown.

That came in April of 989 when I marched to the relief of Abydos with a mixed force of the Russians and some of the European regiments. Constantine rode with me. Bardas took the bulk of his forces away from investing the town to bar our way about three miles from its walls. As the opposing armies faced each other, the pre-battle rituals began: catcalls and profanities, obscene gestures and mooning. A civil war gives much more scope for this as both sides speak the same language and can understand the insults being hurled, although the Russians looked rather bemused. My troops were drawn up around a slight hillock on which I had pitched my tent: it gave a fine view across the straits to Gallipoli and the European side. I was standing with an icon of the Virgin which I had had brought down from Blachernae. I had ordered leather thongs to be fitted on the back so that I could wear it like a shield. Thus everyone could see that I was relying on the protection of Our Lady. I also had my tiny St Demetrius concealed about my person. Constantine had a different way of inspiring the troops. He emerged from his tent bare-chested and brandishing a spear. He bellowed over their heads:

'Come on, Bardas, you cocksucker!'

He then hurled his spear towards the enemy lines (it fell far short) and made a series of energetic pelvic thrusts, to the delight of our side and the mocking derision of the other. This time the Russians got it too and roared with laughter.

Meanwhile, in the midst of Bardas' lines, a figure was elbowing its way to the front. It was Theognostos Melissenos, Constantine's old confederate.

'What are you doing over there, guys?,' he shouted across to our men. 'You should be here with us, serving a real emperor! All you've got over there is a couple of pampered nancy boys. Their mother was a pub keeper's daughter who was still on the game even when she was empress! They may have been born in the purple but they were probably conceived up against a wall in an alley in Perama. There's a good chance that one of the greybeards here is their dad!'

As I looked on impassively, I noticed that someone was attempting to pull Theognostos back into the line. It was his elder brother Leo who was trying to shut him up. Perhaps because he had served under me in Bulgaria, he was visibly wincing at his brother's display. Theognostos did fall silent but it was not because of his brother. At the rear of Bardas' lines, there was blast of trumpets and a murmur of excitement and expectation rippled through his men. In the distance I could see a phalanx of horsemen approaching, the ranks parting to let them through. They were led by a figure with his visor down who must have been Bardas himself to judge by his purple cloak. Like his uncle, he rode a steed that was far too big for him but he managed it superbly. They were at the trot and the troops cheered frantically as they passed. I have to confess then that the sight of him terrified me. It was apparent that he was preparing a charge directed at my tent with a view to killing or capturing me as the best way to decide the issue.

Then something completely unexpected happened. From where I was on the raised ground, there was a clear view of the whole sequence of events from beginning to end. Bardas reined in his horse and rode off to one side away from the other riders. He cantered up a low hillock similar to the one that I was standing on. His men cheered once more – there was going to be a speech. Perhaps he would give Constantine and me generous terms to resign the throne and the battle would never happen. But Bardas said nothing. Instead he rather unsteadily dismounted and then slowly lay down on the ground. Some of his soldiers started to laugh, thinking it was a joke: he was showing his contempt for the feeble princelings by taking his ease. But when he did not move, the laughter died away. The staff officers were clearly concerned and one of them rode over to over to where Bardas lay, jumped from his horse and knelt down by the recumbent figure. When he straightened up, even from where we were, it was plain that it was all over. The ranks before us wavered. Some grasped their weapons and prepared to resist us, most started to draw back, looking uneasily over their shoulders.

I held up the icon of the Virgin and proclaimed that she had delivered us through as miracle. A resounding cheer went up from our side, even from the Russians who had no idea what I was talking about. On Impy's orders, the front rank formed a shield wall and began to move forward. That is a standard gambit in any battle but on this occasion it was the endgame. The troops before us broke ranks and scattered in all directions. Such fighting as there was involved our men chasing the fugitives and grabbing anyone who looked remotely important. There were fewer than ten casualties on both sides. It was indeed a miracle, only the Mother of God had wrought it through the medium of Outis and a servant in Bardas' household who was soon to become a very wealthy landowner in Greece. There were other versions of what had happened to Bardas. Constantine claimed that the rebel had been stuck by the spear that he had thrown and he dined out on the tale ever afterwards. I did not contradict him as he had provided a useful screen to the truth.

15

Chrysis Cheiros (989-1024)

My triumphant weathering of the crisis of 987-9 finally removed any doubts that might have been harboured by my subjects as to my capacity to rule. Henceforth, I would do exactly that, unaided and unimpeded by ambitious soldiers or scheming eunuchs. I suppose that I could have looked for replacements for Nothos and Ouranos and gathered around me a cohort of allies and advisers. There certainly would have been a long queue of eager and well-qualified candidates. I did not do that. Instead, I downgraded the rank of chamberlain so that its incumbent was more of a master of ceremonies than a political adviser and I appointed a series of nobodies to the position. The other officials I choose for their competence not their brilliance, their diligence, not their intellect. They give advice when called upon to do so but it is usually rejected. The pattern of my reign had been set: I alone decide, I alone rule. Had I wished to replace

Spondyles, that might have been more difficult, as people like him are not to be found in palaces. But a way could have been found for there was now no need for circumspection or dissimulation. I could have had as many favourites as I pleased and bought them all vineyards in Psamathia or houses in Hebdomon. But again, I did not do that. I forgot about him, just as I forgot about Ouranos and Nothos.

To start with some of the supporters from the early days remained at my side but as time went on they vanished one by one. Roupenios served me faithfully until age caught up with him. Then he returned to Armenia to become a monk and in due course was interred in a graveyard there under his monastic name, which I have forgotten. Impy Kontostephanos was always a useful tool but he perished when his detachment was ambushed in the Balkan mountains in around 996. He fearlessly battled seven Bulgars, all twice his size, until he was finally overwhelmed. I had always regarded my Aunt Theodora as a friend and ally. She lived to a great age but remained in her apartment for the most part once her brief term as empress had come to an end. I used to visit her there sometimes as, in periods of stress, her non-stop monologues were rather soothing. By the time she finally died, she had collected so many bits and pieces and had grown so huge that men with sledgehammers had to knock down the door lintels to get her out. Then she had to be manoeuvred up the steps in the Brazen Gate to the church of the Saviour so that she could go into the sarcophagus with John Tzimiskes. Ouranos went about fifteen years ago, in his sleep after complaining to his wife about pains in his chest. He is chiefly remembered today for the great victory he achieved against the Bulgars on the River Spercheios in 997 and his very successful period as governor of Antioch. In retirement, he wrote a manual of military tactics which is still in use today.

The fact was that I did not need any of them anymore. When, in the days after the excursion to the Holy Apostles, I had resolved to break free from Nothos' tutelage, I had crossed a line, just as Plutarch says Caesar did when he forded the Rubicon. The affection, support and approbation of others became nothing compared to the exercise of power and the possibilities that it bestowed to ruin and destroy those who had plotted against me, threatened my rights, belittled and despised me. This point should not be misunderstood: power is not to be exercised arbitrarily, for there is nothing sublime about destroying an innocent victim or one who showed genuine remorse. In the decades that followed the battle of Abydos, I was merciful whenever I could be. Most of Bardas' followers escaped from the field and were quietly reabsorbed back into the army as loyal soldiers of the emperor with no questions asked. Even among those who were captured, most were pardoned. Leo Melissenos I forgave because he had tried to stem his brother's tide of abuse. John Tzimiskes' brother-in-law Skleros was also pardoned. He had returned across the border from the caliphate when he heard about Bardas' revolt, in the hope of reviving his own claim to the throne. He was soon apprehended by the troops who were scouring Asia Minor for rebels. When I was told that he was a prisoner and that he was being brought to my tent, I was at first resolved to be harsh. When he was brought in though I was astonished to see that he had become wizened and bent and he could scarcely stay upright without a stick. He was unrecognisable from the tall, distinguished soldier whom I had seen standing behind John two days after Nikephoros' murder. I turned and whispered to Roupenios: 'So this is the man I feared!' He was pardoned and allowed to retire to his country estate where he died not long afterwards. I let his son Romanos return to Constantinople and for a time he was a member of my council. I even refrained from punishing the Phokas family as a whole for Bardas' conduct. Instead, I took more general measures to make it difficult for wealthy dynasties like them to build up large landholdings that might turn into an alternative powerbase.

In many cases, though, it would have been completely inappropriate to show mercy. How could I pardon Theognostos Melissenos after what he had said about my mother at Abydos? He and a few others who had been taken prisoner on the day, were paraded half naked around the Augousteion mounted backwards on donkeys, while the crowd shouted and spat at them. They were then hanged from the Brazen Gate and their corpses left dangling there for the rest of the day. I do not deny that an element in my decision to spare or to punish was lingering memories of how I had been treated in the past. I still could not forget Theognostos sniggering when Constantine made derogatory remarks about me at Hebdomon, even as he twitched at the end of the rope. Then then was the minor official in the Great Palace on whom Outis brought me a report. Apparently, as Bardas' army had drawn near to the Marmara, he had said to some friends that they ought to follow the lion and ditch the monkey. When I saw the name, I realised that he had been one of those who had shared Diaphantes' lessons with Constantine and me. No doubt he had been secretly jeering at me even then. The punishment was an appropriate one. I gave orders that the lions at Blachernae should go without food for a week. Then I had the despiser of monkeys flung into the cage so that he could enjoy the company of his favourite beasts.

On that occasion, I acted on impulse but I was prepared to play a long game where necessary, waiting for years until the right moment to strike, never losing sight of the hurt that had been done to me. That was what happened with Eustathios Maleinos. The man was quite obviously a Phokas supporter and a rebel. It had been in his house that Bardas Phokas had been proclaimed emperor in 987. But there was more to it than that. I blamed his family for turning Constantine into the stranger who returned from Caesarea and still burning in my mind was the crack that Maleinos had made to Nikephoros during the hunt in Philopation: that Constantine would make a good cavalryman but not me. I was almost completely sure that he had been at Abydos with Bardas in 989 but I had no proof. No one would admit to having seen him there. He had probably been well to the rear and he was rich enough to afford a very swift horse. So I bided my time. About six years later, as I was returning from a successful campaigning season on the eastern frontier, I encamped with my army in and around Caesarea. Maleinos came to meet us as we approached and begged that I would stay with my suite in his house. I accepted and we imposed ourselves for rather longer than he had anticipated. Still the hospitality was lavish and no expense was spared for our enjoyment and comfort.

When we were finally packing up to leave, I put my hand on Maleinos' shoulder and said that I had relished his company so much that I would take it as a personal favour if he would return with me to the capital. You cannot refuse a request like that from your emperor, so he came and took up residence in his town house which was in the same street as the old Phokas mansion. The day after his arrival I sent a messenger down there to say that he must not leave the house without my express permission. He remained under house arrest for the remainder of his life. When he died, I confiscated his estates and everything he owned. Fitting acts of vengeance like that gave me a celestial feeling. There was such variety: the punishment of my enemies could be appropriate to their offence, to their deserts or simply a reflection how I felt on the day. Pure theosis, in fact.

The reason why I could deal so harshly with Maleinos was that by then I was delivering victory in battle myself without the need to rely on military strongmen like him. When it came to settling accounts with Tsar Samuel and the Bulgarians, I played the same long game. That embarrassing defeat at Trajan's Gate in 986 had led to Bardas' revolt and Samuel had taken full advantage of my distraction to consolidate his hold on the Balkans. His troops appeared before the walls of Thessalonica and marched as far south as the Gulf of Corinth. Things only got worse in the years after the victory at Abydos. Some prophets of doom claimed that since I had destroyed our greatest general, military catastrophe was sure to follow. They were all proved wrong. I resumed the war against the Bulgars but I knew that it would take time to bring Samuel down, so I abandoned the idea of trying to deal one knockout blow. Instead, I fought a war of attrition. I raided deep into Bulgar territory every year, burning and looting as I went. Orders were given to the troops to do whatever they liked: I leave it to the imagination to fill in the details. Samuel died in 1014, and the war finally came to an end in the summer of 1018 when the Bulgars laid down their arms and accepted Roman rule. Our frontier is now once more at the Danube.

The defeat of the Bulgars took longer than I would have liked because to start with I also had to contend with the Fatimids of Egypt. They thought that the removal of Bardas Phokas was their chance to reassert their influence in northern Syria as there would no longer be anyone capable of opposing them. In 995 while I was campaigning in the Balkans, I received news that the Fatimids were threatening Aleppo, whose emir was our ally and client. I marched east with 17,000 men and arrived in Antioch weeks before anyone had dared hope to expect me. Disconcerted, the Fatimids withdrew but I followed them over the border and wreaked vengeance on the towns of Syria. But you can read all about these victories in great detail in the bishop of Side's history of my reign.

Although my victories have excelled even those of Nikephoros, John Tzimiskes and Bardas, I am proudest of my bloodless conquests, such as the extension of the border to the northeast. Initially this was done by force. In 990, I marched against David, prince of the Armenian principality of Tao, because he had supported Bardas in his rebellion. But he soon sued for peace and he agreed to leave me his lands in his will, as he had no son and heir. Ten years later, he died and Tao was incorporated. With that precedent established, I met with other Armenian princes and persuaded them in their own language that life would be much easier as one my prominent subjects than as the ruler of a small, weak and vulnerable state. Thanks to me, the Roman border now stretches further eastwards than it ever did in the past. I resolved the rivalry with the Fatimids in much the same way. My forays across the border into Syria convinced the caliph that it was better to have me as a friend than an enemy and we concluded the truce which fixed our borders in Syria and has lasted, with a few hiccups, until today.

For both my military and diplomatic victories, I have relied heavily on the Office of the Wine Steward. I am now on my sixth Outis and I have expanded his department at Petrion to involve it in a much greater range of activities. One of them is disinformation. An operative has the job of disseminating rumours which will be useful to me. I had better say here and now that the story of how I blinded 15,000 Bulgar captives, apart from a selected group who lost only one eye, is one such rumour. I did defeat a Bulgar force at Kleidion in 1014 and I did have some of the officers mutilated to make an example of them. By that time, I was growing impatient at the continued resistance when it was quite obvious that the Bulgars had lost the war. Moreover, I was starting to wonder whether I could keep my own people on side as it dragged on. So the Office of the Wine Steward circulated this complete fabrication about mass blinding to show everyone just how determined I was. It seems to have been widely believed and has become a central element in my mystique. For it to work though, I had to make it credible. That was why I had to be as ruthless with my own people as I was with the Bulgars. When my commander of the castle at Vodena abandoned his post, I ordered that he be impaled and made sure that the punishment was carried out in the main square in Thessalonica. A skilled impaler knows how to insert the stake in just such a way as to avoid all the vital organs. That way the victim will linger for days in indescribable agony. No one doubted my resolve after that.

As well as helping me to win wars, the people at Petrion have enabled me to avoid them. I will give an example. Not long ago, one of our sources in Cairo indicated that after the death of the very competent regent Sitt al-Mulk, the council that advises the young Fatimid caliph Ali az-Zahir had come to be dominated by hawks who wanted to abrogate the longstanding truce and eject us from Antioch and northern Syria. They planned to send an envoy called Sayyid al-Wuzara to Constantinople, ostensibly to begin negotiations towards renewing the truce. Meanwhile troops were to be secretly massed on the border and intelligence was to be gathered on our state of readiness. If it appeared that the defences were weak, they were to invade. Naturally, our first move on receiving this intelligence was to send reinforcements ostentatiously to Syria but it seemed to me that we might derive some advantage from the situation.

Al-Wuzara arrived and had his initial meeting with my chamberlain, the eunuch John the Paphlagonian. I should not have trusted that John. The man is a lout, the product of the Black Sea coast where they breed like rabbits and castrate a spare son in the hope that he will get a post in the palace and make the family fortune. He overplayed his hand and nearly gave the whole thing away. Thanks to him blurting out certain facts that he should not have known, al-Wuzara smelt a rat and he decided that his Christian Coptic interpreter must be disloyal and leaking information to us. He was quite wrong on that. We had another source much closer to him whom he never suspected. So to check up on the interpreter, al-Wuzara got the caretaker of the mosque next to where he was staying to come with him to his first meeting with me. He was hoping that the caretaker would report anything suspicious that the interpreter said in Greek but he had no idea that the caretaker was one of our agents too!

We staged the meeting in the Magnavra hall and it was along the same lines as the reception that I had laid on for Nothos all those years ago. The place was packed with off-duty guards and their families all of whom had been carefully primed on their role beforehand. I even got Constantine to play a part. By wandering in late and leading al-Wuzara to think that he was me, we got the envoy disoriented and on the back foot even before I delivered my angry speech. I told him that the Fatimid invasion had already happened, a complete fabrication of course. The crowd then erupted in fury. Al-Wuzara had been warned that the invasion might begin while he was in Constantinople but that he would be well clear before news could reach us. He naturally assumed that we had been given prior warning, which in a way we had. He was sent back to the merchants' hostel by the Gate of St Eugenios to cool his heels for a few weeks. A guard was placed outside, though we knew perfectly well that he would send a message out with one of the merchants to report to his masters what had happened. They would then fear that I was about to march east as I did in '95 and would soon be scrambling to reinforce their Syrian border.

After an appropriate interval, I invited him to the Petrion and handed him our terms. I had long remembered how, in the autumn of 975, John Tzimiskes had come close to Jerusalem but had not been able to capture it. Now I saw a way of protecting the site of the resurrection of Our Lord and I insisted that we must be given guardianship of the Holy Sepulchre in Jerusalem if there was to be any renewal of the truce. To mark the resumption of amity, I could not resist asking whether he would put aside the precepts of his religion and drink a goblet of Ganos red with me. I knew perfectly well from our source that he had got through two large jars of the same vintage during his weeks of confinement at the hostel. He carried our terms back to Cairo, the truce was renewed, Antioch is safe and Jerusalem is under our care. Perhaps even Nikephoros would have approved.

287

* * *

Having come this far and described my victories and my vengeance, I now have to move on to something else. Over the past few years, I have started to look back on the past again and to see it differently. That was what prompted me to write this. As far as I can tell, the change began in the late summer of 1018. That was when I achieved the final victory over the Bulgars and received the submission of the widow of their last tsar at Ohrid. I was acutely aware that few leaders have ever enjoyed a triumph so complete. Alexander the Great and Caesar did, I suppose, and there has never been any shortage of flattering courtiers eager to assure me that I excel both. In the days that followed, though, I felt a deep sense of anti-climax and was not sure what to do next. I hesitated before returning to Constantinople, knowing that I would have to stage a triumph and endure all the wearisome ceremonial that went with it. So after I had marched my army south over the mountains, I sent most of the men back to their quarters. Then, with an appropriate contingent of picked troops, I headed south. I wanted to take a tour of some parts of the Roman empire that I had never seen before. I went as far down as Athens and installed myself in the archbishop's palace there. We attended a service of thanksgiving for the victory in the cathedral of the Virgin Mary. It is a remarkable edifice, perched on a rock above the town, built long ago by pagans in honour of one of their gods. There are wonderful marble carvings of men and mythical beasts on the pediment and all around the outside wall. They look so realistic that you almost expect them to move.

It would hardly have been appropriate to linger too long at Athens though, so after a few days I had to give orders for us to begin the journey to the capital. It was when we were two or three days out of Athens that one of my officers pointed out that we were riding through the pass of Thermopylae. I remembered reading the story in Herodotus of how Leonidas and three hundred Spartans had fought to the death holding up the vast Persian army there. Then I saw that a wall that had been built relatively recently across the pass. It is odd that I was surprised to see it as I had ordered its construction. That was back in the 990s when Tsar Samuel was still master of much of the Balkans and I feared he was going to invade Greece as well. So I had given Roupenios the task of erecting a defensive wall across the pass and now I could see what a good job he had done of it. I had not thought about him for years and memories welled up of how I had first met him with John Tzimiskes in the Great Palace gardens and how he had come to collect me from Hebdomon. That was the beginning of my rediscovery of the past.

We rode on and came to a river. We forded it easily enough but I had noticed that the ground sloping down to the bank was strewn with whitened bones as if some great slaughter had taken place there. I enquired and was told that the river was the Spercheios and the bones were those of the thousands of Bulgars slain in the battle with Ouranos' army in 997. It had been an extraordinary victory. Ouranos had been encamped on the north side of the river and the Bulgars on the other. Night had fallen, it had begun to rain heavily and the waters became swollen into a churning torrent. Judging that in these conditions no battle would be fought, the Bulgars had taken to their tents to sleep. Ouranos, however, had reconnoitred and found a place a little upstream where his men could cross. In the depths of the night they had burst into the Bulgar camp and killed almost all of them. The association of the place with Ouranos naturally got me thinking about how I had first encountered him in Philopation, a few weeks before the murder of Nikephoros Phokas, when my pony had bolted. I would have been hopelessly lost had it not been for him. More to the point, had I not met him like that I would never have dared to make the challenge that eventually brought me to the supreme power which was my birth right.

From there, ineluctably, I had to think of Nothos. For years, I had tried not to do so, though whether to avoid feelings of resentment or guilt I cannot say. Yet I found now, as the column plodded northwards from Thermopylae, that I could at last consider him dispassionately. I could admit to myself that whenever I made a decision, I secretly asked myself what he would have done in the same situation. True, he had been ruthless and callous at times. He had cynically manipulated my mother's infatuation with Tzimiskes to bring Nikephoros to Constantinople so that Bringas could be ousted from the office of chamberlain. He had done so again when the time came to remove Nikephoros and then when she became inconvenient, he had not hesitated to consign her to a living hell in an island nunnery. But his cruel deeds were always the carefully calculated minimum. He never acted on impulse or gave way to emotion. He had carried the burden of rule for over twenty years without being recognised as the emperor he was in all but name. The manner of his passing proved his greatness. Ever since his death, I had been convinced that he had known all along that I was marshalling Outis and the Phokas family to bring about his downfall. So why did he do nothing? If he had known that he was ill, why did he not just ask to retire and spare himself the agony and indignity of that scene in the Magnavra? I now believe that I have found an answer to the question. My mother been right and the man had loved me like a son and had done to the end in spite of all our differences. In accepting disgrace and humiliation the way he did, he hoped to atone in some way for his treatment of my mother and restore my esteem for him. He yearned until the very end to be reconciled with the child he never had and when that could not be, he offered himself freely as the victim of my vengeance. There was something Christlike in the stoical way that he had kept his eyes fixed on mine when I last saw him in the

Magnavra. Like the suffering servant, he had opened not his mouth.

By now it was late autumn. The road wound on through Thessaly and into Macedonia where we joined the Egnatian Way. That brought us to Thessalonica which we entered by the Gate of Vardar, escorted by a crowd of palm-bearing citizens and clergy who sang and swung censors. During the brief stay, I fulfilled a long-held ambition to visit the tomb of St Demetrius. It is housed in an ancient basilica and is said to exude a sweet-smelling myrrh that has wonderful healing properties. The archbishop presented me with a phial of it on the day we left. It was when we were a day out of Thessalonica and back on the Egnatian Way that my Keeper announced that we would be stopping for at time at Hebdomon.

'It is tradition, Majesty, that the emperor should lodge at Hebdomon before a triumphal entry to the city through the Golden Gate. Your predecessor, the first Basil, did so when he celebrated his triumph in 879.'

True enough but I had for a long time avoided the place. When the armies gathered in the spring for the yearly offensives during that long, grinding Bulgarian war, I never reviewed them at Hebdomon. Rather I would leave through the Gate of Adrianople and catch up with the army at some convenient inland point in Thrace. When returning from the east, I never landed at the harbour of Hebdomon, but had my galley take me straight into the Boukoleon. Nor did I ever use the villa as an overnight staging post for a triumphal entry. Instead, I used to ride out to meet the approaching column then return with it through the Golden Gate. It was a shock when I realised that I would be returning for the first time since I was seventeen. I did not object though. Perhaps the time had come to revisit the place.

That prospect ensured that over the next few days, as we made our stately way eastwards, I stopped thinking about Nothos and turned to Demetrius Spondyles. How odd that the emperor of the Romans and conqueror of Bulgaria should have been so taken with someone so ordinary and undistinguished. I had even hoped to abdicate and to go and live with him in the villa at Hebdomon. One does such ridiculous things when young. Then, as we breasted a hill, the forest of Philopation became visible on the horizon and the fortress of Strongylon, standing on the headland with the sea beyond. Hebdomon, its harbour and parade ground were still hidden by the lie of the land. At that moment, I suddenly felt an intense desire to see his face again. I tried to call it into my mind's eye but I could not recollect it at all. In the Pharos chapel in the Great Palace we have the Mandylion, the cloth on which Our Saviour left an imprint of his face. How I wish we could keep something similar for our friends and family to remind us of how they once were. I took out the tiny icon of St Demetrius, now rather faded. Then, quite unbidden, an image flashed into my mind. Spondyles was standing silhouetted against the red sky with the bearded star hanging there, reaching up to the branches of a tree. I knew at once when and where it was: that summer of 975 on the parade ground at Hebdomon. That had been the moment that I had realised simultaneously both that I was blissfully happy and that my happiness could not possibly last. Then my horse snorted, shook its head and jingled its bridle and the apparition vanished. I looked around at my attendants to see whether they had noticed anything odd about me but they were riding on unconcernedly.

We lodged in Strongylon rather than the villa, as my suite was too large to be accommodated there. The next morning, I rode out with six companions, down the hill to the town and up the slope to the villa. I had given notice of my intention in advance so that my appearance would not cause anyone undue alarm, unlike my first arrival. The building was in very good repair, I noticed, and the fountain in the courtyard was trickling merrily. Constantine must have seen to that during his lazy summer visits while I was enduring the rigours of campaigning in Bulgaria. Out in the garden, the formal terraces stretching down towards the sea were well-tended, the flower beds weeded, the cracked paving stones replaced. When I came to look for the path at the side that led to the statues though, I found that it had become completely overgrown and impenetrable. I had to call for men to come with billhooks to clear the way for me. I sat on a stone bench and waited while they worked. One of them came out to me, mopping his brow, and reported that further progress was blocked by a fallen pillar.

'Climb over it, man,' I snapped testily, 'the path continues on the other side.'

I waited again until he came back and said that he had found some statues. I got to my feet and walked down the newly cleared path until I reached the porphyry column. On my previous visits I had scrambled over it effortlessly but now it presented a formidable obstacle. One of my attendants had to cup his hands for me to place my foot in and he then heaved me up. I sat on the column while they climbed over and then allowed myself to slide down into their waiting arms. It was very undignified. I found myself hoping that the hole in the wall might still be there and that we could return that way via the parade ground. Then I remembered that I had only to give the word and the entire wall would be demolished.

We reached the satyr fountain. No water was coming from the mouth and had evidently not done so for some time. The stone bowl underneath was full of earth and grass was growing thickly in it. I moved on to the enclosure with the lichened statues. They were still there with the inscriptions which I now know are in Latin. One of their heads had fallen off and was lying a few feet away. I looked around me. It was late in the year, not high summer like last time I was there. Cold bare branches formed a sombre background to the figures, rather than the green leaves and motes of sunlight that I recalled. My attendants were standing back, peering at me through the undergrowth, wondering how much longer I would be. I too was starting to ask myself why I had come. But then I saw the stone pediment under the statues where Spondyles had sat and where he had started to speak. Then I was glad I had made the pilgrimage as I now understood why he had been such an object of fascination to me. He was the antithesis of Nothos. His homely incompetence provided the only thing that my great mentor had lacked. So now, after so many decades when I had scarcely thought once about Ouranos, Nothos or Spondyles, I found that I was missing all three of them dreadfully.

✳ ✳ ✳

After the triumphal entry into Constantinople and my return to the Great Palace, I resolved that I would live differently from now on. After all, there were no more campaigns to be fought and I was tired of all the wars and the killing. I settled down to the usual round of day-to-day administration and looked for opportunities to display my benevolence. The first arose early in the new year when a delegation from the nobles of Bulgaria arrived. As they were now subjects rather than representatives of a foreign power, I received them personally in the Magnavra. Their leader spoke in Greek and asked me for a great favour. Traditionally, as long as anyone could remember, the nobles and people of Bulgaria had paid their taxes to their tsar not in coin but in kind, handing over a fixed proportion of the produce of their land. They requested that this custom should continue.

I thought about this. Roman subjects are always required to pay their taxes in gold. That means that whatever is not needed immediately can be stored for future use. In fact, I have built up just such a surplus in recent years and I am having new cellars excavated underneath the Great Palace to accommodate it all. Revenue in produce, on the other hand, has to be used immediately, shipped to a local garrison town to feed the troops. I could feel my Logothete of the Drome shifting restlessly behind me at this potential loss of income.

'We grant your request,' I said.

There was no point in forcing on the Bulgars customs that were strange and alien to them. Their loss of independence has been traumatic enough without that. A few months later, a delegation of Bulgarian clergy arrived with another request. They wanted their Church to be independent and not under the authority of the patriarch of Constantinople. I granted that too. The patriarch was furious but he did not dare challenge my decision publicly.

Since my return, I have been giving more thought to spiritual matters. I have been having twinges of conscience for having knocked down Nothos' monastery so I have been wondering which one I ought to adopt for my special patronage. All emperors have their favourites: Nikephoros and John both chose the Great Lavra on Mount Athos. For my part, originally I had favoured St Theophylact at Sosthenion but its association with Nothos rather put me off it. So I have decided on St John the Evangelist at Hebdomon. That was the one that Ouranos and I used to attend while Constantine and his cronies went to the other one, John the Baptist. The church could doubtless do with some renovation and redecoration and I thought that it might be a good idea to have a small monastery attached to it as well. So I sent to St John Stoudios and asked that their best architect and mosaicist attend on me. The monks arrived a few days later on a galley that I had sent to collect them. The architect came armed with plans for a cloister, refectory and dormitory and with the artist I discussed the new cycle of mosaics to adorn the dome and main body of the church. In such matters, I am very conservative and so I was happy to follow the traditional layout that he advised, with Christ

Pantokrator in the dome, the Virgin and Child in the apse, the life of Christ on the higher levels. Only there was an exception: 'There is one addition I would like to make to the usual cycle, father. I would like a mosaic of St Demetrius in the entrance hall so that he is the first thing that worshippers will see when they arrive. A head and shoulders portrayal, extending over all three doors that lead into the nave.'

'Ah yes indeed,' said the monk eagerly, 'St Demetrius as a beautiful youth!'

I put my finger to my lips and bowed my head for a moment. Then I looked down at the faded icon on a side table.

'No. Just make him ordinary.'

About eighteen months ago, something else happened. I remember that it was a day or two after news arrived from Kiev that my sister Anna had died. It had not been as bad for her as it might have. She had outlived her husband Vladimir by some eight years and her son Yaroslav is the current ruler. She enjoyed great prestige both as queen mother and as a kind of exotic import. The Russians did everything they could to make her life comfortable. I considered taking the news in person to Constantine. He is as hale and hearty as ever and has numerous hobbies and activities to keep him busy. He hunts in the Philopation, enjoys the bucolic delights of Hiereia and Hebdomon and takes very long baths. He also cooks and has become very good at devising savoury sauces to enhance the flavour of meat. The harem at the Petrion still exists but I doubt he goes there very often as his arthritis restricts his movements. His wife Helena is dead now but she provided him with three daughters, Eudokia, Zoe and Theodora, all born in the purple. I am very fond of them and when they were small I used to visit them in the Kainourgion when I was home from campaign. They are grown up now though. Eudokia is a nun and neither Zoe nor Theodora has a husband. It is just too much of a risk. Anyone who married them would consider themselves my heir and might not want to wait for nature to take its course. I do not want another Nikephoros or John Tzimiskes on my hands. To return to the point, in the end I sent a note to Constantine rather then tell him myself about Anna's passing: I still do not relish his company.

In fact, that was why it happened. I was, as usual, striding through the corridors of the palace early one morning, dictating as I went. John the Paphlagonian and a bevy of scribes were behind me, one of the latter scribbling down my words on a tablet as I reeled off some of the business for the day. By force of habit, I have predictable circular route and was heading towards the Nineteen Couches. That morning though, I heard an ominous arf-arf ahead of me and my heart sank. I turned left abruptly, so that John and the scribes carried on with the usual route for a few seconds before turning round and running to catch me up. I carried on dictating as if nothing had happened and we emerged into the upper portico of the Golden Hand. Then both my mouth and my feet came to an abrupt halt, causing John and the scribes to bump into each other.

Down in the courtyard a crowd of young men was milling around the pointing hand. They had clearly been brought in from outside the palace: you could see that from their clothes and general demeanour. My eye had gone straight to one of them who was different. He seemed slightly older than the others, about eighteen or nineteen, short with brown hair, that stuck out in various places and with a straggly beard to match. He was standing on the edge of the group with his hands clasped awkwardly behind his back, staring vacantly up at the sky with a strange look of bewilderment on his face, apparently heedless of the restless figures moving around him. I leaned over the marble balustrade.

'Keeper, who are these people?'

There was instant stillness in the courtyard and the eunuch came puffing up the steps to meet me:

'These are the young men to be trained for palace service, Majesty.' That would explain why most of them, with one exception, were good looking and athletic.

'I see. And who is that?'

I was pointing not at the one who had caught my eye but a younger youth with black hair. The habits of dissimulation acquired in my youth have never left me. From behind my shoulder, John the Paphlagonian put in:

'Why, that is my own brother Michael, Majesty, we hope to train him for the guard.'

He had not wasted much time getting one of his family's snout in the trough then. I indicated a few others. When I heard one name, I said:

'Ah yes, I know the family. I believe his father was with me at Kleidion.'

'His Majesty's powers of memory never fail to amaze us all,' said John.

Nonsense and flattery and he knows it. Only the other day, I called him 'Nothos.'

'What about that one?'

At a loss, the Keeper turned and a younger eunuch stepped up to whisper in his ear.

'He's called Stephen Lagoudes, Majesty,' adding in a lower voice, 'We do not think that he is suitable.'

I wondered how he had ever been included in the group in the first place: there had been a mistake somewhere. It was a moment for decisive action and I gave my orders.

'The Chamberlain's brother should certainly be trained for the guard and that one too. And that one. I could use two new cupbearers as well. Those I have at present have been in the role too long and should progress to other duties. I will have that one,' I indicated someone at random, 'and him.'

So Lagoudes now stands behind me at meetings. I have not yet spoken to him and I have no idea even what his voice sounds like. He is terrified of me and if I even glance at him, he appears ready to flee. He seems afraid of the Chamberlain too and I suspect that John might have hit him. If I ever get proof of that then John will be Chamberlain no more and he will be on the first boat back to Paphlagonia. No, I will bide my time with Lagoudes. A year or so perhaps will do it. Then I could have him accompany me on morning rides and take it from there. I must find out whether he can handle a horse. If not, I will have to devise some stratagem for getting him out to the stables and starting him off on a docile mare. In the long run, I will start spending the summers at Hebdomon once more. I am sure that the satyr fountain can be made to flow again and I might get the head put back on the statue. He will come with me. I'll need to find a suitable house there for him, with a bench outside. That way his mother and wife will be able to come too. The wife's name has slipped my mind: it begins with E. I will make absolutely sure this time that he will not have to leave early to return to the vineyard. I would hate to think of him trudging back along the Egnatian way all by himself. But now I think about it, how am I going to arrange all this? How will I find the house it Hebdomon? Maybe Ouranos could do it? Or better still, I will ask Nothos. He will know. Yes, Nothos will know.

16

The Ambassador
and the Spy (1024)

A l-Wuzara was emerging from the han to be carried in his litter to the dockside. It was September and he was going home on one of the last sailings of the year to Alexandria. The small procession made its way through the Gate of St Eugenios, Jacob and Aziz walking beside the litter and the rest following on behind. As they passed the mosque, the envoy heard the sweep, sweep of Yazid's broom. Aziz reported that he had refused all payment for taking part in that calamitous encounter in the Magnavra hall. All he said was that the honour of serving the Lord al-Wuzara was reward enough and that if he was ever in Cairo he would visit the Lord's household and pay his respects. Al-Wuzara had not set eyes on him since that day. It was as if he had gone into hiding. A curious fellow, he thought.

They made their way along the walkway, passing the busy piers and wharves until they reached the one where the Alexandrine ship was moored. Al-Wuzara left the litter and walked up the gangplank to be ushered by Aziz into a small but cosy cabin at the stern. A comfortable couch with an array of cushions followed the curve of the vessel's lines and there were crimson silk hangings in the unshuttered windows. The ever-vigilant Aziz had even provided a flagon of the Ganos red that he knew his master was partial to. The servant then withdrew and the ambassador assumed that he would take up his accustomed position outside the door, in readiness to respond to his master's call. But Aziz did not stand outside the door today. Instead he climbed up the short ladder to where the rest of the party was looking for space on deck or in the small hold where they would have to rough it for the duration of the voyage. The crew were busying themselves with taking on barrels of water and other last-minute preparations for departure. Aziz walked across the deck and down the gangplank onto the jetty. He returned to the walkway along which they had just come, turned back and looked at the ship and then set off back towards the Gate of St Eugenios. About a hundred yards further on, Angelos was there, sitting on a coil of rope and staring, staring out towards Galata. He did not look in the direction of Aziz but got to his feet and walked away. Aziz followed him and they both passed through the gate and bent their steps towards Petrion.

As the sailors pushed away from the jetty with their long poles, there was a rumbling noise as the oars were slid out of the ports, then a splash as their blades dropped into the water. Al-Wuzara settled down among the cushions. He felt the galley rock as it moved out from the Golden Horn and into swift current of the strait. The breeze wafted it from behind, making the crimson silk hangings over the windows float up, and the captain shouted the order to lower the sail. From his cushions, the ambassador could hear the gulls crying and shrieking as they wheeled around the masthead. Peering out from between the billowing hangings, he saw that the vessel was passing the gardens and pavilions of the Great Palace. Between the trees and parterres, a few isolated and unidentifiable figures seemed to be strolling aimlessly. He knew for certain that the Emperor Basil would not be one of them. He would be locked away from the breeze and the sunshine to hatch his plans in some dark chamber.

The ambassador had encountered many powerful men in his travels but never one who seemed so icily remote from human fellow-feeling with only his snide humour to take the edge off his frigidity. He wondered he had ever been capable of affection or whether he had been like that ever since he was a child. He must have had a mother but perhaps she took no part in his upbringing. That was not the case in the court of the caliph, as each wife fiercely cherished and championed her own son as a possible successor. But perhaps that was how things were done among the Christians. The emperor was old now but had he ever had real friends or lovers? The dead shark eyes seemed to suggest not. Perhaps he had sacrificed all human emotions in some devilish pact on the altar of supreme power. It was then that a strange recollection occurred to al-Wuzara. At the last interview, the one in the Petrion palace, when the rather awkward youth had stepped forward with the wine goblets, something odd had occurred. For one split second the dead eyes of the emperor had come to life and followed him as he walked forward. What could that mean? For a moment, the ambassador wondered whether this was what he had heard about in one of the courts that he had visited. They said that the ruler there kept a harem of young men for his pleasure. But al-Wuzara soon discarded that thought. This cupbearer was no Ganymede – he looked more like a farmhand. In any case, there was no lust in that fleeting glance, as far as he could tell, merely affection. So he concluded that this was probably a natural son, fathered on a servant girl. Now he thought about it, the resemblance between the two was striking. He had been told though that the Romans castrated their emperors' bastards to prevent them having a claim to the throne. Perhaps the emperor did have some shred of humanity after all and it was that which had held him back from so drastic a step. Yet he could hardly have been that fond of his son, if the best provision that he could make for him was a menial job as a servant.

Enough of that, al-Wuzara told himself and gave up the fruitless task of trying to understand someone so detached from his own approach to life. He leaned forward to pour a beaker of the Ganos red and gave himself over to pleasant dreams of Cairo and of home. Perhaps he would call for Aziz and tell him to massage his shoulders. He dwelt no more on that fearsome emperor. He left him to sit alone and unloved among the cold marble halls of his ancestors.

HISTORICAL NOTE

Basil II died on 15 December 1025 and, in accordance with his last wishes, was buried in the Church of St John the Evangelist in Hebdomon: a noticeable break with tradition since emperors were usually interred in the church of the Holy Apostles within the city walls. He was succeeded as sole emperor by his brother, Constantine VIII, who ruled until 1028. After that the succession was provided for by Constantine's daughter Zoe, whose three husbands and one adopted son successively occupied the throne. Her sister Theodora then ruled briefly and on her death in 1056, the Macedonian dynasty came to an end.

When it comes to reconstructing Basil's story, very little now remains of the built environment that he knew, largely thanks to the political upheavals in the centuries that followed. Within fifty years of his death, the Byzantine empire began to lose ground in the east to Turkish invaders and it finally succumbed in 1453 when the Ottoman Turks took Constantinople, now Istanbul. Most Byzantine buildings in the city and its suburbs have long since vanished. Neither the villa nor the church of the Evangelist in Hebdomon can be seen today, as the site is covered by the suburb of Bakirköy. The Great Palace has also largely disappeared although a few structures from the Boukoleon are still visible above ground. Only the cathedral of Hagia Sophia remains from the Augousteion, although these days it serves as a mosque. Because there are so few physical remains, I had to rely on the surviving written texts and my description of the Great Palace is largely based on *The Book of Ceremonies* (listed below). There is a fuller record when it comes to some of the major characters in the story. The works of Liudprand of Cremona and Michael Psellos provide memorable character sketches of Nikephoros II, Nothos, John Tzimiskes and of the older Basil II and Constantine VIII, on which I have drawn freely. The histories written by Leo the Deacon and John Skylitzes narrate the political events that form the background to the story: the usurpation and murder of Nikephoros II Phokas, the reign and death of John I Tzimiskes and Basil II's struggle against first Nothos and then Bardas Phokas the younger. Many episodes are taken directly from them, including the bearded star that Basil saw hanging over Hebdomon and Constantinople in the summer of 975. Now known as Halley's Comet, it will next be observable from Earth in July 2061. Othedr texts have been used occasionally. For example, I have portrayed Nothos citing pages 557 and 589 of *The Taktika of Leo VI* (listed below) when instructing Basil on statecraft.

That said, I have freely augmented, adapted and departed from the historical record on numerous occasions. While the Magnavra hall was probably much as I have envisaged it, the Lausiakos and the Portico of the Golden Hand are almost entirely of my own construction, as is the villa at Hebdomon. Some individuals, such as Roupenios and Kalokyris Delphinas, are no more than names in the sources and no details are given about them, so I have provided them with characters. Others, such as Yazid, Demetrius Spondyles and Leontios Diaphantes, are completely fictitious, as are some episodes and institutions, such as Patriarch Anthony's unopened letter and the Office of the Wine Steward. There are details that have a basis in fact but have been deliberately altered. John the Paphlagonian, better known as John the Orphanotrophos, did indeed hold office in the later years of Basil II but I have promoted him to the post of chamberlain. There is no specific evidence that the Mitaton mosque existed as early as 1024 but then again, it might have done, so I have decided that it did. There are also deliberate anachronisms such as the use of CE (AD) dates. The Byzantines used the Anno Mundi system, which took the year of Creation, the equivalent of 5509 BCE, as its starting point, rather than the birth of Christ. So they would have regarded the period covered by this book not as 958-1025 but 6467-6534. Nor have I rigidly followed the places names used by Basil's contemporaries. Instead they are sometimes given in their modern form (e.g. Plovdiv rather than Philippopolis) and sometimes in the medieval one (e.g. Chalcedon rather than Kadiköy).

Texts, imagination and pure invention aside, the shape that the story ultimately took also owes a great deal to its first readers: Steve Tibble, Faith Tibble, Jonathan Phillips, Nada Zečević, Jane Draycott, Teodora Artimon, Justin Bengry, Suzana Miljan, Mihai Motoarca and Ozren Glaser. It also reflects everyone whose company, whether in person, by post, online or via text, has enlivened the past few years of political uncertainty and pandemic: Derram Attfield, James Desbois, Amanda Harris, Caroline McCluskey, Jan Parkin, Nicola Phillips and Keith Raffan to name but a few. There is a little bit of all of them somewhere or other in the book.

Further Reading (Primary Sources):

Constantine Porphyrogennetos. *The Book of Ceremonies*, trans. Ann Moffatt and Maxeme Tall. Canberra: Australian Association for Byzantine Studies, 2012.
Leo VI. *The Taktika of Leo VI*, trans. George T. Dennis. Washington DC: Dumbarton Oaks, 2010.
Leo the Deacon. *The History of Leo the Deacon: Byzantine Military Expansion in the Tenth Century*, trans. A.-M. Talbot and D. Sullivan. Washington DC: Dumbarton Oaks, 2005.
Liudprand of Cremona. *The Complete Works*, trans. P. Squatriti. Washington DC: Catholic University of America Press, 2007.

Psellos, Michael. *Chronographia*, trans. E.R.A. Sewter, *Fourteen Byzantine Rulers*. London: Penguin, 1966.
Skylitzes, John. *A Synopsis of Byzantine History, 811-1057*, trans. J. Wortley. Cambridge: Cambridge University Press, 2010.

Further Reading (Secondary Works):

Harris, Jonathan. *The Lost World of Byzantium*. New Haven CT and London: Yale University Press, 2015.
—. *Introduction to Byzantium, 602-1453*. Abingdon and New York: Routledge, 2020.
Herrin, Judith. *Byzantium: The Surprising Life of a Medieval Empire*. London: Penguin 2007.
Holmes, Catherine. *Basil II and the Governance of Empire*. Oxford: Oxford University Press, 2005.
Stephenson, Paul. *The Legend of Basil the Bulgar Slayer*. Cambridge: Cambridge University Press, 2003.